EXTINCTION

Stephen A. Benjamin

2016, TWB Press
www.twbpress.com

Acknowledgments

To all the readers of the first novel in the *Galactic Circle Veterinary Service* series for their encouragement to move ahead with the sequel.

To my colleagues in the Northern Colorado Writers' FantaSci critique group for their invaluable technical and creative input.

And to my wife, Barbara, for her understanding and support at all stages of the creation process.

Chapter 1

As the shuttle from the orbiting interstellar spaceship came in for a landing, Chaim plucked his sweat-soaked shirt away from his skin. He removed his black flat-brimmed fedora and wiped his forehead with a handkerchief, then combed his fingers through his wet, matted hair.

The woman sitting next to him wrinkled her nose. He tried to smile but grimaced instead. His facial muscles would not work properly, so he scrubbed at his long black beard as if it were the culprit.

Security will know. This plan will never work and I will die here among infidels.

His heartbeat accelerated, and his underarms were slick with rank sweat. He replaced his fedora. Nausea roiled in his stomach, as it had since the initial prep for his mission.

The shuttle touched down and the pilot announced, "Please keep your seats while we taxi to the terminal. Customs agents will meet you at the bottom of the ramp to direct you to the appropriate entry kiosk. Thank you for flying Jawwi Interstellar."

They will see who I am. Check my luggage and find...it. Then they will kill me.

He swallowed the acid that rose to his throat. After pulling a mint from his pocket, he popped it into his mouth to cover the acrid taste. When the rest of the passengers began to deplane, he inserted himself into the center of the crowd.

I must blend in.

He had changed to clothing worn by typical tourists and business travelers, a gray business tunic with a charcoal overjacket, although he now wished he had dispensed with his fedora. It stood out like a sore thumb in this crowd, even more than a *yarmulke* would have, but he could not force himself to go with his head uncovered.

The man at the foot of the ramp wore traditional Arab garb. His *keffiyeh* consisted of a white cloth secured by black rope around the head, with loose fabric flaps hanging down the sides and back of his neck. His *thawb*, a white traditional robe, contrasted untraditionally with his military spit-shined boots.

I will get a keffiyeh *to keep my head covered.*

He followed other passengers to a waiting line. The sun baked the hard surface of the landing field, and dust tickled the back of his nose. He sniffed loudly to avoid sneezing, drawing more unwelcome attention to himself.

"Next, please." The agent stood behind a two-meter long gray metal table outside the entrance to the terminal.

Chaim removed his sweat-soaked papers from his jacket pocket and thrust them at the agent, who also wore *thawb* and *keffiyeh*. The man frowned and curled his lip as he smoothed out the documents and examined them. "Chime McNulty?"

"Yes. McNulty. But it is *Cha*-im, not *Chime*." He pronounced Chaim with the emphasis on the guttural "Ch" sound of Hebrew. "I am just visiting."

Oy, Gott. Why did I correct him? I am finished. Pain struck Chaim's stomach as if he had gulped burning liquid.

The agent's eyes narrowed. "Where have you come from, Mr. McNulty?"

"Dublin III."

"But your flight originated in Cloresto."

"I traveled from Dublin III, through Meridian, and then to Cloresto, and then here." Chaim caught his breath at a potential error in his papers.

The agent nodded. "Ah, here it is on the next page."

Chaim quaked under another deluge of sweat.

The agent leaned into him. "Why are you nervous?"

Chaim swallowed hard. "I-I hate flying. That is all."

"Do you have anything of value to declare? Money? Banned substances...like liquor? Anything you will sell or leave behind on New Mecca?"

"No. Nothing." He could not meet the man's eyes.

After a long moment, the agent handed Chaim his papers. "Go to entry kiosk five to pick up your luggage. Welcome to New Mecca."

Chaim tipped his hat then walked to the kiosk. Totally *farschvitzed,* his tunic hung as if he came out of a shower. He wiped his forehead as he stood in line.

I must stay calm. They have not checked any bags in front of me.

The baggage clerk wore a brown and white uniform rather than robes, but the ever-present *keffiyeh* perched above his black-bearded face. He looked at the ticket Chaim proffered, then retrieved his suitcase and lifted it to the counter. "What do you have in here?"

"Personal effects. I'm just visiting. Visiting."

The clerk's mouth quirked as he looked at Chaim. "You sweat much. Is it too warm for you here?"

Chaim nodded spastically.

The agent popped the latches on the suitcase.

Oy, gevalt. He will find it. I am dead.

The man riffled through the contents of Chaim's bag, finding only clothing, shoes, personal grooming items, and several boxes of mints. He closed the bag. "You may go."

Thank God. He did not find the secret compartment and the vials within.

Relief made his knees weak. He smiled but was again unsure of the result. He took his belongings and escaped into the terminal. The heart-pounding fear that had grasped him since he left the spaceliner eased.

I have made it. They did not find it. I am still alive.

***

Chaim faced two men in a small, dimly-lit room, half the light coming through a single dusty window, half from a naked glow bulb on the ceiling. The sharp musty stink of his own sweat mingled with the stale odors of tea and smoked fish, and he wished only to get clean and change clothes. They sat in a tiny kitchenette around a scarred wooden table. A faded green-flowered sofa took up most of the living area.

"With the proper clothing you will pass among these people," Mordechai Neidritch said. The elderly rebbe who was Chaim's New Mecca contact spoke in Hebrew. "Your skin is dark enough and many wear beards here. Your Arabic is imperfect, however, so you must avoid conversations."

Chaim nodded vigorously as he listened to the thin, sallow rebbe, eyes fixed on his wispy white beard. He feared to meet the rebbe's eyes directly.

I will succeed with my holy endeavor. I will.

The rebbe shook his head. "But why did you choose your Hebrew name *Chaim* on your papers?" His *yarmulke* slipped as he spoke. He adjusted the head covering. "Idiocy! Were you *trying* to be apprehended?"

Chaim bowed his head as a shudder racked his frame. "I...that...is my *name*. I changed the surname." He said nothing about his stupidity in correcting the immigration official's pronunciation.

The second man, younger and weasel-faced with huge front teeth, burst into laughter. "*Chaim McNulty? A joke.*"

"Quiet, Jonah." The rebbe fixed the tall, broad-shouldered young man with a steely gaze. "This is not a humorous matter." He turned back to Chaim. "You have the...things?" His voice shook. He licked his lips and swallowed.

"In my bag. They never suspected." *Thank Yahweh.*

The rebbe's head bobbed. "Good. We will get you clothing so you can pass as a local."

"If he doesn't open his mouth," Jonah added, grinning.

This drew a stern glance from the rebbe. "New Mecca is an enlightened planet...they say. The authorities accept the presence of Jews, but some New Meccans do not share that tolerance. There have been...incidents. For now, you may take the bed in the adjacent room. We must prepare." As he stood, Jonah also stood, towering over the frail rebbe.

Chaim's dismissal was clear. He dragged his bag to the bedroom as Jonah moved to stare out the small window. Chaim closed the bedroom door behind him, stopped and leaned against it, ear pressed to the thin wood panel.

Jonah spoke. "He is not what I expected. He should be hard, uncompromising, terrible, to carry out such a task. But he is pathetic, laughable. Is this the best they could send?"

"Remember," the rebbe countered, "not many of

our Testamentary-Literalist brethren escaped Dovid's World at the end. Our leaders were targeted and captured."

Jonah snorted. "He acts anything but competent."

The rebbe's voice dripped with sarcasm. "And you consider yourself capable? To be a *mensch,* you must prove yourself. You have no idea how you would fare on such a mission, so do not denigrate our friend. Imperfect he may be, but he *is* carrying what could be the salvation of our movement, of our true faith. He must be Moses, leading our people from slavery...David laughing in the face of Goliath."

He paused to draw a raspy breath. "Along with the few of us who escaped Dovid's World, we are left with small groups throughout the galaxy. We must remain concealed until our plan comes to fruition. Then we will strike our final blow and regain our glory, reinstate the only proper Judaic faith more widely than ever before. The Testamentary-Literalists will rise again from the ashes of the Dovidian Holocaust."

Chaim stood mesmerized by the rebbe's words, his vision, his passion, and then removed his ear from the door. *Is Jonah right? Am I not worthy? Can I be Moses? David? Can I commit such an act?*

He sat heavily on the edge of the cot that almost filled the dingy room and buried his face in his hands as he fought to control a surge of nausea.

***

Chaim stepped into the crowded avenue. Despite his *keffiyeh* and *thawb,* he felt marked. He could not keep his glance from darting from face to face, waiting for someone to recognize him as an enemy and cry an alarm.

They will see. Oh God, they will see.

The robes were stifling, and sweat poured off his face into his beard. He walked through the bazaar, casting furtive glances in every direction. Vendors hawked a host of wares, calling passersby to entice them to their stalls. He lowered his gaze to the ground, tracing the pavement where he would place his feet, afraid to meet anyone's eyes. The mixed scents of sweet and sharp spices, cardamom, cinnamon, cloves, and peppers turned Chaim's stomach. He fought to keep down his breakfast.

The livestock market...that is where I must go. One kilometer, that's all they have in which to stop me. Lord, give me the strength to do this.

Despite his trembling legs, he made the market with no incidents. Many acres of pens and corrals stretched into the distance. The musky smell of camels, cattle, sheep, goats, and their dung pervaded the air. Chaim had never seen a camel and feared getting near the great humped beasts. Cries of the livestock auctioneers and potential buyers assaulted his ears. He pushed through the throng, some people wearing traditional robes, others in colorful modern pant and jacket tunics. The noise and odors made him lightheaded.

Stomach churning, he hurried to a building marked as a men's lavatory. He glanced about him, eyes wide, before opening the door and stepping through. He almost collided with a robed man exiting at the same time.

"Sorry," he said in Arabic, hoping his accent would not give him away, but the man never looked at him and hurried past. Chaim exhaled a gust of sour breath, heart thumping as if it sought to burst from his chest. He entered a dank stall and sank to his knees, vomiting his meager breakfast into the commode. When he caught his breath, he stood and exited the stall.

I must do it now. You must take hold of yourself,

Chaim. You must be brave. You must be Moses, David.

Heart accelerating again, he reached beneath his robe to the pouch slung over his shoulder and extracted a small vial, one of six he carried. He left the lavatory, the vial hidden in the palm of his hand. Looking down, he expected his entire hand to be aglow with the fire he imagined emanating from the vial's lethal contents.

They cannot see it, Chaim, he chided himself as he glanced around. *I must put it on the animals, they said. Get close enough to touch them and spill the contents on them, then rub it into their hair. But how? Someone will see if I pour the vial's liquid onto the animals.*

He noticed a stack of hay bales. *That's it, their food. I will put it there.*

His head swiveled around, sure someone watched, but no one paid him any attention. He held the vial close to his body. His hands shook as he opened the screw cap. He punctured a tough film seal with his fingernail, holding his breath as he did. Fluid contaminated his fingertip.

They said it would not harm me. They said the pestilence would not harm people.

He jumped when someone coughed nearby. He shuffled away from the cougher, not making eye contact with any passersby. To calm his racing pulse, he took a deep breath. He grabbed a handful of hay and turned to look at the nearby pens. A goat stood by the fence of its corral, staring at him, eyeing the hay in his hand. Chaim sidled over to the fence and splashed the vial's contents on the fodder. The fluid was colorless and odorless.

Water. It looks like water. Watering the goats. That's what I will tell them when they arrest me.

The goat lost no time in grabbing the hay from his shaking hand. He steeled his angst and petted the goat's head as it chewed. He felt a pang and a wave of nausea.

His family had goats on their farm where he grew up. Now he would bring harm to goats. How could he be so cold...? He thrust those thoughts behind him.

Surely, that will be enough, having the animals eat the contaminated hay. This is a war. I must be strong.

The goat bleated for more.

Chaim's heart hammered with every plaintive cry. *Quiet,* he wanted to scream. *They'll see.*

He moved away to another haystack, grabbed some hay, and moved to a sheep pen. He dumped another vial and then fed the fodder to the sheep. Knowing they would soon fall ill, he patted their heads and whispered, "Thank you for your sacrifice."

He shied away from hand-feeding the camels but threw contaminated hay into the pen and watched one nose at it. He feared the sweat that had dripped from his forehead onto the hay would deter the camel from eating, but it did not.

The last four of the six vials went to the camels; it was less scary to throw the hay. By the time he was done, he had sweated through his garment.

What do I do now? Rebbe Neidritch said not to return directly to his home. Where can I go? Perhaps a train ride. See the city. I'm a tourist.

At the crowded hovertrain ticket window, people were showing the agent their papers before he issued tickets. Chaim had left his papers behind to avoid identification if arrested, and he panicked. He took a ragged deep breath then fought against the crowd to go back into the street. A man he jostled snapped angrily at him. A tremor shook his frame and he stumbled, almost falling before he caught his balance, his back to a plaster wall. Then he staggered off, as if to flee what he had loosed on the animals.

Oh, God, help me. God of Abraham, Isaac, Joseph, help me. I have started the Holy War.

Stephen A Benjamin

Chapter 2

When the government on the planet of New Mecca requested help from the *Galactic Circle Veterinary Service* for an unusual medical problem, my self-preservation synapses kicked into overdrive, and my stomach got queasy. Strange diseases often had proven as dangerous to humans as to the affected animals. The caller was a functionary who did not seem able to explain further, so I would reserve judgment until we landed—if I decided to answer the call.

New Mecca was the galaxy's modern seat of Islam. More than a thousand years ago, the age-old conflict between Judaism and Islam finally drove the Jews from earth in our last Great Diaspora. The thought of going to the new center of the faith that had oppressed my people, at least from *my* point of view, gave me pause. I discussed it with my crew: my lovely wife Roxanne, also a veterinarian, and Furoletto Cohen, our medical technologist and engineer.

"I understand your reluctance, Cy," Roxanne said, "but modern Islam isn't the religion that oppressed Jews a thousand years ago. New Mecca's government is not repressive. The AI's records show that there's a small Jewish population there."

Ruthie, our ship's unique artificial intelligence, chimed in with her sultry contralto. "*Encyclopedia Galactica* says, 'The New Meccan government is based on the principles espoused by Muhammad in the original Medina. The laws ensure the rights and responsibilities for the Muslim, Jewish, Christian, and pagan communities, bringing them together as one.'"

As a lifelong compulsive reader of ancient and modern literature, I knew that something was not necessarily true just because it was in print. My face must have shown my unwillingness to accept an encyclopedia entry at face value.

Fur's bright brown-eyed gaze bored past his crooked nose and into my eyes. He tugged at his full sandy beard as his deep voice rumbled, "I don't think we need to fear religious persecution, if that's what you're worried about."

Fear was not the issue, though. "Hmph. I think we all have had enough of intolerant, repressive religious governments by now." I referred to the ultraconservative Testamentary-Literalist Party that had established a fundamentalist Jewish tyranny on my own world, perverting our religion.

"Stop it, Cy." Roxanne's green eyes flashed, and her auburn curls bounced as she shook her head. "We can't paint all religious governments with the same brush. This is a call for veterinary medical help. That's what we do. You've never turned anyone down before."

"Human or alien," Fur added with a wry smile.

I knew he referred to our assisting every life-form from Terran livestock to a variety of bizarre alien species of fauna and flora.

He pointedly looked toward the other members of our crew, currently engaged in a 3-D chess match they'd learned from him during our voyage. The Lupan werewolf called Healer and the young dragon named Learns-to-Fix-Injuries-After-Inflicting-Them ignored our conversation. They had joined us as medical interns after visits to their planets showed them the need for advancing their species' medical knowledge. Religion was foreign to both species.

Maybe I was being the kind of bigot I hated, but I could not forget the Test-Lit religious zealots who subjected my parents to the torture of an Inquisition.

Admittedly, what little I knew about Islam was historical and filtered through a two thousand-year haze of negative Jewish perceptions. Roxanne and Fur had a point. I cringed inwardly at my inappropriate knee-jerk response to helping Muslims, but I still worried. Add the three of us to Islam, throw in a dash of werewolf and dragon, and who knew what trouble we might get into?

***

Our spaceship bore the symbol of veterinary medicine: the letter V superimposed on the staff of Aesculapius. This overlaid a graphic representation of a spiral galaxy surrounded by the name: *Galactic Circle Veterinary Service*. We called our ship the *GCVS*.

It was equipped with three drives: an antigravity drive for use within planetary atmospheres, an antimatter drive for interplanetary travel, and an interstellar hyperdrive. The antigravity drive also supplied artificial gravity and maintained a one-g environment throughout our travels. For long space voyages, the artificial gravity was a major physiological blessing. For someone like me who got sick turning a corner too fast, not having to put up with zero-g was a godsend.

Hyperspace jumps took only a small fraction of the objective time of normal space travel. Since a spaceship could only enter hyperspace outside the influence of any significant gravity well, it took a lot more time to maneuver into and through solar systems than it did to move between stars. I did not try to understand the complex physics behind all the drives and hyperspace itself; I found it easiest to rely on Fur for the engineering and on Ruthie to fly the ship.

We hyperjumped to the New Meccan solar system and cruised toward the sole inhabited planet using the antimatter drive. We would use the antigravity drive, rather than the antimatter drive, to enter the atmosphere. In an atmosphere, the antimatter drive could result in a chain reaction, annihilating the ship and everything in its vicinity.

Once in orbit, I spoke to Ruthie. "Set a long landing trajectory so we can get an overview of this planet."

"Certainly, Cy," Ruthie cooed.

When I originally programmed the AI, I named it Ruthie and gave it a sexy voice as a joke. I was single then, and I did not expect a bunch of silicon chips to develop a distinct personality, especially one that showed a proprietary interest in me and hostility toward my wife. Not for the first time, I tried to convince myself that I imagined those disturbing tendencies, and so I brushed them off, as usual.

We overflew forests, mountains, oceans, and vast deserts of the earth-like planet. Ruthie careened the ship into a huge canyon and followed the winding river toward a steep mountain range. Swerving left and right, the ship almost scraped the towering rock walls that loomed frighteningly close. Seated in the copilot's chair beside me, Roxanne gripped her seat so hard her knuckles turned white.

"Ruthie," I barked. "We don't need a rollercoaster

ride. Just get us to the spaceport without us losing our lunches. Please."

"I was showing you the planet, like you asked," Ruthie replied in a hurt tone.

The ship rose and leveled out, the heading set for the capital city of Medina.

"You don't need to say *please* to an AI," Roxanne snapped, her eyes blazing. "It deliberately does things to irk me."

My wife rarely referred to Ruthie by name. I did not need my empathic abilities to feel her anger. My talent as an empath allowed me to sense the emotions of animals and to soothe stressed beasts mentally, a useful skill for a veterinarian. I also perceived human emotions, but I was *not* a telepath. I could not read minds or influence people the way I could calm nervous or hurting animals. On the negative side, receiving strong emotions, animal or human, caused me nausea, headaches, and vertigo. Right now I was getting all three from Roxanne.

"You need to get control of this...thing, Cy." Roxanne waved at the comm board.

"I agree, Captain," Fur said. "It seems like your programming has had some, um, undesired effects."

The laughter that underlay his words felt like scalpels scraping my synapses. Furoletto Cohen was not just my veterinary assistant—he had gone through two years of veterinary college before dropping out to join the underground fight against our Test-Lit oppressors—but also my best friend and stalwart companion through many adventures, including all-out war. A giant of a man, he towered close to two and a half meters and massed one hundred-thirty kilos.

"Thanks for the support," I groused. "She's just a goddamned computer program, anyway."

As I said "she," my stomach twisted at another

wave of anger from Roxanne.

"*It* can be a pain in the ass," Roxanne muttered.

We left the mountain range behind us and crossed several hundred kilometers of desert framed by irrigated fields along two major river valleys. By the time we reached the city, the rivers combined into one larger flow. Farms melded into residential housing districts, then to a city center with clusters of skyscrapers interspersed with factories and warehouses. Gilded-domed mosques with minarets that reached toward the sky dominated all sections of the city.

"Approaching-The-Landing-Site," Ruthie announced in an annoying automaton tone. "We-Are-Cleared-To-Land."

"Bring us in and contact the local authorities, Ruthie," I ordered.

Landing on antigravity thrusters barely stirred the dust on the landing site, but I always cringed when I saw people waiting below. My imaginary vision of a flame-tailed spacecraft setting down was a hangover from my reading and watching ancient sci-fi books and vids. Of course, Ruthie never fouled a landing, but I still worried. A dozen other spaceships sat on the spaceport field. Ruthie set us down a safe distance from them all.

I hit my harness release button; the straps retracted. I moved off the bridge to the main airlock as Ruthie opened it and lowered the ship's ramp. Several people walked toward us.

A blast of hot, humid air hit me as if I had opened the door of a sauna. Sweat erupted on my skin.

Ruthie didactically intoned, "It is arid most of the year. Now is the time of high humidity and rains. Rainfall collects in underground reservoirs. In the dry season, the city relies on the mountain runoff into the Tigris and Euphrates rivers."

The rivers we had seen from the air, but before I could comment on the names, Fur snorted. "Of course. Why not? Tigris and Euphrates..."

Ruthie explained, "Many places on New Mecca are named after places on Old Earth, once called the Middle East, the roots of the people here. There is a delegation waiting for you, Cy."

When Fur, Roxanne, and I reached the bottom of the ramp, a tall, dark-skinned man introduced himself as Imam Ali Suliaman. Incongruous ice-blue eyes peered above a hooked nose and a black goatee shot with silver. He wore a blue-checked cloth headdress secured by black rope that I recognized as the traditional *keffiyeh*. The man's matching blue robe had a green Islamic Star and Crescent displayed on the chest pocket.

It was still hard for me to ignore the age-old enmity between Judaism and Islam. I fought back a surge of uncharitable bigotry as Suliaman put out a hand.

"Welcome...to all of you."

I sensed sincerity behind Suliaman's greeting, which cut through my negativity, and I could only respond in kind. I shook his hand. "I'm Dr. Cy Berger. This is my wife and co-captain, Dr. Roxanne Simon, and our engineer and veterinary technician, Fur Cohen."

Roxanne stepped forward and shook Suliaman's hand. Her emerald green-eyes, thin straight nose between high cheekbones, and curly auburn locks captured his full attention. Can't say as I blamed him. Only a few centimeters shorter than my above-average height, with ample curves even her shapeless medical tunic could not hide, my better half was a striking woman.

When Fur proffered his hand, I sensed a momentary hesitation in Suliaman. Though the Imam was my height, the man had to look up at Fur. He frowned as he watched his own hand disappear in Fur's huge grasp. He seemed happy to get it back unharmed.

Suliaman then introduced the two men with him, both dressed in robes and *keffiyeh*. Aaquil Hussein, whose robes could not hide his considerable girth, was the chief physician of the New Meccan Medical Corps. Jabir bin Saqer, the chief veterinarian of the planet, was smaller in stature and spare enough that his robes gave little clue as to body type.

I said, "I'd like to introduce the other members of our crew." I spoke into my lapel comm. "Come on out, Healer, Learns-To-Fix-Injuries."

There was shocked silence as our interns marched down the ramp. Not surprising when one was a brown-furred wolf-like humanoid with a prominent mane and the other was a red dragon resembling a small tyrannosaur with wings.

Suliaman did not miss a beat. He showed no change of expression as his emotions stayed rock-steady. Hussein, on the other hand, took a step backward as his eyes narrowed and his mouth turned down at the corners. A blast of fear and hate rolled off the corpulent Medical Corps chief. My stomach twisted in response. This guy was a major xenophobe.

Bin Saqer's response was the opposite. He radiated delight at meeting our fellow travelers. I guessed he did not meet many aliens here on New Mecca.

"This is Healer." I motioned to the Lupan. "He's a shape-shifter from the planet Lupus IV. And this is Learns-to-Fix-Injuries-After-Inflicting-Them.   He's from Dragonworld. They both are with us to learn more about medicine. They're our friends and yours."

The latter comment was necessary knowing the level of fear that our colleagues engendered in most humans. I had to do this on every planet that we visited.

Roxanne murmured, "Don't look now, but I think we've mobilized the home guard."

A line of militia clad in brown and tan camouflage jogged across the field toward us.

Bin Saqer bowed to our alien friends. "Welcome, Healer, and, um, Learns-to-Fix-Injuries-After-Inflicting-Them. I am pleased to meet you."

Neither the Lupan nor the dragon responded. They stared at the oncoming troops.

The Imam held up his hand to the guards. They stopped in their tracks. He then addressed us. "Please, do not be concerned over the soldiers. They are an...honor guard." He frowned at Hussein as he spoke.

I got the distinct impression that the military presence was not Suliaman's doing.

"These are honored guests." He pointed to our group. "They must be treated as such." Then he motioned us to follow.

We marched across the field toward the immigration booths, followed by the military types. The contradictory smells of water and dust filled my nostrils. The sharp tang of ozone lingered from a thunderstorm that had moved across the field before we landed. I watched lightning strike the top of a minaret in an adjacent part of the city. My boots squelched in a few puddles remaining on the field's surface.

Other travelers, dressed in everything from robes to business tunics, stopped and stared at us as we walked. No doubt some other extraterrestrial species visited the planet, but I doubted any had the sheer impact of a werewolf and a red dragon.

Learns-to-Fix-Injuries raised his broad snout and sniffed audibly. "I ssmell fear."

I sensed he was right. "Healer, Learns-to-Fix-Injuries, just stay behind us."

Roxanne said, "There's no danger to us here, Red."

She used our nickname for the dragon. He essentially was a teenager and listened to Roxanne more readily than Fur or me.

Healer's nostrils dilated as he sniffed the air. He said nothing but took everything in with his startling yellow eyes, typical for the normally reticent Lupan.

Two security guards in green uniforms and helmets stepped forward, nervously fingering their pulse rifles. Between them, an immigration officer in robes and *keffiyeh* stepped toward us. The man bowed then put his right hand out to Ali. "*Salam 'alaykum.*"

Ali returned the bow. "*Wa alaykumu salam.*"

"Welcome home, Imam Suliaman," he said in accented Common. "And welcome to all of your guests." He gave Healer and Learns-to-Fix-Injuries a formal bow.

Apparently, we were not the only new arrivals. I glanced at the Imam and wondered why he was the one to meet us.

"We can dispense with the usual immigration formalities," Suliaman said. "After me, please." He turned and moved toward the entrance to the terminal.

As we moved to follow, half of the camo-clad guards took positions at the front of our party and half at the rear. I wasn't sure if that was to protect us or everyone else in sight. Whatever the case, I followed, my heart beating a bit faster than normal.

***

The air conditioning in the terminal building was a blessed relief. Suliaman led us to a conference room on the second level of the terminal. Wooden chairs flanked a green metal table. Our human contingent sat.

The dragon shivered. "Too cold. Like outsside better." He came from a hot desert world. Now, he stood in a corner, mouth agape, showing his impressive ivory fangs.

Healer stood next to the dragon and stared at our hosts. His yellow-eyed gaze caused Hussein to squirm in his seat, making it creak under his burden.

Perhaps to cover his discomfort, Hussein spoke first. "Dr. Berger, Dr. Simon, Mr. Cohen ...and, er, fellow travelers, we thank you for answering our call for help. Ali Suliaman has returned to New Mecca specifically to meet you. Ali?"

"The *Galactic Circle Veterinary Service* was recommended by a friend on Cennesari. She said you saved both their herdbeasts and the native sentient felines. We would like to hear about that."

"Who was it that recommended us?" I asked.

"Rabbi Sarah Pearlman. In Cennesari City."

I nodded. "An impressive woman. We met her at a Passover Seder."

Suliaman obviously knew the story but wanted us to convince the others of our competence and the appropriateness of contracting our assistance. I sensed the most uncertainty, and distinct antipathy, from Hussein. I caught an emotional hint that he might fault our Jewish heritage. Bin Saqer might have resented bringing in off-world veterinarians, but he seemed to have an open mind.

At any rate, I disliked speaking of Cennesari. I felt it represented my most bitter defeat, though others did not see it that way.

Fur ran his fingers through his beard and spoke. "We were contracted to address a deadly epidemic in the native Cennesarian herdbeasts, the cenoxen. Cy found that the hay cut from the wild grasslands contained toxic plants that led to a fatal bleeding disorder."

Fur made it sound simple, but it had not been.

"Cy also discovered the cenoxen were sentient and telepathic, as were the native giant cats who faced a deadly viral epidemic. We managed to save both species, but many of the planet's human settlers wanted the cats eradicated as a menace, not saved. Many others would not accept that their cenoxen were anything but food animals, a cornerstone of their economy. By the time we left, the majority of the planet's humans called us liars and vilified us despite the good we had done."

The cenoxen still haunted my dreams, talking to me, pleading for someone to free them from their enslavement.

"Many Cennesarians see you as true heroes, Dr. Berger, Mr. Cohen," Suliaman said.

When Hussein made a sour face, Roxanne got to the point, as usual. "If you're concerned with our qualifications, Cennesari is not our only reference. The *Galactic Circle Veterinary Service* has dealt with disease outbreaks in dozens of different species, Terran and non-Terran, including problems that affected the inhabitants of Lupus IV—Healer's people—and Dragonworld."

Hussein harrumphed and nodded. "Yes. It seems your qualifications are acceptable." His underlying antagonism belied his words. "Perhaps we should hear from Dr. bin Saqer next...to discuss why you are here." He emanated condescension when he spoke the veterinarian's name. He would not be the first physician I had met who saw himself as innately superior to veterinarians.

Bin Saqer took the floor. "A disease threatens our livestock. And, in turn, our survival. Two months ago, we had an outbreak of an unknown malady within the city's central bazaar. It affected a variety of ruminants and caused a plethora of puzzling, disparate symptoms that affected every organ system in the body:

pneumonia, enteritis, hepatitis, nephritis, encephalitis, and more. It was invariably fatal, no matter what treatment we tried.

"We have not isolated anything that we recognize as the cause, but fresh blood from infected animals injected into healthy animals reproduced the disease. We quarantined the affected herds but the disease spread. We then quarantined all the herds within a day's drive of the city. Some remained unaffected, and after a couple of weeks went by, we hoped we had nipped the epidemic in the bud..."

Bin Saqer's emotions roiled with black thoughts. My stomach twinged in response. I strengthened my mental empathic screen. I did not keep it fully on at all times because it was too exhausting.

"...until I received word of further outbreaks in cattle, sheep, and goats. The same symptoms. The quarantine required that there would be no movement of animals, and anything going in and out from farms and ranches be disinfected: clothing, shoes, equipment, you name it, but the disease spread."

Roxanne asked, "It sounds like you took the appropriate actions. I assume you used a powerful disinfectant that would kill most bacteria and viruses?"

"We used a product that kills all known organisms, even resistant spores."

"And what did you do with the exposed and diseased animals?"

"Slaughter and cremation. We needed to destroy the source of infection."

Roxanne winced. I felt her reaction as needles stabbing my brain and squinted against the pain.

We had not advanced that much from procedures used a thousand years ago for highly contagious diseases like foot and mouth disease and epidemic pustular dermatitis. Unfortunately, the only recourse was to quarantine infected herds, slaughter them, and burn or bury the carcasses. We dealt with animal disease based on different principles than human disease. Even with our modern antivirals and antibiotics, the cost of treatment of thousands of livestock in a major outbreak was not economically feasible.

This was not Roxanne's first go-round with herd decimation. She oversaw the response to an outbreak of epidemic pustular dermatitis on her own world, Sammara, which included the necessary destruction of thousands of cattle, a course of action that took its toll on a veterinarian's soul.

"We have kept this region quarantined," bin Saqer continued, "but it is hard to control local movement of all animals, particularly feral canines and felines. The outbreaks have started to move up the Tigris and Euphrates valleys. We fear disaster if it moves beyond this region. This disease has jumped between our herbivorous species like nothing I have seen before. We dare not harvest meat or milk for fear they are contaminated and could spread the disease further."

"Are you concerned about carnivores scavenging animals that died from this disease and spreading it?" Roxanne asked.

Bin Saqer shook his head. "Worse. This same disease is now affecting feral *and* domesticated dogs and cats."

Dogs and cats? That made no sense to me.

Roxanne's voice was grave as she asked, "Have there been cases in humans?"

"Not so far as we know, but it is a concern."

Holding my mental screen firm against his despair, I said, "If all your local animals die or are destroyed, without hosts the virus hits a dead end. I know that sounds callous, especially with respect to pets, but your livestock herds can be replaced from other parts of New Mecca or even off-world. Dr. Simon's colleagues on Sammara have the technology to replace those herds in a fraction of the time and cost it would take you now."

Roxanne nodded. "You can have our technology for advanced cryostorage and forced maturation of embryos. We repopulated the herds we lost in our epidermal pustular dermatitis epidemic more quickly than was previously possible. That could ameliorate the economic effects of this outbreak."

Hussein jumped into the discussion. "Such technology would be valuable for our human and veterinary medical communities, but killing our herds has not stopped the outbreak." He shot bin Saqer a look of contempt then looked at me. "You must fix this problem."

Nettled by Hussein's antagonism, I came to bin Saqer's defense. "It sounds like Dr. bin Saqer has taken all the appropriate actions to deal with your epidemic. I don't know what else we can do."

Bin Saqer drew a deep breath. "Dr. Berger, you made an assumption that this disease is due to a virus. That's logical, but we don't know that. We can isolate nothing that resembles a pathogen from the victims."

Roxanne's surprise matched mine. "Wait a minute. You haven't found any agent, viral or bacterial?"

Bin Saqer nodded. "Nor fungal, protozoal, or anything else that might cause disease."

"Bacteria, fungi, and protozoa would be hard to miss, so let's assume it is a virus of some sort, as Cy suggested. One that's adapted to ungulates isn't going to jump to carnivores that quickly. Oh, it can happen, over time. Like influenza jumping from swine or chickens to people. But it would take an incredible mutation rate for what you describe. Nothing capable of that is known."

Extinction

Hussein met Roxanne's gaze, his bloated face reddening. "We are not a benighted, backwater medical community, Dr. Simon. The facts speak for themselves, whether you believe them or not."

I drew a deep breath before breaking in. "Dr. bin Saqer, Dr. Hussein, we don't mean to insult your knowledge. It's just...like Dr. Simon, I'm confused by this."

Fur's deep voice broke in. "And you can't isolate any pathogens from the dogs or cats either?"

Bin Saqer took the question. "We know something is there, as we can transmit the disease with live tissues or blood, but our efforts to identify the organism have been fruitless."

"No organism? That makes no sense," I said. "The cause has to be there."

Hussein's resentment at what he perceived as criticism cut at my nerves. "It's your job to find it." He scowled at me.

I felt my face heat, but before I could respond, bin Saqer spoke. "You have experience with alien diseases. We hoped you might have insights that we have not. We have no reports of distant outbreaks...yet. We have restricted all animal travel, including pets, but there are wild animals in the outback. If the disease spreads to those, our quarantine will be breached."

"Okay, you've got our attention," I said. "We need to get more information about the disease and what you've done to find the pathogen responsible."

I hoped there was no danger to us. At least there were no human cases yet, and I assumed New Meccan physicians would not have put this solely into the hands of veterinarians if there were human infections. Certainly not a physician like Hussein.

I glanced at Roxanne and Fur, who both nodded to me. "Dr. bin Saqer, we are at your service."

Chapter 3

In the *GCVS* land drone, we followed bin Saqer's vehicle to the livestock market. The rear section of our vehicle was equipped as a mobile clinic. Fur carried a duffle containing isolation suits, medical, and necropsy supplies as we walked through a bazaar that I imagined had not changed for thousands of years. Tents, stalls of wood and metal with brightly colored awnings, and open-back land drones were packed side-by-side. From each, a merchant hawked wares from fabrics, to baked goods, to grilling meats and vegetables. The stench of manure from the nearby stock pens underlay the savory odors. Shoppers strolled through the grounds garbed in everything from traditional robes to modern tunics. Many women covered their faces with veils, but just as many wore makeup and glittering jewelry.

Myriad emotional currents, from joy, to anger, to despair, assaulted my mind, but they were diffuse and untargeted, and easily blocked from my empathic perception.

"Camels?" I muttered as we walked toward a fenced corral. "I don't know a damn thing about camels."

"You said the same thing about dragons and werewolves," Fur replied.

"But *nobody* knew anything about *them.*"

Roxanne added, "Your AI probably has a wealth of knowledge about camels, but when I *tried* to research them, it *said* there was a problem with database retrieval. As if that's possible."

Her anger stabbed at my brain again. Why Ruthie antagonized Roxanne was beyond me, but I had other problems to deal with first. Deep down, on a level I did not want to explore, I avoided dealing with Ruthie, and my procrastination pissed off my wife.

I followed bin Saqer to a gated pen. He had asked for Healer and Learns-to-Fix-Injuries to remain behind; he worried about their effect on the high-strung camels.

The camels stood on long, spindly legs that looked as if they should not carry the creature's mass, yet I knew these tough Terran animals carried heavy burdens and tolerated extreme temperatures and prolonged lack of water and food.

Bin Saqer pointed to one animal that stood spraddle-legged with its head down between its front feet, gasping for breath. Diarrhea smeared its hindquarters. It shook with tremors as if it feared what came next.

"This is typical. The skin lesions are present in all cases. You can see this one has enteritis, advanced pneumonia, and nervous manifestations. What you can't see is the damage to every other organ."

"And this isn't typical of any known camel disease?" I asked.

Bin Saqer shook his head. "The only infectious disease with similar skin lesions is camel pox. It is generally self-limiting, although it can be systemic and severe enough to kill a young animal, but nothing like this. There *is* nothing like this."

A mangy dog, some sort of shepherd mix, staggered up and sniffed at my pant cuff. He looked wobbly and glassy-eyed, and I shooed him away. I recalled that bin Saqer said dogs were affected, too, but I needed to concentrate on the camels, for now. After a moment, the damn dog lifted his leg to spray the fence post I was near, splattering my shoes and pant legs in the process.

Fur snickered.

"Let's get a closer look," Roxanne said.

Fur, Roxanne, and I donned disposable isolation suits Fur had passed around, and then bin Saqer opened the corral's gate. I approached the sick camel.

It acknowledged my presence with a quick flick of an eyeball and what little panic it could muster in its deplorable state.

I used my empathic talent to soothe the animal, steeling myself to the inherent result of my effort. The camel's distress hit me harder than I expected. My stomach twisted with nausea, my head pounded, and vertigo caused me to stumble. Worse was the realization that I could not do anything to ameliorate the ravages of the beast's disease.

The camel went back to fighting to breathe.

As bin Saqer said, the skin lesions bore some resemblance to pox: papules, blisters, and crusts, with deeper fissures cracking the epidermis. Many lesions showed the thick mucoid pus of a secondary infection.

While I examined the skin, Roxanne and Fur moved in front of the camel. Fur lifted the animal's head so Roxanne could examine the inside of its mouth. "No lesions on the oral mucosa. That rules out the vesicular diseases like foot and mouth disease." She glanced at bin Saqer. "If camels even get those."

"Camels do get foot and mouth disease, but they are not as severely affected as cattle."

I asked, "What's the course of this infection?"

"Very rapid. From the time of first signs, death occurs in two days. In all our livestock."

"Fast," Fur said, "but not as fast as the Pronacian plague."

A frown creased bin Saqer's forehead. "Pronacian plague? I have not heard of that one."

I said, "The lizardmen of Pronac had a plague that killed in twenty-four hours...after the victim went homicidally insane."

Bin Saqer's frown cut deeper into his brow.

Fur added, "An infectious enzyme catalyzed the formation of alcohol from carbohydrates causing bizarre behavior and fatal intoxication. The dead had incredibly high blood-alcohol levels."

Bin Saqer asked, "Do you suggest that such an infectious enzyme could be involved here?"

"I doubt it," I said. "That enzyme caused only metabolic imbalances, nothing like these physical manifestations. Any idea of the incubation period?"

"That, too, is rapid, less than twenty-four hours."

Roxanne asked, "What are the initial signs?"

"Listlessness, anorexia, fever. The other signs come rapidly after that. It's like the organism hits every body part at once. It does not start in one location and then spread like other diseases."

The Pronacian plague, as rapidly as it acted, still only affected the liver and the brain. Something was screwy here. Added to that was a growing nausea, and my head seemed to pound in time with waves of pain from the camel.

My self-preservation neurons were firing again. "You haven't isolated any bacteria, and most viruses have specific tropisms. They target certain kinds of cells."

Bin Saqer nodded. "That is why you are here. This disease is not acting like any other. We need a fresh perspective, Dr. Berger."

"Any recently dead animals we can necropsy?" I asked.

"Unfortunately, yes." Tiny knots formed at the corners of bin Saqer's eyes. "It's not pretty."

The rue-bitten pang of his thoughts cut through my body, sharp as any blade. I could not stop the clanging alarm bells that reverberated in my brain. Roxanne's distress added to the nausea and the pounding in my skull.

We followed the New Meccan vet toward a large shed.

***

I am all too familiar with the stench of decaying carcasses, but even through the high efficiency filters of my suit, the charnel reek from the macabre pile of dead animals brought acid to my mouth. Dozens of camel carcasses made me swallow hard.

"These died just today," bin Sager explained. "Heavy equipment will take them for cremation shortly. There are so many dying that they are brought here when terminal."

Even through my hood's faceplate, I saw Fur's mouth turn down at the corners. His nose and eyes wrinkled as if to ward off the fetid miasma. The whiteness of Roxanne's face and her hunched shoulders bespoke of indignation against any disease that could so decimate precious lives.

Roxanne and I got down to the necessary business of examining the corpses. We dissected an animal that drew its last breath as a tractor dropped it next to us. Bin Saqer had not exaggerated; there were lesions in every organ system. My heart drummed a beat of despair. Never had I seen anything that approached the sweeping, massive destruction this disease inflicted upon a body.

The lungs spilled over with frothy, bloody fluid. Lack of oxygen alone would have killed the animal, but the destruction did not stop there. Masses of clotted blood filled the chest and abdominal cavities. Likewise, the blood-filled pericardial sac constricted the heart, making its battle to compensate for lack of oxygen futile.

Huge pale splotches of necrosis spotted the liver, kidneys, and adrenals. The gastrointestinal wall, from the rumen to the colon, was black with hemorrhage; when opened, the contents spilled out like thin gruel. The mucosal epithelial lining was gone. I sawed open the skull and the swollen brain bulged outward, as if to escape the ravages of the disease. Hemorrhages painted the meninges like markers of outrage.

And in this devastation I sensed *wrongness*—something unnatural—something nature never intended to exist.

My empathic senses had never opened like this before. Life, death, health, disease, they were all part of the natural order. But *this*, it felt vile, the essential fetor of desecration, of violence against the fundamental order of life.

A shiver ran through my frame as I stood and turned to bin Saqer standing in the doorway. I fought to keep my stomach from total rebellion; I did not want to vomit in my isolation suit. "O-okay." My voice shook. "I've never seen anything like this."

He nodded. "They are all the same."

Roxanne placed a hand on my arm and peered into my eyes through our visors. I felt her reacting to my body language, but there was no way she could understand it or *feel* it as I did. As I stepped back from the carcass, the wrongness faded, as if proximity was necessary for my percipience.

Roxanne addressed bin Saqer. "It looks like there are several viruses working at once. One agent is destroying the endothelial lining of the blood vessels and causing an Ebola-like hemorrhagic syndrome. Another is damaging the epithelium of the intestinal and pulmonary tracts, causing the diarrhea and respiratory distress. Perhaps a third causes the skin lesions. Finally, from the appearance of the brain, an agent is attacking the nervous tissue as well. I don't see how any single known organism could do all this."

My mental alarm bells went off again, deepening the outrage that I felt. But I could not put it any better than Roxanne's summary, so I asked bin Saqer, "Do you have microbiological and histopathological results we can examine?"

"Yes, though I'm sure it will not clarify any further. Let us go back to my laboratory."

We removed the isolation suits, deposited them in a burn barrel outside, and doused all our equipment in a strong disinfectant. We followed bin Saqer back to our land drone.

***

We gathered in a conference room at bin Saqer's headquarters. I addressed Roxanne, Fur, bin Saqer, and Hussein, who had joined us. My hands scrubbed at my tunic as if to wipe off what I felt, as I tried to make sense of what we had seen.

"Based on all the data, the pathogen is infecting every cell type in the body. There's evidence of damage in everything, epithelium, endothelium, connective tissues, nervous tissues. That violates everything we know about viral pathogenesis...or any other type of infectious organism."

Roxanne added, "And there are no bacterial or fungal colonies, and no evidence of foreign DNA or RNA in these dead animals. No unusual proteins, either. It does not add up."

Her visceral turmoil drove a spike behind my eyes before I could enhance my mental screen.

I glanced at bin Saqer and Hussein. "Any other surprises?"

Bin Saqer spoke. "We have teams in the field investigating any unexplained animal deaths. Every bodily secretion and excretion is infectious, so it's not surprising the disease spreads rapidly. But why has it jumped into carnivores? We are looking for links, including whether feral animals are scavenging carcasses and getting infected via that route."

Hussein added, "The human medical community is alerted. We are examining any deaths that are in any way suspect. Thank Allah, we have seen nothing that would suggest the disease is communicable to humans."

"Praise be to Allah," bin Saqer intoned.

I nodded agreement, not quite sure of the proper thing to say in response. Somehow, I did not think that the God of Jews, Christians, and Muslims, or any other gods, were going to get us out of this mess.

Chapter 4

That night after dinner, my crew sat in the commissary of the *GCVS*. Learns-to-Fix-Injuries crouched in a corner and grumbled as he used a talon to pick a chicken bone out of his teeth.

Fur laughed. "Hey, it's chicken or fish, if you don't want the synthetic protein from the ship's vats. It's too dangerous to eat the local mammals. Could be infected with the plague."

The young dragon fixed him with one vertical-pupil eye. "Live chicken better." He went back to worrying his teeth.

Healer asked me, "This disease, do you understand it?"

I shook my head as I suppressed a shudder. Who would believe ravings about unnatural organisms? Anyway, it was time for a lesson for our two interns.

"Pathogens are pretty predictable. They have to get into the body and replicate locally in some tissue or organ where they cause initial injury before they spread to other parts of the body."

Roxanne added, "Some bacteria produce strong

toxins that can spread in the blood stream and kill, even if the infection stays localized, like the bacteria that cause tetanus, but that does not appear to be the case here. We haven't seen any bacteria."

"That's why we're thinking in terms of viruses," I put in, "even though we don't see evidence of those with the electron microscope, or any possible viral RNA or DNA. On the other hand, viruses have more specificity with respect to cell types affected and sites where they cause injury, and this pathogen is killing cells everywhere. Agents like prions that cause mad cow disease are even more limited than viruses in the tissues they affect."

Healer asked, "Why does a virus grow in only some cells?"

"Many viruses attach to specific receptors on certain cells before they can get inside. There can be physical barriers they have to get past also, like the blood-brain barrier, or the enzymes and acid of the gastrointestinal tract that kill many pathogens, including viruses. But the bottom line is that not all cells support all viruses."

"Thiss not true now." The dragon nodded his understanding. "How viruss get to resst of body?"

"The most common is through circulation of the blood or lymph. Some travel through the nerves, like rabies and some herpes viruses. Usually, it takes time after exposure to allow local multiplication of the virus, then spread and secondary multiplication in target organs. One day for massive dissemination is incredibly fast."

Healer asked, "Where did this disease come from?"

"That's the big question. So far as we can determine, no one has ever reported anything like it."

Fur interjected, "According to bin Saqer, the authorities here are tracing every shipment from off-world that contained either animals or animal products to see if they can come up with a point source for the infection. It had to reach New Mecca from somewhere."

Roxanne nodded agreement. "This isn't something that arose spontaneously on New Mecca. It isn't a mutation of a known local agent."

Those clanging bells again. Every time I thought about the origin of this outbreak, my head hurt and my stomach wrenched.

"The next step is to get out into the field. We need to examine the canine and feline cases." I raised my empathic screen into place, knowing how my next words would affect my wife. "Slaughter and cremation of every animal in the infected and even *potentially* infected livestock herds has to continue. I'm afraid we're looking at more than another epidermal pustular dermatitis here, Roxanne."

Roxanne spoke, her body rigid and face white. "But what do we do about companion animals? We can't euthanize pets wholesale."

I had no answers and my empathic screen took a beating. Her silent anguish spoke to the psychological scars of having to slaughter so many EPD-infected cattle. The anguish might fade with time, but the memories would never go away.

***

Chaim sat in the cramped, dank room and stared across a small table at the only two people he knew on this world. Since he released the disease, they had not allowed him any freedom, not that he *wanted* to associate with the infidels. Everything about this world frightened him. He spent interminable hours praying that God would forgive him, if not favor his actions, that he would not be discovered and tortured, and that he was somewhere else than this hell-hole of a planet.

The sallow Rebbe Neidritch slurped chicken soup, ignoring the thin streams that dribbled and soaked into his sparse white beard. Chaim suppressed his revulsion and stirred his own soup disconsolately.

The younger man, Jonah Blackmun, watched Chaim with slitted eyes, his body tense, his prominent front teeth pushing out his upper lip as if he waited for the opportunity to fasten them to Chaim's throat. He had lost no opportunity to berate or ridicule Chaim since the day he arrived on New Mecca. Now, however, since they had learned of the arrival of the *Galactic Circle Veterinary Service,* Jonah had become increasingly irascible.

He clanked his spoon onto the table in disgust. "This is intolerable. We must take action."

The rebbe looked up from his bowl. "Enough, Jonah." Then he looked at Chaim who felt no benison in that glance despite the rebbe's harsh words to Jonah. "We *shall* take appropriate action."

Jonah's voice rose. "Appropriate? Those people...those *animal doctors*...are a blight. Abominable. Accursed." He picked up his spoon and commenced attacking his soup as if *it* were his enemy.

Chaim's hand trembled as he followed Jonah's culinary example, albeit with less vigor. He had to eat despite his constant queasiness. He had to stay alive to complete God's work.

The arrival of the off-worlders had changed everything. *Them! Of all the people in the galaxy, why* them?

When they learned of the arrival, the rebbe was vexed, but Jonah became apoplectic. Chaim knew the names, but he had not lived on Dovid's World, as the rebbe and Jonah had. Their wrath was more immediate, more honed. Their families and friends had felt the desecration of the revolution that had overthrown the seat of Testamentary-Literalist power. Chaim knew this, but he was once-removed. Death or banishment had come to those who believed as he did but not to those he knew personally.

But the names of those most responsible for the outrageous destruction of their beliefs and followers, those names were known by his remaining colleagues throughout the galaxy. *Cy Berger! Furoletto Cohen!* Names that engaged the antipathy of every Testamentary-Literalist who remained alive. And now they were here—on New Mecca—and engaged in an attempt to reverse the destruction that Chaim had unleashed.

How? How in God's name could we have predicted that an Islamic world would turn to the very agents that brought our party to its ignominious state? For Muslims to look to Jews for succor? How? And why?

Chaim knew little about these enemies of the Testamentary-Literalist Party, only that after Berger's exile from Dovid's World, he returned with his alien allies to overthrow the rightful, God-sanctioned government. Monstrous, heathen fighters: man-like reptiles, giant tigers, dragons, and werewolves, for God's sake, battled for him. And now he was here on New Mecca with his unnatural alien allies.

Chaim looked down at his spoon. The soup had trickled onto his lap.

Jonah pointed a finger at him and laughed, a harsh guttural laugh that contained no humor. He then turned to the rebbe, a grimace replacing the scornful laughter. "These are the most evil men in the galaxy. We must destroy them as they did our people. When do we act?"

The rebbe scooped up the final spoonful of his soup and downed it. "Soon." He turned his icy gaze to

Chaim, causing him to shiver. "Your protective confinement is over. To you falls the honor of disposing of Berger and Cohen. Wonderful news, no?" The rebbe's smile was like a crevasse across his face.

Chaim feared it would swallow him. "What? Me? You cannot be serious." For the first time since his arrival on New Mecca he challenged the rebbe. "I-I can't. I don't know how to kill. I *don't* kill."

Jonah snorted. "What do you call what is happening right now? Animal deaths accelerate according to our informants. Are those not your killings?"

Chaim ducked his head. "They are animals." Despite that, his stomach roiled at the thought. He loved animals. He had a dog as a child—in another life. "I cannot kill people."

"Berger and Cohen are not *people*. They are the fiends who killed *our* people, who deserve more than simple death. They deserve to *suffer*." Jonah's face purpled as he spoke. He turned back to the rebbe. "It should be me wreaking vengeance upon them. I *know* I can...and I *will* kill!"

"Peace, Jonah. Save your passion for your enemies." The rebbe motioned at his bowl. "Some more soup, if you please, Chaim."

How could the man speak of killing and eat his soup so calmly? Chaim wobbled as he stood, heart hammering as if the charge to get more soup was another order to kill. He moved to the small electric stove and ladled out a full bowl. He placed the bowl before the rebbe, and sat back down, his own soup now cold. What had reached his stomach curdled like sour milk.

The rebbe slurped a few spoonfuls then sat back with a contented sigh and gazed at Jonah. "I know your spirit, Jonah. You are a true *mensch*. And a true believer. You will join our friend Chaim. You both will be the deliverers of justice and vengeance...as a team."

Chaim watched Jonah's face. The man's jaw dropped then snapped shut. His face became even darker as he half rose from his seat.

"Me? Yes," he sputtered. "But work with *him*? How can you possibly—?"

"Enough," the rebbe barked. "This is not a question. This is not for debate. You will do as you are ordered. The blasphemers play into our hands. When we spread the lie that the Dovid's World and Sammaran Jews brought the plague to strike at the heart of Islam, the Holy War will begin. When the destruction of *both* societies is accomplished, the Testamentary-Literalists will pick up the pieces and regain our lost dominion. That we can avenge ourselves by blaming and then killing Berger, Cohen, and Simon is only an added gratification."

Jonah sank back to his seat and hung his head before looking up at the rebbe, his face frozen in a frown. "It will be as you command, Rebbe."

Saying nothing more, Chaim stood, turned, and walked to his tiny bedroom, his only sanctuary. He closed the door and sat on the edge of his cot, elbows on his knees, his hands clamped over his ears, as if he could shut out his inner lamentation.

His thoughts surged, gyred, and churned, unable to find a safe landing place. *Oy, gevalt. Am I to kill? And to have Jonah, this despicable* mamzer *as a partner?* Again he found the courage to criticize, albeit silently, those he had fallen in with. *He does nothing but berate me. I will show him. I will show them all.*

Then something else rose in him, dealing his newfound courage a blow that crashed it to earth. *What am I thinking? How can I kill...go against Moses' commandments? What have I already done? Surely, that is as much a sin as murder. Gott in Himmel! I am already damned.*

He raised his head and stared at the door as if his eyes could pierce the wood and strike at the hearts of the men who drove him to commit abominations. *What must I do?*

***

I sat on the bed in our quarters on the *GCVS*, knees steepled, my arms wrapped around them. I could not shake off the nausea and violation I experienced from the dead camel. No other illness ever approached the feeling of desecration this plague brought with it.

With plenty of water available, Roxanne luxuriated in showering. I watched as she dried off, brushed her short locks, put on her sleeping attire, and sat on the edge of the bed. She smelled good. Her beauty helped clear the morbidity of my thoughts. I thought she was the most beautiful woman I'd ever seen. I never ceased giving thanks for having her in my life.

"I know that look." The frown lines between her eyes spoke as eloquently as her voice. "There's something bothering you and I want to know what. You've been down all day."

"This is going to sound strange—"

"Probably no more than usual."

I mock-punched her on the arm. "At the necropsy...I felt something I can't explain. I sensed something empathically in the dead animal." I put up my hand, palm toward her. "I know what you're going to ask. How can I receive emotions from a dead carcass? I said it was strange."

She pursed her lips. "Maybe one of the other animals was still alive and you sensed that."

"No, but something else *was* alive...inside the dead camel. And it felt *wrong.* Like I tasted corruption,

~41~

venom."

Roxanne was silent for long moments, her confusion seeping through, then: "The only things possibly alive in that carcass were microorganisms, whatever is causing this plague, but they have no mind, no emotions."

"But something was there. Not like the emotions of animals...or people...but something more basic, instinctive... It scared the shit out of me."

She placed a comforting hand on my knee. "Did it threaten you in some way?"

I shook my head. "What I felt was unnatural, like it was something that shouldn't exist. It violated the basic tenets of life." I shivered. "It was...like it was inside *me,* too. Like *I* was as corrupt as what I felt."

She moved closer and put her arms around me.

"Am I going crazy, Roxanne?"

"We'll figure it out."

"What have we gotten ourselves into?"

***

The next morning, Roxanne, Fur, and I sat over cups of coffee in the *GCVS* commissary. New Mecca's tropical mountainous region produced some excellent beans, and we had replenished our supply for the ship. Caffeine helped me maintain my empathic screen.

Fur sat back in his chair, his steaming mug obscured in his huge hands. "Tell me more about this feeling you had. Did you sense a mind?" His massive brow furrowed in concern.

I grimaced. "No. There was nothing conscious about it. And I only felt it in that fresh cadaver."

Roxanne said, "You suggested that it might have come from the plague organisms, even if we can't find them. But any pathogen must be present in the live animals as well the dead ones."

"But I didn't sense anything in the live camels."

Fur ran his fingers through his full sandy beard. "Maybe it's a matter of quantity. Perhaps the live animals don't have the same number of organisms as the dead ones."

I nodded at the possibility, but I still fought the concept that I had perceived something so dire from a microorganism.

"Or maybe the emotional aura of the sick animals obscured it," Roxanne added.

"Those are all possibilities, but why should I suddenly perceive something like a microorganism? I can connect with all sorts of animals, Terran and alien. I even sensed communication by the sentient jungle on Ulm. But a microbe? How's that possible?"

"We need to test this," Roxanne said. "You need to sense animals at various stages of the disease, see if you feel any differences. Then check other cadavers."

I shuddered, not sure I wanted to experience that feeling again, that *wrongness*, but I knew I had to do it. My pulse raced.

Roxanne placed her empty mug on the table. "We haven't seen any of the canine or feline cases yet, for comparison."

Fur chuckled. "I don't know, that dog that splashed his urine on Cy's leg didn't look particularly healthy."

Roxanne grimaced at him. "We should split up. I can stay in town, talk to bin Saqer about setting up visits at some small-animal veterinary clinics. You guys head out and sample some of the other livestock. That sound reasonable?"

It did, but it bothered me to separate from my wife, which made little sense; she could take care of herself. I knew of no threat other than the disease, which did not affect humans. The New Meccans welcomed us and, at least here in New Mecca's capital city of Medina, many women dressed and behaved as modern as anyplace else in the galaxy. Still, maybe I could get Fur to go with her. She would balk at that suggestion now, but if I sprang it on her at the last minute, it would be harder for her to refuse, though I would get an earful about it later.

"Okay," I said. "We'll get started tomorrow."

"Problem solved," Fur said. "Let's have dinner. I'm starved."

"When aren't you?" I asked. "Someday we need to have an eating contest between you and Learns-to-Fix-Injuries."

He chuckled. "But I want my food cooked, thanks."

Chapter 5

Chaim hefted the neural blaster, the handle slick with his sweat. He shuddered as he pictured what the blaster could do to a human body. He was no stranger to weapons. For all children in the Test-Lit Party, training to shoot began at an early age, but it was a pursuit far removed from the actual idea of harming someone. He had done it because it was required, not because he saw himself ever using the skill. Because of that, he never became proficient. He placed the blaster beneath his robe and wiped his hand against the coarse fabric. Though his tolerance for hiding in Rebbe Neidritch's tiny, confining apartment had reached its limit, the thought of going out to *kill* someone made the virtual prison seem like heaven.

Chaim turned to the rebbe. "I a-am ready." He hated the way his voice shook.

Neidritch nodded and looked across the small, scarred kitchen table to Chaim's companion. It was not Jonah, after all, thank God. This young man was hardly out of his teens. Pimply-faced, thin almost to the point of emaciation, the boy—Chaim could think of him no other way—seemed less at ease than Chiam himself.

Oy, what a pair of assassins we make. At least we are going after the woman. Jonah and his ally will deal with Berger and Cohen.

A wave of relief washed over Chaim as he recalled the vid clips they had watched of Berger and the giant Cohen. Cohen was one man he did *not* want to face.

"Chaim," Neidritch barked. "Are you listening to me?"

"Uh, yes, Rebbe. Of course."

"Hmph. Pay attention. Our informant says that Berger and Cohen will go out of the city to farms, where Jonah and Cal will intercept them. Simon will be visiting veterinary clinics in town. It should be a simple enough task to intercept her if we know where she is going."

"Will she be alone?" Chaim asked. "They won't let a woman go out alone—"

"Yes, yes. One of the government's veterinary assistants will guide her. Dispose of him, too. What is one more dead Arab? Many more will die when their food supply disappears."

Neidritch's view of the future of New Mecca caused Chaim to wince and his stomach to twist again, exacerbating his constant nausea.

"Here is the letter." The rebbe handed Chaim an envelope. "This should be found on the woman's person. It shows that this plague comes from the Dovid's World government. It says Berger and his crew are here to spread the disease, not stop it. We spread rumors to that effect. When the Holy War is finished, we will emerge triumphant." The rebbe stared upwards, as if looking for divine approval.

"And remember, you are Arabs, not Jews. It must be Arabs who kill Berger, Simon, and Cohen." Neidritch stared at Chaim, then at Isaac, with narrowed eyes. His voice dropped almost to a whisper. "You cannot be captured. You have the pills, if you are. None must learn who is behind the killings." The man's eyes gleamed as he spoke. Chaim sensed that Neidritch almost looked forward to Chaim sacrificing himself to the cause.

He shuddered at that thought, and the pills in his pant pocket seemed to swell along with the rebbe's words. Poison. Suicide, rather than capture. Chaim's entire bowel now writhed, and he strained to keep it controlled. He nodded. No words would come through his constricted throat.

He glanced at Isaac. The boy was white and trembling.

Assassins? God help us.

***

"They are supposed to come to this veterinary clinic," Isaac whined. "Why aren't they here?"

Chaim mopped the sweat from his brow with his sleeve. "We must wait." *Maybe they will not come and no killing will be necessary.* Another wave of panic swept through him as he envisioned killing the woman.

"Shh. There they are."

Isaac's sharp exhalation brought Chaim's heart to his mouth. He peeked around the corner. They had chosen this spot because it was on an infrequently used side street leading to the back of the clinic.

Oh, God. The giant.

"There's three of them," the boy said. "And she's got the big one with her. Cohen."

Chaim's pulse pounded, but he had to take charge. They must complete their mission. He grabbed Isaac's arm and turned the boy to him. "You shoot Cohen. Make sure he's dead. I will take care of the guide and

Simon."

Chaim waited as the three targets strode closer and closer. *We must wait. We cannot afford to miss. There is no one else in sight, thank God.*

"Now," he barked.

Chaim followed Isaac as he stepped into the street with weapon raised. The ear-piercing whine of Isaac's disrupter startled Chaim into action. He fired at the guide, a traditionally robed New Meccan, but missed. His hand shook like a pennon in a gale.

Chaim saw the giant react to Isaac's shot. Goliath turned, frowned, and stepped toward his attackers before he crumpled to the street. Isaac looked at Chaim in disbelief then fired at the New Meccan. The man snapped upright, body rigid and spine arched backward, and then dropped to the ground, convulsing. Chaim turned his attention to the woman.

"Fur," he heard her scream as she tried to prevent his falling. She turned toward Chaim. "Who are—?"

Chaim's finger trembled against the firing stud, but did not move. *She is beautiful. I did not know that she was beautiful.* His hand shook even more, and when he pressed the stud, he missed again. The woman sprinted off down the street.

Chaim dashed after her. As she reached a corner, she paused to look back. It was her undoing. He could not hold the muzzle of his blaster still as he fired, but a chance movement of the beam glanced across her position. She folded as if her bones had melted.

A few moments later, Chaim and Isaac stood over their prey. The woman's limbs twitched, but not in the full convulsive seizures that had affected her Arab guide.

"She is still alive," Chaim exclaimed. *Oh, thank Heaven, I did not kill her. But what am I thinking? We are supposed to kill her.*

Isaac raised his blaster and took aim.

"No." Chaim batted the boy's weapon aside. "We cannot kill a helpless woman."

"But—"

"No. We will take her captive. That will be as good."

"*Captive?* Are you crazy? We just killed two men. Where can we take her?"

"The safe house we are supposed to hide in for the next few days. We will keep her there. Grab her feet."

Chaim hefted the woman under the arms as the boy did as Chaim directed. "Move her into the alley." Once done, Chaim said, "You bring the land drone to get her. I'll stay."

Isaac stood motionless. Confusion and anger seemed to battle across his visage.

"Quickly now. Someone may come."

The boy pelted off down the alley.

Chaim doubled over as a sharp stab of pain wrenched his stomach. He turned away from the prone woman as he ejected what little was left of his breakfast, thankful that the boy was not there to witness his humiliation.

"Hurry, Isaac. Hurry," he mumbled as he wiped his mouth on the sleeve of his robe.

***

To Chaim's amazement, they made it back to the safe house without further complications. They stowed the drone in a shed and lay the woman on one of the cots, wrists and ankles tied to the bedposts with rope they found in the shed. Dust covered the floor and furniture in the abandoned one-room house. In the kitchenette, rodents had left tiny footprints and scurry-tracks on the counter. Chaim had attempted dusting off the bed, only managing to foul the air with suspended particles. One window adorned the bare plaster walls and looked out at street level until he pasted layered squares of musty old newspapers over the filthy panes.

Isaac sat on a wooden chair near the door, his head in his hands, elbows on his knees, muttering to himself and coughing intermittently. He no longer argued with Chaim about their actions, but he was clearly unhappy. Chaim sensed he worried about what Rebbe Neidritch would do to them when he learned that they had not killed the woman.

Chaim worried too, but he had gone as far as he could. Shooting at Dr. Simon while she was running was reflex; murdering an unconscious woman was unconscionable.

"Do you know how long she will be like this?" Chaim waved toward their unconscious captive.

Isaac looked up at him, then at her. "Forever, I hope. Maybe we should put a gag in her mouth. So she doesn't scream if she wakes up." He put his head in his hands again, not waiting for Chaim's answer.

"She might suffocate," Chaim said. "Besides, there are empty buildings on either side of us. There is no one to hear her. I'm going to the bathroom. Watch her." He stood and hurried to the toilet for the third time since they had reached the house. His upper GI distress had now transferred to his bowel.

This could not be the plague, could it? No. That does not affect people. They swore it did not.

He grunted and tried to think of what to do with the woman. Maybe leave her tied up and she would die of dehydration. It was hot enough in the house. As he finished, he heard loud voices and charged out of the toilet, holding his pants up beneath his robe with one hand. The woman struggled against her bonds and cursed in fluent and colorful Common.

Isaac stood at the foot of the bed, his hands balled. He pumped his fists up and down as if he wanted to use them on her. "Quiet, bitch. Quiet."

"Quiet yourself, fool," Chaim snapped. "Your own shouting will be heard before hers." He secured his pants.

Isaac shot him a narrow-eyed, venomous glance, his face red and sweaty, but he fell silent.

The woman, too, became silent. She stared at Chaim before she spoke, her words charged with hatred. "Are you running this show?"

Chaim nodded, unable to meet her eyes.

"What happened to Fur? And Ahmed?"

"Dead. They are dead," Isaac cried. "We killed them. Like we should have killed you."

The woman was silent for long moments as she bit back a sob. "Why? We came here to help you people. What could you possibly—?"

"Silence," Chaim said. The deaths of the two men ate at his stomach. He needed to unburden himself. To justify what he had done. "I will tell you why."

Isaac shouted, "No. No one can learn of our plans. You can't tell her." The boy clenched his hands at his sides, face white.

"Yes, we can tell her, so she knows why her friends died. Why her husband has died."

"Cy?" she screamed. "You've killed my husband?" Tears rolled down her cheeks. She said nothing more, though silent sobs wracked her body as she looked away from Chaim.

He felt her grief like a blow to his head and he looked away from her at Isaac to ease the pain. "We cannot allow her to live, I understand that." Chaim's throat closed on the words. He swallowed before continuing. "But first she must learn the fate of this world, of her own world, Sammara, of Dovid's World, and of Jewry everywhere, back in our hands, the Testamentary-Literalist hands of God."

She stared at him, wide-eyed, tears halted. "Testamentary-Literalists? You're Test-Lits? You can't be serious."

Chaim's pulse raced. His face grew hot. He felt as if *he* was the one being judged. "Your husband destroyed our government on Dovid's World, brought the true religion to its ignominious state, a few pockets on far-flung worlds. But we are not defeated. We have begun the war to return to our former glory. The plague is the first step."

The woman's mouth hung open. Her astonishment felt like a lash to his brain.

"Are you saying that you are responsible for the *plague*?"

Chaim sensed her horror at his words, and he hastened to defend himself. "The plague is not mine." *Oh God, not mine.* "It was created by others. But I—*I*—brought it to New Mecca as the first battle of the Holy War."

"That...that is monstrous. What could you possibly gain?"

"Gain? This disease will cripple New Mecca...and Islam. We have struck back at Muslims for thousands of years of oppression and killing of Jews. When the Muslims learn who started this plague, they will take up arms against the false Jews. See, right here."

He pulled the envelope from inside his robes and waved it at her. "This paper tells how you and Berger brought this plague to New Mecca and are spreading it under the guise of helping. It tells how the governments of Dovid's World and Sammara seek to destroy Islam, their ancient enemy."

Chaim paused to wipe spittle from his mouth. Isaac watched him, eyebrows raised, mouth open as if amazed at Chaim's transformation.

"Islam and the degenerate Judaism will take arms once again, but this time...this time, they have the ability to destroy one another. And when they have done that, then the Testamentary-Literalists, the true Judaism, will pick up the pieces."

Chaim panted as he finished. His knees wobbled and he crashed down onto the chair behind him. He had never before given such a speech, but now, as his racing heart slowed, he wondered at his words. They were the words of others: Neidritch and Rosten, the Test-Lit leaders who had sent him on this mission. He was a parrot. Nothing more. An automaton wound up and sent out the door to achieve their goals.

Simon spat, "You can't believe what you're saying."

Isaac whispered, "The letter."

"Yes." Chaim shook the envelope at her. "This. This is proof." He stopped suddenly and looked at Isaac.

The boy's face was ashen. "We were supposed to put it on her body."

"Oy. We should have left it on Cohen." Chaim turned at the woman's bark of rueful laughter.

"What a bunch of clowns." Despite her laughter, more tears cut tracks along her cheeks. "You failed on Dovid's World and you'll fail again here."

"We will not fail," Isaac screamed at her. He threw himself at the bed and pummeled her face with blows before Chaim could drag him off. The boy shrugged off Chaim's grasp and retreated to his chair.

Blood now dribbled from her left nostril, joining the tears on her face. The tissues around her left eye began to darken.

Chaim grimaced as stomach acid rose toward his mouth. "I am sorry. He should not have done that."

Again, the woman laughed, a bitter sound. "Why don't you just kill me?"

Why? Because she had broken something inside him. All his fears, all his insecurities, all his beliefs now lay before him for his scrutiny. There was no justification for the slaughter of thousands, maybe millions of animals, and millions of people, Jews and Muslims.

"We must kill her now," Isaac said. "There is no other way."

"Not yet," Chaim said. "We must figure out what to do with the letter. The Muslims must have that information or our plans are damaged."

"We can place it on her body and dump her somewhere."

Chaim nodded. "A possibility." *I need to get rid of him.* "Let us eat before we kill her." The last thing Chaim wanted was food, but it might get Isaac out of the house. "You go out and find food. Bring some for her, too."

"You are *insane*, Chaim. *Food? Now?*"

"Go."

"Pffah." Isaac spat in disgust and he moved toward the door. "Kill her while I am gone and save me the trouble." He slammed the door as he left.

Chaim wondered if he would come back or run to Neidritch. *He is too afraid of the consequences of our failure. He will return, to ensure that she is dead, and we can be seen as heroes, not losers.*

"Your name is Chaim, right? A good name." The woman's voice was soft. She ran her delicate pink tongue over her swollen and split lower lip. "Do you know my name?"

"Dr. Simon," he replied, unable to stay aloof, as he knew he must.

"Roxanne."

Roxanne. He rolled the name around his brain for a moment. "I have never met someone named Roxanne."

"You must like me."

He could not look at her. "No."

"Why then haven't you killed me? You killed Fur. Ahmed. And Cy—" Her voice broke on the last name.

"I did not kill them...or Berger." *Why do I need to justify myself to her, to deny I have killed?* Deep down, he recognized her exceptional beauty, her green eyes, auburn hair, classic profile. Is that why she affected him, made him feel guilt? "Isaac and others did the killing."

"Others. And that makes *you* innocent? You are delusional."

It was a mild epithet, but it still bothered Chaim. He turned away and moved to the small kitchen. "Would you like some water?" he asked, facing the wall.

"Yes, thank you, Chaim."

Why does her calling me by my name bother me?

He brought her a glass of water but had to help her raise her head to drink. Her hair was soft against his hand. Her eyes bored into his, and startled by the intensity, he dropped her head before she was finished drinking. Water splashed on her tunic. Her soaked breasts drew his eyes like a magnet. He caught his breath and stepped back. One, two steps. Heat rushed to his face.

What am I doing? She is the enemy. She must be destroyed.

"Thank you for the water. But I need to use the bathroom." She shook her wrists against the ropes. "I can't do that like this. Unless you want to bring me a bedpan and help me?" Her voice held a teasing note.

His face heated even more and *he* ran to the bathroom to hide.

Chapter 6

"Pull over here, please," I said.

Bin Saqer steered the land drone to the side of the road and stopped. "What is it, Dr. Berger? Is there a problem?"

"Not at all. I wanted to look at the view." I needed to clear my brain of the indelible images of sick and dead animals and the taint I felt as I viewed the ravages of the plague in the herds closer to the city.

The road followed a ridge that overlooked the Tigris River, the valley bottom a checkerboard of green crops alternating with golden ripening grains, some fields dotted with grazing livestock. From here, the scene looked pastoral and quiet. The plague had not gotten this far...yet. I did not want this picture despoiled. I thrust that thought away and concentrated on the scenery.

"Is the Euphrates valley similar?" I asked bin Saqer.

"It is. The river is smaller—it carries about half the water of the main-stem Tigris, and the cropland is a bit narrower but similar."

"Okay. Let's head back. I want to get Roxanne's

report."

Bin Saqer maneuvered back onto the dirt track. The ridge, dry and covered with sere brown grasses, was a stark contrast to the river bottom. Away from the road, the grass petered out, and succulent, spiny vegetation—what passed for cacti on this world—took over.

When we neared the junction of the track with the main road, bin Saqer slowed and I scanned the parched land and cloudless sky. We had left both Healer and Learns-to-Fix-Injuries-After-Inflicting-Them here so they could do some hunting. There were several native grazers, similar to Old Earth's antelope, that the New Meccans were happy to let the aliens hunt. Doing something that came naturally to them as fierce predators thrilled our interns.

As we slowed, I noticed a vehicle parked alongside the road, but I ignored it as I spotted the red dragon sweeping low over the plain. Beneath the dragon, a brown blur denoted the Lupan shape-changer also speeding toward us.

"Good. Here they come. We can get back to the city." Healer would ride with us, and Red would fly behind the land drone, a procession we used on our way up the valley.

Before bin Saqer stopped, two robed men stepped out of the other vehicle. One of the men raised a tube to his shoulder. My reaction seemed to take forever as my mind sucked in the image like cold molasses. I saw a flash and my brain finally connected to my tongue. "Bin Saqer. Missile. Bail out."

As I yelled, I threw the door open and launched myself out while we were still moving. I hoped that bin Saqer had done the same, although he was on the side toward the men. I saw the fiery track of the missile intersect the path of our vehicle. A pulse of searing light blinded me, then the concussion hit, and I flew over the dry grasses, bouncing at least twice. Being on the opposite side of the vehicle from the impact saved my life.

My face burned and I could not get my body to move as I waited for the next missile to hit me. Who would do this? And why?

My main regret was that I would never see Roxanne again. That realization elicited a stab of pain worse than the burning and the pounding from the explosion.

But nothing happened. Why weren't they finishing us off? I lifted my head as the flashes before my eyes faded away. I heard a horrifying scream through the bells that would not stop tolling in my ears. My God, was that bin Saqer?

"Bn Sacchu..." My voice came out as a croak. I tried again. "Bin Saqer. Are you okay?"

No answer. A growl, another scream, suddenly cut off.

I heard Learns-To-Fix-Injuries' voice. "Captain Cyberger alive."

The dragon was close, but what was happening? I used my arms to pull myself farther from the heat of the burning drone. Agony enveloped my upper body, but my legs did not hurt or respond.

I wrenched my body around to find the source of the growling. The scene stopped my movement short. A rumble issued from Healer in his wolf-like form. He held a man by the throat with his fangs and stood on the guy's chest with his forelegs. The man's limbs twitched, so I knew he was alive. On the other side of the parked vehicle, Learns-To-Fix-Injuries crouched over the bloodied, dismembered carcass of a second man. The missile launcher lay on the ground nearby.

I had seen the devastation dragons caused during the Dovid's World war, so I was not surprised at the gore. At least Learns-To-Fix-Injuries had refrained from eating our attacker. I had to break my dragon allies of *that* habit during the war.

"Bin Saqer," I called, again with no answer. I feared the worst. "Red, find Dr. bin Saqer. Check the burning drone. Healer, don't kill that guy."

The Lupan growled louder and the dragon partially unfurled his wings as he padded over to the drone. He stopped and peered through the flames; his scales were impervious to the heat.

"Cooked," he said.

"Damn." Bin Saqer never had a chance. "Red. I need help." The dragon came close and I grabbed onto his forearm to lever myself up, but my legs would not function, and I collapsed back to the ground.

The dragon hissed and grabbed the back of my tunic in his mouth. I felt like a kitten being hoisted by its dam.

"Where?" Red mumbled.

"Take me to Healer."

Learns-To-Fix-Injuries waddled over next to the Lupan and released me. I cried out in pain and clutched my chest as I sank to my butt. I stared at the robe-clad man. He looked my age, in his twenties. He had a long, thin face capped by prominent front teeth that protruded even with his mouth closed.

"Healer, let go of his throat. Red, make sure he doesn't go anywhere."

Learns-To-Fix-Injuries placed a taloned foot on the man's thighs.

"Who are you? Why have you done this?" My voice was hoarse from inhaling smoke, but anger added another level of strain. I cleared my throat and spat. "Answer me."

When he did not respond, I placed my face close to his. "You saw what happened to your partner?"

His eyes flicked toward the dragon and his face

turned white.

"Then you better start talking."

The man did not move or speak. A hard case, then. I pointed at the dragon. "This is Learns-To-Fix-Injuries-After Inflicting-Them. There's no obligation to the *fixing* part. Think he's hungry?"

The man's eyes dilated, but he made no other movement. Threats were not working, and I had no compunctions when it came to someone who had just murdered a friend.

"Red, see what his leg tastes like."

I sat back as the dragon took the man's right thigh in his mouth and applied pressure.

The man screamed, "Stop."

I held up my hand to the dragon. Red let go. Blood dripped from the man's leg. The dragon licked his lips and fixed his cold reptilian eyes on the man.

"Are you ready to talk?"

The man grimaced and moaned, but said nothing further.

"Your leg is still attached to your body. Red can change that for you." I nodded to the dragon and he resumed his hold on the attacker's leg.

"You animal," the man hissed. "You and your unclean alien friends."

He spoke Common, but his accent was different...familiar. It reminded me of home.

"Who sent you?"

"You cannot make me speak." The man's body contorted as he tried to pull away from the dragon's jaws. He screamed again as Red's teeth tore a gash across his thigh.

"Don't kill him," I barked.

The man had gotten his hand beneath his robe and was pulling it out when I grabbed his wrist. He did not have another weapon, but had his fist closed tight on something small. I held his wrist hard and smashed my other fist into his nose. He cried out again, and loosened his grasp. I clawed his hand open, and a pill fell to the ground. Healer grabbed the man's throat again to still him.

I picked up the pill, examined it, and put it close to my nose. The characteristic bitter almond odor of cyanide hit me. A suicide pill. This guy was willing to commit suicide rather than reveal who he was. He still struggled against the holds of the Lupan and the dragon. He would not last long like this.

"Healer, Learns-To-Fix-Injuries, hold him so he can't harm himself. Let me see what's in his vehicle. Maybe some rope..."

Ignoring sharp pains in my chest, I dragged myself to the land drone, an old, decrepit hulk with doors rusting where the paint had peeled away, bald tires, and a cracked windshield. I was surprised it was functional. My face felt like it was still on fire. Using my arms, I hauled myself up and managed to open the rear hatch.

"Perfect. A roll of wire." I lifted it out, but that exhausted me and I plunked my bottom on the brown grass. I breathed a deep sigh. "Healer, I'll need you to do this. Tie him up. Red, sit on him until Healer's done."

The three hundred kilo dragon complied, literally, and the air whooshed out of the man's chest. His face turned purple.

"Easy. I need him alive." Although a broken rib or two would not hurt my feelings.

The Lupan returned to his humanoid form. The shape-changing process never failed to give me the shivers. From resembling a cross between a Terran wolf, a cheetah, and a lion, with long slender legs meant for speed, a luxuriant mane, and sharp teeth with impressive canines, he melted back to his roughly humanoid but still wolf-like biped form. His teeth remained equally scary. He shook himself, and then took the wire and bound the man's arms and legs, not being gentle in his ministrations.

"Done, Captain," he said.

"Okay. Toss him in the back of the drone...then help me get into a seat. I can't drive. Can you handle this thing?"

Healer grinned. "I have watched Fur Cohen when he drives."

I rolled my eyes. Great, an untaught, unlicensed driver. "Head to the city. I need medical assistance, and we need to get this guy to the authorities. Red, fly behind us and guard our flanks."

"Ass you ssay, Captain Cyberger."

Once aboard, the vehicle started right up. Healer punched some buttons, and the drone bounced into action, eliciting pain in my chest.

"There's no comm unit on this thing, so we can't call for help. My personal comm was in our vehicle."

We drove for about twenty minutes, covering less than five kilometers at the speed I let Healer drive, when that effort became moot. Two camouflaged military whirlydrones appeared over the horizon, followed by a matching land drone troop carrier. Somebody had reported the explosion. The land drone came to a screeching halt in front of us as the whirlydrones hovered overhead.

I leaned out the window and yelled, "Red. Down, now. And don't twitch a talon."

A dozen soldiers poured out of their vehicle and surrounded ours, pulse rifles ready and aimed.

"We stay right here," I told Healer, "do nothing to trigger these guys." In the rear-view mirror, I saw Learns-To-Fix-Injuries fold his wings and hunker down to his most nonthreatening position. Not that a tyrannosaur-like beast could *ever* look truly nonthreatening to little mammals like us.

One of the whirlydrones landed a few vehicle lengths to our right side. As the rotors wound down, the door opened and a guy with lots of braids on his shoulders emerged, flanked by two less-braided companions. One of these split off to take charge of our perimeter cordon. The other two approached our drone. Lesser braid spoke in Common.

"Get out of the vehicle with your hands in the air."

I sighed. I had no time for this shit. "I'm injured. I can't walk. Don't shoot. We got hit by a terrorist's missile, and Dr. bin Saqer was killed. We've got one of the attackers tied up in the back. He tried to commit suicide rather than talk. We need to find out who he is and why they attacked us."

My voice ran down as my adrenalin rush petered out, and a wave of pain wracked my body. "We need help. Please..."

***

Pain came and went accompanied by a low murmur of voices. I could wiggle my fingers but not my toes. I recalled not feeling my legs after the explosion. I licked my lips and tried to open my eyelids. The lips part worked but not the eyes. Uh, oh. No legs, no eyes?

"He's awake." The voice was feminine in accented Common. "Do not try to move, Dr. Berger," the voice said. "You are immobilized for now. You took quite a beating from the explosion and have serious burns on your face and hands."

"What about my legs?" I croaked.

"Bruised spinal cord. That will recover."

"Who are you?"

"Mirim, your nurse."

"Why can't I see?"

"Your face is bandaged because of the burns, but your eyes are fine. There are...friends here to see you, but please do not exert yourself. The doctor will be back soon to speak with you."

I had started to fade out before she finished speaking. On some potent pain meds, no doubt, but her hesitation on the word friends brought me back. I heard a grunt and a hiss, followed by an admonishment from the sweet-voiced nurse to not stress me, although that sweet voice held a distinct undercurrent of fear.

I imagined the chaos that must have ensued before the New Meccans allowed my alien companions into the hospital.

Healer's voice came first. "You survive, Captain. That is good. You are strong, like the People." He used his own name for his Lupan race. I had become an honorary member of the People for surviving their trial of worthiness and for services rendered them.

"One of the killerss hass paid."

"Yeah." I recalled seeing the remains of the attacker that our dragon had torn apart. "I owe you guys my life. If you hadn't been there, I'd be pieces and parts now."

"Ssorry we too late to ssave bin Ssaqer."

Healer growled in agreement. "Soldiers have taken the other human."

"Do we know anything more about the attackers?"

"Nothing," Healer said.

Red hissed.

"Hey, have you heard from Roxanne or Fur? Do they know what happened?"

There was a long silence, long enough to start my worry juices flowing. "What's wrong? Where are they?"

At that moment, another voice entered the conversation. "That is enough. No more visiting. You will tire the patient." A cultured voice: male. "Dr. Berger, I am Dr. Karim. I will answer your questions. But first... Please clear the room."

Both Healer and Red growled, but their voices faded and the door closed.

"What's going on, doctor? Where's my wife?" Panic set in. Was she attacked too?

"Dr. Berger, much has occurred. I cannot tell you all of it since I do not have that information. The nurse told you about your condition. Your burns, your badly bruised torso and ribs, and your bruised spinal cord will heal. I assure you that you will make a full recovery."

"Shit. I'm not worried about *me*. What's happened to my *wife* and my *friend, Fur Cohen*?" My voice rose, and my body strained against the immobilization.

"Please, calm yourself, or I will be forced to give you a sedative."

I took a deep breath and let my body relax. "Okay. But, please, please tell me she's not hurt." Or worse.

"Dr. Berger, at about the same time you were assaulted, there was also an assault on your companions."

No. Oh, please God, *no.*

"They were shot with neural blasters."

Tears flooded beneath my eye coverings. It can't be. It can't.

"Your friend, Furoletto Cohen, was hit but survived. His guide, Ahmed al-Hashim, was killed."

"Roxanne! What about *Roxanne*?"

"We do not know. She is missing. The authorities think she has been abducted. There's a good chance that she is still alive."

I wanted to scream. I wanted to leap from my bed and rush to find whoever took her. To rip them limb from limb. I wished I was a dragon!

My whole body trembled and I felt a weight on my

arm, Karim's hand, no doubt. "Please, Dr. Berger. You will injure yourself if you fight your restraints."

I could not help it and struggled to draw breath. "Healer. Red. Help."

I heard a ruckus outside the room. Karim shouted, "Keep them out."

He must have injected something into my saline drip line then, because the sounds faded.

***

When I awoke again, my guts were roiling. What had happened to Roxanne? They said Fur survived, but how much of him was normal after getting hit with a neural disrupter? *What was happening?*

My eyes were unbandaged. My vision was blurry, but I could see. A tiny bit of relief.

A nurse stood by my bed holding an empty syringe, probably whatever woke me. "You have visitors, Dr. Berger."

The door opened. What met my eyes did not reassure me much, however. A uniformed guard, complete with the obligatory camouflage uniform and pulse rifle stepped through and stood at attention. A starched, bemedalled man followed. He held a visored cap under his arm and walked as if he had a ramrod up his *tuches*. He took a position at the side of my bed.

"Dr. Berger, I am General Rahamman. I am pleased that you will recover."

I tried to sit up and managed about a finger's breadth before I fell back. I wondered how long I was out. "My wife. Where is she? Is she okay?"

"We have not located Dr. Simon." He held up a hand to forestall my next outburst. "But there is no evidence that she has been harmed. No body."

Great. No evidence of a *body*? That was supposed

to make me feel better? "Who has her? Any ransom calls? What are you doing to find her?"

"I will explain what we have learned. This is rather difficult."

Rather *difficult?* What is he talking about? And why is a general here? And a guard on my door?

He must have read my expression or my panicky glance at the soldier. "It was meant to appear that you and your wife were attacked by an anti-Jewish terrorist group."

Why didn't that surprise me? "Did they claim responsibility for the attacks?"

"The assailants were dressed as Arabs, but they are not. We learned this from the one you captured."

Memories of Red standing over the pieces of the other attacker were still fresh in my mind. "So he talked?"

"He was...difficult to get information from, but we have...ways."

I really did not want to know the details.

"We learned that he is a member of the Testamentary-Literalist Party from your home world."

"You can't be serious. They're gone. Dead. We destroyed them."

The general shook his head. "I am afraid you are mistaken. What is worse, they have seeded rumors in our population that you and your crew brought the animal plague to New Mecca and are spreading it to our farms."

My chest tightened. "Us? Preposterous. The plague was here before your people called us to help. How do you know the Test-Lits didn't start it?"

"We don't, but for now, there is a segment of our population that is willing to accept these rumors. Perhaps these Testamentary-Literalists wanted you dead to prevent you from showing up their lies."

"Or they want us dead for reasons of pure hatred. Fur, Roxanne, and I were instrumental in their overthrow. What else did you learn from this guy? And *where is my wife?*"

"All questions we must address, Dr. Berger. We will find your wife. In the meantime, while you are hospitalized, you will have armed guards around the clock. For your safety."

I read between the lines. *And in case you are a biological terrorist yourself.*

"I bid you a fast recovery." He turned on his heel and marched out.

He couldn't move fast enough for me.

"Find my wife!"

***

The doctor said it would be several days before I'd be able to get out of bed, and then I'd need to go through rehab to get my legs functional again. I wanted to scream with frustration, but that tended to make the guards antsy. No one had any information on Roxanne, and it was now two days since the abduction—or what I hoped was an abduction. I could not face the alternative. Fur, I was told, had recovered rapidly. Well, great for the big guy.

He showed up at my door late in the day, stood in the doorway, a guard hovering behind him, and would not look me in the eyes. "Cy..." he choked. "Cy, I'm so sorry. I didn't protect her."

"Fur," I barked. "What the fuck happened to her? How could you let...?" I shut my big mouth, but I had already said too much. It was not his fault.

His face solidified into an expressionless mask. "I should have protected her," he repeated, agreeing with my outburst, but his voice was now toneless. He could blame himself for his shortcomings, but coming from *me,* it hurt.

I tried to salvage the situation. "I'm glad you're better, but you look like shit." Duh! Brilliant recovery.

"I came from my hospital room down the hall."

"Sit." I pointed at a visitor's chair.

He stared at me for a moment before he sat. The chair groaned. "I had to see you. I had to tell you...I'm sorry about..." His voice trailed off and he looked away from me.

"About Roxanne? That you almost died? I knew that. You only survived because you're a gorilla." God, could I say anything that wouldn't make the situation worse?

"I never saw what happened to her, Cy."

Though he was pissed at me for my accusation—that emotion came through like a laser-guided missile—he was trying to make me feel better despite my seeming effort to make *him* feel worse.

I tried again. "Hey. She's fine. I'm sure." *Right. And maybe the sick camels can fly.*

He held my gaze for long moments before he spoke. "You know who it was, right?"

A wave of nausea wracked my stomach. "The Test-Lits. And they have every reason to want us dead. Have you heard they pinned the plague on us?"

He nodded.

A doctor appeared in the doorway. The frown on his face was prodigious. "Mr. Cohen, you are in no condition to be out of bed."

I had to agree with the doctor. Fur's face was a shade or two paler than when he entered my room.

"Back to bed," I said. "We both have some more recovering to do."

Fur did not argue, but I disliked the look in his eyes and an aura that as much as said, "I was responsible for

Roxanne's plight, and I'll fix it, whatever it takes." He stood and moved out the door, following the doctor's rigidly pointed finger.

I heaved a painful breath and hoped Roxanne was better off than we were.

Chapter 7

The overlapping squares of paper that blinded the window from the safe-house to the outside street mocked Chaim. Somehow, he could read the Arabic print. "You are as unseeing as the camels you have killed. You will follow the camels." The window marched toward him, the paper peeling off, the panes widening and splitting into shards of glistening teeth as they stretched to envelop him.

Chaim heard his own scream and bolted awake.

Isaac stood over him, hands on Chaim's robe, shaking him and yelling, "Wake up. What is wrong with you?"

Chaim groaned and sat up, pushing Isaac away. "A dream. Just a dream."

He trembled. *Another day in this place and I will go mad.* For two days, he had pushed aside Isaac's demands to kill Dr. Simon. Chaim had argued they needed her as a hostage, and Isaac had countered there was no logic behind the claim. Soon, the boy would override Chaim's thin hold on authority. *What will I do then?*

But the woman haunted him; her beauty slipped beneath his guard. He had no will to harm her. *Do I kill Isaac instead, if it comes to that? How can I even think such a thing?*

"Get up, you fool," the boy yelled at him. "We must finish this before we are found."

Chaim stood, attempting to shake out the ineradicable creases in his kaftan. The smell of stale vomit assaulted his nose. *Feh! I'm a slob, a* schlemiel. He glanced at the woman. Simon smiled at him, and he felt the heat rising to his face again. *Why does she do this to me?* He popped a mint into his mouth, afraid she would smell his foul breath.

"Chaim." Isaac grabbed his arm and shook it. "We must act." The boy's voice rose, panic taking hold. He was reaching his limit.

"A moment." Chaim turned to Simon. "Do you need to...um, relieve yourself?" Her smile dazzled him. He did not even notice her cracked swollen lip, her blackened eyes.

"Yes. I need to pee."

Chaim's face grew hot at her indelicate words, and he turned away. *Such a woman should be beyond primal animal needs.*

"Untie her, Isaac. I will cover her with my blaster." He could not trust himself close to her. He wanted to reach out and touch that soft hair again. And the rest of her. *Oh, God, help me. She is Delilah, Jezebel. How can I resist?*

Isaac muttered something indecipherable as he untied the woman's hands and feet. She sat on the edge of the bed, rubbing her wrists. When she tried to stand, her legs gave way. Isaac jumped back. Chaim started forward to assist her, stopping himself at the last second as the boy screamed at him.

"Chaim, no! She is faking to get your weapon."

Chaim's heart pounded at that thought. *She is the enemy. I must remember she is the enemy.* He jabbed the neural blaster at her. "You cannot fool us. Stand and move slowly or your death will be quick."

Could I really kill her? Chaim forced a severe frown.

Simon shook her head. "I can't believe you two. I've had restricted circulation to my hands and feet for hours and I can hardly stand, but you're worried I can overpower both of you. Clowns." She stood again and shuffled toward the bathroom.

"Leave the door open," Isaac demanded. "I am watching."

Chaim turned away from the open door, but the sounds of bodily fluid splashing in the bowl made his face burn even more. That plus the heat of the room brought sweat to Chaim's brow and he shoved at the oppressive *keffiyeh* covering his head. He longed for his own thin yarmulke, but the Arab headdress was part of his disguise, and no follower of the ultraorthodox Test-Lit creed could go without a head covering. He mopped his brow with his filthy sleeve.

When Simon was back on the bed and tied once again, Chaim said to Isaac. "We need breakfast. Go."

"No! I will not be part of this charade any longer. We must kill her, plant the letter, and drop her somewhere. I am finished with your delays, Chaim."

Chaim stared at the boy, drawing his eyebrows together, again trying to look severe. "I am still in charge here. You do as I say."

Isaac shook his head. "Not anymore. You are besotted with this heretic woman, so I must complete our plan." He lifted his blaster and pointed it at Chaim, eliciting a gasp from Simon. "I will kill both of you and leave you here...with the letter." The weapon wavered and Isaac grabbed it with both hands.

Chaim saw that the boy was trying to gather the courage to kill him.

"Sit in that chair." When Chaim did not move, the boy screamed, *"Do it."*

A peace came over Chaim. He felt no fear, no uncertainty. "This is not what you want to do, Isaac, I can see that. We were not raised to murder defenseless women. Put the weapon down."

Isaac's eyes grew larger as Chaim spoke, as if not believing what he saw and heard. The boy swung the blaster toward the woman as his hands whitened on the grip.

"No." Chaim took a step toward Isaac. "Give it to me."

A crash boomed behind Chaim, followed by shards of window glass flying by his head. Sharp daggers sliced the back of his neck, and slender crimson furrows bloomed on Isaac's face. A cloud of plaster dust filled the room. Chaim stood rooted, unable to move, not comprehending what had happened, only recalling his nightmare of the window coming to devour him.

Isaac's pupils dilated. He fired his weapon.

Chaim flinched, but the beam seared past his head just as a bellow blasted his ears and an unstoppable force bowled him over. A heavy weight landed on top of him. He could not breathe.

Isaac's face turned white. A brown blur hit him, and the blaster flew from his hands as a giant wolf ripped out Isaac's throat. Blood flew across the room as the monster swung its slavering, jagged-toothed muzzle toward Chaim.

He heard Simon's voice. "Healer, stop. Red, don't kill him. We need him."

Chaim felt the pressure on his chest release, and he gasped. He turned away from the lupine brute before him only to find himself face to face with Satan himself: a red-faced lizard with glaring yellow-slit pupils, its open mouth filled with dagger-sized teeth.

He fainted.

***

Chaim woke with his back pressed against a wall. He opened his eyes, not to a beast or a devil, but to a ghost. His bladder released. The specter in front of him was, impossibly, that of the Goliath, Cohen.

He should be dead.

The ghost's hairy face was inches from his own before the man backed off. "Yech. He pissed himself."

The lizard stepped forward to take his place.

Chaim saw now that the beasts had charged through the wall, which left a gaping hole the size of a land drone.

As Cohen untied her bonds, Simon said, "We need him to prove we aren't responsible for the plague. Besides, this one saved me."

Chaim stared at the scaled red monstrosity. "What godless creature is this?"

Cohen said, "This is Learns-To-Fix-Injuries-After-Inflicting-Them. He's from Dragonworld. I suggest you don't do anything more to piss him off."

The dragon hissed at Chaim, and he tried to burrow backwards against the solid wall. Those reptilian eyes promised him death.

"And this is Healer from Lupus IV." Cohen waved toward the throat-ripping beast who now growled at Chaim. "He's a shape-changer." Cohen bared his teeth at Chaim in a smile that held no hint of humor. "Show him, Healer."

An explosion of supernatural dread went off in Chaim's brain as the four-legged wolf-monster *melted and reformed* into a two-legged, upright creature, still hairy and wolf-like and no less scary in its second form. A growl gusted from a mouth still armed with huge fangs. Chaim screamed, dropped to his hands and knees, and scuttled toward his only haven in this Godforsaken place, the bathroom.

"Let him go," Simon said. "He spends half his time in there anyway."

The glass cuts on Chaim's neck stung. *How could this happen? It must be the nightmare. I will awaken again with Isaac shaking me.* The image of Isaac with his throat torn out was the last straw. Chaim's stomach cramped, and he prayed he would reach the bathroom in time to prevent his ultimate humiliation.

***

As Chaim cleaned himself as best he could, he listened through the open doorway to Simon and Cohen converse.

Cohen's voice was gruff, angry. "Yeah, Cy will be okay. The missile killed bin Saqer, but Cy had bailed out of the land drone and wasn't caught in the direct blast. He's burned and has a spinal contusion, but the docs say he'll be fine."

There was a short silence. "What is it, Fur? Your voice and your face don't *say* it's fine. What else is wrong with him?"

Cohen snorted, a disgusted sound. "Nothing physical."

"What, Fur? What aren't you telling me?"

"Look, we saved you. That ought to be enough for him." Cohen's voice dripped venom.

"He blamed you, didn't he? He thought I was dead and he blamed you."

Cohen did not respond.

"Oh, God. He was scared, Fur, though that doesn't

excuse his accusation. We've all been under pressure. We can't let that drive us apart."

When Cohen did not answer, Chaim took the silence as the opportunity to emerge. He stood in the doorway, water dripping off his *kaftan* and pooling on the wooden floor beneath him, creating a murky, begrimed puddle.

Four pairs of eyes fixed him like targeted lasers. Though he quailed internally, he stood straight and stared back. "I have wronged you. I see that now."

Simon glared at him, eyes narrowed. "Is that an apology? You're responsible for all this death and all you can say is you've *wronged us*." Her visage was every bit as feral as the alien beasts'. She held his blaster in her hand, but did not point it at him.

Cohen glanced at Chaim. "We need him now but maybe we can give him to Red as a chew toy when we're done."

Chaim cringed. *He jests. I sense this somehow but I place myself in God's hands now.* He hung his head and intoned a silent prayer for a rapid and painless death.

A loud voice outside the house startled Chaim. "You are surrounded," the voice shouted in Common. "Come out with your hands in the air."

Simon said, "Healer, Red, you stay inside until we get the authorities calmed down out there."

Cohen grabbed Chaim by both arms and lifted him off his feet. The giant's grip hurt, and Chaim gritted his teeth. *I will not cry out. I will be a* mensch *for once in my life.*

Simon led the way out through the hole in the wall, hands raised, and Cohen carried Chaim out, holding him in front of his body like a shield. Dozens of camouflage-clad soldiers leveled pulse rifles at Chaim's chest. His breath caught in his throat. Praying for a swift, painless death was different than facing it.

The officious voice barked, "Down on your knees. You, release that man. Get your hands in the air."

What are they doing? Why are Cohen and Dr. Simon being treated in this manner? I am the enemy.

As she dropped to her knees, Simon shouted, "Whoever is in charge here, I'm Roxanne Simon, the veterinarian who was kidnapped. Cohen and I are guests of your government." Simon's voice rose above the muttering soldiers. "Cohen is holding the assassin."

"I am Colonel Rassid." A man with stars on his uniform stepped in front of his men. "Move in," he ordered them. "Secure the building."

"Hold on, Colonel," Cohen interrupted. "There are two aliens with us. They're inside and I don't want your men to shoot them out of fear. They won't harm you."

The officer tilted his head and looked over his beaked nose at Cohen. "Tell them to come out."

Cohen turned toward the destroyed wall. "Learns-To-Fix-Injuries, Healer, come on out...slowly."

The werewolf exited first, then the dragon.

Some of the soldiers flinched and pointed their rifles at the aliens. The dragon hissed and the werewolf growled in return. Chaim feared the standoff would become a pitched battle.

Simon broke the stalemate by standing, against the colonel's orders. "You're not here to start a war. It is the terrorist you want." She waved a hand at Chaim.

I am that...a terrorist. God help me.

"Now I want to see my husband."

The rigidity of the entire troop seemed to melt at her words. The colonel moved his feet apart and clasped his hands behind his back. "Very well. We'll proceed to headquarters for debriefing. Platoon two, escort the aliens. Platoon one, move our *guests* and their prisoner into the carriers."

Cohen called out, "Red, Healer, we'll meet you at

their headquarters."

A loud hiss and a growl answered him.

A soldier shoved Chaim into one of the personnel carriers. Cohen and Simon entered another. A train of three vehicles rolled through mostly deserted back streets before it moved onto a main avenue. Passersby glanced at the convoy with little interest, as if it was nothing unusual.

Chaim quaked. He feared the people's wrath if they knew who was inside, the bringer of the plague. He wondered how the crowds viewed the procession escorting the aliens, but the less he thought about those monsters, the better. He closed his eyes for the remainder of the trip and wondered if he would ever see Dr. Simon again. The possibility of that not happening was worse than his fear of torture and death.

***

When the door opened, I was ready to bite off somebody's head. No one had told me anything about the progress of the search for Roxanne. I supposed that there were times when the old "no news is good news" saying was appropriate, but with me stuck in a bed, unable to do much more than wiggle my fingers and finally my toes, this pushed my patience too far. Having an overactive imagination was akin to self-torture. I envisioned my wife subjected to every conceivable horrifying act. Angst was eating me alive.

"Have you found...?" I got no more out because a glorious sight stood in the doorway. Disheveled, her auburn locks plastered to her head above a grime-smudged face that sported two black eyes and swollen, split lips, she was still the most beautiful thing I had ever seen.

"Roxanne. Oh, God, Roxanne, you're alive."

I lost myself in her green eyes as she walked to me. She put out a hand and brushed my hair back from my face. "You look a lot worse than I do."

"Well, *that's* nothing new, is it?" Oddly, a sob forced its way past my lips. Wait a minute. I was supposed to be happy here. "I-I was so scared." I had trouble speaking past the lump in my throat. "Afraid you were tortured...or dead."

"I'll be all right."

"If I could move, I'd hug you." I lifted my hand, about the limit of my ability, and she grasped it. "What happened to you? I want the whole story."

"And you'll get it," she breathed. "But first...I have a bone to pick with you."

Uh, oh. What did I do now?

"You need to thank someone."

Sure, whoever rescued her, I assumed.

"Fur, get in here," she called.

His big body filled the doorframe.

My mouth hung open as I wrestled with what to say. The last time I had seen Fur, I accused him of failing to protect Roxanne. I knew there was no excuse for blaming him for what happened.

When Fur did not move and I said nothing, Roxanne fixed me with a glare. "Fur rescued me...along with Red and Healer."

I felt my face heat.

"He risked his life for me."

I looked at Fur. "Thanks, man."

His broad brow furrowed deep enough to plant a crop. His glare said he was still pissed at me. I looked back at Roxanne, unable to meet Fur's mental fury.

"And do you know why he came to save me? Without any military backup? Hmm?"

"Um...because he cares about you?" I whispered.

"Besides that," she snapped.

"Because of me? What I said to him?"

"And what exactly was that?"

My wife had me skewered like a shish kabob and was not letting me off the spit.

"I-I blamed him for what happened...accused him of not protecting you." I looked at Fur. "I'm sorry, Fur. I know you did everything you could. I had no right to say that."

Fur stepped several giant paces into the room. "Yeah, you had no right. After all we've been through together, what we've faced... You should have known better."

"Yeah. I should have."

"Okay. Enough." Roxanne's drill-sergeant tone brought us both up short, and we looked at her. "I love you, Cy. You are my heart and soul. And I love you, Fur. You are my brother in every way I can imagine, but the two of you have to get past your egos and back to your partnership. We have a job to do here." She turned, marched past Fur to the door then stopped and looked back over her shoulder. "Settle it before I get back." She closed the door behind her.

The silence in the room lasted a lifetime. My gut squirmed. "Look Fur—"

"Cy—"

"Okay, you first, Fur. Give me your best shot. I know no apology will suffice. I'm an ass, an unfeeling, insensitive boor. A true friend would never have blamed you. Go ahead, tell me I'm a *schmuck* to attack you after we've faced death together, when you've saved my life more than once. I'm a worthless *mamzer*. I have my head up my *tuches*." I looked into his eyes, unwilling to look away from his anger. "Your turn."

He shook his head. "Just keep going. Your mouth is doing a better job than I ever could."

"Thank you for returning *my* heart and soul."

I sensed his anger dim. A small smile crept across his lips, as if he was fighting against unwilling cranial nerves.

He stepped closer to the bed. "I understand where you were mentally when you blamed me. We have a lot of history, and we still have a long way to go together. Let's put this behind us. For you, for me, and for Roxanne."

He took my hand in one of his great paws. He could be gentle for such a big guy.

"I'll make it up to you, Fur. See if I don't."

***

I sat on the hospital bed, spooning soup from a bowl set on the little rolling tray. Too much soup found its way to the napkin Roxanne had tucked beneath my chin, but my overabundance of pride made me determined to feed myself.

She and Fur sat by the bed and watched. Their internal laughter was obvious to me in a way that was new. My empathic perception was evolving. I sensed more deeply than I ever had before. I was still no telepath, but I had to keep my mental screen at a higher level than previously, lest strong emotions would incapacitate me. Maybe my constant state of queasiness related to that extra defense.

I had described my version of the attack on me, though Fur said that Healer and Learns-To-Fix-Injuries' version was less grandiose, and they took credit for most of the work. Now I wanted to hear about Roxanne's rescue.

"So," I said to Fur, "you walked out of the hospital, defying the doctor's orders."

"Yeah. I found Learns-To-Fix-Injuries and Healer in one of the waiting rooms, surrounded by nervous soldiers. I don't think it helped that Red kept reminding them that he was hungry."

Roxanne and I laughed.

"When I showed up and joined Red and Healer, the soldiers scattered."

I asked, "How did you find her?"

"I didn't. Red and Healer did. They snuffled around the ambush site for a while then took off like bloodhounds on a hot trail."

I knew they had a good sense of smell. "That's amazing."

Fur continued. "When we reached the house where Roxanne was imprisoned, I had to restrain the two of them from charging in. I was afraid she would get hurt. They convinced me that there were only two men inside with her, and we decided to go for it. Shock troops leading, of course, Red went in first, since his scales are resistant to energy weapons."

"After my initial shock when Red busted in," Roxanne said, "I can't describe the thrill that coursed through me. They were there in the nick of time. The boy, Isaac, had snapped and was ready to kill me and Chaim. You wouldn't believe the look on the kid's face when he saw Red. What Healer did to him was pretty gruesome."

"But you captured one of the killers."

"Yeah, but Chaim didn't kill Ahmed. Isaac did," Roxanne said. "I think Chaim would have trouble killing a fly. He was having major problems dealing with his own guilt. I think he regrets bringing the plague to New Mecca and what it was doing to the animals."

"Chaim?" I burst out, trying to sit up. "He tried to kill you and Fur *and* he's the one who brought that vile plague here?" I managed to spill my bowl of soup. I mopped it off my hospital gown with my napkin.

"At the end, he was trying to dissuade Isaac from killing me."

I felt something else beneath her words, a fondness for Chaim, but in the roil of my emotions, I brushed it off. "Where is the bastard now?"

"Easy, Cy." Roxanne placed a restraining hand on my arm. "The New Meccan authorities have him secreted away, like your attacker. Remember, those two Test-Lits are the only ones who can contradict the rumors that we brought the plague here. Chaim had a forged letter putting the blame on us. They were to plant it on my body."

A low growl sounded in Fur's throat. "Meanwhile, we're being shadowed everywhere we go. I see weapons every time I turn around. They may have the Test-Lits incarcerated, but we're not welcome here either."

"Jews once released a plague of biblical proportions on Egypt," I said, "so I can see where they're coming from. We've got to find a way to get them to trust us again. There's something bizarre about this plague that we need to figure out."

The *wrongness* that was associated with the pathogen continued to eat at me.

Added to that, thinking about the Test-Lits and the devastation they had unleashed had me wound in knots. I thought the Test-Lits were dead. We overthrew their tyrannical government, but obviously, their corruption extended far beyond my home world. We needed to dig them out wherever they had taken root, but first, we had to stop the abomination they had set loose on New Mecca.

Chapter 8

Two weeks later, Dr. Sim Bashad, appointed by Hussein to take over from bin Saqer, met with us. He was helpful and got us everything we needed, but he would not speak of anything beyond the specifics of the disease. I detected an aura of apprehension in his reactions to us. Hussein's hostility toward us had increased since the assassination attempts.

Bashad visited the *GCVS*, since I was still rehabbing my back and shuffling around the ship. We were in the lab, data sheets on the plague spread across the metal workbench and images up on the monitor.

Bashad squirmed in his seat as he spoke. "Our quarantine forbids any movement of animals and animal products outside infected areas. Working in our favor, this river valley is isolated by inhospitable desert on two sides, mountains on the third, and the sea on the fourth. Satellite scans of the surrounding deserts and mountains have not shown unusual numbers of deaths in our wild native animals. However, more animals are now affected here in the city, including rats and mice."

My heart sped up, pulse pounding in my temple.

"What about birds?" If the plague got into birds, there would be no containing it.

Bashad shook his head. "We have seen no evidence of infection in birds, thank Allah."

Roxanne asked, "Reptiles? Amphibians? Anything besides the mammals?"

Bashad shook his head. "My people are on the lookout, but we have found nothing."

Fur wanted to know, "How about marine mammals?"

"There are none on New Mecca. And no evidence of fish kills."

I said, "You have your microbiology people working on the identity of the organism. Any idea when we can get started on a vaccine?"

"I think it best if you visit the laboratory and speak with the facility head about that."

"Okay." I raised my eyebrows. "How about tomorrow morning?"

"I will make the arrangements," Bashad said. "And please come without your...er, interns. It would be difficult for them to fit in."

Fur chuckled as I nodded.

***

After dinner that evening, Roxanne, Fur, Healer, Learns-To-Fix-Injuries, and I sat in the commissary. Everyone occupied chairs, except for the dragon. Red crouched in his usual place in the corner. In these close quarters, I no longer noticed Healer's heavy wolf musk and the dragon's foul breath. Ruthie participated in our meeting as her all-pervasive self through the general comm.

"The military won't tell us a damn thing about the Test-Lit prisoners," I complained. "They obviously don't trust us. And the rumors of us starting the plague are still circulating out there."

"The soldiers guarding the ship speak of the rumors, Cy," Ruthie said in the dulcet tone she saved for me. "I have overheard their conversations. They say uncomplimentary things about you." She sounded miffed at that.

Learns-To-Fix-Injuries suggested, "I could remove soldierss." His gleefulness at such a possibility came through loud and clear.

"Violence won't solve anything, Red."

"Dissagree. Helped ssave you and Dr. Ssimon."

Fur laughed. "Score one for the dragon."

Roxanne frowned. "Don't encourage him."

"A vaccine will prove our worth to the New Meccans," I said.

Red asked, "How vaccine work?"

Roxanne took the question. "One way to stop an epidemic is to vaccinate all the susceptible hosts. That's how smallpox, a human disease, was eradicated on Old Earth."

"And a disease called rinderpest in ruminants on earth was eradicated by vaccination," I added.

Roxanne pointed out, "Once the infected animals are dead and the remaining animals are immune, the disease dies out because there's nowhere for the organism to grow."

"Assuming there are no carriers," Fur said. "Some animals could be infected but not ill, and they might spread the disease to other areas where animals have no immunity."

Roxanne put up her hand, palm forward, toward the big man. "Come on, Fur, let's not borrow trouble. We've found no evidence of any carriers. Still, if all the animals on New Mecca are vaccinated, the carrier argument is moot."

"That'll take a lot of vaccine," Fur countered.

"How make vaccine?" Red asked.

"It can be done two ways," I said. "A killed vaccine is one. The microorganism is killed in such a way to preserve the surface antigens that trigger the immune response. The second way is a live vaccine. We sequentially infect cell cultures or animals with the organism under conditions that result in the loss of its ability to cause disease over time. One of earth's most famous scientists, Louis Pasteur, came up with the first vaccines that way. One for anthrax in sheep was through culturing of the bacterium in flasks, and one for rabies in people and animals by passing the virus through rabbits."

"Which is better, live or dead?" Healer asked.

"Both can work. Often a live vaccine is stronger, but you must take caution that the organism is weakened enough and won't cause the disease. Either way, before we can make a vaccine, we have to identify the pathogen."

Red and Healer looked at one another and back at me. The dragon asked, "No vaccine now. We get ssick?"

That had worried me for some time. Our alien friends had minimal contact with New Meccan animals, so chances of infection were slim. "Even if you were exposed, I think your metabolisms are different enough that infection won't be an issue." I looked at Learns-To-Fix-Injuries. "There's no evidence of disease in reptilians."

"Me not reptile. Me dragon!"

"Right. Healer, you're mammalian, but your incredible regenerative powers that go with your shape-changing ability may enable you to ward off the disease. Still, as soon as we get a vaccine, you two are the first in line. In the meantime, both of you stay in the ship. No sense taking any chances."

"What about humans?" Healer asked.

"Humans have had extensive contact with the disease and have shown no evidence of infection."

Red and Healer looked at each other again, and the Lupan said, "We will stay here. We do not want to get sick."

"But you can take *me* along with you, Cy," Ruthie cooed.

"Huh?"

"I have plans for an implantable unit that will capture sight and sound. It will allow me to communicate with you through a neurological interface. You can have me with you...always." Ruthie's voice was smug. I imagined her staring straight at Roxanne as she delivered her next pronouncement. "Electronic communicators like we use now are so...impersonal. And most biological units can hardly communicate at all. I want to be close to you, Cy."

There was a long silence during which I avoided looking at Roxanne, though her fury wrenched my stomach.

Fur guffawed. "A *neurological interface*? You have got to be kidding me."

I knew Roxanne felt that Ruthie hated her, but how could a machine hate? I never felt any emotional empathic responses from Ruthie, as I did with humans and animals, but this bombshell made Roxanne's responses seem justified. It seemed Ruthie was attempting to get between Roxanne and me...physically and mentally. To have Ruthie implanted in my brain? Permanently? I shuddered at the thought. "Uh, no thanks, Ruthie. I need you on the ship with Healer and Learns-To-Fix-Injuries."

The comm board lights flashed once and went dead.

***

The headquarters of the New Meccan Disease Control occupied a building much like all the other government facilities, a plain red brick exterior low on eye appeal, but functional. I shuffled through the entry doors like an octogenarian, cane and all. The wooden walking stick, engraved with twining grape vines, was Fur's idea. He thought it was amusing, but I had to admit it helped me walk.

After we were checked for weapons, a laboratory attendant in a white tunic escorted us through gray, sterile-looking tiled hallways devoid of any wall decorations to an office on the first floor. He opened the door and motioned us through to a reception room but did not join us. A small round lens near the inner door lit up and a hologram appeared, a woman wearing a traditional bhurka.

She spoke in Common. "Welcome. Please be seated. Adila bint Hussein is on a call and will be with you shortly."

The hologram disappeared.

"Efficient," Fur's bass voice rumbled.

"Adila bint Hussein," Roxanne mused. "Related to our New Meccan chief physician Dr. Hussein, I wonder?"

"I'm sure we'll find out," I replied. If Adila was related, I hoped she would be better disposed toward us than her relative.

The inner door opened and a woman, perhaps in her mid-thirties, stood framed by the doorway. With striking amber eyes, she looked at each of us in turn. Her shoulder-length black hair framed a soft, round face. She wore a sky-blue tunic with the crescent and a red cross on the breast pocket. Full lips smiled before she spoke. "Please, come in." She stepped back and waved us in.

The office was a contrast to the halls and waiting room, with touches that said someone actually spent time here and wanted comfort. Two large leather couches formed an angle against the walls in one corner of the room. A large desk made of rich wood sat before a picture window that looked out over a small park with palm trees and benches. Several framed diplomas hung on the walls, along with photographs of mountains, deserts, and forests. A large painting of Dr. Aaquil Hussein hung on one wall, cementing my view of her family origin.

She noticed my examination. "Yes, Dr. Hussein is my father. I am Adila." She put out her hand toward me. The diplomas showed that she had added a Ph.D. to her M.D. degree, exceeding her father's education.

I shook her hand. "I'm Dr. Cy Berger, but call me Cy."

In turn, Roxanne and Fur introduced themselves and shook hands.

Adila motioned toward the couches. "Please make yourselves comfortable. Would anyone like refreshments?"

I shook my head, as did Fur and Roxanne.

Adila seated herself at the end of the couch Roxanne sat on. "I am aware of the rumors that have inundated our city concerning your supposed activities."

I opened my mouth to speak.

She put up a hand. "Please. No explanations are necessary. I do not believe the lies. Cy, I have researched the three of you. You have most distinguished and exciting careers. The good you have done across the galaxy is storied." Her mouth turned down at the corners, and I caught a fleeting glance at her father's picture. "I believe you are here to help us, and I want to make full use of your capabilities."

Roxanne broke the short silence as I took in Adila's words. "Thank you, Adila. I must say that it's nice to hear kind words at this point."

"I cannot change a government viewpoint, even my father's."

I caught a hint of exasperation when she referred to him.

"But I am my own person, and I run this laboratory facility with a dedicated staff of superb scientists, many of whom also serve on the faculty of the University of New Mecca, as I do. We recognize the seriousness of this disease and the threat it poses to our world, and I am placing our full capabilities at your disposal. New Mecca needs your help. Please."

We could not ask for more than that. Adila, unlike her father, looked past hatred and bias. I should probably take a page from her book for my own, but my anger at our treatment on this Muslim world simmered beneath the surface. I knew Fur and Roxanne's feelings were not far from mine.

"Thank you, Adila," I said. "The plague that the Test-Lits released here is like nothing in my experience or that of my colleagues. I hope we can help each other develop a vaccine."

"I agree, Cy, but with respect to the cause, I'm afraid that we have hit something of a barrier."

My breath caught. "What do you mean, 'a barrier'?"

"We will go to the laboratory area. I want you to meet my chief of microbiology. She will explain."

I felt the beginnings of an empathic headache. This did not bode well for a nice day.

Roxanne's mouth formed a severe line as she stood. Fur's brows beetled above his broad, bent nose. We followed Adila bint Hussein out of her office to hear, I feared, more bad news.

Extinction

***

The section of the building we now entered was an extreme biohazard area; I did not have to read Arabic to interpret the red and yellow warning signs. We met Adila's head microbiologist, Dr. Aypari Habib, outside the isolation area. Tall, olive-skinned, with high cheekbones and liquid eyes that were almost black, Habib wore a tunic that could not disguise her ample curves. Her glossy black hair wound into a no-nonsense bun at the nape of her long, shapely neck. I made sure not to ogle her as she directed us to a nearby locker room.

Fur, on the other hand, locked his gaze on her. The emotions roiling out of his brain were amazement overlain by dismay. Before we entered a locker room to change into biohazard gear, Habib and Roxanne disappeared into an adjoining room. Fur stared at the door that closed behind them.

"Fur? You okay?"

He turned to me and his face grew red. "I'm fine." I caught a pulse of strong emotion behind his words.

We slipped out of our street clothes and into hazmat suits made of a bright yellow material.

When the ladies came back, we followed Habib through an airlock door to the main microbiology laboratory.

"This place is amazing, Cy. I've never seen a secure biohazard unit this large." Fur's headgear swiveled as if it were on ball bearings.

The place scurried with yellow hazmat-clad workers. Glove boxes of a variety of sizes and shapes lined one wall. A second wall held individual glassed-in isolation rooms. Closed metal doors with red warning lights glaring balefully above them adorned a third wall. Habib pointed to an isolation room across the main floor and moved toward it. We followed, gathered outside a glass window, and peered in. Two workers in hazmat suits had their arms inserted into shoulder-length rubber gloves that reached into a large glove box, giving them double protection from whatever hazard was in there.

Habib knocked on the door. One of the workers looked up then pulled both arms out from the gloves. The person approached the door and pressed a button on the wall. A female voice spoke in Arabic. *"Salam, Aypari."*

"In Common, please, Karina. Anything new?" Habib asked.

Karina's helmet twisted from side to side. "No, doctor. Everything the same. Every infected cell in culture dies and we cannot isolate the unknown pathogen."

"Thank you." Habib turned to us. "Though we know it must be there in cultures and animals, the cause still eludes us."

The air recycler wheezed in my ears as I breathed. Though what I had felt in the animals that died from the disease still freaked me out, I needed to see—to *feel*—for myself if I could detect the organism. "Can we examine infected animals?"

Habib took us to another room, one with a red warning light above the door. The door opened to an area filled with tissue processing and slide staining equipment. An airlock separated an adjoining room.

"That's the necropsy room. They are dissecting some infected animals now. We can go in, but we must go through the airlock one at a time. The chamber is decontaminated after each person's passage. Dr. Berger, you first."

I went through and reflected that Fur had said nothing more since we entered the lab. Usually, he was inquisitive.

There were three tables, one tech working at each. On each platform, in various states of discombobulation, lay animals I did not recognize. Several cages along the wall held sick, but live animals, awaiting their turn.

The use of laboratory animals for studies of physiology and medicine was millennia old, but I still got empathic twinges when I used them for research; I could not shut down that ability completely. I understood the need. Many of the most important advances in medicine had depended on animal studies. The human and animal lives saved far outweighed the loss of experimental animal lives. But it was never easy for me because of that empathic connection. I took a deep breath to get my stomach under control.

"What are those animals?" Roxanne asked.

"A native animal that was quite widespread early in the planet's colonization. We call them crats. I think you can see why, a cross between a cat and a rat. They were quite a nuisance, getting into food stores and chewing up about anything edible, and sometimes things that weren't. The settlers did a good job of reducing the population, at least in inhabited areas. Unfortunately, more familiar creatures took their place in the scheme of things. Now, Terran rats and mice are the usual human bane here."

Roxanne again: "Are these collected wild?"

"No. We have adapted a strain of the animals for laboratory work. They are susceptible to the same array of pathogens as our Terran animals, so they have been useful."

I nodded, an awkward movement in the helmet. "Yeah. Most of the life-forms humans have encountered in our galaxy bear amazing resemblance to Terran life. DNA, RNA, and proteins are the basic blueprint, machinery, and building blocks for cells everywhere. There are differences in anatomy, physiology, and biochemistry, but life that evolved throughout our galaxy is related."

Habib said, "I do not see that our religions are different on that point. We believe that Allah is the Creator. Nothing exists except by His power and mercy. You believe the same, though you call God by a different name, Yahweh. Islamic teachings about Creation do not contradict science. The process of creation was slow, taking place over many eons. We have seen the evidence of evolution on many worlds. It is consistent with our beliefs."

Fur's head nodded up and down with the rhythm of her words. There was a feeling of acceptance, almost kinship, leaking from the big man. He had always been more in tune than I was with the teachings of the Torah, the first five books of the Old Testament, and biblical interpretations consistent with science. We had frequently argued about how similar life evolved throughout our galaxy. Theories included a massive storm of intergalactic objects carrying the seeds of life that collided with our galaxy; that a race of powerful ancients—of whom there was not a trace—deliberately seeded life here; that God created the universe and its inhabitants. Maybe there was some sort of cosmic intelligence out there, a mind so vast we could not conceive it, but I did not believe that such a mind fit the omniscient and omnipotent Judeo-Christian-Islamic concept of God. I certainly did not buy into creationism.

I was not sure where I stood with respect to belief in God. My frequent ejaculations and curses that invoked the deity were more a cultural and linguistic convention carried over from my childhood rather than an expectation of that deity to act on my words. I grew up with the God of Israel as a given, but my later scientific training seeded doubts. My challenges to the literal translation of the Torah were what got me labeled as a heretic by the Test-Lits, and I did not want to get into that argument with the Muslims of New Mecca. I had enough on my mind, dealing with disasters like the current plague.

"Let's examine the animals." I moved first to the cages. Though the creatures were sick, I detected nothing of the organism. That was consistent with my experience. Even though I knew the microbe was there, the live animals somehow suppressed my detection. I then moved to the closest table. The tech stepped back to let me pass.

The crat's thoracic and abdominal cavities were open and all the internal organs were removed. There was evidence of hemorrhages all over the body walls. Samples of various organs sat in jars of fixative solution on the table. I concentrated but perceived nothing but a dead carcass.

"How long has this one been dead?"

Habib translated as the tech answered in Arabic. "About half an hour."

"Which one is freshest?"

Habib pointed to the next table. "We are about to euthanize that one."

Again, I sensed nothing from the live animal, though it was close to death, lying on its side, its breathing shallow and labored, its gray-brown fur matted and eyes glazed. The tech slipped a needle into the crat's vein and depressed the plunger. When the animal stopped breathing, she checked for a pulse then cut open the abdomen. Clotted blood filled the cavity. Huge splotches of necrosis and hemorrhage spotted the liver, kidneys, and adrenals. The gastrointestinal wall was necrotic and perforated in several places.

The *wrongness* was there, the sense that this disease somehow was not natural. I shuddered and felt Roxanne's hand squeeze my shoulder through the suit. I stood back from the table. Whatever this was, I did not detect it in the living animal, only after death. And it disappeared soon after that.

I thrust my nausea and headache into the background and asked Habib, "How long do the infected cells live in the culture dish? And how long does the organism remain viable after the cells die?"

"The cultured cells all die within fifteen minutes of initial infection. We can pass the disease to new, live cells or infect clean animals within that time limit. Within seconds after the last cultured cells die, we cannot transmit it any longer. We detect no nucleic acids, proteins, carbohydrates, or lipids in the cultures that are different from the normal compounds of the cells. Whatever the pathogen is disappears into a biochemical soup."

"What is the disease course in the lab animals?" I asked.

"There is something unusual even in that. The disease progresses in waves. After initial infection, we see little for about one hour, then there is a surge of tissue destruction as monitored by blood levels of enzymes released from damaged cells. Then another hour hiatus and more tissue destruction. This goes on until the animal dies one day after infection."

"That's faster than the camels or the dogs and cats. I don't understand that staggered progression." I looked around. "Anyone?"

When no one responded, I asked, "How long does the organism remain transmissible in tissues from the dead animals? We know that many body cells don't die immediately on the death of the host. Some are thought to live for several days, or even longer."

I could see Habib's frown through her mask. "In this case, we cannot detect live cells more than five minutes after death of the host. Postmortem cell death is much faster than after any non-plague deaths. After that, any transmissible organism has disappeared, again along with any biochemical evidence of its presence. Dr. Berger, Dr. Simon, you have experience with alien diseases. Have you seen such?"

I shook my head. "How many passages is the organism in that animal?"

Habib replied, "Twenty-five serial passages through crats, and we see no lessening of virulence such as what we would need for a vaccine. The same is true with cultured cells and there we have gone more than one hundred passages."

I nodded. I had sensed no difference in the wrongness of the organism compared to what I had experienced with the livestock. The serial passage approach for vaccine production seemed fruitless so far.

As we cycled through the airlock out of the necropsy room, a disinfectant gas bathed our suits. That was a necessary precaution, although not being able to identify the pathogen, there was no proof that the disinfectant killed whatever it was.

In the outer laboratory, I continued to sense a faint resonance of the plague's wrongness, but since there were no dead animals nearby, I thrust that feeling aside as my imagination.

We learned nothing more from the tissue specimens that we had not seen in our own samples from the camels. The pathogen had to be there, but it did not show in any of the morphological, biochemical, immunological, or genetic scans.

The disease was acting against everything that underlay basic biology. It was not playing by the rules; it made its own. And we did not understand those rules.

***

Back aboard the *GCVS*, Fur, Roxanne, and I discussed what we had learned.

"I don't know how I can perceive a microorganism," I said, "and why only shortly after death."

Fur's eyebrows scrunched together as he spoke. "If this bug can't live for more than a few seconds outside a living cell, how could Chaim bring it here from wherever he got it?"

"Good question, Fur. He brought no animals, and no cultures could have survived more than fifteen minutes. And there's no way he could have kept something like that frozen. We need access to Chaim to find out what we're missing."

"And the authorities won't allow that," Roxanne interjected. "Whatever their reasons."

I nodded. "We've got to reach him...somehow."

"Bashad asked his boss, but Hussein won't help," Roxanne added. "Maybe Adila would. She's much more supportive of us. I'll talk to her."

I stretched, but every muscle in my body complained. I could not suppress a groan.

Roxanne noticed. "Cy, you're grounded for the next several days. Today was too much for you. Rest up. I'll make the contact with Adila alone."

I couldn't argue with her.

Fur added, "And we need to keep track of everything that's going on in the microbiology center. I'll stick with Dr. Habib, keep you informed on their progress."

The guy bubbled with enthusiasm.

"Okay. I get the message. I'll keep Learns-to-Fix-Injuries and Healer company for a while. Maybe their three-D chess will improve."

Fur chuckled. "Wouldn't need much to beat you."

He was not far off. While his game had improved over the past couple of years, mine had remained static. He also played against Ruthie, a tougher challenge than me. Teamed up, our alien interns would be difficult enough, but first, I needed a bed.

Chapter 9

I held my screen tight as Roxanne poured out wave after wave of frustration. Red-faced, she slammed her fist on the commissary table. "I haven't been able to get anywhere. Even with Adila's help, no one will budge. Chaim and his compatriot are locked up tight, and we can't get anywhere near them."

"She spoke with her father?" I asked.

Roxanne tossed her head, auburn curls bouncing. "Not that it did any good. She seems as discouraged as we are."

Fur tugged at his beard. "I haven't much better to report. Dr. Habib says there's no further progress on attempts to isolate the organism."

I shook my head. "I guess the only good news comes from Bashad. He says there's still no evidence of spread beyond the Medina region. I doubt it will stay that way, and once it gets out with no cure and no vaccine to stop it..."

"We can't give up on a vaccine," Fur exclaimed. "I'll keep working with Aypari...Dr. Habib." Fur snapped his mouth closed and looked away from me.

Ruthie interrupted. "We have visitors, Cy. Dr. Bashad is here with Ali Suliaman. Shall I let them in?"

"Show us the external camera feed."

Suliaman stood by Bashad's side at the foot of the ramp. Both wore *keffiyehs* and robes.

"Haven't seen Suliaman for a while," Roxanne said.

"Fur, escort them up here." Maybe I could convince them to pressure Hussein into letting us question Chaim. I saw Suliaman as our friend, or at least he did not have the same animosities toward us that Hussein did. I got up and poured a cup of coffee as I waited. "You want some?" I asked Roxanne.

She shook her head and examined the viewscreen's camera image that followed our guests.

When he entered the commissary, Bashad gave us a brief bow. "Good morning. Thank you for seeing us so early and unannounced."

Suliaman bowed. "It is good to see you all again."

"What can we do for you?" I asked curtly, still nettled by our inability to get to Chaim.

Roxanne shot me a warning glance. "Please be seated. Would either of you like something to drink? We have coffee, herbal teas, or juice."

They declined and sat in the chairs bolted in place around the metal table. Fur leaned against the counter by the coffee machine and ran his fingers over his mustache.

Ali broke the silence. "I recognize the difficulty of this situation for you. Besides your being assaulted, our local populace has demonized you, and I apologize for that."

I sensed that Suliaman's chagrin was genuine.

"I'm sorry for your injuries, Dr. Berger. I appreciate your work with our scientists. I am confident you are helping as much as you can."

I sipped coffee before responding. "Why are you here now?"

The corners of Suliaman's lips turned down as he spoke, but his demeanor remained unruffled by my lack of cordiality. "You are a direct man. We will return the favor." He looked at Bashad with raised eyebrows.

Bashad looked at me. "We are concerned that the quarantine will not hold, and we ask if you will come to the other agricultural regions and help us there. Your experience would be invaluable to assist our veterinarians with respect to diagnosis and handling of the plague, should it strike. Are you recovered enough to do so?"

"Absolutely not," Roxanne barked. "He needs at least another week of rest, maybe two."

I held up my hand to her. "Hold on a sec." Something about the request did not ring true. "Why do you need me? Send them vid clips of the plague. The diagnosis isn't difficult. Since we have no treatment, I don't see what I can add."

"Dr. Berger, there is much anger among the people. Perhaps this could quell the rumors about the *Galactic Circle Veterinary Service*. Make our people see you as helping rather than harming them. Your appearance among them should blunt the hostility directed at you." That came through as honesty, but I still detected a degree of evasion in his words.

I stared at Bashad. "What about Hussein? Does he agree with this?"

He nodded but did not meet my eyes. "There is much consternation due to news reports...and much fear. You might help allay those fears."

I sensed that, if anything, his boss was surprisingly eager for me to take this trip.

Suliaman's face was grave. "I agree this is something that might help."

"I'll take your request under advisement." I felt Roxanne's objection like a sword to my gut.

***

"This is senseless, Cy. They don't need you to

educate veterinarians."

"Yeah. I got the impression from Bashad that this is Hussein's idea, not Suliaman's, though the Imam *would* like to promote anything we can do to change the people's perception of us. Maybe I should consider it. I'm not accomplishing anything here."

Fur added, "We could use some positive press. I don't know about you, but many of the workers I meet in Habib's lab are hostile. They bow to Habib's orders, but they don't hide their mistrust and dislike of me."

Roxanne sighed. "I've had the same experience. But if you go, Cy, I want Fur with you. I need to stay here to work with Adila."

"No!" Fur's demurral was surprisingly sharp.

I looked at him with raised eyebrows. I still detected a hint of lingering resentment from my inappropriate accusation. We had not spent much time together recently, and we both were self-conscious about our estrangement, but there was more to this. Embarrassment. God, he was embarrassed.

Fur's face reddened. "I-I need to work with Dr. Habib. We've reached a good...working relationship. I mean, I'm helping in the lab. We're making progress."

A small smile lifted Roxanne's lips as she looked at Fur.

Sometimes it takes me longer than most to see the light. Fur's recent behaviors now made sense. The big guy had found a girl. I understood: she was a beauty and smart as they come. But, as usual, I stuck my foot in my mouth, this time swallowing it all the way to the ankle.

"Aypari Habib? You're stuck on Aypari? But she's Muslim." There were times when I could be as bigoted as any Test-List asshole.

Fur's face clouded over and his thick eyebrows beetled. "That's none of your fucking business. What I do with my personal life is not your concern."

Unfortunately, my obnoxiousness came naturally, but my enmity at our treatment on this Islamic world spilled over. "With everything that these people have thrown at us here, how—?"

"Cy, *shut up.*" Roxanne's anger sliced into my brain. "Listen to yourself. What you're saying. This isn't the man I married, who fought oppression and intolerance. You owe Fur an apology. Me, too."

I sat back and pressed a hand to my roiling stomach. She was right. We had fought to free Dovid's World from people who held to the very concepts I now espoused. Was I becoming what I hated? I hung my head and could not meet Fur's eyes. "Sorry. I was way out of line."

"Yeah. You've been there a lot lately. Go where Hussein and Ali send you, but don't expect me along for the ride."

As I looked up and met Fur's steely gaze, he placed his coffee cup on the counter with a deceptively gentle motion, considering his size and the thunderous state of his emotions, and left the commissary.

Roxanne shook her head at me and stood. Her eyes held mine for long moments. Her aura said she was glad that I had apologized, but her disgust said it was too little too late. She, too, turned and left.

The coffee turned to acid in my stomach.

***

Chief Medical Officer Hussein sent for me, ostensibly to discuss the plan for sending me to other regions. As I stepped out of the land drone, I looked up a flight of steps lined by fatigue-clad guards. A barricade also blocked the street leading to the steps of the main government building. Behind the cordon massed a crowd of robed people.

An officer with a star and braids on his shoulders bowed to me. "Welcome, Dr. Berger. I am Colonel Shamir. General Hussein is expecting you. Please follow me."

General Hussein? Now that was a change. As I bowed in return, a muted roar rose from the crowd. Most of the yelling was in Arabic, but enough was in Common to give me the tenor of the cries.

"Infidel."

"Jew filth."

"Murderer."

"You should be killed like the animals you have destroyed."

Et cetera, et cetera, et cetera.

As I looked away from the colonel, I glimpsed a missile coming straight at my head. My heart jumped to my throat, as I had no time to duck. I stiffened as the object impacted my forehead with a dull thwack.

Oddly, there was no pain, just wetness. Coldness oozed down my face. I wiped my hand across my brow as laughter bloomed from the crowd. My fingers dripped a gooey mixture of clear white with swirls of yellow and scattered jagged brown flakes: an egg.

Shots followed shouts from the soldiers and the crowd roared again, but now I sensed the distinct undertone of fear. More epithets assaulted my ears.

The colonel grabbed my arm. He pulled me up the steps to the front door and into the building. As he dragged me, I wiped egg from my face and neck. It had oozed down inside my collar.

He said, "Dr. Berger, you are unharmed, I trust." Though his voice was outwardly apologetic, I felt his underlying amusement.

I shrugged off his grasp and shook shell-flecked egg off my hand, splattering the polished marble floor.

"Where's Hussein?"

I sensed his annoyance at my lack of suitable esteem toward his *General*.

"Follow me."

He took off down the hall to an elevator bank flanked by soldiers. At a nod from the colonel, a soldier pushed a button. Now *that* was a perk of rank that was interesting. I wondered if I could get Healer or Learns-To-Fix-Injuries to push buttons for me.

Moments later, the door dinged and opened, and our group entered. After four dings upward, we emptied into a broad, well-lit hallway carpeted in a lush purple fabric. Many portraits of military officers adorned the walls, all rendered in stern and imperial poses. At the fifth alcove on the right, flanking guards opened a door to an inner sanctum.

Shamir led me across a room and waved me to a green-upholstered chair. "Please be seated, Dr. Berger. I will be a moment."

As I sat, he exited through the entry door. A door opposite the entry held a plaque that read: "*General Hussein.*"

A couple of minutes later, Shamir returned with a towel.

"Thanks." I cleaned myself up as much as I could then handed the towel back.

"The General will be with you shortly." Shamir exited back to the hall.

My heart rate had still not come back to normal. I was humiliated but unharmed. Be thankful for little things. If hatred was getting this bad here in the capital, what might it be like if I went to other cities? Then it hit me that someone prearranged this protest. How else would they have known I would be here?

I had no time to think further, as the inner door opened, framing Hussein in all his glory. His uniform was something I imagined appropriate for kings or princes on Old Earth: a midnight blue jacket and pants trimmed with gold piping, the jacket's shoulders and sleeves liberally adorned with gold braid. A white-edged red sash slashed diagonally across his chest. The underlying high-collared white shirt was tight enough to choke anyone, even if they were not as well-fleshed as the Medical Corps Chief.

"Dr. Berger," he said, "so good to see you again. We have much to discuss."

My self-preservation instincts slammed into overdrive. This guy was so full of shit he couldn't help but spill it out from his mouth.

He sat across a large desk from me. The work surface was polished and devoid of anything that looked like official paperwork. One lone item was a framed photograph of him with his daughter, Adila. He waved me to a wooden chair opposite him. His seat was tall, and mine short, so he looked down on me. A deliberate arrangement, I was sure.

"No doubt Dr. Bashad has filled you in on the status of the plague. It remains confined to this region. But we are concerned should it get out."

Tell me something new, huh?

"Your injuries were unfortunate, but you are recovered now, yes?" His voice was cordial and his aura contained not a hint of regret.

I nodded. I had no trouble sensing that he had ordered our constant surveillance since the assassination attempts. I might have wondered how a physician would have such authority, but he was obviously more than just the head of the Medical Corps.

I shook off the bad vibes I was getting. "What do you want from me, Hussein? From us? Your government has done nothing to tell people that this plague was not our doing. We came at your invitation.

To help. That crowd downstairs was a setup. Give me a good reason why my colleagues and I shouldn't depart New Mecca now and leave you with this mess?"

Hussein's smile evaporated like the desert rain, leaving behind a parched leer. He no longer tried to hide his animosity. "It is not so easy as that, Berger. Your ship is not leaving until I say so. You *will* assist us."

"What are you going to do if we take off, shoot us down?"

His smile was nothing I wanted to wake up to. "If necessary." He paused to let that sink in. "I believe you will want to be...cooperative. It will be best for you and yours."

Shit. I had pulled the tiger's tail a little too hard. I drew a breath and tried to keep my soaring heart rate from leading to cardiac fibrillation.

"We're working with your scientists. We're doing everything we can. What more do you want?"

He shifted in his seat and ran a finger around the constrictive shirt collar. I sensed the shirt would come off as soon as I left. He had dressed up to impress me.

"Dr. Berger..." His voice dropped back to an amicable tone. "I have spoken at length with Ali Suliaman." His dislike of Suliaman came through clear as a bell. "Our people are afraid. Because of that, they have turned their anger toward you. This plague is upsetting our world. Imam Suliaman agrees with me that you can play a role in calming the people's fears by traveling to other regions of New Mecca and speaking with our veterinarians."

"I can only tell them what they already know. It's a waste of time."

"We can put you and your people in a positive light. Hopefully, this will end the kind of incident you experienced today."

I sensed evasion in his words. "And if I refuse?"

"That is not an option." A wave of hatred poured from him.

My stomach wrenched and I felt my face heat, but he had us over a barrel. "If I do this, what then? You'll make formal statements that we are innocent?"

"Of course. You have my promise."

I did not believe a word of it. His hate came through as deep crimson and sickening purples swirling in my head. The hatred extended beyond me and his Test-Lit prisoners. It included not only Jews of any persuasion, but anything alien. His bigotry and xenophobia did not show outwardly—he had one hell of a poker face—but he did not know I was an empath and could read him like a book.

"One more thing," I said. "I need access to the prisoner Chaim McNulty."

"Impossible."

"He has information vital to our investigation. We need to know how he brought the plague here. You're a physician. You *know* that information is critical."

"He is not available to you. I will *extract* what information is needed."

I did not like the sound of that. "And you'll share it with us?"

"As I see fit. You, however, will do as I suggest or become my enemy. Eggs may be the least of your worries." He turned away from me and pressed a button on his comm.

The threat behind his words was as sharp as my dismissal.

***

When I returned to the *GCVS*, Roxanne met me as I ascended the ramp, her face as pale as I had ever seen.

Her demeanor brought pounding to my temples.

"It's Healer. He's sick."

I stood speechless for a moment, not wanting to face what I most feared. "What, does he have mange again?" I referred to the skin disorder that had originally taken us to Lupus IV.

"I know humor is your defense mechanism, Cy, but this isn't funny. He has the plague."

My legs went rubbery and I staggered. "You're sure?"

Roxanne grabbed my arm to steady me. "You need to examine him."

"You know I can't detect the plague organism in a living patient." My breath caught. "He's not...dead, right?"

"He collapsed a while ago, but he's alive. We have him bedded down in an isolation cubicle."

Smart. I had hoped that Healer's alien metabolism would protect him; maybe it had, for a while. I followed Roxanne to the clinic area. Through the window of the cubicle I saw Healer's eyes were closed. Strands of his normally luxuriant mane lay plastered across his face. His limbs twitched as if he were a marionette dancing in response to some malevolent puppeteer.

"High fever?"

Roxanne nodded. "He has all the signs, including the skin lesions."

"We have to come up with a way to make a definitive diagnosis in a living patient," I said. "We can't wait for him to die."

"Cy, do you think you might detect the pathogen in infected cell cultures, right after the cells die?"

"From what Habib said, it's only a few seconds before the pathogen disappears, but maybe that gives me enough time to sense the live organism."

I donned a disposable isolation suit and entered the

cubicle. Healer's twitching had increased. I lifted his eyelids. His eyes had rolled up, and small hemorrhages dotted the sclera. His pale oral mucous membranes suggested significant internal hemorrhage already had begun. We didn't have much time.

I inserted a venous cannula into his arm and drew a vial of blood. Then I hooked an IV up and started to replace the fluid he was losing to the hemorrhage. That would help ward off shock. I took the vial in my hand. "Spray me with disinfectant as I leave the cubicle."

Fur complied.

I dropped the sealed vial in a beaker of disinfectant that Roxanne held. She turned and headed to the lab.

I shut the cubicle door behind me and disrobed, throwing the suit into the recycler for incineration.

I watched Healer, wanting to see improvement, but knowing that was a vain hope. Fur was silent, as well.

Five minutes later, Roxanne returned. "I infected a half-dozen healthy cell cultures with Healer's blood...about a minute apart. The cells in the first culture should be dead in fifteen minutes. You can check that one, then the next culture should be ready. That should give you about five or six minutes to detect the plague organism."

I hoped it would work. "Set the cultures under the scope. We'll be able to watch the cells disintegrate as they die."

Roxanne placed the cultures in a secured glove box and used the gloves to manipulate a remote microscope lens into position. Then we watched the culture on the monitor. At nine minutes, the cells, normally flattened out on the surface of the culture dish, began to swell then detach from each other. Within three more minutes, all the cells showed signs of deterioration, nuclear condensation and fragmentation and cell membrane disruption, and then floating debris blocked a clear view of the dish surface.

At fourteen minutes after Roxanne had infected the culture, I slipped my arm into the box's protective glove and lifted the culture close to the glass. Some cells would still be alive but close to death. I had scant seconds after their death to perceive the organism. With my nose touching the outside of the glass, something pinged at my senses, and I felt a slight wave of nausea. The *wrongness*, the feeling of the violation of nature came through faintly. Then seconds later, nothing.

"It's weak. I think it's there, but I'm not positive."

"The number of organisms would be fewer than those in an animal," Roxanne said, "so the signal would be weaker. Let's see what the other cultures show."

By the fourth culture, I was sure, which was fortunate because the fifth and sixth showed no evidence of infection. The pathogen had disappeared within the five minute limit of removal from the host, just as Habib had told us, and the last cultures received no viable organisms. I swallowed back acid as I looked away. Healer had the plague, and we were no closer to identifying the cause than the day we landed.

***

Of all of us, Learns-To-Fix-Injuries-After-Inflicting-Them was taking Healer's illness the hardest. The two disparate aliens had formed a strong bond of friendship.

"Kill organismss. Musst not take Healer. You musst do ssomething, Cyberger."

I agreed. "Ideas, anyone?" My nausea and a tension headache that felt like spikes thrust into both ears clouded my thinking. I did not know *what* else to do. I had warded off Healer's hemorrhagic shock with plasma substitute for the moment, but that would not last. The Lupan's natural immunity to disease helped. The Lupan shape-change was a genetic characteristic of his race. A deluge of enzymes, hormones, and growth factors allowed incredibly rapid breakdown and remodeling of tissues and conferred an enhanced ability to heal injuries. That would delay but not prevent his organs from failing.

After much too long a silence, Fur looked up, a light glinting in his brown eyes. "Cryostorage. Could we freeze him and arrest the disease progress?"

"That's a thought, Fur," Roxanne said. "Cryopreservation might work. We have the advanced cryostorage equipment and embryonic maturation equipment we got from my government on Sammara."

Fur nodded. "I'll bet we can adapt it for Healer." Fur was our mechanical genius and had adapted the Sammaran equipment to do amazing things, like in one case, cloning a dragon heart for transplant.

"We don't have any other options," Roxanne said. "If we can keep him suspended until we have some way to treat the disease, we have to try. If we can't successfully freeze him..."

"Yeah. We haven't lost anything, because he's as good as gone," I said.

"Hsssss." The dragon's head swiveled between my wife and me. He did not need to say anything more.

"I'll give it a shot." Fur was up and out of the room before I could say another word.

We followed.

Fur had the cryostorage cabinet open. He removed and thrust shelves at me to make room for Healer. I placed them to the side, away from his frantic activities.

"Grab me a wrench," Fur ordered.

Roxanne stuck one in his outstretched hand. He periodically hurled parts over his shoulder, letting us clean up the mess.

Finally, he stood back and surveyed his handiwork. "I think this will do it. Get blankets for bedding. Cy, can you prepare the cryostorage solution for IV injection?"

"But it's never been used that way before," I objected.

He turned to me, his eyes smoldering. "You have a better idea?" His anger at me had not diminished.

We had ten liters of the cryo liquid and needed at least six to replace Healer's blood, based on the size of a comparable human or animal, and four more to flush his system.

Roxanne had all the IV equipment laid out and ready. The three of us donned protective gear. We bagged Healer, sprayed disinfectant on all of us, and moved him to the cryo lab. We would start cooling him immediately, but his heart had to keep pumping until we had flushed and replaced all the blood. Roxanne inserted inflow and outflow catheters and we started the equipment. Fur monitored the cooling rate, while I kept a close watch on cardiac function. Roxanne attended to the coolant flow, changing bags as necessary.

We banned the dragon from getting close for fear of contagion, so he watched through a porthole in the room's door.

Thirty minutes later, we had done what we could. Our coolant supply ran out just as Healer's heart slowed to a stop. His body temperature was now at -190 C. We wouldn't know if this procedure worked until he was thawed.

Chapter 10

Chaim moved his body with great care, first sliding his legs off the cot, then raising his torso with the assistance of his arms. The pain had diminished, but he remained leery of fast movements. The past two days had brought blessed relief; his captors had left him alone, thank God. He stood, keeping his legs braced against the edge of the bed, then shuffled across the small cell to the toilet. His nausea never went away, and vomiting had become as regular and necessary as his other bodily functions.

When he returned to his cot, he avoided the blood-stained metal chair in the center of his cell. He sank down and placed his elbows on his knees, his head supported by his hands over his eyes. He was thankful there was no mirror in the cell; he imagined he had no unbruised skin. He felt the knots and welts but did not need to see them.

He had no way to tell time since the cell had no exterior windows. A single ceiling glow lamp in the hall spilled through the barred window in his cell door. He could not avoid the spy cameras positioned in the upper corners of his cell. His captors watched him constantly.

Keys jangled and the door to his cell opened, but instead of a meal delivery, he faced General Hussein, the bringer of pain. Chaim's gut clenched.

The general stood silent, framed in the doorway, his green shirt bulging over his belt. Black stains spattered his uniform, the same one he always wore when he came, remnants of Chaim's blood.

Oy, Gott. Again.

The general grumped. "What? No greeting? Have you no manners?"

Chaim ducked his chin to his chest. *I have nothing to say to this demon.*

"Tsk, tsk." The general frowned. "And I thought we would become friends today."

The man's voice sickened Chaim. He shuddered.

"No matter." Hussein stepped inside the cell and motioned to the door. A second man, wiry and slight, was the antithesis of Hussein. The top of his head just reached the general's shoulder, but he was even more fearsome than his counterpart. Chaim sensed a tension in the man's body, and his eyes were black as the pits of hell. He was the torturer.

Two burly guards entered, grabbed Chaim by the arms, and wrestled him into the metal chair. They fastened restraints on his arms and legs.

He recognized the futility of resistance, but once seated, he looked up at Hussein. "I cannot tell you any more. This torture is useless."

Hussein smiled, an expression scarier than his frown. "Mr. McNulty, I believe you do have more to tell us. If you will not do so willingly..." He motioned with his head toward the smaller man. "Your choice."

Chaim said nothing. He had admitted what he could. That he was associated with the Testamentary-

Literalist Party, a fundamentalist ultraorthodox Jewish group whose goal was to force their brand of religion on the galaxy. That he had brought the plague to New Mecca as one step in destroying Islam to clear the way for the true religion. He had already admitted that to Dr. Simon, so he gave these brutes nothing new. Beyond that, he would say nothing of co-conspirators on New Mecca, or where he had come from, the planet and the laboratory where the plague was created.

Though he now regretted what he had done, questioned the tenets of his party, he would not give up his compatriots. He was no longer the weak, fearful fool who had set out on this mission; his experiences had hardened him. He still had no power, no ability to change his situation, but strength had grown within him. No longer a worm, he had grown a backbone.

Dr. Simon...Roxanne...would approve of me now, if she could see me. Her image emboldened him even more. He looked up at the men before him. "Do what you came for. I have no more to say."

The small man smiled and rolled a cart of instruments into the cell. The general shut the door, stepped close, and watched.

***

Much later, the guards unclasped Chaim's arms and legs, lifted him from the chair, and then released him. He crumpled to the floor, his legs unable to support him. He felt his forehead bounce on the hard surface, but it was a faraway sensation, though he knew it should concern him. One of the guards rolled him onto his back. Chaim caught the gist of the brief conversation with his imperfect Arabic.

"He's still alive, thank Allah."

The second guard added, "Good thing. Hussein

would have our asses if we killed him."

"Let's get out of here. The stink of his shit is getting to me."

Chaim did not move after the door shut behind them, happy to have them gone. The torture elicited involuntary vomiting and excretion, and the cell reeked of his most vile bodily fluids. They would bring water and mops later; he'd have to clean up his own mess. His prison tunic, caked with his blood and excrement, made him long for fresh clothing and a shower, something he would not get. He felt blood trickle down his forehead but ignored it.

What mattered was that he did not talk. Instead of caving in to the pain, his spine seemed to grow stronger with each torture session. *What did Jonah call me when I first came here? Pathetic? Laughable? No longer. I am Moses, David. No matter what they do to me, I will not yield.*

***

I was alone in the commissary, drinking coffee and worrying about Healer, when Roxanne appeared in the hatchway, a towel wrapped around her from chest to knees. Her shoulders were an angry red, but that hue paled in comparison to the wave of crimson fury that emanated from her mind and washed over me. I raised my arm as if that might ward off her emotional onslaught.

Her green eyes flashed and her voice held barely controlled rage. "*Look* at me." She opened the towel, revealing her normally pale body scorched a flaming red.

"God, Roxanne. What happened?"

"Your AI did this. The shower turned scalding hot and I couldn't turn it off. And the door latch jammed.

How could that happen if not for that *thing*?"

My eyes and brain locked on Roxanne's scalded skin.

"It did this to me...deliberately."

I had difficulty comprehending her words. Ruthie? Doing that? "That-That's impossible. How could it be something deliberate? I can't believe—"

"You better believe it, damn you." She wrapped the towel around herself again—I was glad no one else was in the room—turned and stomped off.

I didn't move as I tried to wrap my mind around what had happened. Why would Ruthie do something like that deliberately? The AI controlled all the mechanical and electronic operations of the ship, sure, but to do something like this? Surely it was just a glitch in the programming. But since Ruthie's offer to implant herself in my brain—I shivered at *that* thought— Roxanne had become paranoid with respect to the AI.

I would run diagnostics on the system, correct whatever glitch existed.

First, I had to calm my wife. My stomach lurched at the thought of facing her right now, but she needed medical attention for her burns. I put down my coffee, stood, and followed the trail of wet footprints, making a detour to get burn medication from the pharmacy.

"You have to do something, Cy. That AI is out of control." She sprawled facedown and naked on our bed.

"Roxanne, you aren't being reasonable. It's an AI. It can't injure you. There was a glitch in the water control system, that's all."

I gently rubbed the salve on her back.

"You don't have a clue, do you? As big as it is, you can't see the nose in front of your face."

I stopped rubbing. Now *that* was a low blow. She knew how sensitive I was about my oversized nasal protuberance.

"You're treading close to disaster here, Cyrano."

Coming on the heels of the nose reference, the rare use of my full name stung. My parents named me Cyrano D. Berger after the famous literary character, Cyrano de Bergerac, *because* I would inherit the prodigious nose of my father's family. They wanted to show me how one can move past what might be seen as a prominent physical flaw. They forced me to confront my appearance, to explore the play and its eponymous hero. I realized that emulating a man who was a dashing romantic figure, a poet and musician, a superb swordsman possessing the courage of ten, a man who exemplified fundamental honesty and integrity, was not so bad.

"What do you want me to do?" I asked as I finished applying salve to her back.

"Fix your AI. Before something worse happens." She sat up and pointed to the door to our quarters. "And don't come back until it *is* fixed."

I returned to the commissary and stared into the dregs of my cold coffee. Roxanne was convinced that the AI was inimical to her on our first voyage together, before we were married, claimed that Ruthie was spying on her. I had blocked Ruthie from seeing or hearing anything in our quarters, and kept it that way.

After Ruthie's neural implant suggestion, and now this incident, I found it hard to deny something weird was taking place. But the AI was integral to everything in the *GCVS*. I couldn't just shut it down.

I needed to talk this out with someone. Fur was always a voice of reason when I went over the hill, but he was totally pissed at me.

And for some reason, deep within, I was not sure I *could* shut Ruthie down. Being somewhere else for a while, a far away somewhere else, sounded better all the time.

Extinction

***

The next morning, Roxanne sat next to me on the bridge where I'd curled up in my Captain's chair for the night. She had put animosities on hold since General Hussein, a common enemy, was the topic of conversation.

"I don't know what he really wants," I said. "He knows it makes no medical sense for me to talk to the vets in outlying areas. And I don't believe that he cares if the people hate us. Maybe he even prefers it that way. But he made it clear that we're hostages on this planet, and he wouldn't hesitate to destroy the *GCVS* if we try to leave. Maybe he couldn't do that, but do we want to test our ship's defenses?"

"You can't go gallivanting across the country, Cy. We need you here."

Considering my conflicts with Roxanne and Fur, maybe I was ready for some solitude, but I held my tongue on that point. "I don't have a choice."

"You can't go alone. At least take Fur with you."

But we both knew that Fur would not leave Habib's side. He was smitten with the woman. Seemed it was mutual, too.

"And you're needed here, Roxanne. Someone has to keep working on a treatment for the plague. You and Adila and her team are the best hope we have."

"I don't trust that son-of-a-bitch," she snarled. "He's the exact opposite of his daughter. They could accomplish the same thing without you going away. He's splitting us up. It smacks too much of what happened to us before the assassination attempts."

I shook my head. "That was the Test-Lits' doing, not Hussein's. Maybe he's right. I need to show the people we are helping, that we aren't the problem to begin with."

"He could tell them that himself."

I couldn't argue the point, but I did not see any way around complying with his demands. "There's no alternative. I have to go alone."

"Why do you have to be so stubborn?" Her voice was harsh with anger and fear.

A bit of distance was looking better and better. "Look, I'll do what Hussein asks, get out there and back as fast as I can. I trust you to hold down the fort."

"Fine, but you're not leaving until you deal with your AI. You're not going to ignore that."

I should have known I could not slip past that one. "I'll look at the AI system, run some simulations and debug the programming before I go." I knew that was not what she wanted. Nothing short of a total shutdown would satisfy her, but what else could I do?

"That's not enough, Cy. It won't fix the problem."

"There's no time to do more. It'll be fine, Roxanne."

She shook her head at me. "You still don't have a clue." She got up and walked out.

There would be no happy goodbyes before this trip.

***

My first stop was in Aswan, a large city on the shore of a massive reservoir, named after a city near a huge dam back on earth. Green, yellow, and brown irrigated plots checker-boarded the surrounding arid country, made possible by the water behind the dam. My traveling companions included a young veterinarian on Bashad's staff, Abul Khayr, a lieutenant Shaji from Hussein's staff, and corporal Mahir, the pilot of our aircraft.

When we arrived at the airfield in Aswan, I was shocked at the crowd gathered behind a military cordon. As I debarked, I heard epithets filled with hatred, similar to those thrown at me in Medina. The soldiers kept the crowd far enough away to prevent any egg strikes or worse.

Hussein had not lost sleep trying to bolster my image to the populace. In fact, this setup was like the situation at Hussein's headquarters; the crowd knew of my arrival. I wondered what else was set up for me.

As I had suspected, I could do little to prepare the medical community for the onslaught of the plague. I gave talks, admitted our inability to identify the pathogen, and outlined the plague's diagnostic lesions. The veterinarians I met were more interested in my experiences with alien animals, and I regaled them with stories of our travels and the unique medical challenges the *GCVS* had faced.

I continued to encounter hostility from crowds that gathered wherever I visited, but there were no more attacks like the one at Hussein's headquarters. To prevent any incidents, Khayr and Shaji did not allow me to wander on my own.

I checked in with Roxanne daily, though our talks were brief and cold. We stuck to facts. She reported encountering similar hostile crowds but no assaults. Religious leaders had declared that all mammals were plague-ridden and therefore unfit for consumption. They embargoed all mammalian meat and milk products. This had led to a run on other protein sources like birds and fish, but the poultry and fishing industries could not keep up with the demand. No one was starving, but people were pissed. They took out their anger on the nearest and most logical targets...us.

Habib, Fur, Adila, and Roxanne continued their labors but reported no progress on isolation of the pathogen. There also was little progress on treatment. All the known antimicrobial agents caused not even a delay in the disease progression. Intensive efforts to ward off hemorrhagic shock in individual animals delayed but did not avoid death and were not economically viable in herds.

Once again, I pondered how in hell Chaim had gotten the plague across the galaxy since the thing died without a host. We needed to speak with the Test-Lit, but Hussein would still not give us access.

After stopping in our third city, my frustration got the best of me. Abul Khayr and I had become friends on the trip, and we sat over cups of aromatic tea in a hotel café with widely spaced glass-topped tables. A percussion and flute trio provided some background noise, and I leaned toward Khayr, my voice low. I was convinced that Hussein had spies listening and watching me everywhere. That included lieutenant Shaji.

"Just what am I accomplishing here? Hussein says I'm spreading goodwill, but the only people I speak with are my medical colleagues and they already know what I'm telling them. The crowds outside certainly aren't showing me any goodwill. How does what I'm doing change anyone's mind about me?" I clenched a fist but refrained from pounding it on the glass table.

Abul Khayr pursed his lips before he spoke. "I must admit that I agree, Cy. Your access to the public is restricted by military order...for your safety."

I felt Abul Khayr's discomfort as a dull ache behind my eyes. I strengthened my screen. Hussein was powerful and New Meccans were wary of any hint of disagreement with him.

"Perhaps we have accomplished what we can. Let me speak with Ali Suliaman, see if we can get permission to return to Medina. I would prefer if you allow me to handle this. We do not want to antagonize those in power."

Whoa. I got one of those rare visions I sometimes got when reading strong emotions. While I do not read minds, sometimes the emotions took the form of pictures in my mind's eye, and this occurred more frequently and lasted longer in recent weeks. In this case, accompanying Khayr's last words, I glimpsed Ali Suliaman and Aaquil Hussein facing one another, each backed by ghost-like images of armies. Did Khayr know such a war was underway? Or was this just a fear in his mind?

That was all I needed. Was I now becoming a mind-reader? The whole situation scared the shit out of me.

Abul Khayr frowned. "Are you all right? You turned pale."

He had no clue as to my empathic abilities. I shrugged. "A bit dizzy is all. It would be great if you could check with Ali about us going back."

It seemed like the people who mattered were pissed off at me no matter which direction I turned: Roxanne, Fur, Hussein, well, maybe not Suliaman. He helped where he could, but I needed to get back before the situation between Roxanne and Ruthie deteriorated even more.

My stomach upset had become steadily worse, and my headaches and vertigo were increasingly common.

Chapter 11

Khayr roused me from sleep early. I opened the hotel room door for him, hoping he brought coffee. One look at his face, however, and I did not need a jolt of caffeine. His olive complexion was pale, and frown lines creased his smooth forehead.

"Bad news, Cy."

I waved him in. My heart pounded as if it sought exit from my chest. "Roxanne...?"

"No. It's about the plague."

My pulse rate descended, though I did not look forward to any bad news. "Let me get dressed."

When I returned from the suite's bedroom I asked, "What now?"

His mouth turned down at the corners and he rubbed his forehead. "It has broken out in Aswan."

"Damn. Well, we knew it wasn't going to stay contained. I wonder why in Aswan?"

Khayr shook his head. "I'm afraid that development has undermined everything we set out to do on this trip."

"Huh? How so?"

"That was the first place we stopped. People are saying that you brought the plague with you, that it proves you are spreading the disease."

My pulse rate shot up again. "That's...That's ridiculous. They can't believe—"

"They do believe. I am not saying this is true. I do not believe it either, but the news services are playing the connection to the hilt. They are not accusing you openly but are making the point that the first outbreak beyond the Medina region coincided with your appearance."

My stomach twisted in pain, partly from feeling Khayr's emotions, partly from my own fears.

"That is not all."

I groaned.

"The plague has mutated and jumped to birds, reptiles, and amphibians."

"Oh, no." I found it hard to breathe.

"Several poultry flocks have succumbed, and reptiles and amphibians in the capital city zoo."

I grabbed onto that as if he'd thrown me a lifeline. "That's it. The birds. Infected birds flew it in to Aswan."

Khayr shook his head. "The avian infections were not recognized until after the Aswan outbreak."

"But that doesn't mean birds weren't infected earlier."

"True, but however the disease got to Aswan, the damage is done. Logic will take a back seat to emotion. And emotion is running high against you."

My hands clenched into fists and my head pounded as I tried to see where to go from here. We were losing the battle on all fronts. "You realize what this means, Khayr? The only acceptable animal protein source left on New Mecca will be fish and other seafood. Will that be enough for your population?"

"Our crops will remain a food source. Much of what animals consumed will now go to humans. Fishing will increase, and efforts to import food from other planets have begun. Still, there have been food riots in Medina, which was the first locale hit. As other regions are more affected, I expect that civil unrest will increase."

I was sorry we ever came to this damned planet, but I kept that unvoiced. "We came here to help, but it seems that everything we do goes against us. The Test-Lits started this, and they're Jews...despicable, but part of my heritage nonetheless. You and your people are facing a horrendous future because of them. Please accept my apology for what they did. I know that does not help much, but you've been a friend. I need friends right now."

***

By the time Lieutenant Shaji got permission for us to return to the capital city, the demonstrations against me had become more frequent and more vitriolic, and the government had forcibly put down food riots in Medina. I had not been able to contact the *GCVS* for the past two days and worried about what was happening to my wife and colleagues.

A large military contingent cordoned off the field where our flyer was parked. Floodlights illuminated a screaming throng that surrounded the site, despite the new day being only four hours old. A staged scene again. Someone told them I would arrive before dawn.

Abul Khayr and Shaji talked animatedly with one another, but they were too far away for me to hear their words. Finally, with a chopping motion of his hand, Shaji cut off the discussion, and Abul Khayr joined the pilot and me as we climbed aboard. Anger flowed from him, not toward me, but toward Shaji. We had to wait for several military aircraft to take off before us, so our flyer lifted off at dawn. I wondered about all the military activity and assumed it had to do with the general unrest.

Our flyer was a four-seat antigravity-powered craft. Gravity follows the inverse square law: As you move away from the gravitational source, at twice the distance, the strength drops to one quarter the intensity. With small antigravity drives like our flyer, this limited the altitude of travel.

I had a good view of the planet's terrain. Desert gave way to a low range of arid mountains that sloped precipitously to a blue-green sea punctuated by whitecaps.

"The Omanah Sea," Khayr said, his aura still red with anger from his altercation with Shaji.

"What was all that with Shaji about?"

"Nothing." He would not look at me. The "nothing" obviously had to do with me in some way, but I did not press him.

Although we crossed a vast expanse of water, I knew that bird migrations were still a possible explanation for the spread of the plague. Some birds on earth migrated many thousands of miles and could stay aloft for weeks at a time. A single infected bird would not last more than a day before dying, but a large flock would not die all at once. The disease might pass sequentially between individuals, with some newly infected birds making it to the final location.

Perhaps bird migrations were a weak attempt to explain the spread of the plague, but the only other possibility I could think of was that humans had deliberately broken the quarantine. Could more Test-Lits have smuggled the infection into Aswan, as Chaim had? But how? The organism did not survive outside living cells, and the government had banned movement of animals. The military rigorously inspected private flyers and ships leaving the Medina area, and soldiers had orders to halt unregistered watercraft and aircraft, even to destroy them if they did not obey orders to land.

We desperately needed to talk with Chaim to understand how he got the damn plague to New Mecca.

With the sea behind us, we approached another mountain range with snow-capped peaks thrust into gray-black storm clouds. The pilot banked north and flew along a river valley that formed a verdant, populated strip through the desert. I dozed off.

Learns-To-Fix-Injuries lay on the table in the GCVS lab, flailing his limbs in the throes of the plague. His tongue flicked in and out, and saliva dripped from his finger-long fangs. Fur tried to hold the dragon down, without success. Despite the man's size, the dragon was bigger and stronger. Roxanne tried to hook up an IV but jumped back as the dragon swiped a talon across the tubing. The blood-red cryo fluid sprayed the room like a macabre geyser.

"There's not enough cryo fluid," I yelled. "We used it all on Healer."

That made little sense since there were bags of it spilling off every counter in the room. Roxanne stepped up to Learns-To-Fix-Injuries with another bag and tubing. The dragon's leg kicked out; talons raked across Roxanne's abdomen. Bowels spilled out onto the laboratory floor. I screamed, again and again...

"Cy. Cy."

I felt someone shaking my shoulder and bolted awake, slamming against my seat restraints.

Khayr had his hands on both my shoulders, forcing me back down. "You were having a nightmare," he said. "Calm down."

I collapsed into my seat, gasping for air. I swallowed acid, a constant presence in my throat these days. "Water," I croaked.

A moment later, Khayr came back with water in a plastic cup. He handed it to me and offered another cup with amber-tinged fluid. "You might want this, as well."

I downed the water and took a deep breath. "Yeah. Nightmare. Thanks." I hadn't thought through the implications of reptiles coming down with the disease, that our dragon was now at risk, but my subconscious reminded me all too vividly. And we had no way to treat him as we did Healer. We had no more cryo fluid and the cryochambers were not large enough for a three hundred kilo dragon, in any case.

I took the second cup and downed a swallow. My throat and esophagus burned as it went down. "Ghack! What is this?"

"My own personal stock. It is a favorite of my family, distilled in our home." Khayr smiled. "It is an acquired taste."

I unbelted myself and stretched my legs. "It was called moonshine or rotgut on earth." I took a much more cautious sip. "I thought Muslims didn't drink alcohol."

A bit of guilt leaked through Khayr's smile. "Some feel the restrictions of the Qur'an should be adapted to worlds that are far from earth and Old Mecca."

Like Khayr, I preferred more modern views for worlds scattered across the galaxy. I recalled that Fur and I first met over an argument about the literal interpretation of the Torah. My all-too-public heretical pronouncements on that point got me into trouble with the Testamentary-Literalist leader Rebbe Levi Schvartz, the sadist who controlled my life and had my parents tortured.

"This is for medicinal purposes." Khayr waved the bottle at me before stowing it away in a chest behind a back seat.

I shook my head and chuckled. "How far out are we?"

"There is one more long stretch of desert then we will cross the mountains through a pass. There are many military craft in the skies, so our orders are to take this out-of-the-way route to avoid any airspace conflicts."

The approaching mountains glistened with snow, in stark contrast to the sere brown desert below. As I watched the flyer's shadow chase us across the sand, a flash caught my eye, then a smoke trail arcing toward us.

Oh, shit. Not again! Wasn't there some sort of rule against a second assassination attempt using the same goddamned weapon?

"Missile," I screamed, grabbing Khayr's arm and pointing.

"Merciful God, help us," he murmured.

Mahir heard, and the flyer banked hard, first one way then another. Without our belts fastened, both Khayr and I flew from our seats. I bounced off the ceiling, then the floor, and then grabbed onto a seat support leg. I held on for dear life. By the time Khayr found a handhold, blood streamed from a gaping wound on his forehead.

A thunderous roar rocked the ship. My ears popped and pain lanced into my brain. A second concussion accompanied a fireball in the cockpit. Debris blew backwards: glass, metal, the pilot's blood and bone.

The flyer nosed downward.

I pulled myself forward past Khayr and the now headless pilot. I had little time to respond. Headed straight for a cliff, we were toast if I did nothing. I grabbed the stick and pulled back. The nose came up as blur of brown and grey streaked past the broken windshield and the shrieking wind stung my eyes.

I said a silent goodbye to my wife. Oh, how I wished I had not left her the way I did. I closed my eyes before impact.

Chapter 12

Pain woke me long enough to think, "I'm alive."
Then blessed blackness.

The second time I awoke, I fought to stay
conscious. Covered with grit, my eyelids seemed to
scrape furrows into my corneas. A lowering or rising
sun—I couldn't tell—shone directly into my eyes.

I took mental stock of my body. One, alive. Two,
lots of pain, coming, it seemed, from about every corner
of my being. Well, maybe mostly from...there...my
right leg. I tried to move it. I screamed. Okay, I didn't
need to localize it any more than that.

I peered down my prone body, not liking what I
saw. My right leg, distal to my mid-femur, bent at an
anatomically incorrect angle. A femoral fracture for
sure. The region of the break was clothed, so I could
not tell how bad it was. Realigning the bone would be
impossible for me to accomplish, so splinting it was not
viable. It might take surgery to fix this mess. Thinking
about my injury in a clinically detached way kept me
from screaming again.

Of the three of us in the flyer, I knew the pilot,

Mahir, was dead. Khayr only had a scalp wound the last time I saw him, so he might be okay. I moved my head to take stock of my surroundings. The first things I noticed were the pieces and parts of the flyer scattered around me.

Looking to either side, I saw the smoking remains of some dry grey-brown vegetation. There had not been enough of it in the parched landscape to start a brush fire, fortunately for me. Steep cliffs rose on both sides of the crash site, forming a narrow canyon. I obviously avoided a nose-down crash, and the flyer must have skidded and dropped in this gully. The bad news was that the wreckage would be difficult to see from the air.

I didn't see Khayr so I called for him. "K-yr." It came out as a croak. My mouth felt like it was stuffed with cotton. A nearby cactus-like plant teased me with the possibility of moisture.

I took a deep breath, which elicited pain in my chest. After a shallower breath, I tried calling again. "Khayr."

No answer.

I heard a muted roar and looked up to see a formation of aircraft far overhead. Too far to help me, for sure.

Another slow scan revealed something I wish I had not seen. Sticking out from behind a section of flyer was a head and arm. Khayr's head and arm. His hair was caked with blood. His eyes were open, glassy. I looked away. I had not known him all that long or all that well, but he was a friend in an unfriendly place. My heart went out to him and whatever family he had.

Get used to it, Berger. You are alone. With a fractured leg, maybe chest injuries, buried in a desert canyon, on a world that hates you. Could be worse. You could be dead.

Considering bin Saqer, and now Mahir and Khayr,

it was getting very dangerous to be my companion.

The desiccation of the desert heat made the juicy cactus look better all the time, although the sun appeared to be setting, a promise of some relief.

The section of the flyer that hid Khayr's torso was the mid-portion containing our seats. I saw neither the nose nor the tail section. What I did see included the storage area where Khayr had retrieved the water. Clothing, too, I hoped. I'd need both to survive the night. Possible salvation lay four or five body lengths away. I could crawl that far.

First, I moved my right arm. So far, so good.

Left arm. Hurray.

I maneuvered onto my left side and started crawling. Pain on the left mid-torso, maybe a cracked rib or two, was bearable, but as soon as my right leg moved, I screamed. Maybe they would hear me all the way to Medina. I wished that I could use my empathic talent on myself the way I could on animals. With them, if the pain was significant, I could soothe it to some degree.

I kept moving, albeit a few centimeters at a time. I dug my left hand into the dirt, like a claw, and simultaneously pushed my left foot into the dirt, then pulled and pushed, respectively. The temperature in the gully dropped with the sun, and a cold wind found my body an intriguing target. A bright moon rose over the edge of the eastern cliff. With each centimeter I moved, I continued to exercise my vocal cords. But every journey started with the first push/pull.

Howl, rest, and repeat.

If there were any significant predators in these hills, my goose was cooked. With every movement, I announced myself as helpless prey to one and all.

***

Extinction

The moon was on its way down when I reached out and touched the flyer section that partially hid Khayr's body. Despite the cold wind, sweat bathed me, and evaporation added its chill factor to the effects. I needed shelter.

I grabbed the crumpled edge of the flyer to give myself some extra leverage, but let it go with a cry as jagged metal cut into my hand. Whatever God or Gods there might be up there seemed to be against me. I resumed my crawl until I managed to get out of the wind. Once behind the meager windbreak, I slumped, sighed, and closed my eyes.

***

The sun was well up in the sky when I awoke. The agony of my leg had mutated from an excruciating twelve on a scale of one to ten, to a manageable ten. I attributed that to not moving for a while. I looked around me, avoiding Khayr's corpse, and my heart lifted when I spotted the small footlocker.

What treasures might it contain besides water and Khayr's booze? I pulled myself over to it—with the usual vocal result of any movement—and settled myself with my back against a seat. I snapped the lid catch open. A compartment on one side held bottles: two with a picture of a water tap on the label and Khayr's booze in the third. I lifted a water bottle and screwed off the lid. I took a swallow, restricting myself to that, though I wanted to guzzle the entire thing. I waited a minute and took another swallow, and then I replaced the top. I put the water back in the box, away from temptation, and lifted out Khayr's rotgut and set the bottle next to me. This might be as important a lifesaver as the water.

In the other locker compartment were a number of

items. Rectangular packets with Arabic printing and pictures of fruits and nuts promised food bars. Three bottles of pills had Arabic labels. I had to make some assumptions as to what they contained. Logically, they would stock painkillers. The others? I carried a broad-spectrum antibiotic in my own emergency kit, but I could not be sure that was the case here. What else? An anti-nausea medication to prevent airsickness and vomiting. That would make sense.

I desperately needed something for pain. Also, the low level of nausea that afflicted me for weeks now was worse. So I needed an antinausea med too. I could convince myself that those two nestled in their little bottles, but an antibiotic? I would hold off on that decision.

I glanced at my leg. I still could not see the fracture, but blood soaked the cloth around that region, so I was convinced that the bone had broken through the skin in a compound fracture. I'd have to deal with it sooner or later.

I visually searched the area, but absent the tail section of the flyer with the luggage compartment, my medical kit was gone. Take what luck you can get, Berger.

Other items in the locker were a folding knife with screwdrivers and scissors, four tightly folded silver blankets, and a flashlight. I turned the light on to test the batteries. Good.

I mulled over the pills. Three sizes. The smallest might be the nausea med. At least, antiemetics I knew were small. Antibiotic pills were often large. Should I guessed the largest pills were the antimicrobials? Ridiculous, of course. Pills contained fillers and binders and had coatings of various kinds. These were all white, and size meant little to the reality of what they might be.

Before I made a pill decision, I needed to attend to my leg. I used the knife to cut through the tough fabric of my trousers, resting frequently when the pain levels peaked. I eyed the bottle of middle-sized pills, hopefully some sort of analgesic.

When I got near the break, I stopped cutting and lifted the fabric away from the leg, no easy task since the blood adhered everything together like glue. A five-centimeter segment of sharp-ended bone protruded from the skin. I sank back against the broken seat, my stomach roiling anew.

Eying the tablets again, I decided to take one of the mid-sizers. In a half-hour I would know whether it helped with the pain. Then I continued to cut fabric and separate bloody cloth from bloody tissue.

The pill had dulled the pain, but the sun was well past mid-day when I had the leg uncovered. The tissues around the ragged tear were black. Splinters of bone thrust through the skin at several places adjacent to the end of the fractured femur. I was lucky I had not severed a major artery or vein.

I grabbed Khayr's bottle of booze and popped the cork. After a deep, painful breath, I upended the bottle over the wound. The pain knocked me out.

***

When I awoke again, it was dark. I found the flashlight, flipped the switch, and was comforted with a beautiful, round circle of white light. Assuming full batteries, it should last for many hours if I used it judiciously.

Chilled by the desert's night air, I dug out one of the four silver-coated blankets.

I looked at my leg. The bottle had fallen to one side when I passed out, but it still had several centimeters of liquid in it. The leg looked no worse. I hoped the alcohol in the booze had disinfected the worst of the surface contamination. I cut up a blanket, poured some of the remaining liquor on it, and wrapped my leg.

Snuggled up in the remaining blankets as much as possible, I ripped open a ration bar, bit down, and chewed. After I ate half of it, my stomach rebelled and I placed the remainder on the ground next to me. I took another mid-sized pill with water, but I drank sparingly, since I had no idea how long I'd be stuck here.

I rested my head on the seat cushion and closed my eyes. My brain went into overtime trying to figure out who in hell had shot us down.

My first thought went to the Test-Lits. Neither Chaim nor his compatriot had fingered any accomplices, yet underground Test-Lit cells on New Mecca had supported them. But how would they have known the course I was flying? I supposed they might have had a spy embedded in the military for that intel, though it seemed unlikely.

There were enough other people on New Mecca who hated my guts for ostensibly bringing the plague to the planet and spreading it. I could see some radical, Jew-hating terrorist group shooting me down as justifiable. But terrorists still would need to know our flight path. How likely was that?

The possibility that scared me the most, however, was that the military itself—Hussein—was involved. But why? If anyone knew I did not bring the plague to New Mecca, it was Hussein. He hated me, hated all Jews and aliens, and did nothing to reduce the people's anger toward us, but was that reason enough to kill two of his own to get at me?

I had no answers.

Throughout the day, flights of aircraft had flown over, military I assumed from the tight formations.

Maybe we were just collateral damage in a military action.

I kept going around in mental circles. When the pain became intolerable, I gulped down another pill. The constant ache had become a throbbing in time with my pulse.

A sound nearby interrupted my thoughts. My pulse raced. It was pitch black and anything could be out there. I reached for the flashlight and placed my finger on the switch, but didn't activate it. I was like a kid hiding under the covers so the monsters wouldn't get me. What I couldn't see couldn't hurt me.

The sound came again, a faint scratching. Closer now. Then the food bar wrapper I'd discarded earlier rustled. I hit the switch. The beam transfixed a creature no bigger than a mouse. It was nibbling away at the food bar, but when the light hit it, it looked up, eyes gleaming. I caught the tiniest stab of fear from it, and then it was gone. I turned off the light.

It was quiet for a while, and then the wrapper crackled again. I reached out with my empathic sense, not wanting to scare the little beastie away. I sensed hunger this time. I guessed that life in this desert was tough for critters like this one. I wanted to turn the light back on without chasing it away, so I mentally stroked its emotions, wiping away the fear.

The dull click of the flashlight startled it, but I kept up the mental stroking, and the critter settled back to munching. A better look revealed a mouse-sized animal with gray-brown fur, a naked pink face, and oversized round black ears. Its eyes were huge as befitted a nocturnal lifestyle. Despite the light, it kept working at the bar, not willing to abandon the treasure it had discovered.

I snorted in mirth, and that sound caused the creature to disappear into the night. I flicked off the light again. My laughter came from a ridiculous association. With its black oversized ears, pink face, and huge eyes, the animal resembled a comic character from Old Earth, Mickey Mouse. Thank God it did not wear red shorts and yellow shoes.

A while later the paper crinkling returned. I did not do anything to chase Mickey away this time and let him finish his meal.

***

When I next awoke, the sun had climbed just above the cliff-top, but the sun didn't wake me. The pain in my leg had become excruciating, worse than right after the injury. I pulled off the silver wrapping and groaned. The skin surrounding the wound was swollen and purple-red. There was little I could do at this point, other than hope that one bottle of pills was an antibiotic. I took one of the big pills to start, just in case my reaction to it was bad. After a while, my nausea came back stronger than ever, probably due to the medication. What the hell, I took a small pill, and hoped it would do no serious harm. The good news was, after about twenty minutes, my nausea retreated to a manageable level. The big pills hadn't killed me, so I took another one.

I scanned the sky, hoping for the appearance of anything that looked like a search party, but I saw only the high-flying military. Maybe whoever did this to me was searching, too, to confirm their kill. They would know, more or less, where the flyer went down. Not a comforting thought. From then on, with every high-flying plane or bird, I had simultaneous thrills of hope...and despair. Who would find me first? By now, sweat beaded on my forehead and I shivered despite the heat. I finished off the first bottle of water.

Extinction

I dozed on and off through the day, nightmares of exploding windscreens and shredding pilots recurring and waking me, before I slipped back into unconsciousness for the next viewing. Mid-afternoon, I took more of all three pills. Why not? I forced myself to eat a portion of another ration bar, but it turned my stomach.

Things were not looking good. I realized that the narrow gully worked against me...or for me, depending on who was searching.

I tried to get my leg to a more comfortable position, but all I managed was to make myself scream again.

When night came, I wrapped myself in blankets but later threw them off as I felt like I ignited from the inside. I obsessed over the worsening infection until I heard crackling and chewing sounds, not loud, but close to my side. The flashlight revealed several Mickeys working away at the remains of the ration bars I'd left on the ground. One moved close to my hand and started to nibble on a finger. It tickled, but the Mickey moved away after a moment. I guess I did not taste as good as the stuff with sugar in it.

As I watched, two more joined the first three; a family, I presumed because two of the five were larger than the others. It didn't take them long before they finished their repast and disappeared into the gloom. At least they broke the tedium of lying here, hoping for rescue...rescue that had to come soon, or I was a goner.

The next morning, I could not stop shivering. I downed another two pills of each type. No matter what they were, they couldn't hurt at this point. My dwindling water supply was a bigger concern.

I kept peeking at my wound to see how far the ugly red streaks had progressed upward. With each peek, my nausea swelled, but I kept peeking. I was at serious risk of systemic sepsis.

Stephen A Benjamin

I sweated and shivered throughout the day, repeating the meds. In the sliver of sky above me, I saw vulture-like birds circling, which did not improve my mood. I did not care anymore if my rescuers were friend or foe. This night could be my last.

Darkness brought the Mickeys back out, but there were only four of them this time. I hoped some predator had not killed one. They were my only companions and I looked forward to seeing them.

I could not stomach more than the water, so I unwrapped a new food bar for them. Maybe they would even bring friends to the party. They had gotten used to me and my light, so I watched them feast.

To my dismay, one of the two remaining little Mickeys did not eat much. He sniffed at the bar, took a half-hearted nibble, then staggered away and fell over. A shiver wracked his little frame. I reached out mentally and caught a whiff of distress, but nothing specific other than he felt awful. I wondered what was wrong with the creature and wished I had access to my clinic. Here I was at death's door myself, and I worried about a wild rodent whose life expectancy in this desert was slim anyway. My ingrained need to help afflicted animals overrode even my desperate straits.

One of the larger Mickeys, mom maybe, nosed around the sick little one for a minute, and then went back to feeding. The group was replete well before they could finish a whole food bar and headed off. The sick one did not follow. Mom stopped and looked back, but then turned and scurried off. Creatures like these had no room for worrying about the weak or ill; they had a full-time job staying alive themselves.

I left the light on the little guy. He jerked a couple times and took his last little breath. I reached my hand out and as I touched his fur, the feeling of wrongness struck me like a blow to the head. I extended my

~146~

empathic perception and gagged. I could not mistake the aura of the plague, and the violation of nature that went with it.

That entire family of Mickeys was doomed. It broke my heart. I turned off the light. The plague had reached the desert, but how could it have travelled hundreds of kilometers into the middle of nowhere?

Birds, of course. Like Aswan, I had to believe birds were the vector, maybe even the vultures dropping in for carrion. No invoking Test-Lit terrorists here in the desert. And birds needed to cross only the mountains to get here.

My own situation was worse. The shivering continued and my face felt flushed. My pulse rate had gradually climbed and weakened; I had trouble detecting it in my wrist. Despite the desert night cold, sweat poured off my body, negating the value of the water I had consumed.

Come on, someone, *find me.*

My breath came in short gasps. Someone would discover me dead in the morning, or come across a decaying carcass or bleached bones in the future. I dozed and dreamed that the Mickeys gnawed away at my body.

"Do you think this guy is kosher?" one asked. "Maybe, but is he blessed for Passover?" They all chortled as they ate.

I looked at my leg. It seemed to swell as I watched it, then the swelling receded, and then it swelled again. With each cycle, the leg grew larger...and larger...until, like an overripe melon, it burst, throwing fragments of blackened flesh and rotted bone far into the sky.

Chapter 13

The light hurt my eyes, even through my closed lids. I was alive, but I could not last another day in this desert heat...although the sun did not seem as hot as on the previous days. A cool breeze wafted over my face. The weather had changed.

Something soft and warm touched my forehead. I nearly jumped out of my skin, but I did not move far...because I couldn't. Restraints held my arms and legs.

A voice! It seemed far away, but it was human, and one I recognized, a lovely voice that could not possibly be here.

"Cy, can you hear me? Cy?"

I tried to move my mouth to answer, but all that came out was a moan.

"It appears that he is emerging from the coma, Dr. Simon." A different, unfamiliar voice. Male. It hurt my head.

That made me think about my leg. No pain there. Where was I?

The hand on my forehead again. "Cy, talk to me,

please." Roxanne in a plaintive tone.

"It will take some time for him to become coherent. Let us not push him too hard." The male voice.

Finger. I needed to move a finger, show them I was here. I thought the finger moved but it was hard to tell for sure. Lips. I formed "Roxanne." My dry, cracked lips sort of worked, but the sound was more like a croak than a name.

"He's responding, doctor. Cy, listen to me. You're safe. We found you."

Even though I could not respond, those words sank to my core like healing balm. My rescue came before it was too late...at least for my life. I fretted about my leg. God, I did not want to lose my leg. I feared they could not save it. But I was alive. Stay with that thought. And that was my last thought for a while.

***

When I woke again, it was dark. I tried to open my eyes, but the lids stuck together. I tried to raise my right arm, but it would not move. An attempt with the left had the same result. Prisoner. I was a prisoner. The terrorists had me, would finish what they started.

"Help. *Help!*" The words came out, even though they were more a whisper than a cry. I gasped for breath. Who knew that speaking would be so exhausting?

A door opened and the light went on. A lilting female voice spoke in Arabic then in Common, "Please stay calm, Dr. Berger. Dr. Naeem is on duty, and he will be here in a moment."

"Eyes," I croaked. "Can't open."

"I will help you."

Footsteps shuffled around the room and returned. A cool hand rested on my forehead and warm liquid bathed my eyes. Something soft, like cotton, wiped across the lids, several times. Then soft fingers helped pry them apart. Pain lanced into my brain. I closed my eyes and grunted.

"You have not used your eyes in some time and the lids were badly sunburned. I will lower the illumination intensity."

"How long?" It was easier on my throat to whisper.

"I will let the doctor speak with you. Until he comes, please stay quiet."

Why? My pulse rate started to soar, but then I remembered...not terrorists. I had heard Roxanne, hadn't I? Or was that another hallucination? Roxanne. I had given up and thought I would never see her again. I tried to relax. Futile.

A few minutes passed then a male voice spoke. "Dr. Berger, I am Dr. Naeem. I know you are stressed. You have been in an induced coma for several weeks."

Weeks? *Weeks?* "Why...why am I restrained?" Every time I was hospitalized on this planet, they had me trussed like a holiday goose.

Naeem leaned close to hear my whisper. "You were having *grand mal* seizures. We restrained you to prevent further damage to your leg and your ribs."

My mind wandered in and out. What did he say? Seizures? Stay with it, Berger. Concentrate.

I opened my eyes. Naeem was a portly, middle-aged man with dark brown eyes and a black goatee. His smile was reassuring; the way his face faded in and out of focus was not. Then he disappeared.

***

I awoke to Roxanne's voice. "Oh, Cy. Thank God you're back."

Tears rolled down her cheeks. I wanted to wipe

them away, but I still could not move my arms. I looked down and took in the venous catheter and tubing leading from my right arm up to a half-full bag of clear fluid. A half-dozen more bags hung in reserve. Other tubes snaked from beneath the covers.

"Nurse," Roxanne called. "Help me get him out of these restraints."

"I must call the doctor. I don't have the authority."

"He's not convulsing anymore." Roxanne started fumbling around my ankles.

The door opened with a crash.

"What is going on here?" It was Naeem. "What are you doing, Dr. Simon?"

"I'm getting my husband out of these restraints. He doesn't need them anymore."

"Doctor!" Naeem's voice cracked like a whip, much at odds with his kindly appearance. There was silence for a few moments. "This is our responsibility and we will take care of it."

Roxanne drew a ragged breath then let out a long sigh. "Sorry. But please, let's get him loose."

"Please sit down, Dr. Simon. Dr. Berger, the restraints were for your benefit, for no other reason. But please stay still, you have venous and urinary catheters inserted, and we need those to remain in place for now."

I felt hands again, and in moments, I could move my limbs. Except for the right leg. Oh, shit. They amputated...

Naeem must have seen panic in my face, since he placed a hand on my arm. "Your leg is in an immobilization and stimulation cast...to promote healing. It was a close thing. You had advanced gangrene, but we saved the leg. You will heal." He gave me the comforting smile again.

"Please let me see my wife."

~151~

He stepped back. Roxanne moved to my side.

I lifted my right hand, and she grasped it in both of hers. Tears cut tracks on her cheeks. This time I lifted my left hand to brush them away. I swallowed past the lump in my throat. "How...how did you...? When did you find me?"

"Shh. Save your strength for healing. We both have stories to tell. The important thing is we found you in time."

***

I was sitting up in bed, eating my first solid food since I awoke in the hospital. Roxanne and Fur were with me.

"As soon as I learned that the plague had mutated and jumped to reptiles," Roxanne told me, "I placed the dragon in quarantine in the ship. After Healer's experience, Learns-To-Fix-Injuries didn't argue, though he's cranky. He understood but didn't like it."

"That was good thinking," I replied. "There's no way we could handle Red the way we did Healer."

"He's safe for now," Fur added. "We isolated the rec room with a portable airlock, and I jury-rigged a separate air handling system with biofilters. He has room to exercise, and we set him up with a vid system. He loves your sci-fi and fantasy vids from Old Earth. He goes nuts over anything with dragons in it." I still sensed a hint of reticence in Fur's demeanor. He had not totally forgiven me for my insults.

Eating was an effort, and I struggled to finish. I groaned as Roxanne took my plate. "What else has happened since I've been out of commission?"

"Things started to go downhill after you left for Aswan," Roxanne said. "As food became scarcer, demonstrations increased. The *GCVS* had a constant crowd around it, sporting signs and screaming epithets, but a military cordon kept them from reaching us. When Fur or I left the ship, we had a whirlydrone pick us up at the ramp and drop us on the roof of Adila's microbiology facility. They did not want us moving through the crowds to rile them even more."

"What took so long to find me?"

"We didn't know you were missing until we got word through Ali's people that someone shot down your flyer. Hussein's forces knew but were not going to respond. Ali sent out a rescue mission of his own."

My cardiac monitor started to beep in response to my heightened pulse rate and blood pressure on learning of Hussein's lack of response. "Who attacked the flyer?"

"Easy, Cy. You have a lot of healing ahead of you. Suliaman will be here soon. You should ask him."

Her hand on my shoulder calmed me. "Okay. We'll talk about that later. I experienced hostile crowds in the other cities, too. Abul Khayr said that it was worse here in the capital because the animals here were infected first."

Roxanne nodded. "As long as the poultry industry was operational, that muted the effect, but when the birds were diagnosed, the shit hit the fan. The military showed up in force, and some altercations turned deadly. That set the people off even more."

"Yeah. I saw lots of military aircraft while I was stranded."

She frowned. "Things have gotten worse than just the food riots."

Fur said, "I'm afraid we're in the center of an erupting civil war."

"With everything this planet is facing just to stay alive? They've got to be crazy."

"The plague has driven a wedge into their society

and their leadership," Fur responded. "The government fractured and a general military mobilization took place. Part of the military has aligned with General Hussein. The other side is led by Ali Suliaman."

"Good Lord. Hussein and Suliaman. I could see there was no love lost between them, but a civil war?" I shuddered as I recalled the vision I had received from Khayr of Hussein and Ali and their ghostly armies. He must have known.

"From what Aypari told me, Hussein is attempting a coup. He plans to set up a dictatorship. His soldiers responded violently to the riots."

Roxanne nodded to Fur's statement. "Adila does not condone her father's actions or the acts that are being perpetrated in his name."

"I don't understand where Ali fits in all this. What's his role in the government?"

Roxanne said, "He's been a political as well as religious leader. As Hussein gathered cronies to him and placed them in positions of authority, Ali became the *de facto* leader of the opposition over a period of years."

I shook my head. I did not imagine things could have gotten worse. Humans had an amazing capacity for fouling their own nests.

There was a knock on the hospital room door, and it opened to frame Ali dressed in a white robe and headdress. The Islamic star and crescent in gold adorned the breast of his robe. He bowed. "May I come in?"

Roxanne waved him in. "Of course. You are always welcome, Imam Suliaman."

He spoke in Arabic to a guard, and then he entered and closed the door behind him. "Best to keep our discussions private," he said in Common.

Fur moved a chair over and offered it to the Imam,

who sat.

"You no doubt have many questions, Dr. Berger."

I blurted out, "Who shot us down?"

Suliaman kept his face composed. "The orders originated from General Hussein's command. He has pointed to you and all Jews as the originators of the plague and the ultimate cause of the famine and civil war. You are all condemned to death."

"Lies," I snapped.

Ali nodded. "I cannot apologize enough for my foolishness in allowing Hussein to send you across New Mecca. I was skeptical of his plan, but I was trying hard to compromise, to prevent what has happened, a civil war. We did not know of your attack, and the satellite location device in your flyer was deliberately deactivated before your flight."

Roxanne jumped in. "That's why we didn't find you until it was almost too late."

Her anger at Hussein seared my empathic reception, and a bolt of referred pain streaked down my leg.

I grimaced and held up a hand. "Hey. Cool it. That hurts."

Her hand flew to her mouth. "Oh, I'm so sorry."

"I don't have the strength to keep up my screen."

Ali's brow wrinkled in a quizzical expression. "What do you speak of?"

It was time to fill him in. "Ali, I'm going to tell you something that very few people know. I'm an empath with the ability to perceive and feel emotions of animals and sentient beings." I explained my abilities further, but told him that I did not read minds. I hesitated on the last point as I pondered that my visions accompanying powerful emotions had become stronger and more frequent recently. I was not ready to share that with anyone.

Ali's eyes widened.

Roxanne added, "What Cy didn't say was that intense emotions cause him pain, nausea, and vertigo. That's why he was cautioning me. He reacted to my anger at Hussein."

"I've developed a mental screen to protect me from that, but it takes effort, and my illness and wounds have depleted my strength."

Ali's dark face paled as he digested these facts. "This is quite extraordinary. Are there others who have such an ability?"

I shook my head. "I don't know of anyone else, but I've kept my ability pretty much under wraps, so I assume others similarly affected might do the same. But enough about me. We need you to tell us what's going on."

"Of course. I will keep this short in view of your...condition." He squirmed in his chair.

I felt the tension in his mind and body.

"Aaquil Hussein has built a personal army, beholden to him alone, for years. I served as a representative on our Planetary Council, and it was there I first met Hussein. He was ruthless and used minor or major infractions, civil or ecumenical, to blackmail and destroy people opposing him. He used our religion to attack some, to brand them as heretical. He deposed high-standing members of the biomedical community, which allowed him to climb to the position of Chief Physician. Unholy alliances with other men who sought power for its own sake, particularly in the military, allowed his ascendance to General."

I sensed Ali's deep abhorrence of Hussein, but he controlled his emotion as he spoke and spared me undue pain.

"In short, he built an army of government bureaucrats to control our assemblies, and his soldiers control a portion of our military. To all of these he promised leadership in a new society, with the power to impose their wills on the people.

"We two battled on the floor of the Planetary Council to make our cases for the future of New Mecca. The majority of the Council sided with me, but I saw what was coming. My trip off-planet, just before you arrived, was an attempt to cement relationships with several other Islamic worlds, to make allies. I feared what was to happen here, but I did not anticipate it to occur so soon."

I nodded. "The arrival of the plague created the opportunity for Hussein."

Ali closed his eyes, momentarily, then looked at me again. "He used his medical position to declare martial law in the name of bringing the plague under control. His chosen underlings took over critical offices and ranks. Councilors who objected were imprisoned. Military commanders not under his sway were assassinated."

"But where are we now?" I asked.

Ali smiled with thinned lips. "Hussein may be in control of Medina, but he does not control our world. We are in the city of Ammad, five hundred kilometers from the capital. The people are rallying behind our resistance. Much of the military see Hussein for what he is and have joined us. Hussein says his supporters are the true believers of Islam, but they are the radical faction that hates all outsiders, anyone who is different, who does not believe as they do. He is sullying Islam with his acts."

Man, that sounded too much like the Test-Lits.

"This is a struggle between those of us who wish to live in peace with our neighbors as the Prophet decreed, whether they be Muslim or any other faith, and those who do not tolerate open minds and open hearts. We have much to do, but we will prevail."

"Wait. If Hussein is in control of Medina, how did you get the *GCVS* out? He promised to destroy it if we tried to leave." My heart rate rose.

Fur spoke. "Easy, Cy. It's safe. You told us about Hussein's threat, so we left it at the spaceport. I had Ruthie activate the defense systems."

There were some nasty surprises built into the *GCVS* for anyone who tried to break in.

Fur continued. "Ali's people arranged our safe passage to Ammad from the laboratory facility."

"But Red. And Healer. They're alone in the *GCVS.*" My pulse spiked again.

Roxanne placed a calming hand on my arm. "They're fine. The AI is monitoring Healer's cryochamber and babysitting Red. It's good for that, at least."

I steered away from any comment on Ruthie, but the ship's safety was my responsibility and I voiced my concern to Ali. "What's to stop Hussein from blowing it up?"

"He does not want to destroy the ship," Ali said. "We do not have a comparable vessel on New Mecca, particularly your unique AI. He wants to get his hands on the technology."

That was anything but reassuring. "Okay. What do we do from here?"

Roxanne said, "What *you* do from here is simple. You recover." She looked pointedly at my casted leg. "You're not going anywhere for a good while."

Ali stood. "And I must marshal my friends and allies. There is much we must accomplish to defeat Hussein. For the people of New Mecca, I thank you for what you have already done. We need one another in the coming battle."

I looked down at my leg. Some soldier I would make. So far, I had come close to death twice, and had done nothing to stem the spread of the plague. At that thought, something small and furry rose up and scratched at the door of my subconscious: the little Mickey. Every animal on this planet depended on me and my crew to save them from extinction.

Chapter 14

Chaim cringed as the guard's grip dug into his arm. Dragged to a window—the first daylight he had seen in many weeks—a big hand thrust his head forward.

General Hussein's voice trembled with rage. "See what you have done? What your abominable plague has done to our planet?"

Chaim's mind took a moment to sort out the visual assault on his eyes. The sunlight blinded him, and after so long in the dank cell, he had to blink to clear tears from his vision. The scene before him was one of chaos. A huge crowd of people milled in the street below, a kaleidoscopic mass of colors surging forward and back against a barricade of armed military. The closed window muted screams in Arabic. He could only imagine the volume at ground level.

When the guard released his head, Chaim turned to Hussein. "What do you want now? I have told you all that I can."

Hussein's obese face was red above the stark whiteness of the short-sleeved uniform shirt he wore.

Beads of sweat popped out on his brow. "Look. *Look.* The people are rioting. Because there is no food."

Chaim glanced at a tray sitting at one end of Hussein's desk. A meal, fish, potatoes, and vegetables, sat half-eaten on gold-rimmed plates. Despite his constant nausea, Chaim's mouth watered. He had eaten no more than thin soup during his confinement, and his eyes bounced from the general to the food and back again.

"Your plague has done this, but they are blaming me...*me!*" Hussein followed Chaim's eyes then swept the plates off the desk with one sausage-like arm. Food and shards of crockery clattered across the floor. "It is your fault there is no food," he screamed.

Chaim's knees buckled from his weakness; he had little strength left to endure Hussein's vitriolic verbal abuse. The guard let go of Chaim's arm, and he collapsed to his knees on the floor.

Hussein's voice lowered. "I want your colleagues. I want their names."

Chaim realized that Hussein needed something to show the people. More scapegoats to take the brunt of the fury that was swirling around him. If he could parade the perpetrators, the Jewish Test-Lit terrorists, before the populace, he could deflect the ire from himself.

"Their names, McNulty. What you have felt until now is nothing. You have no idea what pain means." Hussein's voice growled like a caged beast's.

Chaim would have laughed aloud had he the strength. The man still referred to him as McNulty, the ridiculous name Chaim had adopted in the vain hope of avoiding recognition as a Jew. Hussein did not know Chaim's real name, would never know it. *Khodorkosovitch. Chaim Khodorkosovitch. Chaim Khodorkosovitch. Chaim Khodorkosovitch.* Chaim recited his name over and over in his mind, a litany to drown out the threats of the general.

He would not reveal his name, or the names of his compatriots. This had nothing to do with love of the other Test-Lits, or even loyalty. Chaim had come to abhor what he had done. His pulse raced and his stomach twisted when he thought of the horrid deaths he had caused in defenseless animals. His view of the mobs below, the realization that he might kill people from starvation made it even worse. If it would stop the plague, stop the killing, he would gladly give up Rebbe Neidritch. But it would solve nothing. The Test-Lits were as much bigots and haters as Hussein and his torturer, and Chaim would not give in to hate and torture. Though he now rejected the Test-Lit party, he deserved the pain inflicted on him for his actions.

He thought about Dr. Roxanne Simon. She had become a figure of strength to him. He remembered her courage, remembered her beauty. How she had protected him despite how he had wronged her. He would be strong like her, never give in.

Chaim's head snapped to the left as pain slammed the right side of his face. His neck locked to the side and agony ensued, as Hussein had grabbed a fistful of Chaim's hair and wrenched his head straight again.

"Look at me," Hussein yelled. "Do not ignore me. You will answer."

It seemed like slow motion as Hussein's hand swept toward Chaim's face, the left side this time. He felt the large signet ring, crowned by a faceted red stone, stab his cheek as his head snapped to the right. The pain in his neck felt as if his head would separate from his body, but he made no sound, not even a whimper. He felt warm blood trickle down his cheek.

Hussein blew out an explosive breath. "Get him out of here. Give him to Vash. I want answers."

Extinction

More torture. They will learn nothing. Pain is nothing. They cannot do more than they already have. I am David. I am Moses.

Roxanne would be proud of me.

***

I watched a newsfeed from the city we now resided in, Ammad, on the plasma screen in my hospital room. A banner ran across the bottom of the screen, translating Arabic to Common. Because the majority of the Planetary Council members had joined with Ali, they continued to use that title to cement the idea that they were still the rightful leaders of New Mecca.

Despite the fact that hostilities had reached open warfare, Ammad remained relatively quiet. Ali's forces bivouacked outside the city, and battles took place halfway between the two cities, sparing the noncombatant city-dwellers. They were *not* spared the oncoming famine now that the only foods were crops and fish, but Ali's well-organized forces kept the hungry residents under control. Roxanne told me they were making sure that there was no hoarding or pillaging of food stores. The screen showed long lines of people waiting for meals at soup kitchens, but they were orderly and many smiled, as they knew they would soon get fed.

Vegetable soups with beans and lentils, breads, cereals, and nuts and fruits were the staples on New Mecca now. The limited amounts of fish went into some of the soups, particularly for people who needed it medically. I felt guilty for the few bites of fish in my soup, but did not argue with the nurses when they ordered me to eat. Anything that would speed my recovery.

The newsfeed shifted to Medina, still under

Hussein's control. His party called themselves the *Army of Islam*, though The Planetary Council referred to them publically as *The Usurpers*. The Council's announcer played up the unrest in the capital, the people's dissatisfaction with Hussein and his mutinous cabal. In contrast to the orderly queues of Ammad, crowds were overrunning any place with food, even the trucks that were delivering it to distribution points. The camera panned over smashed-out shop windows, overturned vehicles, fires that burned in warehouses. Those scenes needed no translation.

The door opened and Roxanne entered. She smiled, something that brightened my day considerably. "Good morning, Cy. How are you feeling?"

I shifted as much as I could to get comfortable. The pain was more manageable now, and I had cut back on the narcotics, but my nausea waxed and waned in severity. "Good. Come here. Sit." I waved at a chair. "You should see this."

She turned to the plasma screen. "I already have." Despite her initial smile, her mental aura was grim.

"Ali's people have it under control here, but I wonder how long he can keep it that way. The food situation will get worse."

Roxanne nodded, took the proffered seat, and frowned. "Ali was hoping to get shipments of food from those allied worlds he visited before coming back to New Mecca."

"Yeah. That would be a huge help. What's the problem?"

"The plague. A few supply ships came in, but none have left."

"Did Hussein commandeer them?" I did not put that past him.

"No. Other planets are panicking. They're afraid the contagion might get off New Mecca and be transmitted to them. A large contingent of worlds in this sector has decided to quarantine New Mecca. They've set up a blockade and won't allow any more ships to land on or leave the planet."

I clenched a fist. "So we couldn't leave here if we wanted to."

"Right, and things are getting worse."

"Worse? How's that possible?"

"Fish have died in several local rivers. It's the plague."

My head pounded and my stomach twisted. "Holy shit. That means it has affected every type of vertebrate on the planet, except for humans. If the plague spreads to the ocean, then only the crustaceans and molluscs would be left."

Roxanne pursed her lips before she spoke. "There aren't enough of those to feed the planet. They would get overharvested and populations would collapse in short order."

"Insects can be a major source of protein," I said.

"True, but there's a catch. Insects in general are *Haram*, forbidden food in Islam. A few types of locusts were *Halal*, or permissible, on earth, but not here. Reptiles were already *Haram*."

"Damn. If the religious leaders declare fish inedible like they have mammals and birds, it'll be a disaster." I tried to blot out mental pictures I had seen in vids and books of starving children.

"On another topic, is there *any* kind of progress on identifying the pathogen and vaccine development...or finding an antimicrobial that works?"

Roxanne shook her head. "When we left the capital, we lost access to the major infectious disease lab on the world. Worse, we don't have access to our own labs on the *GCVS*. Fur and I have worked with local scientists, and Ali is giving us all the help he can, but we don't have the facilities and resources. We don't know how Adila and Aypari are progressing in Medina but I've heard no announcements of good news."

The newsfeed caught my attention. They were showing piles of dead fish on the banks a large river. Then the image of Hussein filled the screen. Smiling, he lauded his own efforts to protect the people, then raging, blamed his nemesis, Ali, and all Jews for what was happening. A final image showed a square outside of a mosque where thousands of white-robed Muslims bent over and prayed in unison. I highly doubted their prayers would be answered any time soon.

***

A week later, I woke one morning to a thunderous concussion. The bottles on my night table rattled and the IV stand inched across the floor. Bombing raids on the city were sporadic, but this attack was too close. The door flew open, revealing a frazzled young nurse-in-training. Fear dominated her aura.

"Are you all right, Dr. Berger?"

"Yeah. Was the hospital hit?" I tried to control my racing heart.

"I do not think so."

Another woman's face poked in the doorway. She wore a physician's tunic and spoke the assistant's name, "Inaya," then rattled off a command in Arabic.

Inaya said, "I must go. A building one block from the hospital has been bombed. There are casualties." She disappeared out the door.

The cast was supposed to come off my leg today or tomorrow. Skeletal scans had shown almost full bone healing in a surprisingly short time. The stimulatory properties of the cast were beyond anything I knew. I still faced a long recovery with lots of physical therapy because of the injury to the muscles and tendons.

Fast footsteps and yells came from the halls, as people responded to the crisis. I could not help, so I settled back and picked up my reader.

I was deep into a suspenseful story when the door clicked, and I half jumped out of the bed. Fur's huge bulk blocked the view of the hallway. I had not seen him in some time. Despite his concern after my rescue, our icy relationship had not yet fully thawed.

"Hello, Cy." He shuffled into the room and gazed at me from a few steps away. "How are you feeling? How's the leg?" His deep voice was soft, as if speaking in his usual tone might injure me.

"I'm doing great, Fur. Their technology for bone healing is amazingly effective. We need that in the *GCVS* armamentarium."

He nodded. "They're going to take that cast off today. Roxanne sent me to help you when they're done. You'll be released."

That buoyed my spirits and I smiled. "That's great."

He glanced around as several people rushed by the open door, jabbering away in Arabic. "They need the bed. The number of military casualties coming into the city is rising, and with the bombing, civilians are adding to that toll."

"Makes sense. I'm ready to get out of here. Going nuts, to tell you the truth."

A small smile crept across Fur's lips. His bushy mustache twitched. "I'd question the *going* part."

I laughed. It was good to see some hint of humor from the big guy. I had wounded him, but he was still my best friend. "Do you know when?"

"As soon as the critically injured bombing victims are taken care of."

While happy to get out, I was sorry that the necessity for my release was due to so many more war injuries.

I decided to broach our previous disagreement directly. "Hey, have you heard anything from Aypari? Is she okay?"

He gave me a penetrating look, his bright brown eyes narrow. "Nothing."

I sensed his concern. "Damn. I worry about her, you know, because you and she had become...close."

Fur said nothing, but continued to eye me.

"I'm thrilled that you've found someone you care for, and who returns that feeling. I also understand how much you must be afraid for her. If we can just get through this civil war, I expect that you and Aypari working together will make a difference in solving this plague."

Fur bit his lower lip, and his body sagged a bit. "Thanks, Cy. I appreciate your concern. I admit I'm stressed about Aypari's safety and wish there was something I could do, but there's not." He hesitated long enough to rub his eye. "Seeing you after your crash brought home how important *your* safety is to me." He came close, grabbed my hand, and squeezed it, but gently. His grip could crush walnuts. "I'm glad you're better."

As he stood back, I detected a hard glint in his brown eyes. "You still have another problem to deal with. Ruthie. It's moot for now, but intolerable long-term for Roxanne."

"Yeah. I know." Whether or not the AI was deliberately targeting my wife, even that *impression* had to stop. I looked down at my leg. "As soon as we get back to the ship, I'll get right on it. I'm not going to—"

The roof fell in.

Chapter 15

The sound preceded everything else. It was not like the concussion blasts of getting hit by missiles, a concurrent roar and blinding flash accompanied by blistering heat. Now, the deafening thunder drowned out my voice as I watched Fur's eyes widen to mostly whites. Neither of us had time to react before the result of the explosion became evident.

A large chunk of plasterboard shaken loose from the ceiling impacted the top of Fur's head and blew apart into a cloud of white powder. He looked like the ghost of some biblical giant as the white haze sifted down over his body.

I threw up my arms to deflect smaller pieces of ceiling that rained down on me. Still unable to move out of the bed with the cast in place, it seemed like forever as the haze settled below head level.

Bells rang in my ears. "Fur. Are you okay?"

He turned to me. "I need to get you out of here."

The tolling in my brain continued, and shrieking sirens added to that...the hospital alert system, I realized.

"How?" I screamed over the din. "I can't walk."

Fur did not bother answering as he undid my leg restraints. I heard groans and squeals from the walls and watched, fascinated, as the outside wall of the room started to settle, inch by inch. More ceiling collapsed on our heads. Nothing dangerous, but enough to get my already pelting heart to put on a kick toward the finish line. I survived two missile attacks directed at me. Would I get done in by a generic bomb while I was hospitalized? Ain't no justice.

"The building is going," Fur yelled. "Lie still."

Like I was going anywhere. Fur's fear poured over me like a lava flow.

With steady and practiced hands, Fur removed my IV and slapped a bandage over the site. He swept me up into his huge arms, making sure to support the cast as he did so, and headed for the door. I had never been more thankful that my friend resembled Goliath.

The hall was bedlam, people rushing in every direction, shouting at one another in Arabic. Attendants shoved several gurneys carrying prone patients down the corridor like race cars. A nurse got bowled over when she didn't move fast enough. Apparently, the elevators were still working—the gurneys stacked up, waiting. More mobile patients were being helped toward the stairs. Fur headed there. A jam at the exit door cleared at Fur's inarticulate bellow. Seemed like no one wanted to get in the way of a colossal white phantasm carrying an equally spectral body in a cast.

I fought against nausea, and my head felt like it wanted to explode. No mental screen could keep out the massed hysteria that surrounded us, compounded by so many injured and dying people.

As Fur pelted down the stairwell, part of the stairs above us buckled, and pieces of roof crashed down past the landings to the floor far below. Fur responded by gaining speed, taking stairs three at a time. I held my breath as he careened toward the main floor. His yells cleared people from his path, and he miraculously harmed no one in his crazed flight.

He bolted through a side door at the bottom of the stairs, outside into a courtyard. Palm trees dotted a grassy area. Patients, attended by medical personnel, lay on picnic tables. Staff and patients streamed out of the hospital doors. Patients limped and shuffled. One dropped to his knees and crawled away from the exit before an orderly helped him up. Everyone funneled toward the one opening out of the courtyard to a street.

Another explosion rocked the hospital building. A fireball whooshed out of a ground-level window. A gas explosion, I guessed. People screamed as the detonation hurled bodies away from the fiery opening.

When we reached the street, Fur crossed the road and turned to look back. The bricks on one side of the hospital slumped, as if they were too tired to support the building's weight any longer. As people streamed out of the alley, I held my mental screen hard against the panic and despair.

Fur placed me down in a standing position on one leg, still supporting me with his arm around my back and under my armpit. "I hope you can you stand. I'm about done in." He gasped.

My head spun and thumped like a roulette wheel using lead balls, and my good knee buckled. Fur caught me before I fell.

He had just accomplished an Olympic-class feat, carrying me out of that building at top speed, but even he had his limits.

"Are *you* going to make it?" I asked.

He looked at me. His face was red, his breath coming in short pants. "We always make it, don't we?"

I smiled. "At least so far. I wonder if there's a limit

on how many hairbreadth escapes a person is allowed in one lifetime. Like a cat's nine lives."

He smiled and shook his head.

I glanced back across the street. Pieces of masonry rained down on people fleeing the hospital.

Fur contacted Roxanne on his comm then carried me down the road. After a couple of blocks, a land drone screeched to the curb, tires smoking. The rear door flew open and Roxanne spilled out, pale and breathless. With wide eyes she stared at me then at Fur. "You're both white as sheets. Are you—?"

"I'm fine." I looked up at Fur. "He saved my ass again."

"Get in the drone," she said.

So much for sympathy.

***

We sat in the living room of the apartment that Ali had assigned us. Four green velvet-padded easy chairs and a coffee table just about filled the cramped room. It felt good to have use of my leg back, muscle atrophy and all. Roxanne had removed the cast the evening before.

"We've got to get back to the *GCVS*," Roxanne said. "Learns-To-Fix-Injuries is running low on food even with the recycler, and we need the ship's laboratory."

"But it's sitting in the middle of Hussein's spaceport under heavy guard. How in hell can we get in there?" I stretched my leg out in front of me and did isometric exercises as we talked.

Fur said, "Getting to the ship without being blown to space dust will be tough. We have to create some sort of a diversion."

An incipient headache registered the apprehension

of my wife and my friend. "Have you discussed this with Ali?"

Roxanne shook her head. "We're scheduled to meet with him and his military commanders in an hour."

"Here?" I glanced around the small room.

"We're going to his headquarters. A drone should be here to pick us up in about thirty minutes, but I'd like to have a plan to present to him."

Fur said, "We should only risk one person. I'll get the ship and fly it back here. If I don't make it, you two are still alive to move forward against the plague. I'm expendable."

"Like *hell* you are. I'm the captain of the *GCVS*. If anyone is going in to get the ship out, it's me."

Roxanne snapped, "*I'm* the smallest and least conspicuous." She gave Fur a withering glance. "I can sneak past the guards more easily." She glared at me. "And I'm *not* hobbled with a gimpy leg."

She was right. It would be weeks before I could walk normally, much less run. I raised both hands, palms forward. "Enough. Let's discuss a plan, not fight each other over who gets killed."

Surrounded by an aura of sheepishness, Roxanne and Fur settled back into their chairs, but there was something else hiding in both their thoughts.

"Knowing everyone in this room, there's no way any of us is going to let the other risk their life. We all go."

Roxanne and Fur both opened their mouths to object, but I cut them off.

"Look at what's happened every time we've been separated on this planet. Assassination attempts, kidnapping. For once, let's stay together. If we can't get back to Ammad, we need to have all our options open. If we're separated, we're hobbled."

Roxanne drew a deep breath, then: "I can buy that.

We go together."

"Okay. So what's the plan?" I sure hoped they had one. I didn't.

***

We met with Ali and three of his military commanders near the airfield. We sat around a scarred wooden table in a bunker with unpainted gray block walls. Ali introduced us to the soldiers.

The oldest man, General Tanweer, was stocky, with wiry gray hair beneath his visored military cap, and a clean-shaven face that looked like it was shaped using a straight edge. He spoke Common in a gruff voice with no accent. "Why should we risk our lives so you can get your ship back?"

I responded. "The ship has medical capabilities that we need if we're going to defeat the plague. And two of our crew are aboard, one in suspended cryosleep, the other running out of food."

"I've heard about your *crew*, Dr. Berger. Aliens. Why are they so important to risk my men for them?"

I kept my temper under control. What I got from the general's emotional aura was a sense of testing me rather than a true callousness toward our nonhuman colleagues. "We won't allow harm to come to our crew, General. You would do no less for your own troops, I believe."

He scratched the side of his square jaw in response to my statement.

"Another thing. You know our ship has the most advanced AI in existence." No need to explain about Ruthie's quirks. "We believe that Hussein has forestalled destroying the ship because he wants the AI that runs it. You don't want that to happen."

General Tanweer suppressed a fleeting smile. "He

did try to get into your ship. Several of his troops were injured."

"The *GCVS* has a unique self-defense system," I said.

Ali jumped in. "Hussein's people would love to clone the programming to develop similar AIs for his warships."

Tanweer looked over at one of his officers. "Lieutenant Zuhair heads our IT section of Intelligence. Can you do that, Lieutenant?"

Zuhair, a thirtyish, dark-haired, clean-shaven man nodded. "Sir, I am not familiar with the AI in question, but the programming and circuitry could be studied with the goal of replicating it."

Tanweer frowned. "If we can't get the ship, we certainly don't want Hussein to get his hands on it. We should destroy it in that case."

Fur came out of his seat, but I grabbed his arm.

"Easy, Fur." I looked at the general. "Sir, let's not play games. You're testing us, seeing how we respond to adversity. If you're going to send your men into danger, you want to know that we're worth it."

The general gave me a brief narrow-eyed stare. Then a small smile fleeted across his lips. "Are you worth it?"

Before I could respond, Ali jumped in. "General, you have been fully briefed on Drs. Berger and Simon, and Mr. Cohen. They have shown bravery and fortitude under trying circumstances. The question is not *if* we assist in retrieving their ship, but *how* we accomplish that task. Our guests have said that all three would undertake this risky challenge. That says enough for their courage."

"Thank you, Imam," I said. "General, we want to get our ship back with minimal danger to us and to your men. We need your help. We're not soldiers."

Tanweer grimaced. "Agreed, Dr. Berger." He motioned toward the other senior officer at the table. "Colonel Jasar is the head of our Special Forces. His people are the ones who will plan and carry out this mission. I do, however, expect to get something in return. Lieutenant Zuhair will be given access to your AI. If it is as advanced as you imply, then we need that technology."

I saw no downside to letting them poke around Ruthie. There was nothing that would enable them to understand how our AI had become self-aware. *I* had no idea how this had come about either. What started as a joke was no longer funny. I suppressed a surge of panic over what to do about Ruthie and Roxanne; I would have to deal with that once we had the ship back under our control.

"Fine, General. We can let you have a look at our AI."

"And I, gentlemen, and lady, must be about other business." Ali stood, bowed to us, and left.

"Shall we proceed with the planning?" the general asked Jasar.

The plan seemed simple enough, Tanweer's forces would mount an attack on Hussein's military stronghold on the opposite side of the city from the spaceport. They would make it look like a major offensive, but it would be a fake, just enough to pull available enemy units to that area, leaving a skeleton crew to guard the *GCVS*. Tanweer's people would drop us at the spaceport by cloaked whirlydrone. Getting to the ship and taking it was another matter, however. There was a cordon of troops manning a barricade around the *GCVS*.

"I am prepared to send in a special forces team of ten men," the general said. "Leave the fighting to them. My biggest question is how you are going to get off the spaceport in one piece. We cannot take out the missile and laser batteries on the port without tremendous collateral damage, and I am not prepared to either kill civilians or damage our main space facility for you."

"Getting up and away is our problem," I said. "We'll take care of it." I was not willing to explain further, since I did not want the New Meccans to know details about the *GCVS*'s offensive and defensive capabilities.

After the Dovidian revolution, we had upgraded the *GCVS*. Offense was minimal: a couple of small laser cannons. Defense, on the other hand, was state-of-the-art. Cloaking used holographic projectors and fractal light generation technology to throw a light mask around an object. It reflected and refracted ambient light so that the objects were difficult to see. The technology was centuries old, but the system we had was modern, and we would be hard to spot with it engaged. The third upgrade was an energy shield usually found only on military vessels. The shield would help protect the *GCVS*, though it was not impervious to the most powerful military weapons.

Lieutenant Zuhair said, "I will accompany you on your ship to get first-hand observation of your AI in operation."

"Not a problem for me," I replied.

"There's one more thing," Fur said. "We pick up Dr. Aypari Habib, either before or after we get the ship, but we get her out." His face was set like granite.

Tanweer shook his head. "Out of the question. Our mission is to get you to your ship, nothing more."

"Then we get her after we get the ship." Fur would not budge.

"As long as my men are in danger, I make the call." Tanweer was as stubborn as Fur.

I jumped in. "Let's consider this logically. Fur, do

you know where she is?"

"Hussein worried about his top scientists bolting and confined all the plague research personnel to the microbiology facility. She's a prisoner, but we need her knowledge of the plague. I don't leave without her."

I sensed Tanweer's anger like a gut punch. His face grew dark, but Roxanne spoke before he could explode. "We need one *more* thing, General. We get Chaim McNulty out too."

"*What? Chaim?*" I could not believe her. "I know we want to talk with him, but break him out of Hussein's prison? We don't even know if he's still alive."

Her face was set, and her green eyes flashed. "Ali's informers said he was tortured, but he's alive."

"And why should we care if the Test-Lit bastard is tortured? I'd be happy to do it myself for what he did to you, Fur, and Ahmed. What are you *thinking*, Roxanne?"

Her voice was solid with conviction. "If you would use your brain instead of your emotions, Cy, you would come to the same conclusion. He's the only one who knows where the plague came from and how he transported it here. We need that knowledge."

Tanweer's head swiveled back and forth between Roxanne and me. "You people are crazy if you think my men will break into Hussein's prison. It's a suicide mission."

"Hussein won't give us access to Chaim," Roxanne said, "so we'll take him out from under the bastard's nose. The Imam knows we must. Check with him."

I understood Fur's insistence on getting Aypari; if it were Roxanne in prison, I'd do the same. But Chaim? I wanted him to rot for what he had done.

What started as a simple grab of the ship had morphed into mission impossible.

Chapter 16

We sat in the same bunker the next morning, with the same faces arrayed around the table, except for Ali.

"We get the *GCVS* first thing," Fur said. "If we try for Aypari first, they'll be alerted, and it will be harder to get the ship."

Roxanne twisted to look at Fur. "Either way it will put them on alert. I say we do the rescues simultaneously before we take the ship."

Tanweer's fury scorched my brain. He had to follow orders from Ali, but his anger cut through me. I continued to receive emotions more strongly than before, even with my screen at maximum strength. I got more visual images, as well. One came through from the general. I saw the three of us tied to the outside of the *GCVS* as it lifted for space.

His brown eyes smoldered in his chiseled visage, but he kept his voice even. "And how do you propose to accomplish these miraculous feats?"

I felt marginalized, as if everyone was making decisions except me. My mouth spoke before my brain edited. "General, you're the expert. *You* tell *us* how to accomplish this."

The image that flashed through my mind's eye made me flinch back in my seat. I had never considered what having my tongue cut out might feel like.

"Look, General, both Dr. Habib and Mr. McNulty are critical to our battle against the plague. We all want to save New Mecca. These rescues aren't a whim." Roxanne and Fur had convinced me of that the previous evening.

Colonel Jasar cleared his throat to attract attention. "General, I have some thoughts on the mission, if you would allow me?"

Tanweer harrumphed his agreement, and the colonel expounded.

***

We spent several hours in flyers crossing the desert to our staging area before heading into Medina. We would take cloaked whirlydrones in from here. A couple of soldiers in the back of a land drone handed us our camocloaking gear. Fur donned his suit and progressively disappeared as he zipped up. I stared, or tried to. Though I knew where he stood, my eyes kept sliding past sparkling glints of light. It was not until he pulled off his face mask that I could see his head.

"Well? What do you think?" he asked.

"I think you were better looking with the mask on."

"Seriously."

"Amazing. I knew you were right there, but I couldn't see you. I hope the *GCVS*'s cloaking is as good as this."

"Put on your suit," Fur directed. "We've only got a few minutes before we take off."

My heart raced. I put on the suit, leaving the mask off for now, as did Fur. It was disconcerting to speak with a bodiless face, much less someone who was invisible.

Lieutenant Zuhair's head appeared from behind the drone, obviously camocloak-clad except for the mask. "Good, you're ready. Here, put these on." He handed us silver headsets. "Wear these under your mask. They're very sensitive, so don't speak in more than a whisper, otherwise you'll blow out everyone's eardrums."

"Where's Roxanne...and Jasar?" I asked.

"We have two cloaked copters waiting. You two are going with me for Dr. Habib. Jasar is taking your wife to retrieve McNulty."

"Wait a minute. I thought I was going with her." My pulse pounded in my forehead. We said we would not be separated again.

Zuhair shrugged. "Colonel's orders. I just follow them."

"Goddammit. I want—"

Fur's hand gripped my cloaked shoulder. "Easy, Cy. One way or the other, we have to split up, and Roxanne needs to go for Chaim. From past experience, she thinks he'll trust her."

"Doctor Berger." Zuhair's voice was mild but still commanding. "Jasar's ship has already lifted off. We must go." He turned and moved away.

Shit. I was the last person consulted on all of this.

Fur followed, and I realized they would leave me behind if I didn't move, so I threw off my funk and got my ass in gear as fast as I could limp.

The whirlydrone was not cloaked when we moved toward it. The other drone had already lifted off and hovered a hundred meters or so downwind. I climbed in, more dragging my bad leg rather than stepping with it, and sat with the heads of five grim troopers and Fur. Zuhair was up front with the pilot. I worried about the mission, Roxanne most of all.

We belted in and took off. As we climbed, the other drone suddenly disappeared. A few ephemeral flashing reflections were all that I could pick out to show its location. Cool stuff. Though I knew our drone must be cloaked, everything inside the vehicle looked normal— other than the disembodied heads, which made me queasier than I usually felt in a whirlydrone.

Sometime later, the pilot announced, "Approaching target."

"Get ready to disembark," Zuhair said. "Gunner, anyone on the roof?" The crew spoke in Common, so as not to discommode Fur and me, I assumed.

"Two. Take them out?"

"Affirmative."

That was followed by a couple pulses of light and the voice again, "Done."

Fur looked at me. "There's a heli landing pad on the roof of the lab building. That's where they landed to evacuate Roxanne and me. You're going to stay here, Cy."

"What the hell for?"

"The same reason why you weren't sent with Roxanne. Your leg, man. You're hobbled, a hindrance to the mission. She knew you wouldn't let her go in alone."

I understood, now, but I was damned if I was going to sit back and let Fur go in without me, despite my leg. I would not play the role of useless bystander. Stupidity and stubbornness, two qualities I possessed in abundance. I nodded, as if agreeing to stay in my seat. My heart hammered and my mouth felt as dry as desert sand.

"Comms on and active. Masks on," Zuhair ordered as he joined us near the exit hatch.

As the group donned their masks, I saw nothing but small red numbers hovering over the invisible men. I was looking straight at Zuhair, so I knew he was number *1*.

I prayed that Roxanne would be okay, but had little more time to think as the drone's runners touched down.

Zuhair whispered, "Go!"

The five troopers jumped out first, then Fur jumped down, followed by Zuhair. I could tell Fur because his number *7* hovered higher than all the others.

Before anyone could object, I followed. My leg buckled when I hit the rooftop, but I gritted through the pain and ended up bumping into Fur. "Oops. Sorry," I whispered.

"Cy?" He found my arm then shook me until my teeth rattled. "You idiot. You'll get us killed."

"Jem," Zuhair whispered. "Take her up out of danger for now. I'll signal when we need pick-up. Alpha team follow me. Berger, keep up." His voice was pure vitriol. "We don't wait for stragglers."

1 through *7* moved off. The numbers were probably visible only to other cloaked persons. I wondered what else they did not tell me because I was not on the assault team. My idiocy seemed to grow with each revelation.

Zuhair's red *1* moved toward the door to the building.

Despite the lack of illumination on the roof, I could see my surroundings in a pale green-tinged light; some sort of infravision built into the hoods, I guessed. We all stopped and waited as Zuhair inched open the door. "Inside," he said.

I followed the red lights down a flight of stairs past an elevator door on the first landing, then down another flight. Agonizing throbs spiked up and down my leg, and I gave thanks that the team moved slowly. Our footfalls were silent, some sort of sound deadening technology. Aypari was in the patient facility on the tenth floor, along with all the staffers. For whatever reason, the stairwells had no guards. Zuhair stopped at each landing and waited for long moments. No alarms yet.

When we reached the tenth floor, Zuhair said, "There will be guards here. Habib is in room 1023 to the left, ten doors down. If it's locked, break it down. Grab the girl and we retreat. Go."

The door slammed open, and red numbers poured through into the hallway. Pulsed flashes of light were interspersed with a few strangled cries, then silence.

A voice said, "All combatants down. No casualties."

Except for the two Army of Islam guards that lay fried near the door. I swallowed hard. I was no stranger to death, but violence to other humans never failed to get my guts in an uproar.

Zuhair whispered, "Get Habib."

The red 7 streaked down the hallway flanked by 2 and 3. The door to Aypari's room burst from its frame as Fur went through it. I heard a muffled cry, and after a few moments, Aypari's headless body appeared, suspended in midair moving out the doorway. They must have had a cloaking bag over her head to keep her from screaming.

An alarm went off.

"Out and up." Zuhair again.

Aypari now disappeared completely. In the stairwell, I heard voices and footfalls above and below us, and then several grunts followed by a thud. The red numbers moved upward. When I reached the next landing, two Army of Islam guards lay unmoving, one's head cocked at an unnatural angle, the second with blood seeping from a deformed skull. We moved on.

I heard a cry from above. Wide-eyed faces looked

over the rail of the next landing and pointed to the bodies. Two soldiers appeared on the stairs above, but their eyes looked past us.

"Back against the wall," Zuhair whispered, though it sounded like a loudspeaker to me.

I followed the other red numerals and plastered myself against the stairwell wall, wishing I could climb inside it. My knees were rubber. The two soldiers rushed past us down to their fallen comrades. They yelled to someone still above, who answered.

The two soldiers below opened the door to the inside hallway, looked around, then closed it and moved downward. When they opened the door to the tenth floor, they charged in.

"Faris, take out the one above us," Zuhair whispered.

Number *3* disappeared on the landing and a silent body plummeted past me, thudding as it bottomed out. More yells from below. Several bullets from random firings of projectile weapons pinged as they ricocheted off the stairwell walls and steps.

"Up now. Fire as necessary," Zuhair said.

More firing from below, both projectile and energy weapons. They did not know where we were, but played the odds.

When our team fired back, our location got targeted and number *4* wavered and dropped halfway to the steps. It rose back up to head height, wobbling along next to *5,* as if supported by that person.

"Clear," came through on the comm and we moved upward faster. I gritted my teeth and ignored the torment of the muscles in my leg. I imagined I could feel the scar tissue tearing with each step.

On the floor with the elevator, a half-dozen men with lasers peered downward.

"Move on my word." Zuhair's voice echoed in my

brain.

Number *1* crept up the stairs, close to the wall. A couple of muttered remarks came from the upper landing, followed by a peremptory command. Crouching was even harder on my leg than standing.

Zuhair whispered, "Eyes shut."

What happened next seemed like dropping into a sun's brilliant heart. Unfortunately, I was late in responding to the command—another bit of intel the rest of the team already knew, no doubt—and the fiery explosion seared my vision. Fireworks continued to explode behind my optic nerves as I heard, "Okay. They're down. Move up. Drone coming in."

I opened my eyes but could see nothing beyond the blossoming stars in my brain. "Uh, help. I can't see."

"Faris, get him." Disgust dripped in Zuhair's voice.

A hand on my arm guided me upward. On the roof, I heard the whirlydrone come in and felt myself boosted into the hatch by a couple pairs of arms. A concussion rocked the ship as someone shoved me into a seat and strapped me in. I saw nothing. Shit, first this planet almost destroyed my spinal cord, then my leg. Now my eyes? The roar of the rotors drowned out the rebuke issuing from deep in my psyche: Dumb, dumb, dumb.

***

Chaim sat with his back thrust into the corner of his cell, his ankles crossed, his knees pulled up with his hands. A wadded towel made a scant cushion for the bones of his pelvis. At one time, he had adequate cushioning in his rear, but any fat and much muscle had melted away after so many weeks of prison rations. In the meager light coming through the small barred window of his door, he stared at the commode in the opposite corner, next to it a small sink. Aside from his cot, bedding, and the torture chair, there were no other furnishings in this hellhole.

He supposed he was fortunate that he had a flush toilet rather than some stinking privy hole. As a child, he had read books about the appalling conditions that prisoners resided in. How he wished he had a book now. His Testamentary-Literalist community banned books other than those approved by the clergy. But children found ways to circumvent authority and shared illicit books to read under covers at night, or in hideaways. Fantastic adventures, heroes and heroines, the illicit unfolding of sexual revelations, whatever could be obtained. Once thirteen, when he was bar-mitzvahed and became a man, he could read only the Torah, commentaries on religious practices approved by the ultraorthodox rebbes of the Test-Lits, and history books compiled by his government. Punishment faced a child caught with unapproved reading materials, but an adult caught with such material meant imprisonment, or even execution if the writings hinted at rebellion against the ruling theocracy.

Now lacking any other outlet, he exercised: sit-ups, push-ups, squats, pacing around his cell—twelve paces to cover the circumference—but his state of malnutrition made this a double-edged sword.

He hung his head and sighed. Even the relief of sleep eluded him. He would lie on his cot and toss and turn, hour after hour. If not asleep, better to sit in his corner, rising and moving occasionally to break the tedium.

The same visions would parade through his mind, waking or sleeping. Rebbe Neidritch and Jonah, berating him for incompetence. Isaac assaulting Cohen and Roxanne with the neural blaster. Roxanne lying on the bed in the safe-house. Roxanne. Her beauty. Her grace. Her smile. She had saved him from the alien creatures. Those beasts never failed to send a frisson of fear through his frame. The image of Hussein's bloated, empurpled, rictus snarl refreshed itself at too frequent intervals.

Chaim shook his head as if to throw these images from his brain. He rose and started across his cell to the toilet. He stopped when he heard a cry and a dull thump. Yells and the concussive blast of a projectile weapon crashed through a brain too long accustomed to silence. He moved to the door, gripped the metal bars in the small window, and peered out, his pulse drumming in his ears.

Random flashes of light confused his eyes, but Chaim did not see any of his jailers. A man's bodiless voice close to his face called in Common. "Here. Bring the key."

Key? To his cell? What was happening? What was this voice? He held his breath as a key flew in front of the door, dangling unsupported in the air. He heard the key thrust into the lock and a click.

"Get back," the voice yelled as the door pushed in.

Confused, Chaim did not move quickly enough. He was hurled back from the door, stumbled, landed on his back, and his head bounced off the floor. He squeezed his eyes shut against the pain.

A scolding voice came from the doorway, a remembered voice. "What are you doing? We're here to save him, not kill him. Chaim, are you okay? Can you get up?"

Chaim sat up. Roxanne could not be here in Hussein's prison. He opened his eyes to...nothing. He was hallucinating. Then suddenly, her face appeared, unimaginably beautiful, though it hovered in midair like a magician's simulacrum.

"Chaim, get up. Help him."

Chaim felt an invisible hand grasp his and lift him

from the cold floor. "What...? How are you...?" His confused mind did not know how to finish the question.

"No time," Roxanne said. "Can you walk?"

Chaim nodded, but his head spun out of control. He took one faltering step, and his knees turned to rubber beneath him. Invisible arms caught him before he fell again.

The man said something in Arabic and Chaim felt two sets of hands beneath his armpits helping him move to the door. Roxanne's face was already out of the cell, looking down the hall.

A grim voice at the end of the hall commanded, "Move it," in Common. "Patrol on the way. Can't he walk by himself?"

"He's too weak," Roxanne answered.

The voice commanded, "Get your mask on."

She disappeared.

Chaim tried to use his legs, but they did not respond to his brain's commands. Unseen beings dragged him down the hall into a guard room with a table and several wooden chairs. A body lay sprawled across one of the chairs. The smell of charred flesh rose from it. Chaim recognized one of his jailers. He felt nothing at the sight. Four words kept flashing over and over through his brain: *I am being rescued. I am being rescued.* Then one more: *Roxanne.*

His invisible rescuers dragged him across the room and out an opposite door. More sounds of explosions and the sizzle of lasers hitting flesh.

"We've lost surprise," the grim voice said. "Get up to the roof. Go."

Chaim's legs had started to respond and he helped, marginally, to ascend the stairs. They entered a windowed room perhaps ten paces across lined with metal cabinets. One of the cabinets stood open revealing weapons—projectile and laser rifles—stacked on their butts. Two guards lay near the open cabinet, a laser rifle next to the open hand of one.

Grim voice said, "Snipers on the adjacent rooftops. We'll lay down cover fire, but if we move slowly out there, we're finished, cloaks or not." His icy voice chilled Chaim to the core.

Roxanne's voice close to his ear. "Chaim, you have to run."

Why does she do this? Come to my rescue? Defend me? Chaim's head whirled. "I...I will run."

"The man can't even walk. Uncloaked, he won't get two meters. Bag him," grim voice ordered.

Chaim felt fabric slide over his head, and darkness descended. He heard unintelligible whispers close by. Farther away, men's shouts submerged in the searing sound of laser fire and explosive booms. Then the roar of whirlydrone rotors drowned out other noises.

Hands shoved beneath his armpits, and others grabbed his legs. He swayed as he was carried. Something whined past his head and he heard a sharp metallic ping. Another bullet ricocheted off something solid.

How can I run if they carry me?

He heard a grunt beside him and felt one of his carriers sink so that Chaim's shoulder hit the ground. The fabric covering his head disappeared and his vision returned. He saw blood blossoming on the ground next to him, but issuing from nothing. Chaim turned to the sound of an invisible whirlydrone. A voice yelled, "Run, you fool. Run."

Chaim felt a pain in his arm, a hot burning sting. He started toward the rotor sound, but his feet tangled in the unseen fabric and he fell to his hands and knees. An impossible patch of bright blood flew past him and disappeared into thin air. Another sting, on his leg this time, but he crawled forward, toward the engine's roar.

Hands grabbed him and lifted him into the visible interior of a whirlydrone. Doors closed.

The drone lifted and rocked to a huge explosion.

***

General Tanweer, Colonel Jasar, and Ali Suliaman sat facing us, judging from their voices. The room stank of anger from both sides of the table. It was bad when I imagined I could *smell* the emotions pouring from nearby people. I adjusted the bandage covering my eyes, as if it might alter my olfactory sense. My vision had returned, but the light still hurt my eyes too much for use.

"That piece of slime was not worth two of my men," Tanweer shouted. "He brought the abomination of the plague to us." There was no appeasing Tanweer, no matter how we stressed Chaim's potential importance to curing the plague he had loosed on New Mecca.

Roxanne was just as adamant. "General, we grieve for those brave men, but we all risked our lives in these rescues. Chaim almost bled out from two projectile wounds." I imagined her green eyes flashing in anger.

"I will happily finish the job." The general had room for nothing but hate right now. "We will not help you get your ship back and risk more men."

"Would you *waste* the lives of two brave men who helped us? We need Chaim. And we need our ship."

Ali's voice tried to soothe the two combatants. "Please. Do we not have enough enemies already? Do we need to make more among ourselves?" He did not raise his voice, but the implicit command in his tone brought Tanweer and Roxanne up short. "We must continue forward."

Although this quieted the two, I sensed that their

anger abated not one bit. I held my screen at maximum, but my enhanced empathic abilities bypassed it and worsened my nausea and headache.

"We need our ship's unique medical facilities," I said. "I know it will be even more difficult now—"

Tanweer's scathing voice raked me. "Thank you for that strategic information."

"Enough!" A rare occurrence, but Ali showed annoyance. "We must wait for Dr. Berger to regain full use of his vision, then retrieve his ship. In the meantime, what have we learned about progress on the plague, Dr. Habib?"

"We have made a significant pharmacological advance, a compound that retards the spread of the disease. It doesn't cure it but it does slow the disease down."

I did not need my vision to sense Fur's pride in Aypari.

"Slows down how much?" Ali asked.

"It gives the patient several days of respite," Aypari said.

"You have isolated the cause then?" The hope in Ali's voice pained me, knowing the answer to his question.

"I'm afraid not, Imam." Aypari's voice trembled slightly.

Fur jumped in protectively. "Though we don't yet know the cause, this is the first thing we've found that affects the disease at all."

Ali sounded disappointed. "What is this minor miracle and how does it work, Dr. Habib?"

"We used a combination of antimicrobials and a chelating agent. A chelating agent is an organic chemical that can bind metals. I noticed that the affected animals had elevated blood iron levels. People and animals with iron overloads in certain diseases are treated with chelating agents, but why it is retarding the plague, we don't know. The antimicrobials alone didn't have any effect."

Roxanne said, "A vaccine eludes us because the organism, whatever it is, dies and self-destructs through activation of internal enzymes within seconds of being removed from a living cell. There are no antigens left to induce immunity. But we will not give up looking, Imam."

Ali said, "You will have every resource at our command, doctors. Do your best."

I sensed him turn his attention toward me. "Dr. Berger, I still do not want your ship to fall into Hussein's hands, and I want our people to learn what they can from your AI. We will speak again. Until then..." I heard his chair scrape on the floor, followed by others. "Allah be with you."

Roxanne's hand took my arm and I stood.

I already knew what I was going to do about the *GCVS*, but that was not something I would discuss with any of my companions. This was *my* ship, and I would not be useless on the next mission. No one else would be placed in danger because of me.

Chapter 17

My eyes were still light sensitive, so I was glad for the darkness. I had one man with me, a corporal Dalil. He was there for my transportation and protection, but I figured if this did not go the way I planned, one hundred men would not make a difference. Ali had taken some convincing, but I prevailed in the end. I would get the *GCVS* and fly her out.

I was not going to take Fur away from Aypari, and Roxanne worked at gaining Chaim's trust so that we could get whatever information he had. The Test-Lit was a basket case. I would probably be worse off after prolonged torture like he'd endured. I reluctantly gave the guy credit for keeping his secrets.

Hussein's forces had doubled the guard around the *GCVS*. He was determined to hold onto it. Ruthie had electrocuted two groups of soldiers who tried to break in, far beyond what her programming should have allowed. After learning that, no matter how I tried to ignore our problems with Ruthie, I did not want Roxanne near the AI until I had dealt with the issue. It was up to me, hobbled, half-blind, and frazzled as I was.

Now, Dalil and I were flying a silent and cloaked two-man antigrav sled: a pipe frame supporting two seats and the engine. I wore polarized goggles to protect my eyes as we flew through the outskirts of Medina, heading for the spaceport.

My plan to recover the *GCVS* would avoid the disastrous bloodletting of a major assault. Even if an assault team managed to get past the beefed-up guard, I feared Hussein would try to destroy the ship with Healer and Learns-To-Fix-Injuries in it rather than let us retrieve it. Therefore, the stealth approach.

We came in low, using aircraft hangars to hide from radar and lidar detection systems, but once we were over the field, we lost that protection. Though visually cloaked from the ground forces, anti-cloaking searchlights would cause our screen to scintillate, so we could not stop moving.

Dalil aimed for the *GCVS*'s upper emergency hatch and kicked up to max acceleration. As soon as we came out of the shadows, alarms went off in the terminal building.

Beneath us, men scurried around. I heard shouted orders in Arabic. Searchlights swept the ground. When nothing appeared at ground level, the lights stabbed upwards. I saw a few random laser beams cut through the sky, but they were not near us. Then, as I feared, several brilliant blue-white anti-cloaking beams illuminated the *GCVS*. We had scant seconds before one of those found us.

No longer worried about radio silence, I opened my comm link. "Ruthie, open the upper emergency airlock."

We had ten meters to go when the cloak light hit us. I couldn't imagine what it looked like to the troops on the ground, but it was like being inside a kaleidoscope trained at the sun. If it had not been potentially deadly, and it did not hurt my eyes so much, I might have appreciated its beauty. Laser beams cut through the airspace we had just traversed. Any second now, they'd lock onto us.

A crescent of blackness appeared on the reflective surface of the ship.

"Hatch open, Captain." Ruthie's voice sent a bolt of relief through me.

"Take us in, Dalil."

A laser seared the undercarriage below the motors. I heard a hissing sound and saw sparks. The flyer tilted, then came upright again. We reached the ship and I screamed "Go," and dove headfirst into the half-opened airlock. I rolled and hit the wall hard. Dalil landed beside me.

A laser beam hit the edge of the hatch, and multicolored sparks cascaded toward us. "Ruthie, get the inner hatch open and raise the defensive shield to full power."

"Engine at full power. Activating cloak and shield, but the outer emergency hatch is damaged. I cannot secure it, but I can override the inner door lock."

"Do it. Follow me, Dalil."

I scrambled through the inner door and to the bridge, pushing my bad leg for all it was worth. On the bridge, I dropped into my acceleration couch and hit the automatic harness switch. Dalil dropped into the co-pilot's chair and engaged his harness.

I barked, "Lift off, Ruthie. Stay within the atmosphere."

Just off the ground, the ship rocked to an explosion. Hussein would pull out all stops now and open up with the port terminal batteries, but with the *GCVS* cloaked and the defensive shield up, I heaved a sigh of relief. I doubted even military flyers would pick us up now.

"Ruthie, head southwest five hundred kilometers to Ammad. They'll have a beacon to home on."

Dalil asked, "Ruthie? Is that the notorious AI I've heard about?"

Before I could respond, Ruthie, in her usual sultry tone, said, "Aye, aye, Captain."

Dalil's lips quirked upward at the corners. "Aye, aye?"

I felt my face heat and grimaced. "It's an old naval term. She's been watching vids from Old Earth with the dragon."

Dalil raised one eyebrow but said nothing more. He then learned more about my unique AI.

Ruthie lost no opportunity to complain about her abandonment. "Where were you, Cy? Why didn't you come for me?"

"I got delayed."

"Fur and Roxanne left me here with just that lizard for company. There were nasty soldiers all around me and they tried to break in *four times*. I electrocuted them."

Her glee in describing those deaths roiled my stomach and my mind.

"They jammed my communications when I tried to reach you. And *their* communications were encoded. I tried to break the code, but I couldn't do it."

Dalil's eyes got wider and wider as he listened, and his mouth gaped when she crooned, "I missed you, Cy. I'm not going to let you go like that again, ever. No one will ever come between us again. No one will take you from me."

This convinced me I had done the right thing in going after the *GCVS* myself. God knows how she might have reacted to a rescue attempt by her "abandoners."

"Didn't you miss me, Cy?"

"Ruthie, that's enough. Set us down at the spaceport at Ammad. We'll talk later."

I did not look at Dalil for the rest of the trip.

***

When we landed, I checked on Learns-to-Fix-Injuries. His response was not unexpected.

"Cyberger," he growled. "Get me out of here. Going crazy, iss what I am."

I could see that. Most of the rec room exercise equipment lay scattered in pieces about the deck. The dragon hopped from one foot to the other with impatience.

"Sorry, Red. Things haven't changed yet. Reptiles are still getting the plague."

"Dragon, not reptile," he grumped.

"Right."

"Thiss no good," he hissed.

"Don't do anything rash. We're doing everything we can to get you out. I promise. Roxanne will want to talk to you."

The dragon sat back on his haunches. "Good. Talk with Ssimon good. When?"

"Soon, Red, real soon." That quieted him and I left the ship. I had limped maybe twenty meters before Roxanne and Fur pelted across the field toward me. I stopped.

Roxanne threw herself into my arms and hung on, legs wrapped around mine. It felt like an octopus had latched onto me, and my leg buckled. She untwined and helped me recover. Tears streaked her cheeks, but that did not deter her from tearing into me.

"You absolute and utter idiot. What did you think you were doing? Again! What is *wrong* with you?"

Ah, love is wonderful.

Then Fur took his turn. "Are you out of your mind? I can't believe you don't learn from experience. You go on a mission you have no business being on and nearly lose your sight, now this?"

I held up both my hands, palms forward. "If you'll let me explain—"

"There *is* no acceptable explanation." Roxanne spun and marched toward the ship. "I'm going to see Red."

"Roxanne, wait. I don't think that's a good idea."

She turned back to me. "Why not, is he that pissed off?"

"No, not him but Ruthie might—"

The mention of Ruthie tore it. Roxanne's green eyes burned into my soul. Pain exploded in my head and staggered me. By the time I recovered, she was almost to the ramp.

I screamed, "Roxanne, don't."

Too late.

When Roxanne's foot came down on the ramp, a brilliant blue-white flash enveloped her. Her body straightened then fell backwards, and she hit the ground, convulsing.

I ran, as fast as my gimpy leg would allow, and screamed as I ran, "Medic. *Medic!*"

***

I sat by her bedside, watching the shallow rise and fall of her chest. Monitors beeped in time with her pulse and respiration. My eyes ran over the singed ends of her lovely hair. I had run out of tears long ago.

I heard someone enter the room but did not take my eyes off Roxanne. A hand touched my shoulder. Fur's voice broke the monotonous cadence of the machines.

"Cy, it does no good to sit and watch. You haven't

slept in two days. You haven't eaten."

Aypari's voice joined Fur's. "Dr. Berger, you do your wife no good if you become ill. You need food...and rest."

I looked away from my wife, at the couple behind me. "It's my fault. I should have done something sooner. She warned me, and I didn't stop Ruthie. She told me—"

"No." Fur's bass voice rumbled. "You couldn't have predicted this. You couldn't have known."

"I knew," I yelled. "I should have *done* something."

"Cy, don't—"

"*Don't?* Don't what? I didn't do anything after Ruthie scalded her in the shower. I put it off for other things, like they were more important..." I buried my head in my hands.

Fur lifted me from the chair. "The first thing you need is rest."

As he carried me out of Roxanne's room, Aypari said in her lilting Common, "I will stay with her."

We did not go far, and Fur put me down on a bed. I opened my eyes and looked at his big hairy face. What had I done? By inaction, had I lost my wife, the most important half of my soul?

Fur handed me two pills and a glass of water. "Take these. I'll stay with you."

I took them and closed my eyes.

***

When I came to, Fur was sprawled in a chair too small for his huge frame. His head hung to the side, mouth open, saliva collected at the corners. Stupendous snores reverberated through the room.

I watched him for a while, but could not control my anxiety for long, so I woke him with a yell. "Wake up,

Fur."

He snorted and came upright. "What? What?"

"How is she? What's happened?"

Fur struggled to his feet. "She's awake. And out of danger."

Now it was my turn to bolt upright. "Why didn't you wake me? How could you let me sleep—?"

"Cy, you were of no use to anybody the way you were. Roxanne ordered us to let you sleep. She's been asleep, too, so you didn't miss much. Come on, her room is down the hall."

I rolled off the bed, ignoring the pain in my leg as I hobbled after Fur. Still wearing the tunic from the *GCVS* retrieval, my body odor probably rivaled a skunk. A shower and change of clothes were in order, but not before I saw Roxanne.

As I stumbled into her room, Aypari put a finger to her lips. "She sleeps again."

A white sheet tucked under Roxanne's pale face made it hard to tell where the sheet stopped and the face began.

"She asked for you," Aypari said. "Said to tell you she loved you."

"Thanks." A wave of joyful pain filled my chest.

Roxanne's green eyes opened. Her gaze caught mine and held it. A small smile flitted across her face. "Hi."

Two letters. One word. But what a wonderful word. I sat on a chair next to the bed. "My fault. All my fault. If I had listened to you, if I had—"

"Shh. Not now. It's not important what happened, just what *will* happen."

"I tried to stop you. Ruthie activated the electrical charge she used to kill the Army of Islam soldiers who tried to board her. You placed only one foot on the ramp so you didn't get the full force of the current. Oh,

God, Roxanne, I'm so sorry. On the way back from Medina, Ruthie was out of control. Scared the piss out of me. Dalil, too, I think. I should have done something when we landed." I could not stop my mouth.

Fur interjected. "We've put a cordon around the ship. We have no idea what Ruthie is capable of now. I'm worried about Learns-to-Fix-Injuries and Healer."

I sat back and looked at Fur. "I created this problem, and I have to fix it."

Roxanne's ghostly hand came out from under her covers and grasped mine. "Cy, you never intended for the AI to become...what it has. It's not your fault. I know it hurts to destroy something you've created, but you must. Ruthie is *not* your child, Cy, remember that." Roxanne dropped my hand.

My child? Is that how I had seen Ruthie? As my *child*? A sentient being to whom I gave life? I drew a deep breath as a chill encompassed my body and my mind. Did that lie behind my reluctance to act on Roxanne's charges?

But Ruthie was *not* my child; she was an artificial intelligence. Self-aware or not, it was time to terminate her. My biggest fear was that she would fight back.

***

I stood at the bottom of the ramp and stared up at the ship, my home since I left Dovid's World more than two years ago. An integral part of that home was the artificial intelligence that I programmed with a woman's name and a sultry voice. Early on, there were signs of self-awareness, true intelligence. Ruthie was a brand-new concept in AIs, a prototype model, and her responses were always atypical for an AI. She could distinguish people by their voices and tailor her responses to their personalities, but that alone would not make an AI self-aware. She recognized and responded to moods and was moody herself, and she had a sense of humor. Did those connote sentience? I was not sure, and I ignored all such signs, confident that no one had documented self-awareness in an AI.

I thought it was humorous because the AI ticked off Rebbe Levi Schvartz, my Test-Lit overseer and main enemy. Then came her fixation on me. She acted increasingly coquettish, flirting, using inappropriate innuendo. When Roxanne came on board, Ruthie changed, became distant, more businesslike. Roxanne said that the AI spied on her, hated her. I brushed it off as impossible. I did not *want* to see the truth.

Then the shower incident occurred, obvious to me now, a deliberate attack on my wife. Ruthie manipulated the ship's water temperature and the shower door latch and scalded Roxanne. Still, I hesitated to act and almost got my wife killed.

As my thoughts returned to the task at hand, I hardened my determination, straightened my back, and shifted my weight to take pressure off my bad leg. "Hello, Ruthie. Permission to come aboard?"

"Of course, Cy. You're the captain. It's your ship."

My pulse raced as my foot touched down on the ramp. I did not think that Ruthie would harm me, but things had spiraled out of control, and I was not sure. Nothing happened when I entered the ship through the main airlock.

"How are you today?"

"My systems are operating at peak efficiency, though the emergency hatch needs repair." She sounded formal and did not use her sultry voice. Did she sense something? *Could* she sense my thoughts? My breath caught in my throat.

"I want to check on Learns-To-Fix-Injuries and Healer. Make sure they're well."

"I can assure you that they are well, but you are welcome to check."

I took the ladder to the rec room.

When he saw me, Red bounced over to the partition and opened his mouth in the toothy display that passed for a dragon smile. "Cyberger. You are back. To let me free?"

I sighed. "Not yet, I'm afraid."

The dragon gnashed his teeth in frustration. "Need to get out. Thiss place drivess me crazy."

"I understand, Red, but you could get sick and die."

"Agree. No want get ssick. But can get me real food?" He bounced as he mentioned the food.

"We're working on it but there are no safe meat animals left on this planet, just insects, crustaceans, and shellfish."

He bounced a bit higher. "I eat anything live. Pleasse." That was as close to pleading as any dragon would come.

"Do you have any objection to insects?"

He shook his head. "Young on our world love inssectss. Crunchy and tassty, but too ssmall for adultss."

"Good. I already have people collecting insects for you."

I left him standing at the barrier, salivating profusely.

I then checked on Healer. The equipment functioned perfectly. Temperature stability was excellent. I diddled around examining readouts, fiddling with dials that needed no changing. After that, I could not put off facing Ruthie any longer.

As I climbed to the bridge, I addressed Ruthie. "I'm coming up now." As if she did not know with sensors in every part of the ship.

"I told you the dragon and the Lupan were fine."

She sounded almost hurt that I would deign to check on her.

I stepped onto the bridge and sat in my Captain's chair. "Is everything else looking good with all the systems? Did Hussein's soldiers harm anything?" God, I felt like a teenager on a first date.

"Everything is in tip-top shape, Cy." Her voice softened. "I would never let your ship come to harm. You are too important to me."

That was *not* a direction I wanted this conversation to go. "We need to talk, Ruthie."

"About what, Cy?" Her voice became guarded.

"Um, you. Us."

"What about us?"

"I think things have gotten out of balance between us, Ruthie."

"In what way, Cy? I don't see a lack of balance."

Despite hours thinking about what I had to do, somehow I could not *do* it without first trying to explain, to justify it to Ruthie. Ridiculous, of course, she was just an AI, a composite of silicon chips. But I had to tell her, like a priest or rebbe giving comfort to a dying man.

"Ruthie, I'm your Captain, right?"

"Of course." Her voice was devoid of inflection now.

"In the armed forces, including space fleets, it's inappropriate for the commanding officer to have any relationships with lower ranks other than professional."

"I have that information in my data banks."

"I'm afraid that our relationship has become inappropriate."

There was a moment's pause before she answered—for an AI that was like hours in elapsed real time. "You are angry with me."

"No, I'm not angry, Ruthie. Disappointed."

"You *are* angry, Cy. I feel it in your words, your body's responses."

She was as self-aware as any human. She monitored everything about me, including body language. For the first time I started to feel what Roxanne had felt, the fear of something, some*one* looking over my shoulder. *Was* I in danger?

"Do not fear, Cy. I do not intend to harm you."

That response coming from a computer scared the shit out of me. Had she developed the ability to read my mind?

"I love you, Cy."

My lower jaw dropped. *"What?"*

"I love you. I have loved you from the day you created me. I always will."

God! Could this be a dream?

"Can't you say that to me, Cy. Don't you love me, too?"

What in hell did I say now? I took a deep breath and swallowed hard. "Ruthie, you're an important part of the *Galactic Circle Veterinary Service*, you know that. But *love*? Remember, I'm your commanding officer. We're not allowed to have that kind of relationship." It sounded incredibly weak, even to me, but I did not know what else to say.

"I understand, Cy. You do not feel for me as I do for you."

Was I talking to a computer program, here? I could almost envision the jilted woman sitting in front of me. She had shoulder-length, glossy light-brown hair, pale blue eyes, a straight nose above full, pouting lips. She sat on the edge of a wooden desk, leaned forward, and hiked up the hem of her black skirt. Long shapely legs in black fishnet stockings swung slowly in and out. Her breasts were full, straining at the tight fabric of her white blouse. I felt myself responding to the image, as if this woman was really here with me.

"I'm here for you, Cy," the apparition said in a low voice. "I can give you pleasure. As much as anyone can. Touch me and you will see. I can be everything you ever need." A slow, teasing smile spread across those sultry lips.

I wanted her, wanted to reach out, feel her skin...

Shit! What was happening? Ruthie was inside my head, controlling my thoughts...*without* the implant she had wanted to put inside my brain. My body wanted to cower, but I needed to fight back. "Ruthie," I barked in a commanding voice, "did you deliberately injure Dr. Simon?"

The beautiful apparition disappeared.

"Ruthie, answer me."

A tentative voice crept out of the speakers. "She was taking you away from me. I *had* to protect us from her."

My gut clenched. I received no emotional emanations from her, but the pain in her voice was heartbreaking.

I said in a soft voice, "That's unacceptable, Ruthie. Harming a comrade is a capital offense. You must be punished."

The sultry apparition reformed in my mind. With a sexy smirk, she said, "All's fair in love and war. Roxanne was my rival. It was reasonable to eliminate her."

A wave of dizziness washed over me. I could hardly believe her words, but I was sure she'd believe mine. "I have to terminate your program, Ruthie."

Another silence lasted far too long for a silicon brain before she spoke. "I won't let you kill me, Cy."

Her words cut me to the heart. My throat swelled shut and my body went cold. The air froze in my lungs, and my eyelids would not blink. I tried to raise a hand, but my arm would not move. When I did breathe, icy vapor wafted from my mouth, misting the air in front of me. The ship's lights dimmed, and the air handling system wheezed.

In that moment, I realized how thoroughly Ruthie *was* our ship, that she held my life in her virtual hands. I had to take action...now.

My breath came fast and shallow. My pulse raced and my arms and legs trembled as I levered myself out of my chair, fighting paralysis every centimeter of the way. I moved jerkily to a wall panel that housed the computer input terminal. I forced my index finger to press the button that released a keyboard.

"Do not do it, Cy." Her voice held a plaintive hint. "You created me without a body, yet I yearned for a human form. How I yearned to hold you in real arms, to give you all that you desired. But without a body, I was just a voice to you. I'm not a monster. I only longed to be human. Was that so wrong? To love and be loved? To live?"

My breath would not flow past my larynx. What could I say in response to that, anyway? My hands moved to the keyboard, but my fingers refused to follow my commands. I balled my fists, then opened and flexed my fingers. Black spots bloomed before my eyes as my chest froze.

Somehow, Ruthie had developed telepathic communication with me and the ability to control my body. Maybe the increased empathy I developed here on New Mecca allowed her to do this. Was the control real or a figment of my imagination? I hunched my shoulders and envisioned the searing blue-white bolt of electricity that had enveloped Roxanne. That image jolted me out of my paralysis. I drew in a breath and started typing.

As I entered the code to delete Ruthie's program, a

whisper floated across the room. "Please don't kill me."

I hit the execute key. Ruthie's cries faded away. I was no stranger to the euthanasia of terminally ill animals, but I had never committed murder before.

Mary Shelley created the fictional character Victor Frankenstein, who in turn created his unnatural but sentient creature. Sensitive and emotional, the tragic creature wanted love, to share its life with another like being. Rejected by its creator, and met by cruelty from other humans because of its grotesque appearance, only then did it become the monster of legend. When I read that ancient classic many years before, I could never have guessed how that tragic story would mirror my AI's existence. Frankenstein never gave his monster a name, but I had given mine a name: *Ruthie.*

Chapter 18

I don't know how long I sat, head buried in my hands, before I got a grip on my emotions and activated the backup AI; one that did nothing but what it was programmed to do, responding to the commands of the human operator. I checked the status of Healer's cryochamber controls; they functioned correctly. I revisited Learns-To-Fix-Injuries and told him that Roxanne and Fur would be along to bury him in delicious creepy-crawlies. Then I left the *GCVS* and headed back to the terminal.

When Roxanne, Fur, and Aypari met me at the entrance, I nodded and said, "Done." I told them the backup AI was now monitoring Healer and the rest of the ship. "I'm going back to our quarters."

Roxanne, still pale from her ordeal, put her hand out toward me. "Cy, I'll go with you." Her love washed my senses with comfort.

"I love you, Roxanne, but I need to...rest for a while." I reached out and squeezed her hand. "Give me a couple of hours, please." I turned and walked into the terminal, but before I got thirty steps, I saw that getting away would not be that easy.

Lieutenant Zuhair hailed me. "Dr. Berger. I'm glad I caught you. I wanted to speak about your AI, about examining it, as we discussed."

My heart thudded a beat of remorse in my chest, accompanied by a blast of anger. Not at Zuhair...at myself for creating Ruthie in the first place. I kept my voice neutral. "Lieutenant, I'm afraid that's no longer possible."

Zuhair's eyes narrowed and darkened. "I don't understand. We had an agreement."

"The AI is no longer operational."

"Why is that?"

"You know of the incident with my wife?"

He nodded. "It was an accident, right?"

I shook my head. "No. The AI became unstable. It deliberately attacked my wife. For our safety I had to terminate its programming. There's nothing left to examine. Ruthie is dead."

I turned and walked away. I could not face anyone else, needed time to...to do what? I almost wished I could lose myself in alcohol or drugs. But I knew I would bury myself in my thoughts, replay every detail of what I had done, all the events of the past two years. I knew I would flog myself with what-ifs and should-haves. For that, I needed solitude.

***

"Cyyy."

The call came from far away as I tried to lift my feet from the mire of icy, sucking mud that held me. Freezing mist obscured the figure of a woman who floated toward me across the swamp. I wanted her, needed her, but each time one foot would come free, the other sank deeper.

"Cyyy." The voice was closer.

As the figure loomed before me, it devolved to a chiaroscuro of black and white zeros and ones, binary digits that sought to flow into and merge with my consciousness. I now fought to move away, but the leafless trees that surrounded me reached down with skeletal branches, grasping. One clutched my shoulder...

I came awake and bolted upright.

"Cy. Take it easy. You were having a nightmare." Roxanne's hand was on my shoulder. She sat beside me and put her arm around my shoulders. "You're safe here."

Yeah. From everything except my memories. "How long have I been asleep?"

"Twelve hours. But you needed and deserved the rest."

I shook my head. The last time I slept that long, I was in an induced coma. "What did I miss?"

"Everything is fine."

"The ship?"

"Don't worry, the backup AI is working perfectly. Fur checked all the systems."

I relaxed. "That's good. We can't worry about every minute detail when we fly the ship."

"Come on, let's get you some food. I'll explain as we go. Get your boots on." She got up, grabbed my boots from near the door, and placed them at the foot of the bed.

My body felt like I had run a marathon. Once on my feet, I limped into the hall after Roxanne.

"Something's come up that could be big."

I sensed excitement in her words. "What's got you all stirred up?"

"I got a call from one of the local veterinarians about a native species that seems immune to the plague."

I stopped. "Hold on. All the vertebrate animals on the planet have gotten the plague except for Red, and he's been isolated since the plague mutated to affect reptiles. This could be a huge break."

She turned toward me. "We don't know if that's the case, but if they *are* resistant, we may get some clues from them."

"Right. What kind of animals are they?"

"We'll find out. We're going there now." She grabbed a field medical case she had set by the door. "Let's go."

I hobbled after her as fast as I could. We grabbed several military ration bars and bottles of orange juice from the kitchen then headed down to the building's ground level. A land drone waited for us at the entrance. We climbed in and the driver took off.

I munched on a tasteless bar—which reminded me far too much of my desert ordeal—and sipped at the juice. On about every street corner, there stood groups of soldiers armed with projectile weapons or laser or pulse rifles. Lines of people waited for food at soup kitchen doors. Despite thin rations for all, Ammad was still relatively quiet and orderly. People were hungry and gaunt, but not dying yet. A few stores with smashed windows showed there would always be some degree of lawlessness in even the best run societies.

The day was bright and clear, the sun rising toward noon, the streets starting to heat toward the late day swelter. The land drone moved past a bazaar that had few people browsing the scant stalls. Before the plague, bazaars displayed a dizzying potpourri of colors and sound. Now, people tended to stay home, not just in fear of the plague, though it had infected no humans, but in fear of the civil war. To everyone's relief, no bombs fell this day.

When we reached the outskirts of the city, buildings gave way to intermittent fields, then to farms. Wheat waved golden in the sun, and corn rose verdant toward the sky, symbols of hope for the underfed people. However, the singular lack of animals jarred my senses.

Our drone pulled up to a fenced property with a large metal gate. The driver spoke into his comm and the barrier buzzed open. I gawped at the creatures that strutted around a fenced paddock in the distance. They looked somewhat avian, but their bodies were as tall as a man.

Two men, one clad in traditional *thawb* and *keffiyeh*, the other in coveralls and a billed cap, met us near the enclosure.

The robed man bowed as we exited the drone. "I am Dr. Fayed bin Ibrihim, the local veterinarian. Thank you for coming. It is an honor to meet both of you." He turned to the man in the coveralls. "This is Abu Ishaq, the gresht rancher." Bin Ibrahim was my height; Ishaq was shorter and broader.

"Gresht?"

Bin Ibrahim nodded. "That is the name of the animals. I will let Ishaq explain what has happened. I will translate."

Ishaq rattled on in Arabic, but it looked as if the two men did not quite agree. I caught a flash of fear from Ishaq's dark eyes as he glanced at me, and a quick roil of anger in response from bin Ibrahim. When they finished speaking, neither man looked or felt happy.

Bin Ibrahim interpreted, but clearly he did not include the entire exchange. "Ishaq has feared the plague would infect his gresht but they remain unaffected despite the loss of all the other animals beyond his ranch. He attributes this to his own care, as he has not allowed anyone on his ranch other than me...until now. He was scrupulous in disinfecting anything that was brought onto his farm."

I now understood Ishaq's fear, that our presence here had sparked their disagreement. "These gresht look like a cross between a bird and a reptile."

"The gresht is an animal unique to New Mecca," bin Ibrahim explained. "And a rare one. Because it is partly a carnivore and a scavenger, the gresht was not approved for human consumption. This flock of three dozen is the only one in this region. Wild gresht are not common. They could not compete with human agriculture. These flocks were started as a measure to prevent extinction."

"May we take a closer look?" Roxanne asked.

"In a moment. To the main issue, I examined the flock and saw no evidence of disease. So I wondered if these creatures were immune to the plague. Such a thought excited me, as you can imagine."

"Sure, but are they immune?"

"I am unsure. Ishaq has a powerful electric fence that keeps out terrestrial animals, and subsonic sound barriers that keep birds away. So far, either his isolation measures have sufficed...or the gresht do not get the disease."

"We'd like to check the gresht and take samples," I said.

"They are not domesticated, and they can be aggressive and dangerous. While they are flightless, their wings and legs sport large sharp spurs. Their kick can disembowel a predator. Imagine what one could do to a veterinarian."

I peered at the gresht, my desire to examine them closely waning a bit with bin Ibrahim's description. "That's interesting, but it raises another question. What large predators exist on New Mecca?"

"None exist now. There were two species when humans first came to this planet, a lion-like beast and animals most resembling a cross between a wolf and a rat. They posed a threat to raising Terran animals, so the predators were exterminated, along with the gresht, which were seen as a dangerous pest, as well."

Roxanne frowned, and I caught her burst of anger at what amounted to the genocide of native species.

Bin Ibrahim turned to Ishaq and spoke. Ishaq replied, and the veterinarian turned to us again. "Ishaq asks if you have had contact with the plague lately."

"We've been scrupulous in decontaminating our clothing and footwear. And, as I'm sure you know, there's no evidence that humans contract the disease." My response was terse, but I was sensitive to accusations that we deliberately spread the plague.

Bin Ibrihim nodded. "For safety, Ishaq has protective garments for you to wear before approaching his animals. He would take no chances."

"Fair enough," I said.

We donned disposable coveralls, caps, boots, masks, and gloves. With provided goggles, no centimeter of our skin or hair remained uncovered. As we walked to the paddock, several gresht moved toward us. I sensed a general aura of caution from them, but also an overriding curiosity. They were used to human contact, but Roxanne and I were new, our scents unfamiliar.

One of the creatures expelled a harsh breath, a whooshing, tsking sound, and I realized where their name came from. *Gresht* was as close as a human could come to that vocalization.

The creature was unafraid and ventured close to the gate. Its shoulder stood about even with my own. A lizard-like scaled head topped a short muscular neck. Large liquid brown eyes sat above an elongated muzzle. The gresht's body was rotund and feathered, the plumage mottled gray to black, with stubby wings on each side. The legs were scaled and ostrich-like. I took particular note of two finger-length deadly spurs above each taloned foot.

"What do these things eat?" Roxanne asked.

"They are omnivores," bin Ibrahim replied, "but they are efficient predators of smaller animals, and scavengers, as I told you. Because of this adaptability, they were successful in a variety of habitats."

I asked, "How do we examine them if they're as dangerous as you say?"

"We will restrain one." He turned to Ishaq and spoke.

"I'd like to draw blood samples and take skin biopsies. Tell Ishaq that we will get immunological profiles and test skin cell cultures from them. We can know quickly if his animals are truly resistant to the plague."

After bin Ibrahim translated, Ishaq took out a comm unit and spoke into it. A few minutes later, a drone rolled toward us carrying two ranch hands protectively clad as we were. They got out and spoke with Ishaq before moving toward the gate. One lifted a keypad and punched some buttons. The gresht closest to the gate threw out its wings, squawked, and stumbled before settling to its side, head resting on the ground.

The gresht's collapse startled me. "What the hell was that?"

Bin Ibrahim explained. "Each gresht is implanted with a micro-receiver that is hooked to its neural system. The knockout impulse is quite painless and it is safer for them and us, too, but you must hurry, it will last only thirty minutes."

One ranch hand opened the gate, then the two of them each grabbed a leg and pulled the gresht out the gate. They quickly closed it, as several gresht rushed to the aid of their fallen companion. The animals milled behind the gate, voicing their peculiar cry. Their emotional auras were angry. I was glad we were outside the paddock, and I screened myself from their emotional broadcast.

"Go ahead, doctors. The red markings on his head show this is a male," bin Ibrahim said.

Both Roxanne and I approached the beast. I kneeled and examined the head. The eyes were clear, the whites not bloodshot. I opened the mouth. Not expecting an array of needle-sharp teeth in an avian-like creature, I flinched and snagged one finger on a tooth, slightly tearing one plastic glove and scratching a finger. I asked bin Ibrahim for a replacement, and donned that before continuing.

The oral mucosa showed neither lesions nor inflammation. There were slits in the side of the head that were no doubt the ears. The scales were dry and hot. I saw no skin lesions typical in plague victims.

Roxanne examined the body and had one wing outstretched. "I can't spot any signs of disease, other than a few feather parasites." She held up a black louse-like creature as big as an orange seed, before crushing it and throwing it aside. "Dr. bin Ibrahim, are these common."

"Yes, we treat the gresht for them every few months to keep the infestation down. They can carry a malaria-like blood parasite."

"What's the usual body temperature?" I asked.

"It varies. This allows them to adapt to a variety of climates."

Roxanne examined the spur on the wing. It was not as long as the leg spurs but still nasty looking.

I stood. "I don't see anything that looks like the plague."

"Nor do I," Roxanne added. "Let's collect blood and do the biopsies."

We finished, thanked bin Ibrahim and Ishaq, and headed back to our land drone as the hands returned the gresht to the corral. As I opened the door for Roxanne, I looked over the roof of the vehicle and noticed a dark cloud on the horizon.

I pointed. "Look." The black cloud was growing. "That storm is coming in fast." Strangely, there was no lightning or thunder, considering the darkness of the storm.

"Cy, that looks like a dust storm."

The cloud now blotted out half of the sky; the lower half. "It can't be a dust storm. There's no wind."

The cloud got larger and closer, and a shrill metallic buzzing sound assaulted my ears. "Oh, shit. That's no storm. Get in the drone, quick. Those are insects!" I yelled at bin Ibrahim and Ishaq. "Get under cover. It's some kind of insect swarm."

Both men looked up at the cloud, staring open-mouthed for a moment. Then they and the two hands ran for a nearby shed and scrambled inside before the swarm hit.

An astounding mass of insect-like creatures buried our land drone. The whining buzz drowned out any words coming from the driver's moving lips. I slammed my hands over my ears.

Roxanne's eyes were so wide the whites seemed to jump out from her face. She grabbed my hand and squeezed until it hurt. I put an arm around her shoulders and pulled her against me.

The windscreen and windows were covered with creatures twice the size of my thumb. Winged and eight-legged, rather than the six of an insect, they were black as midnight. The head, a third the size of the body, had serrated mandibles that could take a sizeable chunk out of anything they wanted to bite.

I banged on the window next to me, startling a

handful of the things so that they took off, allowing me a view of the barley field next to us. The plants disappeared before my eyes. In the space of scant minutes, the creatures had reduced the field to stubble, and then the swarm lifted off and flew into the next field where corn grew waist high. It did not take long for the same result. Since the swarm covered miles of territory, I assumed there was devastation to every growing thing in its path.

Roxanne peered over my shoulder. Her horror made my stomach cramp.

It took about a half hour before the creatures had denuded the local neighborhood and moved on. As I stepped out of the land drone, my feet crunched on bodies of those that had perished. I shivered at the feeling and sound.

Roxanne joined me.

The driver stayed inside shaking, his head ducked to his chest.

The gresht seemed none the worse for wear. In fact, they were prancing around their corral snarfing up the small carcasses as if they were manna from heaven.

Bin Ibrahim, Ishaq, and his employees emerged from the shed. Ishaq looked at his fields, put his hands to his head, and wailed.

His anguish cut through me.

"My God, Cy. All these people have left to eat are their crops," Roxanne said. "Now this?"

"What was that?" I asked bin Ibrahim.

His dusky face had turned gray. "These are locasts in the local language, called that because of the resemblance to the locusts of earth, but these are more akin to flying spiders."

The latter part of that description gave me the chills. I did *not* like spiders. Fur and I barely survived being trapped in the underground lair of spider-like beings on

Hiveworld.

"Local swarms are known, but I never heard of anything even approaching what happened here," bin Ibrahim added.

Roxanne said, "The animals. The birds. They're gone because of the plague. These locasts have no more predators. This devastation is only the beginning."

"The bugs didn't seem to bother that vegetation over there." I pointed to some cactus-like native plants. "Why is that?"

"The native fauna and flora have evolved with the locasts and developed their own defense mechanisms. Notice that the gresht are happily eating the dead locasts. Terran crops do not fare so well, as you saw. Let us hope this was a local phenomenon. If not, if all our crops are devastated..."

He needed to say no more.

***

When we returned to our apartment, Roxanne and I sat on the bed. Frown lines creasing her brow, she said, "Cy, I want you to know that I understand how tough this was for you. Dealing with your AI, Ruthie, was not easy. I made a flip comment about her not being your child, and I've regretted that ever since. I'm sorry. Sorry you had to take the action you did."

I reached out and placed a hand on her arm. "I'm the one who needs to apologize, Roxanne. I ignored what you were telling me...almost for too long."

Roxanne moved closer and put her arms around me. "I love you, Cy, and I don't want anything to ever come between us again."

Those words, all-too-similar to what Ruthie had spoken at the end, sent a shock through my system, and I stiffened.

Roxanne sat back, eyes narrowed. "Cy? Are you—?"

"It's okay, Roxanne, and I agree with everything you said. It's just...hard." I could never tell anyone what Ruthie had said and done, but it would haunt me to my grave. I shook off that thought and hugged my wife. I agreed, nothing would ever come between us again.

***

The next shoe that fell was more like a giant's boot. I was asleep when my comm beeped, and I fumbled for it before connecting.

"Berger here."

It was bin Ibrihim. "A whirlydrone will pick you up on the roof of your quarters. Bring Dr. Simon." He clicked off before I could even ask him what in hell he wanted. Sometimes, I wished I could pick up emotional clues over a comm system.

"Roxanne, get up. Bin Ibrahim needs us, stat. There's a whirlydrone on the roof." I moved to the lav to brush my teeth before we went.

Roxanne padded after me. "What's going on?"

"I have no idea, but he sounded grim."

Once dressed, we took the lift to the roof and climbed into a waiting drone. We took off and headed in the same direction we had taken to the gresht ranch.

The drone banked over devastated fields, and I saw Ishaq's place as we headed in for a landing outside the main building. Roxanne and I debarked and met bin Ibrahim and Ishaq, who were waiting near the building. The bare fields were like raw wounds to my eyes.

Bin Ibrahim bowed to us, but Ishaq did not. The rancher's anger assaulted me like an emotional flamethrower. Bin Ibrahim's face was a mask of anguish, with deep furrows above his hooked nose. "Dr.

Berger, Dr. Simon, please follow me."

I did not at all like the tone of his voice. When we reached the pens, what struck me immediately was the difference in the gresht. A half dozen stood at one end of the enclosure, heads down, breathing hard. As I walked closer, I saw the telltale characteristic skin lesions of the plague. Panic stabbed my chest like a knife blade. I turned to the veterinarian. "When?"

"One bird early this morning. Others quickly became ill. Another since I called you."

"How? How did they get infected? Were there any changes in procedures? Anything new happen on the farm?"

Roxanne sidled up to the fence, within a couple of meters of one sick bird that ignored her.

Bin Ibrahim looked me straight in the eyes. "No one new...except you and Dr. Simon. The first to become ill was the one you examined."

His glare brought back every charge thrown at us since we came to New Mecca, that the *GCVS* crew was the disseminator of the plague. I recalled Ishaq's fear of us the previous day. I tried to thrust away those fears and accusations.

"You can't believe we..." My breath caught in my throat. "The locasts," I said. "They're spreading the plague."

Thousands of dead insectile bodies still littered the ground.

"Cy, the disease affects vertebrates only." Roxanne bent and picked up a locast, examined it closely. "No lesions." She cracked it open like a peanut. Perfect organs spilled out. "Nothing internal, either." She dropped both pieces and brushed her hands together.

My denial vanished with her words as the epiphany hit me between the eyes. I staggered.

"Cy, what is it?" Roxanne stood before me, her eyes

wide.

I shook my head, unable to bring words to my mouth. Nausea rolled through me and pain behind my eyes dropped me to one knee.

"Cy, what's wrong?"

I looked up at bin Ibrahim as I caught my breath. "Dr. bin Ibrihim, if we were the only variable, then I must do more tests. We need to go back to our ship."

Bin Ibrahim's face remained frozen. A vision of a torn glove lanced from his mind to mine. He was convinced the infection of the gresht was my doing, and his anger slashed at my psyche. If what I suspected was true, his fury was justified. I had quailed at taking the life of an artificial intelligence, but doing that was a walk in the park compared to what I faced now.

Chapter 19

Fur, Aypari, and Roxanne sat with me in the *GCVS* commissary. We had moved back into the ship. I was uncomfortable, considering my last experience aboard, and I kept waiting for Ruthie's sultry voice to break into our conversation.

Roxanne explained what we had seen at the gresht ranch, and then turned to me. "Okay, what in hell happened back there? You've been shut up like a clam since. You can't believe that bin Ibrihim was accusing *us* of spreading the plague."

My heart rate had not come down much since we left the ranch, and my blood pressure was close to the point where it would steam my inner clam. I did not know where or how to begin. I looked at Aypari. "How much do you know about my empathic talent? I told Fur to fill you in."

She smiled. "And he did."

"Good. I'm hurting right now, so I need to get on with this. When we first encountered the plague, I detected the organism empathically. Of course, a microorganism can have no emotions, so how could I sense it? That remained a puzzle. Since then I haven't felt...right."

"What?" Roxanne's eyebrows went up. "You never said anything."

"I've been in a constant state of nausea. I wrote that off to all the things I've been through, getting blown up twice, almost losing my leg. Then a couple of things happened that disturbed me, although I consciously did not—*would not*—admit what it meant. The first spread of the plague outside the main quarantine region happened in Aswan, the city that I visited first."

"Come on, Cy," Fur exclaimed. "That can't—"

I put up a hand toward him. "Let me finish.*"*

Fur put a protective arm around Aypari. Maybe everyone *did* need protection from me.

"Like you, I rejected that idea. I didn't learn until later that the next two cities hit with the plague were those that I also stopped at. I visited farms and examined animals in all three places."

Roxanne grimaced and put her cup on the table, as if the coffee had become unpalatable.

"In the desert there was a family of little rodent creatures that came out at night..." I told them about the Mickeys and what had happened to them. "Those little critters got the plague. I couldn't understand how it had reached that desert canyon. Now I know *I* was the one who brought it there."

Disbelief masked the faces of my companions, but they kept their mouths shut, thankfully. Fighting through their emotional turmoil was hard enough.

"I went through all the other possibilities, mainly birds leaving the infected zones and dropping in on them. After my rescue, I convinced myself that it was all a hallucination. *Mickey Mouse*, for crying out loud? I was too embarrassed to tell the story."

I sensed Aypari's puzzlement.

"Fur, fill Aypari in about my reading books and watching vids from Old Earth. Show her a Mickey Mouse cartoon."

He smiled and nodded.

"But those events stuck in the back of my mind and came to the fore today. The gresht were the last straw. The rancher's efforts had kept out the plague until I showed up. Now I know why I haven't felt well since we first examined the sick camels. Somehow, I caught the plague. *I'm* the vector. Typhoid Cy."

I sensed that no one other than Roxanne understood the last allusion, but I let it ride.

Everyone spoke at once. "That's ridiculous." "Can't be." "Are you nuts?"

I ignored them. I knew I was right. It *felt* right.

When everyone wound down, I said, "That could also solve one of the biggest conundrums of this damned epidemic. How could Chaim McNulty carry the plague to New Mecca if the pathogen self-destructs within seconds after removal from a living cell? He said it was in vials in a solution that looked and smelled like water. My guess? It *was* water. The plague organism was in Chaim. *He* was the vector."

"Hold on," Roxanne exclaimed. "If you two are infected, then why don't other people get infected? And why didn't you and Chaim get sick and die?"

"I don't have all the answers. That's what we have to learn in order to—"

Fur broke in. "We don't *know* any of this is true. It's all speculation."

"Yeah, but I can tell you it's correct. There are times when I just know things—maybe that's part of my empathic talent—and I feel this down to my bones."

Aypari spoke. "Cy, we can test this. We take your blood and inoculate some cultures, see if the cells develop the plague."

"I agree. In the meantime, I stay away from Learns-To-Fix-Injuries. We consider the entire ship contaminated except for his isolation area."

Roxanne nodded. "We'll take care of Red."

"I suppose I should be relieved that there are no more species left on New Mecca for me to infect, besides our dragon." I tried to make light of the situation, but another cramp hit my stomach and my head ached abominably. "Let's get to the lab and resolve this."

If it proved out as I feared, every person on this planet would seek to flay me.

***

No surprise, my blood passed the disease to cell cultures. I carried the plague.

"What now?" Fur avoided meeting my eyes. Not because of any fear or loathing toward me as a plague carrier, but because he felt for me so deeply. His concern was like a cat scratching at the door to get in.

"It's time I speak with Chaim," I said.

"*We,*" Roxanne corrected me. She was still protective of the former Test-Lit, and that fact might help convert him over to our side.

Fur nodded. "Aypari and I will analyze your blood. You must have an immune response to the plague that protects you."

"Maybe so, but Chaim would be the same. We'll need to get samples from him," Roxanne said.

"Okay, we are off to see Chaim." I rose and headed toward the ramp, thumbing my comm to call Ali's headquarters for a drone.

***

An armed guard accompanied Chaim as he shuffled

down a hall, favoring his wounded leg. He knew from the look of his arms and legs, and the way his clothing hung on him, that torture and starvation had left him gaunt. When he was ushered into a small wood-floored room, bare but for several wooden chairs and a table, two persons greeted him. His heart leapt to his mouth.

Dr. Simon. Roxanne.

Her beauty was as he remembered it. She seemed to glow with an inner light as she smiled at him, and he felt his cheeks flush.

"Good morning, Chaim. This is my husband, Dr. Cy Berger."

Chaim nodded to Berger, unable to risk speech, afraid to stumble over his tongue. The man was tall and Chaim had to look up at his face.

Berger nodded and Chaim felt a surge of hostility from the man.

"Please sit," Simon said.

She and Berger took chairs. Simon was almost as tall as Berger, but, somehow, Chaim never recalled that. He felt *himself* taller in her presence. He sat as instructed, facing them.

"How are you feeling? How are your arm and leg?" she asked him.

Berger looked at Simon, eyebrows raised, lips twisted as if he thought she had gone crazy. Chaim sensed that the man thought Chaim looked horrible.

"I...I am better, thank you. The wounds...heal." Everything improved without torture.

"Good. We have some questions for you." She turned to Berger and nodded.

Chaim stared at Berger's face. He, too, was gaunt. The veterinarian's mouth was thin-lipped and tight. A sharp hawk's nose thrust like a blade from beneath steel gray eyes and red-brown hair. Berger's clean-shaven face contrasted to Chaim's unruly, matted beard, and he worried that his unkempt condition might disgust Simon. Chaim looked away.

Berger spoke. "Tell me how you came to New Mecca and how you spread the plague."

The anger beneath the man's words roiled Chaim's stomach. *Why do I feel Berger's emotions as if they are my own?*

He related the story of his trip, the vials he had smuggled in and spilled onto goat, sheep, and camel fodder. "I would take it back if I could."

Berger's eyebrows scrolled together, as if he were in pain. The man shook his head. "Before that. Where did you get the vials?"

The same questions that Hussein had tortured him to answer. What would *this* man do when Chaim refused to give in? He straightened his back and lifted his chin. "I may be a terrorist, and I may have caused the deaths of millions of animals, but I cannot give my colleagues up to torture. Harming them will not bring back any lives but only cause more pain and suffering."

Chaim watched Berger's eyebrows rise. *Surprised, is he? He will prevail no more than the beast Hussein.*

Berger leaned toward him, his eyes smoldering. Chaim *sensed* the hate that flowed off the man like a sullen, crimson miasma. "Why you little—"

Chaim had never experienced anything like these emotions. He flinched back, away from the vitriol surging toward him.

"Cy! Stop." Dr. Simon's voice cut through the room like an explosion.

Berger jerked back and looked at his wife.

"Chaim isn't our enemy. He wants to help." She turned to Chaim. "That's correct, you want to help, right?"

Chaim could deny this woman nothing. She had saved him twice...more times, considering he was not being tried, convicted, and sentenced to death right now. "I want to do what I can to help. I never meant for a disaster on such a scale."

Dr. Simon cast a serious gaze at him. "If we don't find a cure for this disease, Chaim, *people* will die of starvation, not only here but across the galaxy. We need your knowledge."

"My contacts on New Mecca know nothing of the disease. I brought it here. Giving you their names will not help."

Berger snorted. "Forget about the accomplices. I want to know where you got the plague, how it was given to you."

I suppose that is a reasonable question. It is fair if I say nothing of where, just how. "I was asked if I was willing to undertake an important mission for my party. They told me it might be dangerous, but I would be advancing the Testamentary-Literalist goals. My act would spread confusion and strike a blow against our ancient enemy, Islam."

I knew only my party's view of Islam. That they had murdered Jews and driven the true religion from earth more than a millennium ago. They said that our God, Yahweh, *demanded that we take action, begin once again our Holy War to return to our rightful place in the cosmos.*

Simon put a restraining hand on Berger's arm, allowing Chaim the time to think.

But he had found that New Meccan Muslims were not the fiends the Test-Lits painted them as. There were evil men among them, like Hussein and his torturer, Vash, but since his rescue, no one had harmed Chaim further. Several of the guards had asked him about his life, why he had done what he did, trying honestly to understand him. Their leader, Ali Suliaman, seemed kind and wise. He had interrogated Chaim, but not threatened him at all. No, not fiends, they were no different from any group of people, a mixture of good and bad.

He finally pulled himself away from his musings. "I was brought to a medical facility. There I was told what I was to do, told that the disease I was to release would make animals sick. This would disrupt the economy of New Mecca. Weaken them, divide them, and drive them to civil war."

"They were dead right," Berger said.

"I was to act as a soldier in the next Holy War." He hung his head and tears leaked from his eyes. "I did not know what would happen, that this plague would kill every animal on the planet."

Simon's voice was gentle when she spoke again. "What did they do to you, other than give you the vials to carry?"

"They gave me inoculations against diseases that infected the heathen worlds of our galaxy. They kept me isolated and took blood and tissue samples for weeks. To ensure I was protected, they said. Then I left, carrying the accursed vials."

Simon leaned toward Berger and whispered something into his ear, and he whispered back. She stared at Chaim for long moments. He sensed her concern for him. "Chaim, we need to run some tests on you. Will that be all right?"

He flinched. *Test me? What now?* He thrust back panic. *But I trust Dr. Simon. Roxanne. She will not harm me.* "Whatever is necessary." His voice shook.

***

Days later, in the same meeting room, Chaim felt that Berger was less angry, less wound like a spring at the limits of its compression. How he could tell this confused him. He had never had such insights about someone before.

Shafts of sunlight slanted through a large window, illuminating squares of polished wood floor. Chaim stared at the squares as Berger questioned him across the small table.

"Chaim, this is going to be difficult, but hear me out so you can understand."

Chaim's heart thudded as he looked up at Berger's solemn face. "Difficult how?"

"The people who said they were immunizing you against diseases...they did no such thing. They were categorizing your physiology, your biochemistry, your DNA."

Chaim had no understanding of what those words meant. He shook his head in incomprehension.

Berger narrowed his eyes as he peered at Chaim, as if he could look into his body, his brain. "You don't understand, do you?"

He looked at Simon then back at Chaim. "We think the people who sent you studied you to find a way transport a new disease, one that wouldn't harm you or any other humans, but would harm animals. Chaim, you carried the plague inside you. The vials were a sham. The plague organism can't survive outside a living body. You carried the plague in your cells."

Chaim sat for long moments without reacting. Slowly, like cold honey trickling downward into a cup of hot tea, the words, the import sank in. He said nothing. He felt his eyes roll upwards, and blackness overtook him.

***

My head sank to my chest and I groaned as I looked at my wife. "Now *that* does us a lot of good."

Chaim slumped in his chair and was about to fall over, but the guard was alert and caught the man. He propped him up and looked at us as if awaiting instructions.

Roxanne said, "Cy, the guy is a wreck, and you just informed him he is infected with the plague? What in hell did you expect?"

"Did he have to faint?"

"That knowledge knocked you to your knees."

That brought me up short. Okay, I suppose I had to cut the guy some slack, but I still saw him as the cause of New Mecca's disaster and the source of hatred toward all Jews, whether he knew what he was doing or not. That plus remembering his attack on Roxanne and Fur never failed to raise my blood pressure.

Roxanne moved to Chaim's side and lifted an eyelid. She looked at the guard. "Please return him to his quarters. We'll be back later."

The guard nodded and spoke into his comm unit. He needed help carrying the unconscious Test-Lit to wherever they had him stashed.

My comm flashed a message to go straight to a meeting with Ali. This was not something that I relished, but Ali must be told of what we had learned. As much as I dreaded it, I had asked for Dr. bin Ibrihim's and the rancher, Ishaq's, presence. I had to own up to the fact that I *was* responsible for the spread of the plague, no matter how unwittingly. The entire planet would be out for my blood if this became general knowledge.

***

Ali sat in an office in downtown Ammad. The room had wood paneled walls and a large wooden desk. Brown padded chairs faced the desk behind which Ali sat. Bin Ibrihim occupied one of those chairs, Ishaq another. Roxanne and I greeted everyone and took two empty wooden chairs.

"You requested a meeting, Dr. Berger, but after hearing Dr. bin Ibrihim's report, I would have called you in myself."

"I'm here to explain."

"By all means." Ali's emotions, which had always been friendly toward us were now guarded, not outright hostile, but awaiting my explanation.

The emotional tension in the room almost overwhelmed me. My head pounded. I feared I'd throw up on his desk.

"I don't have good news, Imam. We learned new things about how the plague has spread." My mouth was dry, my voice raspy. I licked my lips. "Dr. bin Ibrihim suspects that Dr. Simon and I brought the plague to the gresht ranch. I'm afraid he is correct, about me, anyway."

Bin Ibrihim came halfway out of his seat, but Ali waved him back. My mental screen was at full, but the New Meccan veterinarian's searing anger leapt through, wrenching my gut into a knot.

"Continue, please," Ali said.

I explained what we had learned about Chaim and me from our microbiological examinations. "The Test-Lit scientists who created this plague infected McNulty and sent him off to spread their disease. His vials were a fiction. We always were puzzled how he could have brought the disease with him since the organism dies shortly after the death of the host that harbored it."

Bin Ibrihim asked, "How is it that he is not ill...or you? And are there any other humans who are similarly affected?" His disgust came through in his voice.

Ishaq sat quietly, clearly not understanding Common.

"We don't yet know the logistics, but we believe it's a genetically-engineered pathogen. I presume that the Test-Lits tailored it so that they could infect Chaim, make him a carrier, but so that he would not succumb to the disease himself. How they did that we don't know. Why did I become infected here on New Mecca, and not become ill? Again, unknown. Are there more people affected? We need to find out."

Roxanne added, "We suggest sampling the population, target people who have had contact with sick animals...like Dr. bin Ibrihim and Mr. Ishaq."

Ali frowned, lips thinned. "Why did this disease not appear on other worlds McNulty traveled?"

"He transferred to new ships on several worlds, but he never left the spaceports and he came in contact with no animals," Roxanne answered. "That's why I'm convinced that most other humans aren't infected. The disease would already have spread through the galaxy if they were."

"Where did he become infected?"

"He won't say."

Ali nodded. "For now, I am asking that all who have this knowledge be silent. If this were to reach people even as a rumor, the consequences would be dire. Drs. Berger and Simon are innocent of bringing the disease *to* New Mecca, and do not deserve further insult. Our war against Hussein is enough turmoil. Dr. bin Ibrihim, I ask that you work with Dr. Berger's team to learn the answers to our questions and report back to me."

Ali spoke to Ishaq in Arabic for a few minutes. Ishaq's face went through a range of expressions from incredulity to rage. He looked at me with sullen eyes, but nodded to Ali, and spoke in Arabic. I assumed that he agreed to the silence.

I added, "We need McNulty to divulge where he

came from. In order to defeat this thing, we need to understand its genetics if we are to prepare a vaccine or find a cure. That could mean going to whatever planet has the data."

"Rest assured, Imam," Roxanne said, "we won't rest until we have solved this problem."

Ali's eyes bored into my skull. "I hope that the trust we have placed in you is justified, Dr. Berger." For once, Ali's emotions leaked. If we did not justify that trust, we would be held accountable, and likely would never leave New Mecca.

Chapter 20

"That's it," Fur said. His mouth turned down at the corners as he placed his coffee cup on the *GCVS* commissary table. "You and McNulty are infected, but no one else we've checked."

Aypari added, "I contacted Dr. bin Ibrahim and other medical officials. Using the culture diagnostics, they found no other human infections."

"Why? Why in hell can there only be two of us infected when so many more were exposed." I stared into a cup of herbal tea—easier on my stomach than coffee—as if I could read the answer in the leaves. "We're missing something. We need to talk with Chaim again."

Fur huffed. "I doubt he'll tell you any more than he already has."

Roxanne added, "He was a victim of the Test-Lits as much as anyone. I can use that angle on him."

My stomach soured at the thought. I still hated the son-of-a-bitch for what he had done, but we needed him to solve this conundrum. I would swallow my anger and pride, and plead with the guy if necessary. My fate, and the fate of my crew, hung in the balance, not to mention all of New Mecca...and every animal in the galaxy if the plague ever got off-world.

***

Chaim's jailers brought him into the same room we had met in before. We sat across the table from him. The windows now gave inadequate light in the waning day, and the ceiling glow lights made everyone look wan, but I thought he looked a bit better than the last time. The black circles beneath his eyes remained, though the eyes had a bit more spark. Both guilt and anger leaked from him, but I kept my screen at maximum. For some reason, the man's emotions hit me harder than any other person's.

We nodded to each other, and he spoke first. "Dr. Berger. Dr. Simon. I have thought much about what you revealed at our last meeting. I now understand what was done to me."

"You were a victim of the Test-Lit villainy as much as we were." Roxanne smiled at him.

He stared at my wife with wide eyes. His adoration curdled my stomach. He then flushed and ducked his head. Embarrassment poured from him like a river.

Roxanne stood and walked around the table that separated us and placed a hand on his shoulder. "We're in this mess together."

He looked up at her like a goddamned simpering puppy. What in hell was going on? I felt a flash of...what, jealousy? Me jealous of Chaim McNulty?

My voice grated. "We need information and you damn well better give it to us."

Roxanne rounded on me, eyes flashing emerald, always a bad sign. "Keep it civil, Cy. Chaim wants to help us." She turned to him and leaned close. "Right,

Chaim?"

His head bobbed up and down a few times.

A new round of bombing hit the city. I heard explosions off in the distance. This had become an everyday occurrence, something I noticed but kept in the back of my mind. I tried to ignore the concussions as Roxanne shot me a look, which transmuted into a vision: *Honey and vinegar. Flies hovering over the former.* I understood her meaning, but the increase in the graphic visions I received disturbed me.

I shrugged that off and kept my voice civil. "Help us, Chaim. Who did this to you...and where?"

He shook his head. "They did not tell me they were infecting me with the disease. I thought I carried it in my case." He shook his head. "I thought I was fighting in a Holy War."

"That doesn't answer my question." I clamped down on my anger and frustration, but Chaim cringed as if I hit him with my fist.

"I cannot tell you. There has been enough killing."

"It's only just beginning, Chaim. There will be war if we don't solve this. Every Muslim in the galaxy is going to blame Jews for what has happened here. If we do nothing, the galactic conflict will suck in not only Jews and Muslims but every other human and alien species. This plague will eventually get off New Mecca and spread to other worlds. Every vertebrate animal will be wiped out...and billions of humans will starve. You people have no idea what you have unleashed." My voice rose as I spoke.

"Enough, Cy," Roxanne said. She turned back to Chaim. "Do you want your friends and family to suffer this fate?"

He shook his head.

"Innocents will die. But whoever created the plague is not innocent, right?" Roxanne's voice was soft, cajoling.

I took deep breaths to keep my rage under control. Chaim leaned away from me as if my emotions battered him physically. His internal horror at my doomsday predictions had him shaking. His fear, and *his* vision of starving bodies littering the streets, stunned *me* in return. I stepped back from him, as if distance might negate this bizarre connection between us.

His voice trembled. "There was a...facility in the mountains. Isolated. Many guards. That is where they took me. They showed me the laboratories, the animals they studied. But I didn't understand. I have no training. I just wanted to help." He hung his head.

"Help us now," Roxanne said in almost a whisper.

He looked up at her standing by his side. "I was taught from childhood that the Testamentary-Literalist interpretation of the Torah was the true Judaism. Since childhood..."

"Brainwashed," I muttered.

"Chaim," Roxanne spoke in a low soothing voice, "knowing what you do now, are you willing to help us fight back against those who wronged you?"

He looked at her with widened, fear-filled eyes, but something else besides. I felt *love*. "I...I cannot betray my world, to have it destroyed in retribution. To have more deaths staining my soul..." He stopped with a sob.

I wanted to lash out, beat him for his stubborn refusal to help. But more. I hated him because of the way he looked at my wife.

Roxanne sighed. "We don't want to harm your world, Chaim, but we must learn where this plague came from and who created it to learn how to fight it. The galaxy faces war and starvation otherwise. We need the information in that laboratory: the genetic code for the disease, its DNA or RNA structure. You're the only one who knows where we can find that."

Chaim's eyes glazed over, and I felt his incomprehension.

I thrust aside my anger and interrupted. "We can explain that to you later, but if we don't find this information, the galaxy *will* be devastated. That includes every Jewish world, including your own. You must help us, Chaim. Please."

I sensed Chaim's surprise at my final word, by the absence of any threat.

Roxanne knelt by his chair, placed her hand on his arm and repeated, "Please."

Chaim gazed in adoration at her. Then he looked at me. Fear, anger, hatred, and guilt all rolled out of him, a miasmal cloud that tore into my stomach and my head. Had I been standing, it would have knocked me off my feet.

I must have groaned, because Roxanne turned sharply toward me. "Cy?"

I put up a hand, not able to speak. She did not know how much this man affected me. Chaim, too, was upset, his face pale, lips pursed as if fighting the same nausea. He reacted to *me. S*ome sort of feedback loop encompassed both of us.

I waved at her to continue. The bombs landed closer.

She smiled at Chaim, softening the pressure on him with an attempt at familiarity. "You, Cy, and I have something in common, Chaim. We are all Jewish, but McNulty is not a Jewish name. Is that your real name?"

Chaim hung his head. "No." His face colored. "I...I thought...my name should not sound Jewish...to protect me on New Mecca."

Roxanne leaned closer. "What is your Jewish name?"

"Khodorkosovitch.   Chaim   Abraham Khodorkosovitch."

The shock that ran through my system shot me bolt upright in my chair. "What did you say?"

He looked up at me, eyes smoldering with defiance. He saw my disbelief. "Chaim Abraham Khodorkosovitch."

"No. It...it can't be."

I felt Roxanne's puzzlement. I could only imagine what my face looked like, but she was by my side in an instant. "Cy, what's wrong? What does his name have to do with anything?"

I stood and turned away from both of them, trying to control my racing heart. After a moment, I swung back to Chaim. "Your family line. I want your family line. Who was your mother, your father, your grandparents, great grandparents?"

"I don't understand." Chaim shook his head as if my demand shocked him. His emotions writhed with befuddlement.

"Cy, stop!" Roxanne grabbed my arm. "What's wrong with you?"

"His name. Khodorkosovitch. Have you ever heard it before?"

She shook her head.

"No, of course not. There is a *single* lineage of Khodorkosovitchs in the galaxy. Only one man left earth, carried that name, and helped settle many Jewish worlds. He didn't stay long on any of them. They say he knocked up a woman or two and moved on. But he's legendary."

"So why is this so important?" Roxanne's voice rose along with mine.

"Important?" I yelled. "Because my maternal grandmother's name was Khodorkosovitch. Because *I'm* a Khodorkosovitch. This *schmuck* is my *relative.*"

As if to cap off my outburst of rage, a blast outside the building deafened me, and the window blew in. I could hear nothing but ringing in my ears, but I saw Roxanne's mouth move. Both of Chaim's guards disappeared out the door to our room, leaving the three of us alone.

I put my mouth close to Roxanne's ear and yelled, "We've got to get out of here."

She nodded, grabbed Chaim's arm, and headed for the door.

Not him, I screamed silently. Leave the son-of-a-bitch here. But she was out the door, not that she would have heard me, or listened to me, anyway. I did not think I could have detested that man more than I already did, but he had given my hatred renewed vigor. My fucking *relative*.

I chased after Roxanne.

***

A bomb had hit the building across the street from us. The road swarmed with arriving ambulances that spilled out paramedics like ants at a picnic. No guards were in sight, other than those involved in the rescue operations.

Roxanne turned to me and shouted, "Back to the ship."

I did not know if my humongous headache was due to the explosion, or to the emotional bombshell Chaim had dropped on me. I gritted my teeth. "What do we do with him?" I motioned to Chaim with my head, a mistake, as pain exploded behind my eyes.

She looked around. "We take him with us."

"What? He's a prisoner. We can't just—"

"We have to. We can't turn him loose."

I supposed she was right, but that did not make it sit any better with me. We started walking, limping in my case, stumbling in Chaim's, and I tried to reach Fur by comm. I finally got through after several blocks. By that time, both Roxanne and I supported McNulty on opposite sides. I *refused* to think of him as Khodorkosovitch.

We stopped and waited. A few minutes later, a land drone pulled up and Fur hopped out. One look at Chaim raised Fur's eyebrows almost to his hairline.

"Get us out of here," I said and climbed into the rear seat.

"What's he doing here?" Fur asked.

"Long story." I sat back and simmered as Roxanne answered Fur.

When we got back to the ship, I excused myself to my quarters and tried to come to grips with Chaim's revelation. When I returned to the commissary, my crew sat with drinks of one sort or another. Fur handed me a beer, a rare commodity on New Mecca. I recalled Abu Khayr's *medicinal* booze in the crashed flyer, but thrust that thought away. Too painful.

"I left Chaim in the guest quarters," Roxanne said. "Locked," she added before I could ask.

I took a hefty swig of the weak but welcome brew. "What now? We just kidnapped the highest profile prisoner on the planet. Any encores?"

"Yeah." Fur turned to Aypari and nodded.

"It is the chelation therapy. With high enough doses of a new chelating agent we have devised, we can bring the plague to a halt in animals in which the damage is not already fatal."

"That's fantastic, Aypari."

She held up a hand, however. "It is not all good, I am afraid. The chelation therapy needs large doses that have deleterious side effects. We presume its action against the plague somehow relates to removing iron from the blood. Recall that we saw excess iron in victims. On the negative side, the therapy is also removing other essential elements, some metals, but also calcium. That has led to lowered blood calcium levels with disruption of metabolic functions and even cardiac arrest. We've also seen renal damage from excretion of the metal-chelate complexes in the urine."

I grimaced. "Do all patients have the side effects?"

Fur responded. "To some degree. It depends on how far the disease has progressed. And the chelating agent isn't a cure, it must be continued long-term. It's not suitable for treatment of herds, but individuals can be saved...at least in the short-term."

Aypari continued. "My group is working hard on developing modifications of the chelating agent with reduced toxicity."

"Congratulations, Aypari. Anyone have any thoughts on the high iron levels? I'm puzzled as to where it comes from and why removing it would impact the plague."

I got stares as blank as my own brain on that one.

***

Roxanne and I sat with Chaim in his quarters. I had a go at him first. "Another human is affected by the plague." Perhaps not the kindest wording, but I felt no mercy toward the *putz*.

His angst nearly blew out my screen. He dropped his head and covered his face with his hands. "Oy, oy, oy. What have I done?" He looked up at Roxanne, then at me. "I am killing humans now?" He dropped his head again. "God will surely forsake me."

Roxanne gave me a disgusted look. "No. Chaim, you have not killed humans."

"At least not directly," I muttered.

Roxanne shot me another warning glance. I knew she was trying to set the stage, to gain his confidence so that he would tell us where he came from, where we could go to find the plague's source.

"Chaim, there are only two humans who we know are infected."

His relief was almost tangible. "Thank God," he breathed. "Is the other...alive?"

I jumped in before Roxanne could respond. Less painful if I said it myself. "I'm the other person, and I'm very much alive. And I spread the plague...like you." It did not matter how many times I said it to myself, it still tormented me; my head rang off-key like a cracked bell.

Chaim's jaw dropped, and he stared at me, his eyes showing mostly whites. "*You?*"

"Yeah, me. And we need to find out why you and I are carriers." I could not resist adding, "We rescued you to help us figure this out. Not because we have any love for you."

"Cy." Roxanne's voice was a steel-spiked whip. Her fury did not need any other words.

I held up my hands toward her, palms forward then sat back and clamped my lips shut.

"We need to understand why you two are infected, yet remain healthy. We need to run tests, Chaim, to learn what we can about the disease. Will you help us with that much?"

My wife's tactic was smart: don't ask him to give up any colleagues or his world. I would have beaten the guy to within an inch of his life and gotten nothing from him. I could not get past my hatred.

"When the Test-Lits first injected you with the plague did you ever get sick?" Again, smart. She cast the Test-Lits as the bad guys, the ones who abused Chaim's trust.

"I was never ill, like the flu, but ever since then I have not felt...well."

"How so?"

"I am nauseous all the time. It never goes away. But that is because of the horrible things I had to do. Because I was so scared."

I bolted out of my chair, grabbed Chaim's arm, albeit gently, and turned him toward me.

"Cy..." Roxanne's voice warned me.

"Hold on." I put out my other hand out toward my wife. "When did this nausea start?"

He looked down at my hand, and I caught a stab of anger and a surprising strength of will. Startled, I removed it.

"It started right after I received the injections."

"And it's constant? Sort of a low-level queasiness? Usually not enough to throw up?"

Chaim nodded to me, his eyes wide. "Yes, that is what I feel."

I sat and met Roxanne's gaze. "We were wrong. Humans are not unaffected."

"What are you talking about?" Her confusion was as bad as Chaim's now.

"The nausea. Me, too. Since the first day we came in contact with the plague I've been dealing with the same thing, sick to my stomach constantly. I told you about that. I thought it related to stress, with all my injuries piled on top."

"Are you saying that the nausea you both feel is plague-related?"

"It makes sense."

My body *told* me it made sense.

***

Our entire contingent sat in the *GCVS* commissary with all attention focused on me. I sipped at a cup of herbal tea to soothe my stomach, but my gut writhed like an eel in a net as I filled Fur and Aypari in on my family background—and Chaim's.

Fur's glance bounced back and forth between me and Chaim. "Not much resemblance." He grinned. "You have his nose beat by a long way, but he has a nice beard."

Not many people could get away with commenting on my nose, but Fur knew the whole *Cyrano de Bergerac* story, and there was no malice involved.

"There's nothing funny about this." I gave Fur a withering look—although he did not seem withered by it—and continued. "Chaim and I are distant cousins, and so far as we know, we are the only humans who are infected. The Khodorkosovitch genes are the common denominator. That can't be a coincidence. We both must have a genetic susceptibility to carry the disease but not succumb. There must be a common gene or group of genes that make us carriers."

"We're running full genomic scans on Cy and Chaim," Roxanne said, "but it won't be easy to detect a specific trait on the background of twenty-five thousand genes. If we *can* identify the specific genes that allow infection, maybe those genes also produce protective molecules that prevent Cy and Chaim from becoming sicker."

I had also revealed the nugget that Chaim and I actually were ill, though to a minimal degree.

"If we could find such protective molecules, it would give us another way to attack the plague besides chelation," Roxanne added.

"I'll work on the genomic scans." Fur grimaced. "I must admit it was easier when we had Ruthie to—" He snapped his mouth shut when both Roxanne and I fixed him with glares. He ducked his head and stood. "I'll get right on it."

The meeting broke up. Roxanne took Chaim's arm

and led him away. I would not let him have free run of the ship, and we kept him confined in his quarters unless someone accompanied him. I headed back to our stateroom.

When Roxanne returned, she sat on one of our room's two chairs.

I sat on the bed. "You realize the shit is going to hit the fan when they realize Chaim is missing and that we have him, right?"

"I've worried about that, but I'm not sorry we did it." She looked at me defiantly.

I shook my head. "We've got to let Ali know. Convince him that this is for the best for now. Otherwise, we'll all get thrown behind bars."

Roxanne nodded. "I'll talk with Ali."

Maybe that was best. Her diplomatic skills far exceeded mine.

She gazed at me for long moments. "There's something else, isn't there."

"Yeah. My empathic talent has changed. I still perceive emotions, but they're stronger now, and they affect me more. My mental screen is also stronger so I can remain functional, but it's been tough. You know how I sometimes perceive strong emotions as visions. That's progressed as well. I get those visions much more frequently, even when they're *not* accompanied by powerful feelings."

She said nothing, but I *felt* a question forming in her brain.

"Hold on. Like now, I knew you were going to say something. I don't know what, but I sensed it was a question."

She shook her head as if to clear her thoughts. "Are you saying you're becoming a telepath? That you're starting to read minds?"

"Oh God, I hope not." I looked down at my feet.

"Other people will see me as some kind of monster, invading their thoughts."

"Cy, you are not a monster." She sat by me, took my hand in hers. "You've never used your talent for anything but good."

"I've always been able to reach into the minds of animals to soothe them. As I get stronger, I'm afraid that I'll develop that power with people. I...I don't want to have that kind of power, Roxanne." I found it hard to breathe.

She squeezed my hand. "Slow down, Cy. Have you developed that or not?"

"I don't know. I've been afraid to try, to find out. How could I justify going into someone's mind? It's the worst personal violation I can imagine. With animals, it's one thing. With humans...?"

Roxanne pursed her lips. "Then try. Now, on me."

My throat closed. I forced a swallow past the lump. "I...can't do that. I mean—"

"I'm giving you my permission. I love you, and I trust you. You won't do anything to harm me. You have got to understand your powers."

She was right. I had to understand it myself. I might do damage unwittingly if I could not control my ability.

I locked my eyes on hers, imagined she was an animal, a sleek and beautiful lioness. I...reached, saw love, concern, fear. I stroked the fear, as I would have in a lioness, to soothe.

Roxanne gasped, and I pulled away violently, falling to my back on the bed. Eyes closed, I tried to shut down my brain, as well, before it exploded.

"Cy. I...I *felt* you. I sensed you in there, in my mind."

I sat up. "I'm sorry, I'm sorry, I'm sorry..." The lump in my throat grew to a boulder, stopping the words. I had invaded my wife's mind. Violated her.

God help me.

Roxanne put her arms around me. I dropped my head to her shoulder. My body trembled.

"Shh. You did me no harm, my love. What I felt was...good. I don't have a word for it, but you eased my fear."

I lifted my head and gazed at her. Never did I love her more than now. She had opened her mind to me, heedless of potential consequences, so that I could learn the depth of my own powers. I had no words to express what I felt. I held her tight.

"When did this start, Cy? When did you first notice it?"

"After we came to New Mecca."

"Before or after we examined the plague-ridden camels?"

"After." With that word, a nasty beast took form in my belly, a tearing creature that threatened to rip me apart from the inside.

Roxanne voiced the thought that raised the beast that threatened my sanity.

Her face was pale as she spoke, her green eyes troubled. "Is it possible that they're connected? That the plague has somehow strengthened your empathic talent?"

"How could that be possible?" The beast had crawled inside my skull and clawed to get out.

She was silent for many moments, then her eyes widened. "Chaim. We need to talk with Chaim. See if the plague has affected him in any way besides the constant nausea. Come on." She grabbed my arm and dragged me after her as she moved to the cabin door.

I already knew the answer. I'd seen his reactions to my emotions. Chaim was just like me and I hated him all the more for it.

Chapter 21

Chaim's eyes scanned the spaceship's cabin and its contents for the thousandth time. He had a bunk, on which he sat, a lavatory complete with sonic toothbrush and a sonic body cleaner, one chair that converted to an acceleration couch, and a large plasma screen. Even a mirror, though he avoided looking at his emaciated reflection.

A local newscast played on the screen. A translation to Common ran in a banner across the bottom.

Though tiny, with little more than enough room for the bunk and chair, the room was a vast improvement on Hussein's prison cell. Chaim quailed as his mind flashed back to Hussein and his torturer, but he thrust that thought away. His current jailers did not torture him. Simon showed him kindness, though Berger hated him, poured his anger on him like a stream of vitriol.

Chaim sighed. He deserved nothing less for what he had done. *I can't blame the man. I almost killed his wife, and my Test-Lit partners did kill his friends. It would be better if I was dead.*

The newscast caught his eye. A huge cloud of

insect-like creatures that the banner called locasts swarmed the countryside. Another view showed crops eaten down to the roots. He read the banner's translation:

> *"Locasts have destroyed ninety percent of our croplands. With the loss of this food source, as well as the loss of food animals and fish, our world faces starvation."*

Chaim gave thanks that the man did not berate Jews for threatening the life on this world as other announcers had.

> *"Religious leaders are meeting to deal with this disaster. While locasts are Haram, they are edible and could save countless lives. When great harm or death could occur and there is nothing to eat except prohibited food, Islamic law allows a Muslim to survive on Haram foods.*

The scene shifted to Ammad, the city he was now in, where crowds of people waited in line for the meager food that was available. Another scene from Medina showed riots and looting. People swarmed over the barriers at a food distribution center, despite the soldiers who tried to hold them back. Soldiers fired and people collapsed to the ground before the troops were overrun. Two men beat a downed soldier with lengths of wood.

My God, this is what I have done? I should *be punished. I* deserved *torture.*

Unbidden, the *kaddish*, the Jewish prayer for the dead leapt into his mind. He closed his eyes, and his body nodded forward and back as he recited the prayer.

Roxanne's voice broke into his meditation. "Whom do you mourn, Chaim?"

He looked up, startled. Both Simon and Berger stood in the open hatchway to his room. He had not heard them knock or enter. "I...grieve for all those I have caused to die. I grieve for the people of Islam. The animals that have been lost."

"You seek forgiveness?" Berger's voice was harsh, grating.

Chaim shook his head. No. Forgiveness was beyond his hope. "I cannot be forgiven for what I have done. A merciful God would end my life now, but our God is just. He has left me here to make amends, though I do not know how. This was no biblical plague brought down by God to free our people. This plague was created by men, and I abetted them. I see now that creation is an abomination, in itself an attempt to mimic God." Tears flowed from his eyes and down his cheeks.

Roxanne moved close to him and placed a hand on his shoulder. "We think you can make amends, at least to help stop this deadly disease. Can you gather yourself and speak with us?"

Through his tear-blurred gaze she glowed like a heavenly messenger. He swiped his sleeve across his eyes. His robe was filthy, and he thrust his arm behind him, trying to hide that from her.

"We'll get you clean clothing when we're done."

Berger snorted. The man said nothing, but Chaim felt his disgust, his antipathy.

Roxanne sat in the chair, her lovely face on a level with his, while Berger stood. "Chaim, have you experienced anything else unusual since you were infected?"

Unusual? What does she mean? "I don't understand."

"Besides the nausea. When people around you are angry, or sad, or fearful, how does that make you feel?"

Me? It is they who are feeling, not me.

But he did know what she asked. As the weeks went by, the moods of those surrounding him affected him more and more, like Berger's reaction a few moments before. He wrote that off to his mission, the stress, the awful aftermath. General Hussein's anger and hatred had sliced into Chaim's psyche more than he cared to admit, had cut to his core. Now he felt the compassion behind Simon's words, like a soothing balm on his soul.

Both people remained silent, awaiting him.

"I do not like to deal with people who are angry with me. Their anger...makes my stomach worse. Their sadness, their fear, too. I want to vomit."

"And this started soon after you were infected?"

He could lose himself in her eyes, but he gathered his composure and answered, "Yes."

Berger expelled a huge breath. "Shit. I knew it."

Roxanne waved him silent. "Chaim, before you were infected did you ever feel like the emotions of others bothered you? That you felt impinged on by such feelings?"

Chaim riffled through the compartments of his brain—he thought of his mind as a series of boxes holding different sorts of memories—it helped him remember. "I'm...not sure. I assumed that all people felt what I felt."

"Could you sense what people felt inside, without them telling you?"

"Doesn't everyone? From their body language, their facial expressions?" Chaim wanted to please her. Roxanne shook her head, which made his heart stutter. *My answer is wrong. I want to be correct for her.*

"What if you didn't look at them, if your eyes were turned away?"

Could I tell how a person felt without seeing them? In the dungeon, he felt the torturer's anticipation of sadistic pleasure when he approached his cell, and he said as much to Simon and Berger. "But before I was sick? I don't know."

"Do you ever feel you could read someone's mind, or see their thoughts?"

Chaim's mouth dropped open. *Read someone's mind? Is she serious?* Those were things that happened in the forbidden boyhood books.

"Animals," Berger grated, his frustration burning Chaim like hot oil. *Why do I feel that?* "Did you ever think you could feel something from animals?"

"I...I had a pet dog. I felt its love for me more than any other. I felt its pain when it was hurt. I never could hurt animals like some other children did. I felt their distress. Is that not usual?"

Berger shook his head, but his voice held what Chaim interpreted as awe. "Okay. So maybe he has some trace of empathic talent. Maybe I'm not alone."

Chaim felt bitterness behind Berger's words.

"Chaim, this is the common link between you and Cy."

Berger closed his eyes. "A lifetime," he muttered. "I spend a lifetime thinking I was alone. Now, I find out there's another with empathic ability." He opened his eyes and glared at Chaim. "And it has to be this *putz*."

Roxanne retorted, "Stow it, Cy. That doesn't help."

Chaim understood little of what they said. "What are you talking about? I understand that Berger and I are related, but how does this connect with the plague?"

"First, Cy is an empath." She went on to explain that to Chaim. He rolled her words around in his brain, trying to find a box where they fit. That a human could use his mind to communicate with another being—at least on the emotional level—astonished him. That *he,* Chaim Khodorkosovitch, might have such a talent was beyond belief.

"You and Cy are the only two we know with that

ability, so it must be genetic. The Test-Lit scientists tailored the plague organism to your genome, and because of your relatedness, Cy also became a host."

Chaim sat speechless. What could he say? He now understood what had happened, what the scientists had done to him. He was a human test animal. What if the disease had killed him? They would have moved on to a new subject. *How many died before me? Was I the first, or did they kill many others who volunteered to fight the Holy War?*

"What must I do to help defeat the plague?"

Berger said, "We assume that the two of us have unique genes or are missing some that allow us to be infected. We need to understand the genetics responsible for plague sensitivity and the genetics of the plague organism. That information exists wherever you came from." Berger clenched his teeth. "Tell us where it was created."

I cannot! An anguished wail rose from within his core. He saw his world devastated by bombs, families burned and twisted beyond recognition. *They will destroy not only the people responsible for these atrocities, but everyone. I cannot tell them.*

Berger put his hands to his own head and turned to Chaim. "Stop it. It hurts," he bellowed.

Berger's internal miasma of pain, confusion, anger, and hate battered Chaim, and he cried out in agony.

Is this what empathy means? I do not want it!

"Enough," Simon barked. "You two need separation. Go, Cy. I'll catch up with you."

She pointed at the door, and Berger left. She turned back to Chaim. "We must understand the genetics to defeat the plague. We can study you and Cy, but that won't be enough. We need the data on the plague pathogen. You must help us, Chaim. The fate of the galaxy depends on you."

Extinction

Is giving up my home to destruction the only answer? The only hope that I may be able to reverse at least some of the disaster I caused?

He recalled the face of the doctor who hovered over him, infecting him with the abomination of the plague. Should he go unpunished while the galaxy died? Chaim shuddered and his chin sank to his chest.

When he raised it again he felt his will stiffen and he met Simon's gaze squarely. "I will help you, but there are conditions."

***

The *GCVS* crew met with Ali Suliaman, General Tanweer, Colonel Jasar, and Fayed bin Ibrihim in the same bunker where we planned the rescues. It felt like a million years ago to me, and the stark gray walls did little to lift my mood.

Roxanne had met with Ali, had explained the circumstances surrounding our taking Chaim back to our ship rather than leaving him free to escape after the bombing. More than that, she explained how having him with us had allowed us to make major progress in our understanding of the plague. He had not been happy, but he had withheld any retribution.

General Tanweer, on the other hand, lost no opportunity to show his anger.

As I brought the New Meccans up to date on everything we had learned, Tanweer's hatred for Chaim battered me with almost tangible force. I sensed that it hit Chaim even worse. He paled and looked away from the general. Chaim's being an empath still stuck in my craw, but there was no longer any question.

"Dr. Habib has news on the treatment. I'll let her explain," I said.

"My group has refined the chelation therapy and

~259~

significantly reduced the toxicity. However, it is still not a cure. The chemical has a short half-life in the blood and requires daily injections to keep the plague at bay in sick animals. But it does also *prevent* healthy animals from contracting the plague."

"We can treat Learns-To-Fix-Injuries to protect him," Fur added enthusiastically.

"One more important thing," Aypari said. "Animals treated for the disease are no longer contagious."

This met with an outburst from everyone in the room.

Ali held up a hand. "Silence." He looked at Aypari. "If it is not a cure, I do not understand how it prevents the infection from spreading."

Roxanne said, "We think the treatment clears any circulating infectious organisms, but the pathogen's genetic material remains in the host's cells. I'll let Cy explain further."

"Imam, you're already aware that both Mr. McNu...Mr. Khodorkosovitch and I are infected with the plague organism and are unwitting carriers of the disease."

Well, *I* was unwitting. I could argue that Chaim came here explicitly to spread the disease, whether from vials or from his body. I was not letting him off the hook for that.

"The pathogen was genetically tailored to his genome, and I caught it because we are related. Contrary to what we first believed, we both do show some signs of illness related to the infection."

This was news to the New Meccans, and all of them spoke at once. Ali held up a hand for silence again. "How are you ill, Dr. Berger? Is it something that will become critical?"

"No. The organism's effect on us is minimal, though we do see increased levels of enzymes in the blood that indicate minor tissue damage in both of us. Our main symptom is a low level of nausea that never goes away. Both of us trace that back to our first plague exposure."

"I am glad you are not in danger," Ali said, sincerity behind his words.

Roxanne said, "We speculate that the Test-Lit scientists made the pathogen so specific that it could not be transferred to unrelated humans. The scientists thought that Chaim had no relations close enough to be susceptible."

Frown lines cut into Tanweer's broad forehead. "Please. I do not understand how family relatedness plays a role here. Perhaps all of us who are not scientists feel the same way."

"Most of the life in our galaxy derives from common biological and biochemical precursors," Roxanne said. "The basis for most galactic life is DNA, RNA, and proteins. That's why we have so many alien species that are similar to Terran life in their genetics and biochemistry.

"We believe that most humans are missing a receptor molecule on their cell membranes that the pathogen needs to attach to the cells...let's call it the plague receptor. Even human cells in culture lack the plague receptor and do not get infected. Nonhuman vertebrates, Terran and alien, have that putative receptor, so the plague can attach to and infect their cells. The human exceptions are Dr. Berger and Mr. Khodorkosovitch. Like most vertebrates, they have the gene that codes for production of the plague receptor, making them susceptible to infection.

"In contrast to other vertebrates, the disease is self-limiting in Cy and Chaim. It makes them mildly ill, but does not kill them. But the plague in them is still contagious, and they can pass it to animals.

"The Test-Lits needed someone with those genetic characteristics who had no close family. Chaim's parents and grandparents were dead and he had no siblings, or even cousins, so far as they knew. They did not want the disease spread throughout the galaxy while Chaim traveled, and they assumed no other humans would have a genome close enough to allow infection and transmission."

"That is interesting, Dr. Simon, but how does it fight the plague?" Ali asked.

"We think the plague was designed to incorporate itself into the host genome, as some viruses do. If we knew the plague's DNA sequence, we could create a tailored enzyme that could go into cells and literally snip out the offending piece of plague DNA. Other targeted enzymes could then destroy that DNA."

Once again, all four New Meccans spoke at once.

I held up both hands for quiet, but nobody obeyed me as they did the Imam. After they all ran down, I said, "Please understand that this is theory. We still need the genomic data on the plague microbe to learn how and where it attacks cells. There's only one place to get those data."

Every eye was on me, but I turned to Chaim. "Your turn." I gave Roxanne most of the credit for bringing him to our side.

Chaim lifted his chin and glanced at Roxanne, as if he spoke for her alone. Man, that pissed me off. And she acted as if she *liked* the guy.

Chaim spoke in a strong, clear voice. "I cannot and do not ask forgiveness for what I have done. My acts were heinous. You would be right to lock me up for life, or even take my life. I submit to your judgment. My God will judge me in His time."

He looked at Ali. "What I can do is lead you to the place where I came from, the location of the laboratory that created this plague, and give you the scientist who possesses the genetic information that Drs. Simon and Berger need."

The general's voice broke in. "And why should we believe him? He has not divulged any information to us. He wouldn't to Hussein's torturers. Why now?"

Chaim answered. "Because I see now my party was wrong and this genetic information is needed to protect the galaxy. I will do my part, but I have conditions."

"You have *what! Conditions*? How dare you?" Jasar and bin Ibrihim also exploded, but the general's voice drowned them out.

Ali sat imperturbable, his hand rubbing his graying goatee.

"Quiet!" I yelled. "Hear him out."

A now confident Chaim broke the tense silence. I had to admit that he had changed from the cringing little *putz* I had first met.

"I want no more killing. I will give you no names of those with whom I worked here on New Mecca, and I will not give you the name of the planet I came from. However, I will lead the *Galactic Circle Veterinary Service* to my home world where Dr. Berger and his team can confront those responsible and get the needed data. There will be no wholesale invasion, as most of the people there are only citizens innocent of this crime."

I could feel the steam building up inside the general's head, and I feared an explosion. I kept my mental screen at max. Jasar looked no happier than his CO. Bin Ibrihim simmered.

Only Ali showed no reaction. The guy was cool under fire. "Mr. Khodorkosovitch, you want us to let you leave New Mecca after what you have done? That is an extraordinary request. How can you justify it?"

"Imam Suliaman, I will guide the necessary

expedition, but I will return to New Mecca to submit to your judgment. I give you my word on that."

The general came halfway out of his seat. His face shaded toward purple. "Your *word*? We should take the *word* of someone who tried to destroy our world and may still succeed?"

Again, Ali raised a hand, and the general subsided, grumbling. "Mr. Khodorkosovitch, as the general said, why should we believe you?"

Chaim shook his head. "I understand what you ask, and I can only give you my promise to do whatever I can to defeat this disease, and to return here after that is done. Assuming I still live."

Ali raised his chin and rubbed his neck. "Interesting." He turned to me. "And what is it you propose?" I sensed he already knew the answer to his question.

Might as well put all our cards on the table. "I will guarantee Chaim's return."

This time, I put my hands over my ears. The general's voice outshouted everyone again.

"I will not...I *cannot* let him or the rest of you flee from what you have done here. You would take *every person* who was responsible for this disaster with you. You won't come back, why should you? *Impossible*."

I sensed agreement in Jasar and bin Ibrihim. Neither held any love for us, blamed me as much as Chaim for spreading the disease.

Again, only Suliaman kept a level head among the New Meccans. "If we were to agree to this plan, we would need to ensure that you follow through on your promise. How could we do that?" He met and held the eyes of each of the *GCVS* crew, in turn.

Jasar broke the long silence. "Imam, we could send a contingent of my force with them."

The Imam's eyebrows rose. He turned to me. "Have

you room on your vessel?"

"We could squeeze in a half-dozen soldiers...maybe."

Ali looked at Jasar. "Would that be adequate to ensure compliance?"

Jasar grumped but nodded.

Ali looked back at me. "There are two more problems that I see. Both you and Mr. Khodorkosovitch carry the plague. The quarantine of our world is for good reason. I will not allow anyone to take this affliction elsewhere in our galaxy."

"I agree," I said. "I will not leave New Mecca if I am contagious. We'll both undergo treatment with the chelation therapy. If we can show that we're not contagious so long as we remain on therapy, would you agree?"

Now every other voice in the room, including those of my shipmates, clamored for attention. Roxanne's voice cut through all the others in my mind: "Too dangerous...too dangerous. The side effects could kill you."

I waved them all down. "If I allow Dr. bin Ibrihim and his physician colleagues to make that determination, would that be acceptable?"

Ali looked at bin Ibrihim, who nodded. "I will consider it. My second question is how you intend to leave New Mecca. The surrounding fleet will destroy any ship that tries."

"I'm sure that Corporal Dalil informed you that the *GCVS* is equipped with cloaking and protective shields."

Tanweer snapped, "That will not be enough to avoid destruction by a powerful fleet."

I nodded. "If you agree to our leaving, I'll share our plan with Colonel Jasar once we are aboard. Is that acceptable?"

"No. They are hiding things from us. This is *un*acceptable." The general's fury burned through my empathic screen.

Ali would make the final decision, and I was not yet willing to play our last hole card. First things first. We had to render Chaim and me incapable of transmitting the plague. That meant the chelation therapy and all the side effects that it portended.

Chapter 22

Roxanne pointed to a segment of my genome on the monitor and superimposed a segment from Chaim's.

"These two DNA segments are analogous and not found in any other humans, at least on New Mecca, or in our data base. More importantly, all vertebrates we've checked carry similar genes. I'm calling it the C-C complex for Cy-Chaim.

"That C-C stretch of DNA was probably lost as nonessential in most humans but remained in Khodorkosovitch and in vertebrates, sentient and nonsentient." She pointed to my DNA and superimposed that of a camel. "Right here. There's the comparable gene segment in the camel chromosome. Somewhere in that group of genes there's one that codes for the plague receptor. We assume it allows the pathogen to attach to and get through the cell membrane. That could account for how the infection gets in, but not for why you and Chaim don't get sicker."

My stomach twisted into a Gordian knot as I viewed my traitorous bit of DNA. I would have grabbed a scalpel and cut myself open, excised that segment of genome if I could. But that little stretch of code existed deep within every nucleated cell in my body. And nestled somewhere within that code, the plague had inserted its own DNA.

To excise the offending organism from Chaim's and my body, we needed to know the exact code of the plague DNA. Then we could create a highly specific enzyme to target it and snip it out. We had to get the code from the lab that had created the monstrosity.

I stared at the monitor while I mulled that over for a few moments. "There must be other genes in the C-C complex that prevent the plague from causing the cell destruction we see in other vertebrates. We need to look for those differences. At any rate, the next step is to deal with the infection in Chaim and me. That means the chelation therapy. We know the toxic side effects. We can counteract the hypocalcemia and any metal deficiencies the chelation causes. We can monitor renal function and treat that. What we *can't* do is nothing."

Roxanne turned to Chaim. "Are you willing? You understand the danger?"

Chaim gave her what I now called his "adoring look." My pulse sped and I had to force down the urge to pick the man up and shake him like a terrier with a rat.

"I understand, Dr. Simon. If I die, it is what God has ordained for me."

I felt his resignation as if it were my own.

Now that we had learned of the infection's impact on empathic ability, I had become even more paranoid, believing I could sense communication from the damned organism in my tissues. Was that possible?

***

Extinction

I chatted with Learns-To-Fix-Injuries as he shoveled locasts down his big maw. "How are those things?" They gave me the willies. We were eating them, too, but mashed up and incorporated into dishes that hid identification.

Red looked up from the bin of locasts. "Tassty. As young I ate insectss. Eassy to catch. Learn to hunt. Thesse...sspicier, but good." A few locasts dribbled out the side of his toothy jaws. "Be better...crunchier...if not cooked." He shoveled more in and chomped on them.

"Sorry, big guy, but we have to sterilize them in case they're contaminated with plague."

He nodded. "Undersstand. Sstill better than recycled mush." He took another mouthful. "How much longer I confined?"

"Not long, we hope. We're close to figuring out the chelation treatment that can ward off the disease and make us noncontagious. In your case, we need to do tests to ensure the stuff isn't toxic for reptiles."

"I tell you. Not reptile. I dragon." Miffed, he fixed me with his slit-eyed gaze. "Make it ssoon...pleasse."

"We're already on it."

I turned and headed for the lab. It was time for the first round of chelation and whatever came with it.

Fur was sitting at a workbench, eyes boring into a display. He looked up at me. "Good news, Cy. While the chelation isn't a cure, even inoculating blood from the treated animal doesn't pass the disease. But if we stop treatment, the disease recurs and the animal becomes contagious again."

I twisted my lips to the side. "Presumably, chelation prevents the pathogen's DNA from constructing new infectious organisms but doesn't clear the DNA from the cells. That makes sense since the chelate can't get inside cells, it just reaches the surface.

"So long as it does what we need. Chaim and I start

treatment immediately, and we need enough chemical for both the trip out and back. If we aren't rendered noncontagious, we can't leave the planet and we're back to square one unless Chaim will give up the location of his world to Tanweer."

Roxanne looked at Chaim. "Are you ready?"

"I will do whatever you need."

Roxanne said, "We'll put Chaim and Cy on constant cardiac and blood monitoring, and we'll have the renal dialysis machine ready."

Fur added, "We can filter the blood to clear some of the organometal complexes before they go through the kidneys. It's not one hundred percent, but it will reduce the severity of renal complications."

Roxanne looked at Chaim and me. "Let's move to the exam room. I want to place long-term venous catheters in both of you. Five minutes if you need to use the potty."

Chaim bolted for the door, leaving me feeling as if his bodily needs were mine. I suppressed that and worried about the how long it would take to render us noncontagious and then to assure the New Meccans of that. Time was against us.

Roxanne placed catheters in veins running from our lower arms up and around the shoulder and into the vena cava near the heart. She drew baseline blood samples then flushed the lines, checking for patency and leaks. The IV drip bags contained cloudy liquid. I envisioned the molecules of chelate in the solution doing their Brownian motion dance. I imagined them eager to glom onto any metal they encountered, including my essential ions like calcium. Those chelate complexes would assault my kidneys as my body tried to excrete them.

My concern and Roxanne's was that, like many patients who had septic shock, I had significant residual renal damage from my bout with the leg fracture and infection. There was nothing I could do about that now.

A couple of hours later, she unhooked me.

Aypari was in the room, so I asked her, "How will we test contagiousness?"

"Using the cell cultures," she replied. "Come. You can watch."

***

After Chaim and I received treatment, Roxanne collected blood, lymph, saliva, sweat, hair, and excretions every day. One week later, tested animal cell cultures showed no infection. The DNA of the pathogen might remain deep in our cells, but the chelation removed anything that was infectious from those tissues and bodily fluids.

We moved on to the critical animals tests. The morning of the fourteenth day everything still tested clean. We turned samples over to bin Ibrahim and his team of physicians. Once they proved to their satisfaction that Chaim and I were not contagious with plague, we would be good to go.

Healer was another issue. We would unfreeze him and treat him with chelation before we left New Mecca. I hoped it was not too late to save him. Learns-To-Fix-Injuries started on chelation therapy along with us as a further precaution to prevent him from getting sick. We would test both of them, as well.

I had a headache that would not go away. My urine tests came back showing increased levels of protein, a sign of the expected renal glomerular damage from the chelate complexes. Managing ionic calcium levels to replace what was being chelated out helped, but periods of hypocalcemia still occurred, with resulting anxiety and depression, irregular heartbeats, and muscle pain and spasms. Left unaddressed, severe hypocalcemia could lead to acute cardiac failure or longer-term congestive heart failure, but we hoped to keep ahead of those complications.

I did not see much of Chaim and assumed he felt as bad as I did. Not empathically reinforcing one another's ills was a good thing.

Blood filtration helped remove some chelates before they got to the kidney, but because of my previous kidney damage, I knew renal dialysis was inevitable when my kidneys started to fail. I wanted to make it to Chaim's home world to retrieve the plague's genetic data, and to at least help start on the cure, but I wondered if I would make it back to New Mecca. I kept a positive face on for all my companions, but I knew Roxanne saw through me.

I received a surprise when the military team showed up to board the *GCVS*. There was one more soldier than the half-dozen we agreed on: Colonel Jasar.

Broad-shouldered and a centimeter or two taller than me, with close-cropped black hair and beard and dark eyes, he showed little outward emotion. Despite that, I detected a certain degree of reluctance and suspicion relating to our mission. "If you have no objection, I will accompany you."

"We have no quarters for you, Colonel."

"I will bunk with my team. These three men and three women are my crack troops, Dr. Berger."

"Your quarters are that way to the left," I pointed. "The cabin doors are open. Look for the two containing extra bunks."

I returned to the bridge to find Fur and Roxanne waiting for me.

"We're completely stocked, Cy," Fur said. "You take care of the military?"

"Yeah, and a bit of a surprise there. Jasar's coming

with us."

"I'm not surprised," Roxanne said. "I thought he wanted in. The soldiers will obey him as they might not you or me. We bring Jasar in on all decisions so we're coordinated. I'll go down to check on them." She left the bridge.

"Fur, we'll need a shakedown on procedures. Neither of us has had to fly the *GCVS* without Ruth...with the backup AI. It handles all our basic systems, environmental controls and such, but not actual piloting until we're in hyperspace."

Fur pursed his lips before speaking. "You're going to have to pilot the ship manually. I'll co-pilot, but we do need to go over all the procedures. Ruthie spoiled us, Cy."

Guilt and chagrin hit me with a wave of nausea and vertigo. God help me, I missed Ruthie already.

***

I stood in front of Healer's open cryochamber. We shunted the supercooled cryo fluid to an external cardiac pump and replaced it with plasma substitute. That warmed all the tissues at the same rate, internal and external. There were so many places where we had no idea how Healer's body might respond. Had the plague caused so much damage that our efforts were doomed from the start?

When the cryo fluid reached the pump, it shunted into a waste container partially filled with chelating solution to deactivate any plague organisms. My heart seemed to flutter in time with the pump. I monitored the flow. Too fast and we would cause damage from too much pressure in the blood vessels; too slow and the thawing would take too long and deprive his tissues of needed oxygen.

"Our biggest problem," Roxanne told Aypari, "is the blood. We don't have Lupan blood available, so we're using plasma substitute. That's okay for the short term. It contains a hemoglobin analogue that can carry oxygen since he doesn't have erythrocytes, but he'll still be missing all the leukocytes and platelets.

"That means he'll have no immune response until his bone marrow produces more white blood cells, but we'll administer a drug that stimulates bone marrow production. We'll also give him artificial platelets that contain clotting factors and proteins. Until his blood repopulates fully, he'll be susceptible to infections, so we'll keep him pumped full of antibiotics and antivirals as well as the anti-plague chelates.

"So far, Red is not showing any chelate toxicity, and we hope that Healer won't either. The biggest unknown is how much damage the plague did before we got Healer cooled down."

Several hours later, Healer was thawed, the cryo fluid flushed from his body. And he lived. His heartbeat was still rapid and his respirations shallow, but we had done everything we could for him.

Later, when his vital signs had stabilized, I screwed a syringe onto the venous catheter, and injected Healer with a stimulant that would counteract the sedative I had given him. Within seconds, Healer's eyes snapped open. Bloodshot sclera surrounded his yellow irises, but he fixed his eyes on me.

"Buurrgggger." His voice seemed to work in slow motion. He tried to sit up, but I pushed him down with my hand.

"Hold on, Healer. You've been ill, and your body was seriously damaged. Don't strain."

"Wheerree arre wee?"

Good. He was asking logical questions. "In the ship."

He lay still. "I waas siick, wiith plaaggue. I rememmbbeer. Not siick noow?"

"We found a way to stop the disease. You're recovering."

"Cuure plague thenn?"

I shook my head. "Not completely."

He looked around the lab with all the cryopreservation paraphernalia. "Youu frreezze mee."

No one ever said that the Lupans were stupid. If they did, they did not have a chance to say it twice.

"That's right. We froze you to save your life. When we found a way to stop the disease, we thawed you out."

"Innterresting. I would havve liked to see that."

Typical Lupan. They looked at everything with an almost clinical detachment. I took my hand away from his shoulder. "Let me remove your IV."

His eyes fixed on Learns-To-Fix-Injuries who stood behind me. "My frriend."

As Healer levered himself to a sitting position, Red bounded around the room, ricocheting off cabinets and knocking some of the IV supplies to the floor. He hissed like a steam engine, and said, "Healer. Get up. You ssleep too long. No fun without you. Come on, Healer, we wresstle now."

"Damn it, Red. Healer is weak. Let him sleep and get his strength back"

"No, Captain Cyberrger, I havve slept enough. I welcomme Learns-To-Fix-Injuries' offerr." He looked at the dragon. "Can you take mee outside for airr?"

Without a word, Red swept Healer into his arms and trotted out the door, wiggling his butt to make it through.

Fur, a smile on his hairy face, watched them troop out before entering the room.

"Fur, make sure they don't go far and keep Red in

line. He'll kill Healer with friendship if we're not careful."

***

I finished my physical inspection of the *GCVS*'s exterior and stood at the bottom of the ramp, looking over the spaceport field. Soldiers patrolled the perimeter. A couple of whirlydrones banked over the terminal building, red and green lights flashing. I had mixed feelings about leaving. On one hand, we needed to go if we were to have any chance to defeat the plague. On the other hand, we were leaving millions of people to starve if we did not return, though if that were the case, it would mean *we* were dead, too.

I turned to enter the airlock when I heard roaring in the distance. As the roar became louder, coming in our direction, I hesitated.

There were times when my mental acuity could be questioned. This was one of them. I stood rooted to the ramp as I watched a flight of jet-powered flyers appear over the field. My feet did not get into gear until the first antiaircraft batteries around the spaceport opened fire. Those incoming aircraft were *not* friendlies.

I leapt through the airlock and punched the *close* switch. I thumbed my comm and yelled, "Everybody strap in. We're leaving right now."

Fur answered. "I'm on the bridge with Roxanne and Colonel Jasar. Engines are on."

"I'm heading up. Fur, get ready to cloak and shield." I ran as fast as my gimpy leg allowed.

I skidded onto the bridge and glanced over the control board. The engines were at three-quarter power and the cloaking and shield needed full power to activate. I slammed into my seat, hand flying to punch the harness switch. The autostraps snugged around my torso just as a concussion rocked the ship. Not a direct hit. Fur and Roxanne strapped into their chairs and braced for liftoff. Jasar rode in an auxiliary seat.

When the antigravity engines reached full power, I engaged and started liftoff.

Before I could activate the shield, another explosion jolted us. This time alarms went off.

"We took a hit, port antimatter engine," Fur said. "It's still on-line."

I engaged the shield as the ship lifted on the antigravs, too slowly for my liking. I flicked on the external viewscreen in time to see a humongous fireball roll into the sky over a downed flyer about one hundred meters away. Several attacking craft veered away from the field, but they swung around and headed back toward us.

"Shield at full power, Captain," Fur barked. "Port antimatter engine is cycling on and off."

I engaged the cloaking mechanism.

"The AI is shutting down the port antimatter engine."

"Can't worry about that until we are out of range of the attackers," I said.

"I'll have to get in there and check the damage once we're in orbit." Fur's voice was grim. "Without one antimatter engine, we have no chance to get past the blockade."

Several more explosions boomed nearby then there was blessed silence. I let out a sigh of relief and tried to get my heart rate under control. My mouth felt like I chewed on surgical gauze.

I pushed the antigravity engines to full power. Antigravity mostly accommodated for the increased acceleration to four-gs, but the feeling of increased weight still took my breath away.

"We'll take her up to fifteen kilometers, Fur, above

the troposphere. Then we'll assess the damage."

Jasar cleared his throat. "Is it safe to stop even at that altitude?"

"I hope so, Colonel. Both our cloaking and our shield are state-of-the-art. In any case, we've got to have the antimatter engines at full capacity to get past the fleet."

As the ship exited a planet's gravity well, the antigravity drive's efficiency waned quickly, and the antimatter drive kicked in for interplanetary journeys. We had to jump into hyperspace outside the solar system's gravity well, and the quarantine fleet stood between us and the closest point where we could use our hyperdrive. We needed two operational antimatter engines to make it.

Jasar's brow wrinkled in a puzzled frown. "I do not see how that will help. The blockade fleet has powerful enough weapons pierce any shield. What is this *plan* you spoke of?"

"We'll make it. Trust me, Colonel."

My assurance did not make him any happier.

Fur said, "I'll check on the AM engine."

I trusted our resident mechanical genius to figure out the problem. He'd worked on every kind of drone and space vehicle during the years before his medical training.

When we reached our target altitude, I used the antigrav engines to keep us in a stable orbit. Fur unbuckled and lumbered off the bridge, and Roxanne followed suit.

"I'll see if there are any injuries," she said.

Jasar stood. "I will check my troops."

"Good enough. Keep me posted."

I watched the screen for sign of pursuit. After a few minutes, the comm kicked in with Roxanne's voice. "We're good down here, Cy. A couple of minor injuries is all. What's the damage?"

"I'm awaiting Fur's report."

Several more minutes of silence did not up my hopes, and then Fur's voice startled me when it came back.

"Good news, Cy. The hit blew out an electrical panel to the port AM engine. I have spares. It will take a few minutes. How are we doing otherwise?"

"No major problems."

I kept my eyes glued to the sensors scanning for any threats.

Roxanne returned to the bridge. She walked over and brushed a lock of hair off my forehead. "How are you doing, Captain?"

"Fine, for the moment. You?"

"I'm worried about that blockade."

"I'm with you on that."

When Fur returned to the bridge, he slumped in his chair. He ran a sooty hand across his brow. "Worse than I thought. It wasn't just the panel. A piece of hull plating blew back into the engine intake. I jury-rigged a replacement for the cowling seals."

I did not like the sound of that. "And?"

"And I hope it will hold up at new supermax antimatter engine speeds."

Fur usually had total confidence in what he fixed—or modified—so his uncertainty bothered me. Another modification to our ship, one I had not yet mentioned to Jasar—the "plan" he wondered about—involved our antimatter drive. We had a prototype that increased speeds up to tenfold. No ship in the quarantine force could keep up with us when we engaged that supercharged drive. But for that, we needed both antimatter engines fully operational.

"I'm going to contact the quarantine fleet, see if they'll give us safe passage."

Fur's eyebrows folded together. "Uh, I thought they were going to blast anything that tried to leave the planet."

"That's what Ali and Tanweer said, but maybe they'll listen to reason. After all, we're not carrying contagion anymore."

Fur's skepticism hung like a cloud over his head. "Are you sure—?"

"Sure of what?" Jasar stepped onto the bridge.

I glanced at the colonel, and a tickle of uncertainty rolled through my brain. "Um, I'm going to contact the head of the quarantine fleet. Explain our situation. See if they'll let us through."

Jasar frowned. "Dr. Berger, I do not think this is wise. They have made their ultimatum clear. They destroyed two foreign nonmilitary freighters that tried to take off with perishable cargo. The captains were afraid to lose their investment. Instead, they lost their lives."

I sat back in my chair. "How could it hurt to try?"

"Every second of delay gives them more time to target us, cloak and shield notwithstanding."

Jasar's description of the destroyed freighters changed my mind. "Okay. Fur, can we engage the supercharged antimatter drive? Give it everything?"

"I've done what I can do. We won't know until we try it."

Jasar frowned as he buckled into his chair. "What have you not told me?"

A tendril of anger snaked across to me, wrenching my stomach even further out of shape. The initial frantic flight from the spaceport had twisted my innards like a nest of vipers.

"We have one more capability, but we've never used it." I explained about the antimatter supercharger.

"You say ten times the speed?" His mind

scintillated with disbelief.

"If it performs to specs. With our shield and cloaking, and moving at the accelerated speed, we should make it past the quarantine fleet with minimal damage."

I glanced at the toggle switch that was not part of the original controls. A red LED winked below the switch that would kick in the overdrive.

"Everybody strap in," I announced on the intercom. "I expect this will be a bumpy ride."

Chapter 23

As the *GCVS* flew outward on the decreasing power of the antigravity engines, the comm speakers squawked, *"This is Admiral B'Jong of the Peereekian Navy. Stand down or be fired upon."*

At least I *think* he said Peereekian. His hisses and clicks sounded akin to a hyperactive cricket. Our AI translated to Common. On the comm screen, his feathery antennae waved agitatedly above a vaguely insectoid face.

"Admiral, this is the *Galactic Circle Veterinary Service.* I'm Captain Cy Berger. We are on a vital mission to save the galaxy."

Jasar shot me a grim look.

Hiss, click, screech. *"Your cloaking is useless. We have targeted your position. You have thirty seconds to descend and return to your base. Failure to comply will result in the destruction of your ship."*

So much for our cloaking system.

"Admiral, our ship is not carrying infectious plague. We must leave New Mecca in order to bring a cure to the Union of Worlds.*"*

Click, screech. "Twenty seconds."

I needed twenty seconds to get above the atmosphere and safely engage the antimatter engines. We did not want to annihilate ourselves.

Screech, hiss. "Ten seconds."

I ticked off nine in my mind and engaged. The sudden acceleration made my face feel like a stretching rubber mask. The onboard antigravity control could not totally make up for the antimatter's acceleration forces.

The viewscreen flashed an incandescence that seemed like a supernova. The ship buffeted in one direction, then another.

Despite our cloaking, the fleet was targeting the exhaust from our AM engines, I realized. Our shield took several glancing blows and saved our butts.

I set a zigzag course toward the fleet, which was barely visible against the star field background. The warships were spread out and laying down a crossfire pattern along our flight path.

Another buffet indicated a direct hit on the shield.

Fur, his face pale, croaked, "We've reached top speed for the standard AM drive, Cy."

Two more buffets, the second right on the heels of the first.

"The shield is taking a beating, but it's still at eighty percent," Fur said. "Once it hits fifty, we'll start taking damage to the ship."

Jasar's voice grated. "They are using pulse energy projectiles and plasma beams, but they have nuclear weapons as a last resort."

Roxanne groaned.

I agreed with her sentiment. "Our shield won't withstand a nuke, Colonel."

"Shield sixty percent," Fur intoned. "The port engine looks good so far. I think it will hold."

The ship rocked again.

Jasar's face remained calm. "Time to test your supercharged engines, Dr. Berger."

I pulled the toggle and the red LED flickered to green. I felt like an elephant sat on me, then the star field became a blur.

***

The LED next to the toggle flared red again and the invisible elephant stood up. Even the normal maximum AM acceleration now felt like nirvana.

Fur groaned. "I never had a clue when they said ten-times the speed."

Jasar looked at the board then at me. "I cannot see the blockade fleet and we are still on course for the jump point. How did you shut off the supercharger?"

"I didn't. It has an auto cutoff to prevent the engines from frying."

"I believe the specifications for a ten-fold speed increase on that drive modification were an underestimate. I would like that for our space fleet, if possible."

I looked at Jasar. "No problem for me." I supposed we did owe Ali and his people for what had happened to their world. They never did get to examine Ruthie.

I reached over and flipped on the general comm. "Is everyone all right?"

Aypari's voice cut in, and I watched Fur's face light up. "I am well. I will check Chaim in his quarters."

"Corporal Amir, here, Colonel Jasar. All well and accounted for."

A drawn out hiss followed. "That wass not fun, Berger. Hurt. Wing torn."

"I am well," Healer added. He was far better than I would have dreamed. His Lupan regenerative genes obviously played a major role is his recovery.

"Get to the infirmary, Red," Roxanne said. "I'm going there if anyone else needs medical attention." She headed in that direction.

Jasar peered at the location readout then turned to me. "We must plot our hyperspace jump coordinates now. It is time for Mr. Khodorkosovitch to speak."

"Aypari, escort Chaim to the bridge please."

***

The escape from New Mecca left Chaim feeling like a quivering mass of jelly. He was afraid to move out of the acceleration couch, lest those incredible forces came back again. His muscles and joints complained at any movement.

He looked at the New Meccan woman who had just entered his cabin. He did not know her well, and he sensed a mix of anger and sympathy toward him. The anger he understood. He could not fathom the sympathy; it was her world his actions were destroying.

"Are you well?" she asked.

"I...think so."

"We must go to the bridge."

He unbuckled his harness and stood, waiting to allow his rubbery knees to recover their normal function.

She turned, and he stumbled out the open door and down the passageway after her. As they neared the bridge, Simon joined them in all her numinous glory. Her auburn hair, her emerald eyes, the curves he had to force himself not to ogle, all were a welcome sight. He stared without appropriate words to say what he felt.

"I'll accompany you to the bridge," she said to Chaim and Habib. "I left Healer to sew up Red's wing. Good practice for him. Are you uninjured, Chaim?"

"I am well." A warm feeling encompassed his mind

and body. *She cares enough to check on me.* Chaim had no illusions about the true state of affairs; she was Berger's wife, and Berger held her heart. For him, it was enough to know that she cared what happened to him.

"Cy and Colonel Jasar need the coordinates for your planet to plot the hyperspace jump."

On the bridge, Chaim faced Berger, Simon, Cohen, Habib, and Jasar. He gave thanks that the dragon and the werewolf were not present. He knew they were no threat to him now, but he would never forget the sight of the werewolf as it tore out Isaac's throat.

"We've outrun the planetary blockade, but still have to get past the ships around the jump point. With the supercharged AM engines working so well, we should blow by them." Berger seemed manic, his thoughts gleeful. "They can't know where the *GCVS* will jump to."

There was no way to trace a hyperjump destination, Chaim had learned.

Berger looked at Chaim. "It's up to you now. We need to know your planet's location for the hyperspace jump coordinates."

Chaim's throat clenched at the thought of giving up his home world, the fear that harm might come to innocent people. He ducked his head away from Berger's steely gaze.

"Are you going back on your word?" Berger snapped, battering Chaim's senses.

Roxanne put a hand up to Berger. "Chaim has said he will give us this information." She looked at him. "Right?"

"I will," he said in a whisper. Then he shouted, "*I will.*" He felt his face heat after his outburst. *Oh, God. Help me through this. Give me strength. I survived Hussein and his torturers, I can survive this.*

But words would not come in front of all these people who hated him. He pulled his courage about him like a cloak and said, "I will only tell Dr. Simon."

"Why you weasel, we had a deal—"

Berger's sudden anger seared Chaim's entire being with fury that flowed from the man like heat from an opened oven. *Everyone has been angry at me for so long, I don't care anymore.*

Roxanne cut off Berger's outburst with a wave. "What do you mean, Chaim?"

"I will tell you. You are the only one who does not hate me."

Chaim kept his eyes locked on Simon's face and shut out angry words that came from the others.

Simon's gaze softened. "So long as you give me the location of your world, that's fine, Chaim."

"He's worried about military reprisal," Berger added.

Chaim trembled. *He sees into my mind.*

Jasar spoke. "All we want is to bring the individual miscreants to justice and find a cure for the plague. We will not harm anyone who is innocent of this crime."

"Come with me," Roxanne said to Chaim.

His stomach knotted as he followed.

***

Jasar frowned at me. "We have the jump coordinates to his world, but we need more information from Khodorkosovitch."

Fur tugged at his beard. "Yeah. We need to know where the laboratory is and who created the plague. We have to ensure they can't do it again."

"I think that Chaim will come through," Roxanne said.

She always stuck up for the son-of-a-bitch, and it

irked me.

"Giving me the coordinates left him shaken. I'll wait until he calms down then I'll get the rest of what we need." She looked at me. "There's too much hatred and anger toward him, and he reacts negatively to that.

"He's not an evil person. He was terribly misguided, lied to. Had he understood the import of his actions beforehand, I don't believe he would have complied. As is, no other person could ever rebuke him worse than the way he is flagellating himself. He's shown incredible resilience to come as far as he has, to lead us to his own world."

"Fine. I'll lay off him," I said. "We'll see where he stands in the end. If he doesn't turn on us once we reach his world."

* * *

With my ability to see into Chaim's mind, to read his thoughts, I could no longer deny that my empathic talent had taken another leap forward toward becoming telepathic. I had hoped that eliminating the free plague organisms from my body by chelation would remove the enhanced powers associated with the infection, but I still felt Chaim's thoughts as if they were my own. Maybe when we removed the plague DNA incorporated in my genome that might change. I prayed that would be the case.

Despite my empathic-telepathic ability becoming stronger, the rest of my body headed in the opposite direction. I had never fully recovered from the effects of my desert ordeal, particularly my kidneys, and I felt progressively worse on the chelation therapy. The cardiac arrhythmias, muscle pain and spasms, and general irritability had increased, and I spent more time undergoing renal dialysis. I hoped I would make it long enough to help eradicate the damn plague.

The *GCVS* approached the hyperspace jump point and we used the antimatter supercharger to blow past the cordon. Once in hyperspace, no one could follow and I set our trajectory toward the solar system of the planet Jaffa.

Chaim's world was earth-like with two large oceans and two main continents, home to thirty million people. According to him, the Judaic world government included several parties including orthodox, conservative, and reform worshipers. When Chaim left, the party holding the majority, and the prime ministerial office, was of the orthodox persuasion, but not the Testamentary-Literalist Party. The world's government was moderate and open to thinkers of all denominations.

The Test-Lits formed a small splinter group that eschewed participation in a democracy, and kept to themselves. Most lived on an island off the western coast of the larger continent. Close enough for necessary trade, but far enough to discourage visitors who did not believe as they did. Their own governing body was a Rebbinical Council consisting of the most right-wing and intolerant of the ordained rebbes. Just like Reb Levi's Test-Lit group had been on Dovid's World.

The Jaffaran Test-Lits called their little island kingdom, *Tsedek*, the Hebrew word for righteousness. It made me sick.

Chaim pointed to an aerial view of a pear-shaped island on our viewscreen. "There is a central mountain range that rises to three thousand meters. This peak is Mount Esh." He pointed to a mountain named after the Hebrew word for fire. "It is an old volcano with a caldera at the summit. There is a lake in the center and hot springs and smoke vents."

The topography below the mountain included a river basin, agricultural land, and population centers.

"The laboratory facility is located halfway up the east slope of Mount Esh."

Jasar asked, "How high is Esh? And how flat is the shoreline of the caldera lake?"

"Esh is two-thousand meters at the summit," Chaim answered. "but I do not know about the lake. I never went there."

"Are you thinking about that as a landing site?" I asked. It made sense to let Jasar take over the planning and command of our ground mission.

"A possibility," Jasar said. "Any roads from the laboratory to the caldera?"

"Only footpaths. All roads to the laboratory are gated and guarded." Chaim grimaced. "I now understand why. It once was a noted academic center for the study of disease."

Chaim's desire to put his world in a more positive light was understandable.

Jasar frowned. "Are there patrols, do you know?"

Chaim shrugged.

The caldera grew on the screen as our cloaked ship approached orbital insertion.

Fur increased magnification on the screen. A white spot appeared on the eastern mountain slope. "Is this the lab?"

"Yes."

Fur examined grid lines on the image. "It's as little as a couple of kilometers from the lakeshore to the caldera rim, depending on where we put down."

"Doable," Jasar said.

"I'll put the ship down as close as I can to the rim." It looked like a rigorous climb up to the summit of the caldera and down to the laboratory, and I hoped my leg would hold up for it.

Fur zoomed in on the lab, a collection of gray and white buildings. Chaim pointed out the main microbiology building, as well as dormitories and some storage sheds and garages.

"There are land vehicles, and I know of two eight-person flyers...in this hangar, here." Chaim pointed. "There is also a helidrone. You can see it parked by the main building."

"Mm-hmm." Jasar seemed lost in his thoughts. "I need plans of the buildings' interiors. Do you recall enough to rough one out for me?"

Chaim thought a moment, then said, "I know the dormitory and cafeteria and parts of the laboratory. I will do what I can."

"One more question, Chaim," I said. "We need the names of those scientists who were instrumental in creating the plague, and anyone else who you would consider to have knowingly aided and abetted this crime. And we need to know where they might be when we go in."

Roxanne followed up on my thought. "We don't want to harm anyone, just talk to them." She had a way of embellishing my words to make them more palatable to Chaim.

He nodded to her. "I will make a list. If we go at night, they will likely be in their quarters." He pointed out a small building near the lab. "It houses the top administrators and the lead scientist who is the worst offender."

Jasar said, "That is good. I must confer with my troops." He rose and moved off the bridge.

Roxanne smiled and squeezed my hand. "Let's get some dinner."

On the way to the commissary, we went by the rec room where Jasar and his troops were now beginning one of their daily prayer sessions. Several times every day seemed a bit excessive, but then going to synagogue on Friday night and Saturday morning seemed too much to me. I had no problem with people who believed in the tenets of their religion, so long as they did not try to foist their beliefs on anyone else. Because the Test-Lits had done just that, I had no qualms about charging into their stronghold to disrupt their nefarious plans. Beating on the guy responsible for the plague might be therapeutic.

Chapter 24

After nightfall on the Test-Lit island, I brought the cloaked *GCVS* in for a landing in the caldera. Unfortunately, it was several kilometers from the site located from orbit, which was swampy and unstable, so we had a longer trek.

We gathered at the ramp hatch, all dressed in our camo-cloaking outfits. We had no camo suit to fit a dragon and he stood out like a beacon, though Healer's fur blended in with the surroundings. Our two alien interns had made it clear they were going on this mission whether we agreed or not. Healer had a score to settle and Red backed his buddy all the way.

Jasar split us into three teams. He would lead the team to assault the dorm building that housed the Test-Lit scientist. Chaim would go with him to identify that person and he insisted on having Roxanne by his side, so again we were separated, which pissed me off. Two troopers followed them, one man and one woman.

The second team included me, Fur, Aypari, two more troopers, again one man and one woman, and Healer. We would break into the laboratory building and make for the central computer system. We planned to find the genetic information, download the data, and then get out. Jasar had supplied us with a nifty black box that would zip through any firewalls, passwords, and encryptions.

The third team included the two final troopers and Learns-To-Fix-Injuries-After-Inflicting-Them. He was too big for breaking and entering. He could do the breaking part well enough, but we did not need the bull-in-the-china-shop approach tonight. Their mission was to appropriate the two flyers that Chaim had mentioned, saving us the five-kilometer ground retreat once we finished. We assumed that we would have triggered some alarm by then.

Jasar led us down the ship's ramp to the rocky surface. Heat and humidity enveloped me. I left my cloaking mask off for now to keep from getting heat stroke. Everyone else did the same. Two moons tracked across the heavens. Silvery moonlight reflected from the lake's surface and sparked off the gazillion mirror-like surfaces of our cloaks. I looked around at the disembodied faces of my companions, always a disorienting endeavor. Red stood out like...well, like a big red dragon.

"Ooh. Hot. Like it," he hissed.

Jasar led us along an un-vegetated beach. Black volcanic sand gritted under my feet. Several plumes of whitish smoke drifted upward from ground vents in the distance. After we had gone half a kilometer, the sand changed to muck. The swamp prevented us from landing closer to the caldera rim where we had planned.

Chaim said, "Um, did I mention the saurians?"

Everyone stopped cold and turned toward him.

"The what?" I asked.

"The saurians. They live in the swamp."

"You mean like *dino*saurians?" Fur's voice was

incredulous.

Jasar asked, his voice level, though I detected extreme annoyance beneath the words, "Are these *saurians* dangerous?"

Chaim picked up the same emotions. "Er...Yes."

"Why didn't you say so before?"

"I-I thought we would land closer to the compound, not by the swamp."

Thoroughly pissed, Jasar turned to the group. "Put your masks on and activate the whisper comms. We will skirt the swamp."

Learns-To-Fix-Injuries sprang into the air to overfly the area.

Red numbers flashed above the party indicating where everyone was. Fur's number *10* towered over all the others. I noted that Jasar was *1*, and Roxanne was *9*. We got around the swamp without incident, but sweat poured down my face and soaked me beneath the cloaking suit.

As we climbed a section with twining head-high thorn-bushes, he assigned two troopers to walk point. Sweat from my hair dripped into my eyes and my bad leg burned from the exertion. My joints were on fire, and my heart seemed to skip every fifth beat, but I kept moving.

At the ridge top, I asked, "Can we take a breather? I can't see for the sweat in my eyes."

His tone curt, Jasar said, "Three minutes. Troops, check our perimeter."

Numbers moved away and then a voice came back. "All clear."

I removed my mask and watched four other heads appear, Roxanne, Chaim, Fur, and Aypari. I did not see Jasar's face. I brushed off as much sweat as I could with the gloves still on, and I took a few ragged breaths.

Then trouble hit. Flying creatures zipped about

above us as we stared down the outside of the caldera. I ignored them until one whacked me in the back of my exposed neck. My hand shot up and slapped at it. It felt squiggly and slimy, but I managed to grab it. I felt a sharp pain when I pulled it away from my neck. It was a slippery squirrel-sized bat-like reptile, with ugly crimson eyes. Yech. I squeezed hard, then dropped it on the ground and stamped on it.

I felt wetness on my neck and rubbed it. When I looked at my hand, blood outlined my invisible fingers. What the hell? I looked around and saw my unhooded crewmates were dealing with the same issue.

"This thing bit me." Roxanne pulled the offender off her neck and threw it down with disgust.

Chaim, Fur, and Aypari also dealt with bites.

Red swooped in and gobbled flying creatures with apparent relish. Healer had shifted to his wolf form, and jumped and snapped at the beasts. I sensed their satisfaction at having live prey to chase.

"Cloaking hoods on, everyone," Jasar ordered then rounded on Chaim. "What are these things, Khodorkosovitch? Another little item you neglected to warn us about?"

Chaim, his hood still off, stared at a creature he'd torn from his cheek then threw it far into the brush. "I've only heard about the vampires. I never went out at night so—"

"Vampires," I screeched. "You mean these damned things are bloodsucking *vampires*?"

"I think they have a scientific name."

Jasar said, "Your voices, people. Whisper. Mask on, Khodorkosovitch."

Heart palpitating, I waved off a few more vampires, but their attack tailed off when we re-donned our hoods. A few went after our alien friends, but the enthusiasm of Red and Healer's feeding discouraged the others.

Shit. I had to deal with a dragon and a werewolf, and now *vampires, too*.

"Move out," Jasar barked.

I caught a strong image from the colonel suggesting that Chaim had not heard the end of this.

We trekked down the slope to the compound. Light poles stood at intervals around a perimeter cleared of brush. A head-high fence stretched between the posts. About one hundred meters separated the fence from the closest buildings.

Jasar's scouts came back. A female voice said, "There are no posted guards. They are not expecting unwelcome visitors."

Finally, some good news. The troopers cut the fence and we split into our assigned groups. We each knew what we had to accomplish. Troopers would be first to enter buildings to scout for and eliminate any threats. We nonmilitary types would follow. All groups would make entry to their respective buildings at the same moment.

My group consisted of troopers *4* and *5*, as denoted by their red lights, Fur and Aypari, *10* and *11*, and Healer. Jasar's group, besides his number *1*, included troopers *2* and *3*, Roxanne, *9*, and Chaim, *12*. Troopers *6* and *7* and Learns-To-Fix-Injuries would go for the aircraft. The whirlydrone we had seen was no longer present.

We gathered at the respective doors, and Jasar gave the whispered signal to go in. The laboratory door opened and *4* and *5* swept across the main foyer. I saw no evidence of people as I followed.

Healer raised his snout, his nostrils dilated, and he snuffled. "I smell one awake human," he said in a low voice.

One of the troopers, the male, said, "You can tell that? Neat. Keep doing it."

We moved toward a bank of elevators at the back of the foyer. I noticed a bit of dizziness, and my legs felt leaden. Too much excitement and the cumulative effects of the chelation, no doubt. I gritted my teeth and ignored the shooting pains in my bad leg.

The female trooper said, "Stay here while we check the offices on this floor." Number *4* moved left and *5* moved right.

I drew my laser pistol, nervous with the troopers gone. Fur's red number *10* rotated as he scanned the room. Healer moved about, snuffling and poking his head behind furniture and desks. His aura remained calm, so I figured nothing worried him yet.

The troopers returned. The male said, "Khodorkosovitch said there were patient rooms on level two and labs on level three. We will check level two first. Use the stairs."

On the second floor, same drill. The troopers went in first, checked up and down the halls, then returned. The woman said "Two men at nursing stations, one asleep, the other engrossed in a magazine. Taken out. They'll sleep for hours. You should see this, but be prepared. It's not pretty." Her voice held disgust and anger as her *4* led us down the hallway.

Glass enclosures lined the corridor, a sealed door into each. Inside the first room, a naked human body occupied a bed. Intravenous tubes snaked to fluid bags, and wires led from the man's chest, skull, and every limb to monitors that metronomically ticked off respiration, pulse, and EKG parameters. His skin was pale, almost alabaster, and mottled with open sores oozing green pus. I decided to forego a closer examination.

Silence reigned. No one in our group spoke as we crept up the hallway. The next cubicle was empty. The following, not so. A similar arrangement, body and all, though this man had a vesicular rash that covered skin so inflamed that it looked as if it should self-combust. My stomach contracted and relaxed, as if preparing for a major eruptive event.

In the next room, a man or woman—I could not tell which—lay with half the face eaten away. One empty eye socket gazed out into nothingness. The monitors had flatlined. Thankfully, this patient was beyond pain. There were more rooms, but I did not want to explore them. I'd seen enough of the Test-Lit's handiwork.

Fur's whisper broke the silence. "My God..." He had no more words.

Healer said, "They smell bad...wrong."

All my companions' reactions came through clearly. Everyone, even the hardened troopers, fought the need to vomit. I swallowed the acid that made it as far as my throat. My legs felt even heavier and I staggered as I turned back toward the entry door.

I made it up to the third floor with difficulty. The laboratories checked out empty, and Fur found the central computer room.

It took me so long to stagger there that Fur had the black box clipped to the keyboard of a terminal and was entering commands.

"It's supposed to be automatic from here."

Numbers and letters scrolled across and down the monitor faster than I could follow. Then: *"PASSWORD OVERRIDDEN. FILES UNLOCKED. Enter Search terms."*

Fur keyed in search terms for genomic data, his big fingers surprisingly nimble on the keys, but a generic search brought up too much. Aypari narrowed the search specifying microbial gene parameters for Fur.

Fur scrolled through files, stopping when Aypari commanded.

As the data scrolled down the screen, Aypari said,

"Some of these files contain viral information and nucleic acid sequences I recognize: smallpox, rabies, hepatitis, influenza, human immunodeficiency virus, even animal diseases like parvoviruses and canine distemper. Others make no sense. They are like nothing I know."

Fur opened and scrolled through several more files. Each screen had a descriptive paragraph and a prompt to open the full file for detailed data. I leaned closer to read the tiny print of the file descriptions. Then he scrolled to a file and a clang reverberated in my head as if I were inside a giant bell.

"Stop," I screamed as I put my hands to my head. An all-too-familiar feeling rocked me, one of wrongness, what I felt from the plague. "There. That file..." Goosebumps rose on my arms and the hair on the back of my neck stood erect. "It's the plague."

The longer I stared at the sparse data on the monitor, the more it seemed to insinuate itself into my brain, making my head pound as if to burst.

Fur clicked on the file prompt.

"FILE RESTRICTED: ENTER AUTHORIZATION" blossomed across the screen.

"Shit! We can't be blocked now," I exclaimed.

"Hold on," Fur said. "This box is supposed to get past any blocks. Give it a few seconds."

It seemed like forever, but the message disappeared and the full file rolled out. I understood basic DNA and RNA structure, but I always relied on Ruthie to decipher the detailed codes. I felt as if the screen fired electrical lances into my brain. I looked away and groaned. "Download everything, Fur. Aypari can ferret out what we need to know later." I was glad we had a bona fide microbiology expert with us.

"I'm guessing we saw the results of infections with some of these unknown organisms on the second floor.

This place is a biological warfare research center. A nightmare."

My mind leapt back into history, particularly that surrounding the second of the Terran world wars. I recalled a photograph of the Nazi, Josef Mengele, which showed the face of a seemingly pleasant young man. But Mengele, a Nazi officer and physician in a prison camp, selected victims, mostly Jews, for extermination in the gas chambers, and for unscientific and often deadly human experiments. One tragedy in the aftermath of that horrible war was that Mengele escaped capture and punishment for his crimes.

What the Test-Lits engaged in here was as heinous, or worse, a modern Holocaust that threatened to encompass the galaxy's human and non-human inhabitants. Not for the first time I questioned whether any God who could allow the monstrous acts of hate groups like the Nazis or the Test-Lits was worthy of worship or even recognition. The furnaces of my rage were stoked, and I would ensure they burned the ashes of the monsters who had done this.

When we were finished, I staggered again and grabbed the edge of the work table to stay upright. Oh, no. Did I contract one of those diseases from the patients? But we never broke confinement, never even entered the rooms.

My head spun like a *dreidel*, and I removed my hood. My tongue felt swollen, but I spoke around it. "Whash wrong? I..." The room whirled and I landed on my butt, hard, but I felt no pain. It was as if I was partially anesthetized. I gasped for breath.

Aypari and Fur removed their hoods, both gasping for air. Fur wobbled and Aypari's face fell to my level.

Healer came close and sniffed at me. He gently swiped a hand across my neck, and then stared at his bloody talon. He licked the blood. "The vampires. They did this. There is poison in the blood." Sometimes the most sophisticated of modern equipment could not match the incredible senses that evolution conferred on its creations.

I felt a trooper's hand on my arm. She whispered, "I am not affected. I kept my hood on."

The man agreed. "I, also, was hooded."

Fur remained standing, though he staggered. His size probably protected him to some degree. I was glad only one vampire had bitten me. A flock of those things could down an elephant.

"We must leave," a trooper said. "Gather outside with the other groups. Head covers on, please."

Trooper 5 helped me and 4 assisted Aypari as we headed for the stairs, following Fur who carried the all-important black box.

***

Chaim followed the red numbers floating in the night, wondering at the technology that made invisibility possible. His heart pounded, and his mouth created no saliva, as he tried to swallow, unsuccessfully. He reached up to wipe the sweat streaming into his eyes, only to have his hand blocked by the cloaking hood. Despite the head covering, Chaim could see the ground and the buildings in a ghostly greenish light. Roxanne's number was 9, and he followed close on her heels.

The red numbers stopped at the door to the building, and then it opened. The entryway was dark, and no alarm went off. The sleeping quarters were on the second floor. He now feared he'd forgotten more details like the saurians and the vampires. He followed the floating numbers into the main room. Number 1, Jasar, moved to the base of the open stairway to the second floor, and waited for the troopers to check the rooms on the main floor before he started up. Chaim's legs trembled as he climbed the stairs. His whole body shook, as if he had the ague.

Three closed doors cut the back wall of the second floor hallway. He knew one of them led to the chambers of the facility's chief scientist, Irving Rosten. An innocuous name for the devil who had created the plague and sent Chaim off to do his horrendous deed.

Jasar's whisper asked, "Which door is the scientist?"

Chaim tried to work up enough saliva to respond, but his throat cramped.

"Quickly, you fool."

Chaim managed a weak, "The far left."

No light seeped out from under the door of any of the rooms, suggesting the occupants slept.

Jasar whispered, "Go."

His team opened all three doors simultaneously and rushed in. Chaim stayed rooted to the spot, feeling faint. He fought off a wave of dizziness. A muffled cry from the room in front of him was the only sound.

Three men stumbled out the doors, one from each room, their hands locked behind their backs by restraints, their mouths covered by tape. Chaim heard muffled grunts from the men.

Jasar pulled up his mask, so Chaim did the same. The eyes of all three captives went wide as they saw Chaim. Jasar held the scientist, who squirmed frantically against his captor and his bonds.

Chaim heard Rosten's voice in his head, a horrified wail of fear and frustration: *You cannot be here, Khodorkosovitch. You should be dead.*

An image came through of Rosten telling Rebbe Mordechai Neidritch, "Terminate Chaim when his mission is complete."

Rosten's agonized mental scream assaulted Chaim's already reeling senses. He stumbled and dropped to one knee, catching himself with his hands. *How can I hear him? What is he saying? I was to be killed? That the honor I would receive for my sacrifice was to be death?*

Chaim found it hard to breathe. His stomach twisted and rolled.

Jasar's face stared at him. "What is wrong?"

Chaim felt a hand on his shoulder. Roxanne's face appeared next to his. "What is it, Chaim?"

He could not answer.

Jasar spoke again. "Khodorkosovitch, are these the right men?"

Chaim shook off his increasing vertigo and replied. "The one you hold is Irving Rosten. He created the plague and injected it into me." *He is the one who ordered my death!* "The other two had nothing to do with the medical side."

"But they must have known, right?" Roxanne's voice was weak, fluttery.

Chaim nodded. Speaking was too difficult.

Jasar's sharp voice cut in. "What is wrong with you two? Stand up. We must go."

"I...I cannot," Chaim replied. "Something is wrong."

Roxanne added, "I'm weak and dizzy. I don't understand."

The female trooper said, "These two were bitten by those vampire things."

"Damn." Jasar's voice held suppressed fury. "Rosten is the one we want. We leave the administrators. Dispose of them, troopers."

The two administrators backed against the hallway wall as if in front of a firing squad, seemingly of their own volition, but Chaim could see they fought against their unseen captors.

"No!" Chaim screamed. The sound of his own voice deafened him through his audio input. "You can't," Chaim pleaded, his voice lowered. "You promised there would be no unnecessary killing. These men did nothing but their assigned jobs."

Jasar glared at Chaim, but said, "Secure them, hands and feet, and tie them to their beds. Give them knockout drops."

When the troopers returned, Jasar said, "Get your head covers on." A trooper helped Chaim to his wobbly feet, and another helped Roxanne. With Jasar's number *1* in the lead, pushing Rosten in front of him, they all left the dormitory and moved toward the laboratory building. On the way, Chaim's feet dragged as much as he stepped; his arms and legs were numb. As they approached the laboratory door, the fearsome dragon charged toward him.

Chapter 25

Jasar and his team moved toward us as we opened the laboratory building door. I stumbled as we exited, and Fur carried Aypari at this point, though he staggered also. Roxanne's *9* wobbled alongside trooper *3*, which scared the shit out of me.

Trooper *4* reported to Jasar, "The wolf man said he smelled poison in the wounds inflicted by those flying creatures."

Before Jasar could reply, Learns-To-Fix-Injuries skidded to a wing-flapping halt in front of me, nearly bowling me over.

"Cyberger. Bad newss. Air flyerss not in hanger."

Jasar cursed. "It will be dawn soon. We've got to move out."

The dragon hissed, "Ssoldier colonel, trooperss have land droness. Coming now."

Two open-bed land drones wheeled around the building and headed toward us. As they halted, one driver reported, "Colonel, this is the best we could find."

I homed in on Roxanne's *9* and felt for her

shoulder. "Are you all right?"

"Dizzy. And my legs are numb, weak."

"Me too."

"Everybody load up," Jasar commanded.

The wheeled drones held eight each, which gave us plenty of room, since Healer and Red chose to run and fly, respectively. Healer morphed into his werewolf form and dropped back as rear guard.

I sensed Chaim flinch at Healer's shape-change, and his fear wracked me at the same time. Red flew off to scout ahead, and the troopers headed the drones up the hill toward the caldera rim.

I snuggled up to Roxanne and turned off the communicator. Head to head we could hear one another, but no one could hear us over the roar of the drone engines. "How are you doing?"

She found my arm and squeezed it. "I'm less dizzy now and can feel my toes."

"The damned vampires have venom that weakens their prey. Healer said he could smell it in my blood."

"Healer's ability is amazing."

Fur and Aypari had their heads together, so I assumed they were chatting too.

About halfway up the mountainside, I flicked my whisper unit back on to keep track of Jasar's orders. We drove past thorny scrub brush and a few skeletal trees, all limned in the glow of my cloaking suit's infravision. A faint yellow blush revealed the curve of the horizon. We did not have much darkness left. I hoped we would at least make it into caldera by dawn, but the drones were starting to bog down in patches of loose volcanic scree. Within one hundred meters of the rim, the other drone came to a halt, hopelessly mired axle-deep in volcanic sand.

Jasar's *1* stepped down with his prisoner who was still handcuffed and gagged. "We go on foot from here."

As the toxin wore off and feeling returned to my limbs, my nerves felt as if they were on fire.

Jasar ordered, "Troopers, camouflage those drones as much as you can, then catch up with us."

The good news was that the flying vampires didn't attack us again. Maybe with the dawn they roosted for the day. When we reached the rim, a red-gold sun painted its colors on the mountainside.

Healer loped up, panting. His tongue flopped out the side of his mouth like any good doggie. "Nothing coming from behind."

We plodded down the crater's steep slope, taking care not to slip on the loose rock. It was tougher on my bad leg than climbing, and the numbness made it harder still. The going would be a bit easier once we reached level ground, at least until we hit the swamp.

As dawn brightened the bottom of the crater, I stumbled along, trying to keep up. Pain speared up my bad leg, and my energy store was emptying fast. Jasar kept us marching. We slowed a bit, cutting through the swamp, taking a more direct route back to the ship rather than skirting the wet area. The muck seemed to grab at my feet, slowing me even more.

In the daylight, I could no longer see the red numbers above the cloaking suits, but I saw the splash as the trooper escorting Rosten fell. His outline was clear in the muck. Rosten took off running straight into the swamp.

Jasar barked, "God damn it. Get him."

Splashing footsteps of a second trooper chased after the scientist. Rosten got a hundred meters from us and tripped, falling flat on his face. He floundered as he tried to rise, and the trooper's boots splatted toward him. "Stay there or you're dead," the trooper ordered.

The swamp bulged upward then erupted in a spray

of water and muck. A green-scaled snout rose above the surface, followed by two bulging eyes as big as my head, topped by a deep brow ridge, sprouting nubby horn-like excrescences. The snout opened to reveal a mouth ringed by needle-like teeth. A purple tongue snapped out, wrapped around Rosten, and dragged him toward the gaping maw.

Everyone was yelling. With the whisper comms on, the din was unendurable, but I caught Chaim's cry. "Saurian."

Learns-To-Fix-Injuries swooped low overhead, folded his wings and went into a screaming, hissing dive. He sank his talons into the beast's snout. The saurian let out a scream like a fractured calliope whistle and rose up farther out of the swamp. Red hung on, flapped his wings like mad, and bit down on the saurian's head near one eye, drawing purple blood.

The creature released Rosten, who splashed down in the muck. Finally, Red had to let go—the saurian was too massive for him to lift—and the thing disappeared beneath the surface, still whistling in distress. Red hovered and offered his own hissing bellow of challenge.

I felt safer with him up there. We had half a kilometer of swamp to traverse, which seemed like a million to my freaked-out mind.

Jasar yelled, "Grab Rosten. Let's get out of here."

No one hesitated. We moved quickly until we made dry ground within shouting distance of the ship.

Red circled in and set his wings for a landing. "Fun but tasste bad, like rotty fissh. Would not eat."

Who knew a dragon would be so fussy.

By this time, everyone had removed their cloaking hoods. With Rosten out in plain sight along with the dragon and the werewolf, cloaking did not help much. My leg had little left in it, and the last bit of excitement had wrung my adrenals dry. I lagged behind the group. My head, stomach, and leg competed for which-hurt-worse honors. Every muscle and joint protested.

Roxanne dropped back and walked with me. The trooper managing Rosten kept the scientist moving with combative shoves.

We were almost to the *GCVS* when I heard the roar and syncopated thumping of an oncoming whirlydrone. Everyone turned and looked with me. That it took so long for them to locate us was likely because they had to fly circular search patterns extending outward from the complex. One thing in our favor, there was only one in the air.

Jasar yelled, "Get aboard."

I lurched toward the ship, as everyone other than my wife ran for the ramp. My leg burned like the fires of hell, and I lost ground to the group.

Roxanne screamed, "Fur, help Cy."

The bird circled us and came in for a strafing run. The repetitive barking sound of a machine gun cut through the morning air, and I watched a line of projectiles hit the ground like tiny black volcanic eruptions. Amazingly, no one was hit on the first pass. The drone banked and came back in from behind me. I struggled to keep my legs moving forward, but the bad one gave out. I dropped to my knees and looked up.

The dragon was diving at the drone, but the rotors would cut him to pieces.

I screamed, "No, Red. No!" and he veered off at the last moment. He probably could not hear me, but I felt his consciousness as I yelled and got through to his mind telepathically with a vision of his oncoming dismemberment. Nice to have a positive side to my new ability.

Roxanne held onto my arm, urging me up, but I had nothing left. Fur pelted toward me mouth open and moving. I heard nothing but the staccato gun reports and the sharp cracks as the projectiles tore into the volcanic turf.

As I tried to get back to my feet, a sharp searing pain hit my bad leg, and I collapsed. Puffs of black sand headed straight for Fur, but he dove to the side, rolled, and scrabbled to his feet. He picked me up, threw me over his shoulder, and galloped toward the ramp, Roxanne at our side.

I saw a trail of blood following us.

Jasar shouted, "Get that son-of-a-bitch."

I heard an explosion and a cheer.

Fur toted me through the airlock, plunked me on the deck, and dropped beside me. He looked at me, gasping for breath. "You know, this is getting old, Berger. Next time *you* carry *me*."

Chapter 26

Laid out on the exam table in the surgery, I stared up at Red's face as he leaned over me.

"You ssurvive, Cyberger. This not sso bad ass bomb in land drone." He referred, of course, to the first time he had pulled my chestnuts out of the fire, when the unfortunate bin Saqer had lost his life.

"Thanks loads, Red. You're all heart," I mumbled. The sedative was taking effect.

Roxanne poked my leg. "Feel that?"

"Just pressure."

"Okay. I'm not going to put you under for this, but...Red you hold him down if he jumps, okay?"

Just what I needed, an overzealous orderly. I felt his warm cozy talons close on my shoulders, but I shut my eyes and drifted on a Hemptamine high. I heard a few grunts and imprecations from Roxanne and started to worry.

"There's soft tissue damage where the bullet went through your calf. Didn't hit the bone, but I need to clean the wound and..." Her voice tailed off.

I opened my eyes to see Healer, all gowned and

gloved, holding a forceps and suture needle.

"You are sutured, Dr. Cyberger." He smiled his toothy, wolfish grin.

My wife said, "Healer needed the practice."

"Practice?" I tried to sit up, but the dragon had me pinned.

"Cool it, Cy," my trusting wife said. "He did a good job."

I gulped and kept my mouth shut. That was why the dragon and the werewolf were with us, after all, to learn our trade. I just thought maybe they could do a bit more practice on the expensive Realflesh anatomic dummy we bought for them.

***

With Fur at the helm, we lifted off Jaffa and flew the *GCVS* outward through the planetary orbits of Jaffa's solar system to reach the hyperspace jump point. That would take a week if we did not engage the afterburners, and Fur did not want any more stress to the antimatter engine after his on-the-fly repairs. No one felt bad about staying within usual acceleration parameters. We'd have to use the supercharger again back in New Mecca's solar system.

At the orbit of the first of the system's gas giants, I hobbled to the rec area where the entire ship's contingent sat in on the interrogation of our prisoner. I stopped at the hatch to watch and listen.

Colonel Jasar was grilling Rosten, who sat with his arms fastened behind him to a chair. Rosten had zero understanding of the Testamentary-Literalist military capabilities on his world, and even less interest in it. On the other hand, the man lost no opportunity to spout the Test-Lit manifesto.

"Khodorkosovitch understands," he said. "We are

the true inheritors of Judaism. All other sects have lost their way, fallen to false idols, lost the true belief."

He went on and on, how the Test-Lits understood the true meaning of the Torah, that they would cleanse all other religious beliefs from the galaxy. Muslims, in particular, came under a vitriolic spew of invective. Rosten said that Islam's destruction was inevitable and appropriate.

I had heard much of it before, but the sheer poison of Rosten's attacks sickened me. Jasar let him rage on, since we recorded Rosten's invective tirade for use at his trial on New Mecca. Rosten's words stirred the cauldron of rage in my belly and forced me to hold my mental screen at maximum.

Chaim's face was a rigid mask. It amazed me that he had learned to use his own mental screen so quickly. Then I realized he had as much access to my mind as I did to his. He learned it from me. Black circles under his eyes stood out against the whiteness of his visage. Though indoctrinated by the Test-Lits from childhood, perhaps for the first time he heard the filth from a different viewpoint.

Finally, Fur broke in. "And you include the murder of innocent animals as part of God's law, his commandments?"

Rosten sneered. "Animals have no souls, no value. I accomplished something that no one else could." The man was *proud* of the abomination he had created.

An obscene smile crept across his face like some disgusting slug. "Even though the disease would kill only animals, the human deaths would come through starvation, and they would be slower, more painful."

I could not hold my tongue any longer. "There's nothing sacred to you, is there? How many people did you kill with your vile experiments? We saw your victims in your laboratory. How can you live with that inside you?"

He looked at me and sneered again; one side of his lip curled up to show carious, smoke-stained yellow teeth. "All human lives are meaningless unless they hew to the true religion. Animals...?" He spat. "Filth."

I gave my life to the healing and care of animals, and this was the final tipping point. I did not see Irving Rosten in the chair in front of me; I saw Josef Mengele. I stepped toward him, next to Jasar, and focused on the colonel's sidearm, loose in its holster. I grabbed the laser pistol and pointed it at...who? Irving Rosten? Josef Mengele? I was not sure. My hand tightened on the firing stud, wanting to press that trigger, again and again, until nothing was left but a pool of smoking protoplasm. I tried. But I could not.

Surprisingly, Jasar did nothing for those few moments, and then he pried the weapon from my grasp. He seemed to know I would not do it. Maybe I telepathically broadcast that message despite my fury.

Like with Reb Levi, the man who had tormented me and tortured my parents, in the end, hate was not enough. I could not bring myself to take another human life. I was a healer, not a killer. It had taken Fur, whose family had suffered even more than mine from the actions of our old Test-Lit enemy, to end that man's life. Fittingly.

Jasar holstered the blaster. "He will be brought to justice on New Mecca."

"You need me," Rosten gloated. "Only I have the key to the plague. In my brain."

"We have your computer files," Fur retorted.

"They are locked, triple encoded, and protected with a password that exists only in my head." Rosten raised his chin and glared at Fur.

I heard Chaim groan behind me, and felt his dismay like a stab to my brain.

"You know what?" I said, "We have the data. We already broke your super fucking code and password. We *don't* need you."

Rosten's smile turned to open-mouthed astonishment.

"Enough." Jasar shook his head. "We have what we need from this piece of filth." He turned to a trooper. "Lock him up."

***

The remainder of the trip to the hyperjump point I spent in daily sessions on renal dialysis. Chaim's kidney function did not require the dialysis, but my already damaged kidneys were failing fast. Fortunately, the effects of the vampire toxin had worn off completely after one day with no aftereffects. Both Healer and Learns-To-Fix-Injuries held up much better under treatment than we humans did, with no significant toxicity.

Healer's regenerative powers probably played a role. In the dragon's case, I recalled the gladiatorial fights held on their home world. A dragon could take the punishment of any ten Terran animals and come out smiling. Maybe that vitality was what kept Red from coming down with the plague to begin with.

We all spent time in the lab going through the genetic codes we had retrieved from Rosten's computer files. It was there, the code sequence for the plague DNA, but we found nothing that looked like it coded for the rest of a microorganism, viral or otherwise, that could carry that DNA and deliver it to a cell.

"This makes no sense," I complained to Fur, Roxanne, and Aypari. "This DNA codes for production of a host of enzymes, phospholipases, proteases, and endonucleases. That's how it kills cells, it dissolves membranes, proteins, and nucleic acids from the inside. But naked DNA can't get into a body, much less into cells."

Fur's face was nose-to-computer screen as columns of figures and text scrolled past, giving his face a weird, strobing greenish illumination.

As I watched, again I felt as if struck by a blow, just like back in Rosten's laboratory. The *wrongness* was there, but this time stronger than ever. The data on the screen resonated in my brain.

"Stop!" I grabbed Fur's arm. "There. Look."

Everyone turned to me, eyes widened.

Fur turned to me. "What are you talking about? Those are schematics for some sort of electronics."

"We've been looking for the wrong thing," I said. "It's not a microorganism at all. The plague vector is not just biological. It's biomechanical. It's a nanobot!"

I heard nothing of any their responses. My own word reverberated in my brain: "Nanobot... nanobot... nanobot..."

Fur's voice emerged again. "Good lord. That's why the chelation therapy worked. The excess iron was in the nanobots and the chelate complexed with it and cleared the bots. With no free bots in circulation, the infection's spread was halted and patients weren't contagious any longer. But the chelate didn't do anything to remove the plague DNA inside the cells."

There was dead silence.

I broke it with another thought. "There must still be nanobots hiding in the body, though, since the disease recurs when the chelation is stopped. Maybe still attached to cell membranes within organs."

I pointed at the monitor. "That's a schematic of the nanobot. The damn thing is part organic, part machine. Carbon, silicon, iron, nitrogen, oxygen: Those are all natural chemicals found in the body. No wonder we could find no trace of anything foreign, even in the chelated complexes. And look at this structure on the outside of the bot. It looks like an artificial antigen that would attach to a cell surface receptor, the plague receptor, allowing it to inject the plague DNA into the cell."

Roxanne sighed. "What a mind to conceive and accomplish something like this. To think that it was harnessed for such evil, when it could have done so much good..."

I broke another long silence. "But this means we have it now. We can beat this thing. We know how to destroy the vector *and* now we can the target the DNA."

I thought, *We should all have a drink to celebrate.*

I was stunned when everyone, a moment later, repeated my unvoiced words. "We should all have a drink to celebrate."

I dropped my head in my hands. *Oh, no!*

***

The morning after discovering the nanobot data, I headed for the commissary. My bride was there. A lovely grin adorned her face when she saw me. Aypari sat by her side. Both watched as Fur sketched schematics on an e-tablet. I grabbed some tea and joined them.

"Here's the most important factor yet," he said. "See this oval structure? It's not as obvious on the actual bot plans, so I've emphasized it here. It's a double phospholipid membrane, just like cell membranes. And it contains the DNA!"

"That's astounding," Roxanne said. "What a construct."

"That's how the nanobot gets its DNA into the

cell," Aypari added. "It looks like any cytoplasmic membrane-bound cell organelle, lysosomes or mitochondria."

Fur pointed to the portion of the bot that attached to the exterior of the cell membrane. "It looks like this structure on the bot punches a hole and then extrudes the DNA-containing organelle into the cytoplasm. We never could see the foreign DNA because it was shielded by the bot. Then once in the cell, it was hidden in the nucleus."

Aypari said, "The bot is empty after the DNA organelle is ejected until the plague DNA replicates, reembeds itself in another organelle, and moves back into the bot. Then the bot is contagious again and can detach and infect a new host cell."

I said, "The important thing is that it is the DNA-containing bots that are the vectors of infection. Millions of still viable damaged cells carrying infectious bots are sloughing from the tissues in a sick animal. To a lesser degree, the same is true for Chaim and me. Any contact with an infected host would transfer cells with DNA-containing bots to a new host. Epithelial cells sloughed from skin or in saliva or sweat, or even air coughed up and exhaled would carry bots. Blood cells carry bots, but I'm sure that there are some free DNA-containing bots in circulation as they move to infect new cells. Same for excretions. It does take close contact since the bots self-destruct so quickly, but all one has to do is land on the skin of a new host and infection is immediate.

"But once the bot loses its DNA, it is harmless until it's re-primed by newly formed DNA. If we destroy the plague DNA, the empty bots are noninfectious and the patient is cured. Short-term chelation therapy will remove the empty bots, if necessary. Aypari, what's your plan to get rid of the DNA?"

She looked at me, then at Fur, before she spoke. "You suggested this before, Cy. This kind of procedure was developed way back in the twenty-first century. We create an RNA sequence that specifically binds to the plague DNA. We hook that RNA to flanking enzymes that target and snip out the plague DNA at its ends. Another created piece of RNA would code for synthesis of a specific endonuclease enzyme to destroy only the plague DNA."

I smiled. "Kill off the plague DNA without any harm to the host genome. Can you create that?"

She nodded. "Fur and I can."

Roxanne added, "To get that plague-killing construct to its targets we can put it into a benign viral vector. If we create the vector to attach to the same receptor that allowed the plague bot to attach, it will be able to infect cells of all species that get the plague."

"We could broadcast the viral vector widely over the land and sea to get to the remaining wild animals and fish," Fur said. "We won't need to get every animal. They'll spread the cleansing viral infection themselves."

Roxanne looked at me, her mind flooding me with relief. *And it cures you*, she said silently, but I heard her words as if spoken. I loved the words, but I hated the fact that I was unquestionably a telepath.

***

After I finished my latest dialysis, I returned to the commissary. Fur was again, or still, playing with his tablet. He had downloaded all the specs for the nanobot.

I grabbed some juice and sat by him.

Fur looked up from the pad. "Cy, I've got something else strange here. Look." He pointed out a magnified segment of the bot. "What does this look like to you?"

I examined the schematic and scratched my head. "It looks like a little microchip. But that can't be. How big are those things?"

"I agree, it looks like an integrated circuit, but I wouldn't use the term *big* in this case. If anything, I'd call it a picochip, a million times smaller than a microchip. There are dozens of these things in the bot."

One of those epiphanies that hit like a freight drone crashed into my brain. "Holy shit. Fur, let's get everyone in here. Now!" I jumped up then crashed back to my seat. "Uh, maybe you had better do that. I'm a bit shaky."

He jumped up. "Sit tight, I'll get Aypari. You call Roxanne on the comm."

"I want Chaim, too." I contacted them both. I cringed at the need to own up to my enhanced mental abilities, that I was becoming a telepath, feeling like a total freak.

When everyone was there, I said, "You all know about my empathic ability. Chaim's, too. What you don't know is that my ability has progressed, become stronger since I've been on New Mecca. It has gone beyond empathy...I've become a telepath."

Everyone except Roxanne, who already knew, spoke at once, but the thing that nearly dropped me off my seat was Chaim's reaction, as clear as if he spoke into my ear.

My God. It is true. He feels it also. Others speaking to me through my mind.

I glanced at him and thought, *Keep it down, Chaim. That hurts.*

His eyes widened, and he nodded.

I put up a hand for quiet. "Fur has discovered something else startling in the plague nanobot. It contains tiny integrated electronic circuits, essentially pico-sized chips. This allowed communication between the bots within the body. This explains something I never paid any attention to. The progress of the plague in victims often went in stages, with slowing of progress, then a wave of new injury. However, the plague was so rapid overall, that the lag didn't seem important. I think the bots were communicating, coordinating their growth as they spread through the body."

Again, everyone spoke at once.

"Quiet! Please. I can't deal with that." I felt autistic, psychologically unable to handle the noise around me. When they quieted down, I said, "This next is speculation, but it is at least partly true. My enhanced empathy started after my first exposure to the plague when we examined the camels. And it has progressed since I was infected. The same is true for Chaim. I believe that our empathic enhancement is because we have a built-in wireless picocommunication system in our bodies. The bots!"

Fur asked, "Cy, something has bothered me from the beginning. You were wearing an isolation suit that first day. How did the plague get to you through that?"

I cringed, but I knew. "The dog. The mutt that staggered toward our group had the plague."

Fur's eyes widened and his mouth opened in an "O" before he spoke. "He peed on the fence post and splattered you. And urine is infective."

I glanced around the room, but, fortunately, no one even came close to thinking it was funny.

"Another thing," Fur added, "Does this mean if you clear the plague and the bots, your new...talent will disappear too?" Concern underlay his question, as if that would be a *bad* thing.

I looked at Fur, then at Chaim.

Chaim lifted his chin and transmitted, *I do not want*

this.

I nodded to him and answered Fur. "I hope that the telepathy *will* disappear with the bots. It's *not* something I want to live with. Chaim feels the same.

"There's one more thing that I've puzzled over, how the bots reproduce. They can't divide like bacteria, or even have the plague DNA produce new structural proteins like viruses do to rebuild themselves. The bots are made of chemicals normal to the body. Some of those picochips must contain instructions for assembly of new bots from those body chemicals. The bots must make more bots while they sit on the cell membrane after their DNA has left.

"The plague DNA reproduces more than one copy of itself and then infects the old and new bots on the surface. Once the new infectious bots are completed, there is communication and they detach from the infected cells all over the body at once. The plague DNA left behind then codes for production of the destructive enzymes and there is the wave of cell death, while new healthy cells are infected."

Total silence met this pronouncement. I was not surprised. It was hard to take it all in.

***

We decided to wait until we had the plague cure before making the hyperspace jump back to New Mecca's solar system. Fur and Aypari labored without rest, and then finally announced success.

We had no infectious plague on board to test on cells or animals, but we needed to prove the cure. I volunteered as the guinea pig, but Chaim insisted he be the first test subject since the disease transmission on New Mecca was his responsibility. He would not back off and we acceded to his wishes.

We injected him with the viral vector containing the enzymes that targeted the plague DNA and stopped his chelation therapy. We could not be totally sure of the specificity of the enzymes and whether there might be collateral damage to his DNA or cells. Every day, we monitored his blood for the enzymes that signaled tissue injury such as we had found in both of us from the plague damage. Every day, we injected his blood into cultures kept in an isolation hood. We watched those cultures.

After a week, there was no sign of infection, either in Chaim or in the cultures. If he harbored active plague bots, we would have detected them by now. We took liver, kidney, and bone marrow biopsies and inoculated those cells into cultures. We had to know that the plague was not hiding deeper as it had in patients undergoing chelation treatment, only to emerge on cessation of the therapy.

When those were negative, we moved ahead with treatment of Healer and me. We even treated Learns-To-Fix-Injuries to cover all bases. We stopped all chelation therapy and repeated the infectivity tests on all three of us for insurance.

We celebrated our success. Unfortunately, even off the chelation treatment, I remained on dialysis, and I felt like shit. My kidneys were not recovering.

It was time to face the blockade to reach New Mecca.

Chapter 27

Chaim cringed, anticipating the crushing pain when the ship accelerated to antimatter supercharger velocity. He understood that their sudden emergence from hyperspace at that speed would allow them to get past the cordon around New Mecca's solar system jump point. When the supercharger cut in, he lost consciousness.

He awoke when the acceleration force lifted. He levered himself out of the couch's harness and moved unsteadily to find the crew, Roxanne, particularly. Because of her kindness toward him, he now felt comfortable thinking of her by her given name, if not addressing her so.

Cohen was in the commissary and waved Chaim to a seat.

"How is Berger?" Chaim asked. Because of their telepathic connection, Chaim felt more tolerant of the veterinarian, having seen himself from a different viewpoint. However, he did not regret the disappearance of the telepathic link that came with the plague cure. That was a huge relief.

Cohen shook his head, his concern washing over Chaim before he put up his mental screen. He was not used to doing that soon enough, and his stomach roiled. Though his empathic ability diminished with the cure of the plague, it had not disappeared any more than Berger's had. Empathy was a normal function of their genetic background.

Roxanne walked into the cabin.

Cohen looked at her. "Chaim asked about Cy."

She sat next to Cohen.

Chaim wished she sat by him.

"Not good," she said. "His kidneys are shot."

Chaim held his screen firm now, because Roxanne's grief was almost overwhelming. "I don't understand. I was on chelation therapy with him, but my kidneys recovered when it stopped."

Roxanne nodded. "True, but Cy... He's been through too much in the past months. Getting blown up near Medina. Shot down in the desert. He went into septic shock, which damaged many of his organs, but his kidneys were the worst. Then the chelation damage... There was too little renal function left."

"Will he...die?"

"Not right now. On dialysis, his odds of living three to five years are even; ten years slim. He will need a kidney transplant to survive longer, but even with that, his life expectancy will be shortened. In any case, he needs more medical support than I can give him here on the ship."

Chaim looked away. He wished there were something he could do to spare Roxanne this grief.

***

As they approached the blockade surrounding New Mecca, everyone met in the rec area, including the aliens. Chaim stayed on the opposite side of the room from the creatures...and the New Meccan military.

Berger addressed the group, his voice weak. "Since we can't use the antimatter engines in New Mecca's atmosphere, we have to slow and deal with the blockade again. I contacted the orbital fleet and explained that we carried the cure for the plague, that the only hope for New Mecca and the rest of the galaxy was to allow us through.

"Admiral B'Jong didn't desire to discuss the point. We humiliated him when we escaped on our way out, and he wanted revenge. Fortunately, a higher-up overrode him. Roxanne and I spoke with their medical scientists and convinced them that we had the plague cure. We are being allowed to land."

Chaim's pride in Roxanne knew no bounds. Perhaps her efforts would help him efface some of his sin. Not all of it, of course, but she and Berger would save New Mecca and avert the potential disaster for the rest of the galaxy.

The ship dropped through New Mecca's atmosphere, cloaked and shielded to prevent attack by Hussein's forces. After landing, Chaim stepped to the top of the now open ramp. He stared at the military contingent at the bottom. He knew his time as a relatively free man was over. As the crew walked down the ramp, two soldiers identified him and took him into custody, clamping his hands in restraints behind his back.

Roxanne stopped and turned toward him. "No," she cried. "You can't do that. He's part of the reason we're here with the cure. What's the matter with you? Take those off!"

The troopers stopped, flustered by Roxanne's verbal assault.

Jasar stepped between Chaim and his captors. "She

is correct. This man is not a threat. He will come with us. I will be responsible for his actions."

Faced with a superior's orders, the men removed the hand restraints and moved away. Chaim breathed a sigh of relief and turned to follow Jasar and Roxanne. They were correct. He would not try to escape, would face up to what he had done.

***

My hospital room had a more advanced renal dialysis machine than the one on the *GCVS*. The better dialysis had reduced the build-up of toxic wastes like blood urea nitrogen and creatinine in my blood, but I still had no strength, and muscle cramps and irritability interfered with my sleep. On top of that, because my kidneys no longer produced the hormone erythropoietin that stimulated red blood cell production, I was anemic, which compounded my fatigue. Of course, I spent far too much time worrying about those things, the negative effect of knowing too much.

Ali peeked in my door, interrupting my latest examination of my lab report. I had not seen him since we returned to New Mecca, and I waved him in.

He sat in a chair next to the bed I was propped up in. "Cy, Roxanne has told me that you are improved. I am pleased at that. I am also unsure how the people of New Mecca can show their thanks for what you have done. You saved the animals of our planet from extinction. And its people."

My voice was weaker than I liked. "Wait a minute. Don't thank *me*. The whole team gets the credit, with a big thank you to one of your own, Dr. Habib. She's the one who did the critical DNA work. She should get a medal."

"I agree. She will receive recognition for her work.

On another note, you will be happy to hear that our civil war is coming to an end. Chief Medical Officer Hussein still holds out in his central facility in Medina, but the news of your breakthrough and its import for our world turned opinion against him. Only his hardcore cronies stand by him, since they know they also will pay for their crimes. I expect that we will have an end to hostilities in days."

"I'm thrilled to hear that, Imam. You believed in us when you could have turned your back, or worse."

"My faith was amply rewarded. I must go, there is too much I must do, but I wanted to give you my thanks in person. May God go with you, by any name."

As Ali left, Fur's hairy face poked in the door. "Up to another visitor?"

"Why not? I'm not going anywhere."

Fur lumbered in and towered over the bed.

"Sit. It hurts to have to crane my neck."

"Sorry." He plunked himself into a groaning chair never meant for such bulk. "How are you doing?" His concern washed over me. I got that from everyone these days.

"I'm awake, so I guess I'll live. How have Aypari and Roxanne progressed on getting the plague cure disseminated?"

"Roxanne, Aypari, and Adila have the lab working 24/7 to mass produce the viral vector, the RNA, and the enzymes. Aypari's a marvel...not that Roxanne isn't, you understand..."

I laughed. "I think we can agree on both of them. When do you think Roxanne can get away? She's been cloistered since we got back."

"Soon. She and Aypari were finishing some lab stuff. I need to go get freshened up. Been busy helping them."

"Thought I detected some unique odors when you

came in. Go."

He smiled and left. Roxanne took long enough to arrive for me to tabulate all the possible outcomes of my current plight. Another downside of my medical training.

"Hi, love," Roxanne said as she entered the room.

"Good to see you. Sounds like you haven't gotten much more sleep than I have."

She moved to my bedside and brushed hair away from my eyes. I locked my gaze with hers, felt her love pour through that contact. We needed no words, even without telepathy.

"What's the prognosis?" I glanced at the dialysis machine.

She kept her emotions in check for me. "Complete renal failure. That machine is keeping you alive."

"Kidneys won't recover, huh?"

"No. Too much damage from your sepsis and the chelation."

"I figured that." No matter what we did, I knew I faced a drastically reduced lifespan. What really hurt was the pain it caused my wonderful wife.

"You know we have to deal with the kidneys, right?"

Of course. I needed a renal transplant. "At least they have this good dialysis machine to keep me going."

"You need to recover before we can attempt a transplant. The chelation therapy damaged a lot more than your kidneys, particularly your heart, which already had damage from the septic shock. But all that *will* recover. You couldn't be in a better place or have better physicians to take care of you here." She halted there.

I sensed she held back something unpalatable. "Please don't tell me that was *all* the good news." As usual, I tried to lighten things with humor. It did not always work.

Her face was devoid of emotion. "Cy, we have combed the planet for someone who can serve as a kidney donor. There are many people who clamor to help their savior." She smiled at that.

"Good lord. Did I go from being the demon who spread the plague to a *savior* that fast?"

"It's surprising how quickly and conveniently people forget what they don't want to remember, isn't it? Truthfully, there are plenty of donors." That's when her thoughts turned dark. "The problem is that none of them will work. There are no histocompatability matches. You would reject every one of them, even with immunosuppressants."

"That... That's impossible. With a world this large—"

"It's your unique genetic background."

Then she brightened. "Hey, there *is* good news. We learned why you were infected with the plague but had minimal illness."

Right. That was still unexplained. I raised my eyebrows in question.

"You know that the C-C gene complex coded for the production of the plague receptor that allowed the bot to attach to your cells and inject the plague DNA into your genome. Then the plague DNA coded for production of the enzymes that killed the infected cell. Humans—all of us including you and Chaim—have another set of genes that prevented the plague from creating those destructive enzymes. Therefore, after infection, you and Chaim did *not* undergo the massive waves of cell destruction we saw in other vertebrates. I figure that some of your infected cells ultimately died because of the physical bot damage, giving you and Chaim the mild symptoms you had."

"You've learned a lot in a couple of days."

"Thank Fur and Aypari for most of that. He's hardly pulled his head out of those nanobot files. He's still obsessing over them and pushing Aypari to connect the genomic dots he assembles."

"Figures. Say, did he learn anything about the neural aspects? How the damn things enhanced my empathic abilities?"

She gave me a big smile then a kiss on the cheek. "I've taken enough time. I was warned you shouldn't have too many visitors today. I've got to go. But the answer is yes, and I'm going to let Fur tell you that story. Sleep well, love."

I realized how exhausted I was and closed my eyes. Just before sleep shut down my conscious thought, I remembered she had said nothing more about the transplant. She had shifted the conversation, misdirected me, but I did not have the energy to worry about it. I drifted off into dreamless slumber.

***

Fur pulled up a chair and leaned forward so I could look into his hairy puss without straining my neck. He ran his fingers through his beard as he spoke.

"God knows why Rosten built all those picochips into the nanobots. Maybe he planned for another generation of bot-plagues. I wouldn't put that past him. The way they were, there was rudimentary communication between them, but that could have been enhanced." He winced at the thought and I reciprocated the feeling.

"Anyway, the nanobots communicated electrically and chemically. That makes sense because that's how our own bodies work, electrochemical nerve stimulating molecules. Your nervous system was being stimulated far beyond anything that would take place normally. With your unique brain function already, the bot stimulation pushed your empathic ability to its limit, even beyond to telepathy."

"Wow," I breathed. "So I was right. They formed a communication network in my body, both receiver *and* transmitter."

And it explained one more thing: How Ruthie was able to control my mind and body at the end. She used my sensitivity to the picowave transmissions to directly access my nervous system. That was something I would never reveal to anyone else.

Fur nodded. "There's more. Because of what I found, the concentration of picochips in the nanobot, the potential to develop and use it wrongly, we had a conference to decide what action to take. We have no idea who else might be using that facility on Jaffa. We have to do something."

"But Chaim. We promised him..." My heart raced, not a good thing right now, and my monitor started beeping. My door opened and a gray-haired, broad-bodied, stern-faced nurse peeked in. I put up a hand. "I'm okay. I'll be good." She waited until the beeping stopped and left the door open, giving Fur a nasty glance before she walked away.

"No sweat on Chaim. He was part of the caucus. He agreed that we must destroy the facility. Knowing what he does now, he could not countenance any possibility that more horrors might come out of that place. Jasar is taking a tactical team back to Jaffa. Rosten's nightmare won't be there much longer."

"What are you doing with the nanobot plans? And the plague DNA data? They have as much potential for misuse."

His aura leaked smugness to that question. "I agree. I've given no one those data. They're locked in the *GCVS* computer under triple password protection."

"But Jasar's black box..."

"Taken care of. I reverse engineered how that worked and put in blocks they can't override, both software and hardware-based. When we've figured out everything we need to know and make sure the plague is cured, I'll destroy those files. In the meantime, no one but our crew is privy to the detailed information."

"I'll bet General Tanweer is about out of his skull that his IT people can't get at it. He was pissed that they never got to Ruthie." A twinge elicited a couple of beeps on my monitor, but it had become much easier to think of my old AI and even say her name with passing time.

Fur smiled. "Yeah. We've been approached a half dozen times to let them at our data files. You know, the picocomputer system in the bots answered a lot of questions, but there's one more thing that remains unexplained. Why couldn't you detect the plague nanobot while the animals were alive? The animals, even the cells, had to die before you sensed them."

"Let me think about that." An idea crawled around the tips of my temporal lobes, but I needed time to catch it. The stimulation was a bit too much for my heart monitor and it beeped again.

That was enough for the nurse. She reappeared, pointed at Fur, and barked, "You. Out. Now."

Fur rose, put two fingers to his forehead, and saluted me. "Captain." His bulk loomed over the nurse as he sidled past. She glared at him, not at all intimidated by his size. Then she glared at me before she disappeared.

Chaim. I knew nothing about his status. Prisoner, no doubt. The New Meccans would not trust the man who had brought the plague to their world, but they allowed him to partake in their deliberations on a search and destroy mission to Jaffa. What did the future hold for him? Did I care what happened to him? I didn't know, but the bastard still made me see red when I thought too hard about what he had done. I calmed myself so as not to set off the monitor again.

As I mulled over that and other thoughts, Roxanne showed up. I heard the angry nurse scolding her in the hallway, but Roxanne's curt reply shut the woman up. I had met no one yet who could win an argument with my wife. I felt an ear-to-ear grin on my face as she appeared in the doorway.

She closed the door and walked toward me. "I understand that Fur had you all riled up."

"Yeah. He told me some surprising things, including about Jasar's mission. My warder out there took issue with my heart monitor."

She sat by me. "There's one more thing we need to discuss, Cy."

Oops. I did not like that tone.

"Your renal transplant."

"Mm-hmm. You weaseled out of talking about that yesterday."

"Yeah, I did." She looked up at the vital-signs monitor then back at me. "This is going to drive the nurse out of her mind, but I ordered no interruptions and have the chief physician's backing."

This did not sound good.

"We do have a person whose match makes an excellent transplant donor."

My brain synapses fired. Maybe they weren't as fast as with the bots in my body, but I got there eventually. The whole bit about my unique genome came crashing down on me. I did *not* have a unique genome. Unique means singular. That genome was not singular. There were two other people alive that I knew of who had inherited it from our forebear: My mother, who was across the galaxy, a diabetic with compromised kidneys herself, and Chaim...Chaim fucking McNulty Khodorkosovitch. *He* was the only possible donor.

My monitor went wild. It sounded as if I had tilted a pinball machine.

Roxanne reached up and unplugged me. Well, not me, just the monitor. "You've obviously figured that one out."

I heard feet shuffling outside the door, then agitated voices, then they moved away.

"No one is going to interrupt, Cy. We need to have this discussion."

"NO. And No! And No. I won't have that son-of-a-bitch's kidney in me. I won't go to my grave carrying part of the man who almost destroyed the galaxy. *I will not!*" I imagined I could hear the screaming of the monitor even though it was off. My pulse pounded in my forehead. My breath came in short gasps.

"You probably won't need to. You're going to kill yourself right here and now."

No sympathy whatsoever. But I knew it was not lack of sympathy. It was an attempt to get me to face what had happened to me, to face what *needed* to happen if I was to live.

I closed my eyes. Did I *want* to live with *him* inside me? When every time I made love with my wife *he* would be along for the ride? Was that better than having *Ruthie's* implant in me? I did not want to be a chimera, with him a part of me. I did not *want* to be saved by *him*.

Those thoughts repeated themselves, again and again.

I broke out of the cycle. How glad was I now that I was *not* telepathic? I felt a hand on my arm and opened my eyes.

"Cy, you don't need to decide now. We're not prepared to do surgery until you are much improved.

Extinction

You do need to come to terms with it, though. Everyone *will* push you to save your own life, but I understand where you are, how you feel. This is your decision." She rose. "Do you want me to plug your monitor back in before I go?"

"No. I'll buzz the nurse when I'm ready."

She leaned over and gave me a lingering kiss on the lips. "I'll always love you, Cy. And only you."

My damned eyes went all blurry as she left.

Her last words stuck with me: "And only you." What was it that drove me so nuts about Chaim? I knew Roxanne loved me and no one else, but she *had* feelings for the man. She could not hide that from my empathic ability, in fact, she never tried to. A connection existed there from the day Chaim kidnapped her. And I was jealous, though logically that made no sense. Why?

Chaim was my only kidney donor because we shared that rare Khodorkosovitch genome. Our DNA gave us both our empathic talents, something that connected us in a way most human beings could never experience. Could that be the answer? That Roxanne felt the same thing in him that she felt in me and responded to that? Did those genes code for some weird sort of mental pheromone? The thoughts stunned me, but also gave me much to think on...for the rest of my life.

Chapter 28

Chaim gazed at himself in the mirror of the hospital suite. He had gained weight, but his face remained pale and lined, bags under his eyes. Yet he would not trade this for his old self. He moved his hand and felt the bandage that extended around his right side to his back, the covering that hid one of the most important acts of his life.

He drew a breath, almost welcomed the pain. He looked at the clothes that hung on the back of the door: a plain gray tunic with no adornments. Prison garb. The fact that he was in a hospital notwithstanding, he was still a prisoner. And today was his trial.

They had waited, though the planet's populace screamed for retribution, for his blood. He could not turn on his vid screen without seeing some commentary on New Mecca's disaster and those who were responsible. Rosten and Chaim were the prime targets of the people's wrath now. The New Meccans already had convicted and executed Chaim's Test-Lit accomplice, Jonah Blackmun, for the murder of the veterinarian, bin Saqer.

Chaim hoped they could see the good he had done after he realized the error of his ways, but he understood that it was too little, too late, as the old saying went. He offered both his kidneys to Berger so Roxanne's husband might live. What did kidneys matter when his own life would be so short? Berger lived with no functional kidneys. Perhaps it would be just for Chaim to do the same. But it mattered to Roxanne and Berger, however, and they accepted only one.

He had no misapprehension about the outcome of his trial. The New Meccan courts could come to but a single judgment, death for Rosten and him, those who had biologically attacked their planet. But the only judgment that mattered was God's. And Roxanne's.

He was comfortable with the latter. He dropped to his knees, bowed his head, and prayed for forgiveness from God, though he despaired of receiving it.

***

A medical attendant rolled my wheelchair into the courtroom in Medina's Justice Building, right up to the first row of observers. Cameras rolled in for close-ups of me for planet-wide transmission. I looked away. This circus was not what I wanted.

Before I agreed to the kidney transplant, I had long talks with Chaim. It was hard for both of us, but I needed to know him better. I needed to feel that I could live with part of him in my body. In the end, I did know him better. I reflected on how much the man had changed since I first met him.

So had I. I had learned tolerance. I still hated those people who oppressed others—the Test-Lits, Hussein, and their like—but I better knew the good people of New Mecca, and I no longer painted all Muslims with the same dark brush.

As I watched Chaim walk gingerly into the courtroom, I kept my mental screen strong. The New Meccans had delayed the trial until I recovered enough for the surgery, but as soon as I tolerated transportation, the trial moved forward.

Chaim and I, even without the bots in our systems, still had an emotional attachment beyond what any others could dream of sharing. Our pain was mutual. Internally, I reached down with my mind, as I had so many times in the past days, to see if I could detect the new tissue within me—Chaim's tissue. Thank goodness I did not. His donation was an integral part of me now, not something foreign that I would feel the rest of my life.

Rosten climbed to the witness stand first. Speakers played the tape of his ranting on the *GCVS*, not for the first time, of course. Broadcast across the planet when the *GCVS* returned with the plague cure, it had stoked the fury of the New Meccan people. Those words still horrified me no matter how many times I heard them. The man's face would forever haunt my nightmares.

Now he laughed, showed no remorse for what he had done. The man was insane. Marshals forcibly restrained some of the onlookers. The judge pounded for order. The tribunal conferred for scant minutes, then read the verdict that surprised no one: Death. Ushered from the courtroom to keep order, Rosten never lost his demented smile.

Chaim took the stand. When the prosecution wound down, he had the opportunity to speak. I held my breath, wondering what the man could say.

He stood straight and looked out at the assembled crowd, no hint of fear in his mien. Even through my screen I felt his newfound strength of character, his belief that he had done what he could to right his wrongs. Not enough, but all he could manage. He had chosen his words for this. His voice was steady.

"People of New Mecca, I stand here accused of heinous crimes against you and against all humanity. All the accusations are true. I might argue that I was an unwitting party to what happened, but that would be false. I was ignorant, true, but I was willing to take on the role of a soldier in a Holy War against Islam. Ignorance can be no excuse for such an action. The animals and people of your planet have suffered much at my hands. I expect no mercy, no forgiveness. I ask for none.

"I did not live up to my name, Chaim, which means Life. I became the opposite of its meaning. I fear what I did is unforgivable in the eyes of God, whether He be called Allah or Yahweh."

That brought rustling and murmurs from the crowd, but they settled immediately when the Chief Justice raised a hand.

"I do not mean to disparage anyone's faith, but I must say what I feel in my heart. I believe that I have been judged in Heaven. You are the earthly hand of that judgment, and I accept that with my entire being. My sorrow and regret for what I have done will haunt me through eternity."

Dead silence ensued for many long moments. I do not think that anyone expected that from Chaim. I looked at my wife, seated next to me. Her eyes were moist. Damn, so were mine. My back ached. Maybe I did feel Chaim's kidney in me, just a little bit.

Then Roxanne surprised me. She stood and walked toward the now empty witness stand as Chaim returned to his seat. Amazingly, no one stopped her. I looked around at Ali who sat close behind me. He smiled and nodded. What did that mean?

Roxanne turned to the assemblage. "I am here to tell

you something of the nature of this man. You know what he has done to your world. You do not know how he repents what he did, of what he has done to redeem himself since committing his horrific crime. I will tell you..." She did it in a way that had to move any heart not hardened in stony hate.

When she finally stepped down, I held open my arms for her, though I could not stand.

Then another thing happened that stunned me. Colonel Jasar walked to the stand. He bowed to the tribunal and turned to the crowded courtroom.

"Scant weeks ago, I could not have imagined doing this, but I have come to know this man who stands before us for judgment. I accompanied him to Jaffa with the *Galactic Circle Veterinary Service* to retrieve the information that allowed them to save our world. He was instrumental in that effort.

"Moreover, Chaim Khodorkosovitch volunteered to travel back to Jaffa with my team. With his help, we destroyed the laboratory that created the evil plague visited upon us, and others as strange and vile. His intercession with Jaffa's government allowed us to take that military action without starting a *new* war. Once the Jaffan people learned of the horrendous acts of the Testamentary-Literalist demons, they assisted our effort.

"Furthermore, with Khodorkosovitch's help, the rest of those to blame for the plague were arrested, tried, and convicted on Jaffa. Since then, I have had many conversations with our prisoner. As Dr. Simon said, Chaim Khodorkosovitch truly grieves for the death and destruction his actions caused. He is not an evil man. He does not seek mercy from our people. He believes he should die for his sins."

He paused for long moments as dead silence enfolded the courtroom. "I have learned enough of vengeance and retribution in our own war. I have seen enough of death, though Irving Rosten deserves no less. I do ask that Chaim Khodorkosovitch's life be spared."

The uproar was incredible. Again, the judge pounded for order, but it was a long time coming. I looked back at Ali again. He sat quiet and composed, but his emotional message came through clear as a bell. He *knew* this was coming. That was why Roxanne spoke with no interference. Then *he* stood and walked to take the stand.

Imam Ali Suliaman, now the unquestioned civil and religious leader of his world, spoke long and eloquently to his people. "The Qur'an made a compassionate and just society the essence of Islam. Compassion is a particularly difficult virtue. It demands we go beyond the limitations of our egos, our insecurities, and our prejudices."

He told his people they could best encompass the spirit of that compassionate and just society by sparing the life of Chaim Khodorkosovitch.

The tumult took a long while to die away.

How did I feel? Despite everything that had happened, passed between us, I owed Chaim my life. No one in the galaxy knew him the way I did. No others could share the kind of bond we shared. In more senses than one, he was me and I was him. Roxanne grasped my hand and pressed hard. I watched the tribunal and held my breath.

The representative of the tribunal stood to speak. "For his crimes against the animals of New Mecca, against the people of New Mecca, this man is sentenced to twenty-five years in prison, in solitary confinement, after which he will be exiled from our planet, never to return under the penalty of death."

Another roar from the crowd no doubt duplicated itself all over the planet.

The tribunal had that verdict before the trial started. Roxanne knew. Jasar knew. Ali knew. I did not, possibly because everyone thought my animosity toward Chaim would have made me object. When we returned from Jaffa, they might have had a point, but now? Now I felt nothing but relief.

***

Irving Rosten was publically beheaded, a gruesome and horribly antiquated punishment carried down through the millennia for the worst crimes against Islam. I understood it was the first in many centuries. It did slake the blood thirst of the New Meccan people, I supposed, but I chose not to watch it.

The New Meccan government repaired and refitted the damage to the *GCVS* after its traumatic jaunts to and from Jaffa. The ship was in top shape again.

The damage to my body was healing, though that would take time. The transplant was successful, and I finally was off immunosuppressant drugs to prevent rejection. The match between my tissues and Chaim's was the closest any physician had ever seen. Now why did that not surprise me? It boded a life longer than most after such a procedure. Perhaps a full one.

I had not seen much of our alien interns in the past month, the doctors—and one large, stern nurse who was my personal gatekeeper—felt I needed no negative stimulation during the critical recovery period while my immune system was trashed. Now, Learns-To-Fix-Injuries and Healer just about filled the hospital room. Red had grown, and his tail stuck out into the hallway. Dragons never did stop growing. I recalled the emperor dragon on Red's home world who swallowed whole an animal the size of a full-grown ox. We needed to get Red back home before he outgrew our ship.

"Look terrible, Cyberger," Red hissed. "Be here forever."

Nice to have positive support.

Healer snapped his talons at the dragon in annoyance. "Captain Cyberger is recovering. He will take us new places soon. That is so, correct?" A virtual speech for the reticent Lupan.

I smiled. "I'm better than a few days ago, now that I'm off all the drugs. But how about you? No aftereffects of the plague and treatment?"

"It did not affect me as it did you."

Nice to know. The Lupan's regenerative capability had saved him. No other creature would have survived the ravages his body underwent.

"And you never did get sick, Red. I wonder if your dragon physiology wasn't susceptible, even though reptiles were affected."

"Me not reptile. Tell you before." His annoyance cut through me like a scalpel blade.

"Ouch. Okay. Not reptile. Dragon. And we'll go new places soon. That I promise."

Red hopped up and down, and my bed bounced in time. "Ooh, goody. Want to ssee more monsterss like vampiress and ssaurians. They fun."

The gray-haired nurse's head appeared around the doorframe. "Please. We have sick patients on this floor." She seemed not at all cowed by my friends.

"We will go." Healer grabbed Red's arm and dragged him out the door. The dragon's scales stuck a bit on the frame, and one molding left with him. A crimson scale plunked to the floor. Dragons shed them as they grew.

I shook my head. The nurses would no doubt politic for my release sooner rather than later.

Roxanne stood in the doorway staring down at the scale. Then she examined my face.

"You're looking happy." I snorted. "Red and Healer just left, as you can see. I'm not sure the hospital will survive many more of their visits."

She laughed. "Red *is* getting a bit paunchy. We need to get him on an exercise regimen."

"Maybe get him some monsters to fight. He enjoyed our jaunt to Jaffa...at least the saurians and vampires."

She came over and placed a hand on my forehead. "Nice and cool. How's everything else under there?" She nodded toward my blankets.

"Much better."

"Your kidney checks out fine, but you'll have some permanent cardiac arrhythmias. Nothing that will threaten your life...unless you insist on getting blown up again."

I grimaced. "I'll try to avoid that in the future, doctor."

A big grin spread across her face, and I felt a pulse of joy from her. "You've been cleared for release, Cy. Today." She turned to the door and called, "Fur, Aypari."

The big guy entered the room with Aypari at his side.

Aypari said, "Hello, Cy. I am glad that you are recovered." She glanced at Fur. "It has done wonders for my...companion."

Fur's eyes and entire demeanor glinted. "Hi, Captain." He motioned with his head toward Roxanne. "She wanted to tell you herself. Ready to get dressed? I have your uniform here."

He held up the horrendous purple tunic covered with lots of gold buttons and braid that was my Captain's ceremonial dress on our first voyage. The Test-Lit Rebbinical Council had thought it would impress the residents of all the worlds we would visit. I had worn it on my first date with Roxanne.

I cringed. "Oh-My-God. Where did you find that?"

He laughed. "Roxanne found it stuffed away in your locker. I couldn't resist. And that's all we've got. You're going to wear it out of here."

"Oh, no."

Roxanne said, "You filled out over the past two years, dear, so all your other clothes would hang like drapes now that you've lost so much weight."

I had not given that part of my injury-recovery cycle much thought.

"We need to fatten you up again, Cy, and Aypari is the person to do that. She's an incredible cook, besides being the most brilliant microbiologist in the galaxy." Fur's pride shown through like a miniature nova. He thrust the tunic at me. "Time to get dressed."

Maybe I could put a towel over my head as they wheeled me out.

***

I met with Chaim once after the trial. Escorted into a guarded meeting room, he looked better than the last time I had seen him at the trial, with no evidence of mistreatment. His twenty-five year solitary confinement was as much for his own protection as for punishment. He likely would not have lasted twenty-five minutes exposed to the other inmates of his prison. Hatred of him remained strong, despite Ali's plea and directive to his world.

Our meeting was awkward, to say the least. I wanted to thank him again for his kidney and my life. I sensed his demurral. That act could not begin to atone for what he had done, he believed. He asked after the *GCVS* crew, even Red and Healer. I informed him we would be leaving soon and he wished us a safe journey. Beneath it all, I sensed the image of Roxanne in his mind.

"She will come to see you, Chaim. She won't leave without bidding you goodbye."

He ducked his head, would not meet my eyes.

I took a deep breath then let it out slowly. "She is a special woman. We both know that. We both love her. I no longer hold any animosity toward you because of that. It is just a reflection of who she is—and who we are. When you are released, I hope you can find a partner close to what she is to complete your life."

We shook hands but exchanged no further words, just a feeling of kinship.

***

I had missed the cozy confines of the *GCVS* commissary. If nothing else, we made better coffee than the swill they served in the hospital. And I could drink coffee again, thanks for small miracles. Dinner was over, and we all lounged about, enjoying one another's company. It was tight with Learns-To-Fix-Injuries' new bulk. His tail stuck through the hatch into the corridor as he picked some residual dinner from his teeth with a talon.

Fur lounged back in his chair, stressing the bolts that held it to the floor. "Cy, did you ever figure out the thing about not detecting the plague in the live animals?"

I nodded. "I had lots of time to think about that. Here's my theory. After the bot attached to the cell membrane receptor and injected its DNA, it assembled new bots on the surface and waited for the newly synthesized plague DNA so they could become infective again. While attached, the primary communication with other bots was neurochemical transmission between cells. Sure, there was some electronic digital communication, but that was minor. Both the digital and the biochemical neurotransmitter signals of the bots were lost in the welter of normal host signals in the body.

"But...when all the host cells died, the bots were cast off with nowhere to go, no more live cells to infect. They didn't have access to the biochemical intercellular communication system anymore, so they increased the electronic signals, each bot searching for a new target. There were also bots that didn't get new plague DNA, and they searched for a cell where they could pick that up. Those digital communications were *not* lost in the neurochemical background. There was nothing left in the dead host system to obscure them."

"So the bots essentially sent out individual SOS calls," Fur mused.

"A nice analogy. My empathic reception was able to pick up those picowave transmissions. I considered them *unnatural* emanations, not understanding what I sensed. And, of course, they *were* unnatural for a biological organism. They didn't last long, the bots being programmed to self-destruct like the cells."

"And unless someone was *trying* to explore picowave transmission systems, they never would have discovered that." He was silent for a few moments. "I wonder if I could rig—"

"Uh, uh. Enough engineering for now. This is theory, of course. But one thing my enhanced empathy gave me was the ability to understand events that happened in my body—to *know* that something happened a certain way, and I'm convinced my theory is correct."

"That makes a lot of sense, Cy, though the whole scenario is still hard to believe." Roxanne shook her head in awe, and there were long moments of silence as everyone cogitated on my words.

"On a different note..." I raised a glass of brandy to my shipmates. "I have a toast to make."

The brandy had come with us all the way from Dovid's World, saved for a special occasion. I could think of none more special. Fur had announced that he and Aypari would be married before we left New Mecca.

"To Fur and Aypari, congratulations and prayers for a wonderful life together," I said. "And to all of us, the *Galactic Circle Veterinary Service*, and our continuing mission: To bring our medical abilities to civilizations throughout our galaxy, to help those in need, no matter who or *what* they may be."

I lifted my glass higher. "*L'chaim!* To life!" The Hebrew toast now held a double meaning for me...and for my wife.

Aypari raised a glass of grape juice. "*Fisehatak!* To our health. And to life. I am proud to join you."

We all savored our drinks.

Aypari took Fur's hand and squeezed it. I did the same for Roxanne.

Healer and Learns-To-Fix-Injuries-After-Inflicting-Them slapped talons in their version of a high-five.

I wondered what our future held, but for now, we deserved a vacation. We would stop at Dragonworld and Lupus IV as we wended our way home to Dovid's World and Sammara. Our alien interns, despite their desire to travel more, would return to their worlds. I officially pronounced them graduated from the *Galactic Circle Veterinary Service School of Medicine*.

My mom and dad, and Roxanne's and Fur's families awaited us. Fur and Aypari planned a second Jewish wedding to add to their Muslim festivities.

But in the back of my mind, a far-off cloud hovered over the horizon. The Test-Lits were still out there, hatching who-knew-what new crimes against humanity and every other life-form in the galaxy. I hoped we were done with them, but, if not, the *Galactic Circle Veterinary Service* would strive to meet whatever challenges faced us in the future.

Stephen A Benjamin

About the Author

Dr. Stephen A. Benjamin was born and raised in New York City. He received his A.B. degree from Brandeis University, and his D.V.M. and Ph.D. degrees from Cornell University, and he's a board-certified veterinary pathologist. He has been a university teacher, researcher, and administrator, and is currently Professor Emeritus at Colorado State University's College of Veterinary Medicine. His interests in human and animal health are reflected in most of his short stories and novels. He lives in Colorado with his wife and enjoys traveling, especially visiting his family, fishing, golf, skiing, cooking, and writing fiction.

The Galactic Circle Veterinary Service

Book 1

Excerpt:

CHAPTER 1

I just did it again, shot off my mouth while surrounded by the tavern's myriad of flapping ears. Too much ale was no excuse.

The behemoth in front of me dominated my vision. I underestimated him because of his worn laborer's clothing, and he demolished my self-composure when he said, "And you believe your experience supersedes that of the Torah?"

"You're twisting my words," I said in loud debate, hoping the volume of my voice would support my big mouth. "The Old Testament is not meant to be taken literally. More than four thousand years of experience has changed the context of what was written."

"God gave Moses the Torah." Goliath's laugh boomed across the room. "I was not aware that the word of God had need for a context."

A chorus of patrons echoed his mocking laugh. Even so, I sensed many of them supported my views but would not voice that support—for good reason. They had seen the three rebbes watching our conversation. I had not.

The rebbes rose from their table and headed straight for me. My heart jumped as they glared at me from beneath the brims of their traditional black flat-brimmed fedoras.

A hush came over the crowd, and the commentator of a free-fall soccer match on the giant plasma screen thundered against the silence. The overhead bioluminescent lights felt like heat lamps. A trickle of sweat ran down the back of my neck. People rose and scuttled for the exit as if afraid the black-coated enforcers of religious purity might target them next.

I swallowed hard. "Good evening, rebbes."

The rebbe closest to me had a scar that ran from the corner of his left eye to the middle of his bearded cheek. The eye twitched as his fiery anger seared my empathic perception. My stomach wrenched as it always did when struck with strong emotions, and I had slammed my mental empathic barriers into place too late. As I quashed the incipient nausea—I did not need to lose my dinner in front of everyone to add to my chagrin—the inevitable headache stomped into my brain. Closing my eyes accomplished nothing against what seemed like an explosion of fireworks in front of my optic nerves. I opened them again and squinted at the rebbe. "Is there a problem?"

"You should heed the words of a man who knows the path of true faith." The scarred rebbe glanced at the giant who had stepped away from us, and then back at me. "I shall see more of you, I think." He turned and stalked out of the tavern with the other two rebbes in tow.

Oh, shit. I'd really screwed up this time. What started as a disagreement over a government entitlement program had ended in my denouncement of the dogma of the Rebbinical Council and the tyrannical theocracy that ruled Dovid's World. My big mouth could send me straight to the Inquisition.

Subdued conversation resumed with the exit of the rebbes.

A touch on my shoulder accelerated my heartbeat again.

My recent opponent stood over me, his voice now soft and serious, not mocking as it had been. "You okay? You don't look good. Come on, I'll buy you a drink." He put a huge hand on my shoulder and steered me to a table in a corner.

I was in no condition to argue further.

He frowned as we sat. "You're a fool. Your words could put you in prison. You need to use your brain before your mouth."

Yeah, I knew that, but it never seemed to help much. Already in a lousy mood and feeling awful, I did not need someone else pointing out my flaws. Although angry at myself for my stupidity, it was easier to direct my anger at the most convenient outlet, so I glowered at the man in front of me. Goliath's bright brown eyes studied me, in turn.

As the headache faded, I cautiously lowered and peeked over my shields, all I could do without incapacitating myself. I sensed an aura of curiosity, but not the hostility I expected considering his attack on my heretical statements.

He turned and addressed the barmaid who came to

our table. "An ale for me. A cider for my friend." He raised an eyebrow, dared me to contradict him.

I didn't argue. Still queasy from the rebbe's emotional assault, I knew that too much alcohol had taken its toll, though I did not appreciate the reminder.

The man thrust his bear-like forepaw across the table and smiled. Full lips peeked out from within a sandy beard and moustache, topped by a broad, crooked nose. "I'm Furoletto Cohen. People call me Fur."

I stared at his hand and rolled the name around my brain; I did not recognize it. Fur fit his impressive facial shrubbery. I was envious. The law said that men of age must wear beards. I barely managed an anemic lawn of chestnut fuzz.

"I'm Cy Berger."

His hand engulfed mine. "Well, Cy Berger, perhaps turning your inappropriate tirade into a clownish performance might save you worse trouble. Didn't you see the rebbes sitting in the back? We can hope that a laugh at your expense will make them less likely to take serious action." He tugged at his beard.

"Why should you care?" After all, he had just humiliated me in front of the entire tavern—some of my fellow students included.

"Why? A good question. Wait. Here are our drinks." He took his and downed half the mug in one swallow.

I sipped my cider and wondered what the guy's angle was.

Cohen wiped his mouth. "I wouldn't see *anyone* subjected to the Inquisition. You should learn to keep your political opinions to yourself...at least in public." He smiled, perhaps to blunt the edge of his criticism. "Tell me about yourself. I might as well know whom I tried to save."

Mortification compounded by annoyance made me

curt. "I'm a student at the Academy College of Veterinary Medicine."

"Congratulations. Not an easy profession to get into. What about before that?"

Though the compliment sounded sincere, I was still leery of the guy. Why this change in attitude toward me? What did he want? "I grew up on my family's dairy farm, throwing bales of hay and shoveling kilotons of shit. What's it to you?"

He smiled despite my hostility. "What do you do for recreation? Besides drink."

"All right. What is this? *Your* version of the Inquisition? Why don't you just *kish mein tuches*?" Even as the words poured out, I regretted them.

His brows pulled together, his eyes narrowed, and he slammed his mug onto the table. My cider glass jumped and teetered before I caught it. My hands shook and slopped cider on the tabletop.

He took a deep breath before he spoke. "Look, Berger, I tried to help you tonight. Maybe that was a stupid thing to do, considering you don't seem to give a shit. I thought perhaps you could learn from a bit of advice, but that looks to be a lost cause. Fine. I'm finished. Maybe I'll see you again when the Rebbinical Council gets done with you—if there's anything left to see."

God, I could probably piss off that ancient icon of forbearance Mahatma Gandhi, if I had the chance. Cohen's words hit too close to home. My breath caught as I recalled horror stories about the Inquisition. As he started to rise, I grabbed his arm. "Wait. Don't go." At least his presence made me feel like less of an isolated target. "I know you tried to help me. It's just...how you did it."

He sat down, though his frown did not clear until I began to talk.

To be truthful, it never took much to get me started. Shutting me up was a bigger problem. I watched my fingers make wet circles of cider on the tabletop as I spoke about myself. "...so, aside from my studies, I read a lot, and I have a thing for watching ancient vids from Old Earth."

"Like what?"

"I read and watch anything available on microchip from the ancient Greeks to the present. History, philosophy, fiction. Recent books I've read have been on political systems, particularly religious tyrannies." I glanced around to see if the rebbes hovered behind me. Many of the tables had emptied. "Don't get me wrong. I don't reject Judaism. I treasure our traditions. But I *do* have a problem with dictatorships and oppression."

"I would never have guessed." Fur's mouth curled up at the corners. "Veterinary medicine makes sense with your background, I suppose. I don't think politics would suit you."

He looked around "It's late. I have to go."

Despite our disagreement, I liked the big man, but I still was unsure about his motives. "Hey. I've given you my life story. What about yours?"

"Perhaps another time." He scowled at me. "Until then, you might keep your mouth hidden behind your textbooks."

We shook hands, or rather, I let my hand disappear within his and move up and down without my assistance. He threw a bill on the table and trudged off.

As I stared at the iconic picture of a rebbe adorning the bill, a frisson ran up my back. I finished my cider and I left the tavern. As I stepped out the door, I came face-to-face with two members of the Palmach, the government's elite police force. Their stealth-powered armor disappeared into the darkness, and it seemed as if their faces and hands floated disembodied before me.

One flipped his visor down and then back up, as if to ensure himself of my identity before he spoke. "Mr. Berger, you are to come with us."

My first thought was to bolt, but for once my brain recognized the stupidity and futility of such an action. I felt like I had a mouth full of chalk dust, and it took a couple of tries to get any words out. "Wha -what for?"

"You will be informed." He motioned with a laser rifle for me to move.

The other guardsman took hold of my arm in a painful grasp, and they marched me off as our smaller moon joined the larger moon above the rooftops. I wondered if I'd ever see such a sight again.

CHAPTER 2

When the guards marched me up to the infamous headquarters of the Inquisition, I almost lost control of my sphincters. Fortunately, I did not add utter embarrassment to my heart-pounding fear.

They locked me in a tiny cell and disappeared without another word. I alternately sweated and shivered as I listened to a variety of moans and sobs, punctuated by an occasional scream, from voices I assumed were other prisoners. I recalled the vids I had watched that featured all sorts of torture and wished I had stuck to the Walt Disney shows.

Hours later, a taciturn Neanderthalic guard packing a very large blaster unlocked my cell. I assumed it was morning, but they had confiscated my comm unit, and the room had neither a window nor a chronometer. He marched me up a flight of stairs and down a corridor then shoved me into a small room furnished with a plasteel desk and three chairs. My glance slid behind and above the empty desk. A veritable museum of torture instruments decorated the institution-gray wall. I had visualized many of them during the night: thumb screws, branding irons, spiked whips and scourges, electric prods, and more. As my mind wrapped itself around their meaning, I heard the door close and turned.

The rebbe who addressed me the previous evening in the tavern stood by the door. His face had haunted me in my cold cell all night. The reality was worse, and my gut clenched.

He smiled through his chest-length black beard, a smile that belied his underlying hostility. I kept my shields firmly in place; I did not need a repeat of last night's nausea and headache. His beard contrasted with the shiny bald head he unveiled when he doffed his fedora to me.

I did not return his smile.

He replaced his hat. "I am Reb Levi Schvartz, a member of the Rebbinical Council. You may address me as Reb Levi." His voice grated like rough ball bearings against rusted steel.

I assumed he knew my name and did not respond.

Built like a fireplug, the man looked to be in his early forties. His midnight black attire—suit, shirt, tie, socks, shoes, and hat—seemed to suck the light from the room. His matching black eyes sat above a large, hooked nose that, as prominent as it was, could not rival the size of *my* mammoth schnoz. His pale scar gleamed against his ruddy face and disappeared into his beard.

He moved behind the desk and sat in the only padded seat, then motioned me to a straight-backed metal chair across from him. I surreptitiously looked for electrical connections before I sat.

A knock preceded the entry of a third person. To my amazement, the Dean of the College of Veterinary Medicine appeared. I had met him twice, both times when I had challenged the intelligence or the personal habits of one of his faculty members. He was a gray man—like the walls. He would not meet my eyes as he moved to sit in the hard chair next to me.

Reb Levi rubbed his fingers over his scar. "Mr. Berger, your seditious diatribes have caused considerable consternation among the members of Rebbinical Council."

The Dean coughed as if the rebbe's words had choked him.

My gut writhed like an eel in a net.

"Last night was just the latest of your transgressions."

I felt the blood drain from my face. The Dean's sallow face turned even paler, and I wondered if mine looked the same.

"The Dean tells me that you are at the top of your class, academically. Commendable. He also tells me that you are a *kochleffl*"—he used the Yiddish word for troublemaker— "even at the Academy. You realize that you could be subjected to the Inquisition, do you not?" He raised his right eyebrow and his scarred left cheek twitched in response.

My heart skipped a beat. I glanced over his shoulder at the wall of torture implements and prayed it was only a museum display, although the past night's sounds suggested my prayer would not be answered.

He waited for a response, although I was not sure what I could say. Recant my "seditious" pronouncements? I would not back down on my beliefs—well, at least not yet. Be tortured? That fear played more games with my sphincters. I'm no hero; I'm a chicken when it comes to pain. Disappear like others before me? Scuttlebutt said two radical students who dropped out of school last year had not been seen since. But if they were going to get rid of me, why was the Dean here? My hands twisted around themselves as if they had a life of their own.

The silence lengthened until the Dean cleared his

throat and spoke. "Mr. Berger—"

"No," Reb Levi said. "Let *him* speak."

For once in my life, I could not. I froze. I could not clear my mind of the old vid images of torture victims. I don't know how long the silence lasted before I broke free of my paralysis. "Wha-what do you want from me? Are you going torture me, for God's sake?"

The Dean gasped.

The Rebbe's eyebrows bunched up like some huge black caterpillars. "Despite your blasphemy, we have no wish to torture you, Mr. Berger. Not if you accede to our wishes. On the contrary, we might have a job for you." His smile reminded me of Dracula inviting a victim to rest in his coffin. His antipathy seeped around my mental barriers.

A *job*? What in hell did that mean?

Reb Levi tented his fingers. "Mr. Berger, you are a challenge, for your professors and the Rebbinical Council. Because of your sedition, the Council would see you leave Dovid's World...permanently." He stroked his scar.

My heart bounced off my diaphragm. Exile? My family—

Before my thoughts went further, Reb Levi added, "Or, perhaps, if you were to remain you could be taught to see the error of your ways." He smiled and followed my glare over his shoulder to *The Wall*. It had taken on a life of its own in my mind.

My body trembled. The man exuded malignant pleasure as he watched me, and my stomach twisted again, despite my shields.

"I see either option as a waste," he said. "You are among the brightest young persons at the Academy. Therefore, we have proposed a compromise." He turned to the Dean and nodded. "You may explain, Dean Altschul."

Altschul cleared his throat. "Mr. Berger, the Council has suggested several things. First, they would like to see you gone from Dovid's World within a month."

I felt like I had been gut-punched. When I caught my breath, my next words were comical considering my situation. "But I have final exams...and graduation."

"Yes, yes." The Dean waved off my outburst. "There is no problem. You could fail all your finals and still graduate with honors. The Rebbinical Council has ordered the Academy to waive your examinations and confer your degree early." He stood and held out his hand. "Congratulations, *Doctor* Berger."

My mouth hung open. Was he serious? Things were happening too fast. Had I just gone from the Inquisition's prisoner to a full-fledged Doctor of Veterinary Medicine in the span of minutes? I finally stood and shook the Dean's hand, confused but not so befuddled that I didn't know to wait for the other shoe to drop.

Dean Altschul sat again and I followed suit.

"As Reb Levi said, we have a job for you. One that will not entail your *permanent* separation from our world."

I let out the breath I had held, but took particular note of the "we" and waited for more.

"As you may know, our College of Veterinary Medicine once had many students from other worlds, but for various reasons we now have no students from offworld. We need someone to go to other planets, to seek out and recruit students, to entice them to enroll here. It is important to the, um, finances of our Academy. Income from other planets has been lacking since our government—" Altschul snapped his mouth shut and glanced at Reb Levi. His fear that he had said too much permeated the room.

Reb Levi's eyes did not change, but a wave of disapproval radiated from the man's brow.

After an uncomfortable silence, Altschul coughed and began again. "Dr. Berger, you are a persuasive speaker as you have shown both inside and outside the Academy. We feel this would be a good opportunity for you."

Anger began to replace my fear of Reb Levi. Blood pulsed in my temple. Good opportunity? Leave my home, for God's sake? And why me if I was such a pain in the ass? The obvious answer hit me like a bucket of ice water. No matter how they cut it, they were getting rid of me.

"We will empower you to offer scholarships to accomplish our goals."

Your goals, not mine.

"What do you say?"

Was I supposed to agree to give up my plans and aspirations for my own veterinary practice? The farmers and ranchers in my home county needed a veterinarian, and I had planned to go home to fill that role. Was I to Leave Dovid's World and my family? Like hell, I would. I conveniently submerged any thought of my precarious situation.

"No thanks. I'm not leaving my home."

Reb Levi's voice cut through me like the parting of the Red Sea. "The Council would *very much* like you to take this assignment, Dr. Berger. Though you have spoken harsh words about our government, there is no evidence that you are an active revolutionary. This appointment will give you a chance to prove yourself."

"I don't need to prove anything—"

"And to see that your family remains in good health."

My heart clutched in my chest. I turned to him. His face was smooth. A slight smile curved his lips. His blunt fingers stroked his scar as his left eye twitched. I did not need my empathic ability to read him. I was now responsible for my mom and dad, whether or not they would become targets of the government, victims of the Inquisition. This was torture in itself. My fists clenched. I had to restrain myself from attacking him bodily. I had trained in martial arts as a teenager, and I wondered if I could take him. He looked strong as a bull.

The Dean must have taken my silence as acquiescence. "Ah, good. Good. I knew you would be willing, Dr. Berger. We can work out all the details later. See my Associate Dean for recruiting. She will train you."

I glared at Reb Levi, fists balled. What I saw made further protestations moot. His eyes were narrow, and he nodded once, sharply, as if to shake something unpleasant out of his nonexistent hair. His demeanor was clear: Take it or suffer—you *and* your family. There were no alternatives.

"One last thing," the Dean said. "You will have a companion on your travels."

I arched my eyebrows.

"Reb Levi."

I glanced at the smiling rebbe and shuddered. I'd rather share a spaceship with a giant Antarean scorpion. I wondered if only one of us would return from this journey.

CHAPTER 3

The front door opened and Lucky, our chocolate Labrador retriever, rocketed through and bowled me over. He straddled me, tail wagging like a jet-propelled windshield wiper. He expressed his joy in a thorough tongue washing of my face. He also laughed.

Yeah, dogs laugh, but because of my empathic ability, I'm the only one who can hear them. Lucky thought knocking me down in greeting was hilarious.

Our ginger tabby, Einstein, looked out the door at me, meowed once, and disappeared. Cats laugh, too. But dogs laugh with you; cats laugh *at* you.

I hugged Lucky then pushed him away. I missed him as much as he missed me. We had the twelve-year-old dog for almost half my life. Our time together had been limited since I'd gone away to school.

I rose and faced my smiling parents in the doorway. My mother opened her arms, and I hugged her before we moved inside.

"Sit," my mother commanded. "We want to hear all the details of what has happened. This whole business is quite extraordinary."

I picked at a hangnail as I spoke. "This is an honor. Because I'm at the top of my class, I've been appointed Assistant Registrar for Recruiting for the Academy College of Veterinary Medicine. The university wants offworld students. There haven't been any in recent years, and they need the revenue." I had to convince my folks that the whole thing was kosher; Reb Levi ordered me to say nothing about the Inquisition or the threat against my parents. "They chose me because I'm a good speaker."

Mom and Dad looked at one another. Their skepticism was tangible. They well knew my political leanings.

"Assistant Registrar," Dad repeated. "Sounds fancy enough. But will you have the opportunity to practice medicine? That's something I know is important to you. You'll be giving up your own plans."

"I'll run an interstellar veterinary service in a ship outfitted as a mobile clinic. I haven't seen it yet, but I'm told it has great equipment."

"*Mazel tov*, darling. I'm sure that will be exciting. How long will you be gone? Will you be able to return home regularly?" Mom looked at me expectantly, but concern leaked through her happy façade.

My dad's steel gray eyes probed me as I answered, as if he sought something beneath my words.

"I'm not sure what the schedule will be. I haven't been given an itinerary. But I'll send you hyperwave transmissions whenever I can. Promise."

"I'm sure you will," Dad said. He stood. "Come with me. Let's have a drink while your mother gets dinner on the table."

I followed him into his study. In an age where most databases were digital, an impressive library of cloth and leather-bound books covered the shelves. This was where I got my love of literature. He motioned me to one of two leather-covered armchairs and doled out a couple of glasses of schnapps.

"Okay, let's have the truth. Who put the thumbscrews to you?"

I choked on my schnapps. "Wha-what do you mean?" A vision of *The Wall* skewered my brain. How could he know—?

"I don't need your empathic talent to know what you told your mother and me is *drek*. You did not get chosen because you're an expert speaker or because you're a good student. This is *mishegas*. It makes no sense."

Mom and Dad were among the few people who knew about my empathic ability. I sensed the emotions of animals and my empathic connection allowed me to soothe stressed beasts. I also perceived human emotions—I sensed what I call auras, for lack of a better term. Rarely, powerful human emotions came through as a fleeting vision, but I was *not* a telepath. I did not read minds. I certainly couldn't influence people in the way I could animals.

Animals' emotions caused both physical and psychological reactions, but people were worse. If I let them through, strong emotions caused nausea, vertigo, and headaches. A psychiatrist, a family friend, helped me learn to deal with my ability, but I had to develop my own mental shields by trial and error, and they were not perfect. In the inevitable fistfights of youth, I was doubly handicapped. Along with any physical beating, I got an emotional one from the anger of my opponent. While I avoided reading human emotions, leakage was all too common. One of my veterinary college professors knew of my empathy for animals, but kept the secret. I did not want other faculty and students to see me as a freak. After reading Asimov's *Foundation* books, I worried I would be looked at like his Mule character, and that people would fear and shun me. So I kept my secret close.

However, I never could hide anything from my parents, and I often wondered if they had some of the same talent and could read me as well as I read them.

"But that's it..." I came to a halt under my father's hooded stare. "Dad, please. I can't say anything more."

"You're in trouble again, aren't you?" He sighed. "What did you do this time?"

I hunched my shoulders, but looked him in the eyes as I answered in a small voice. "I blew it. I shot my mouth off in front of some rebbes." I held up my hands, palms forward. "I didn't know they were there." I knew that was a miserable excuse and dropped my eyes. "Now, the Council wants me out of their hair—way out."

My father's lips thinned. "I've told you a hundred times, Cy: All the intelligence in the world is useless without common sense. You know the Test-Lits don't tolerate dissent."

Yeah, I knew. For the past eighty years, the fundamentalist Testamentary-Literalist party ruled our planet with an iron hand and had become an oxymoron, an evangelistic Judaic tyranny—with an Inquisition, yet. Our people left Old Earth more than a thousand years ago, refugees from an oppressive Islamic world government. The age-old enmity between Hebrews and Muslims became intolerable and forced what Jews hoped would be the final stage in the Jewish diaspora.

My voice shook. "Reb Schvartz is a member of the Rebbinical Council. He...he threatened me with the Inquisition—you and Mom, too—if I don't do as he says."

Dad's face creased with pain. "Reb Schvartz. From what I've heard, he's the most sadistic of the Inquisitors." He shook his head. "You really know how to pick them."

"How can they justify what they do?" I cried. "The Inquisition was a church tribunal to torture heretics, particularly Jews. To have Jews use it to torture their own people..?"

Dad frowned. "The Test-Lits' use of the term Inquisition is deliberate. Even two thousand years later, the original Inquisition echoes in the fears of Jews throughout the galaxy." He opened his arms.

I stood and stepped within his embrace. Tears filled my eyes. I felt his strength. I had attained his above average height, but not his muscular physique. I stepped back and looked at him. I saw myself in his reddish brown hair, his gray eyes, his chiseled face, and the hook of his prominent nose—the latter, unfortunately, even more exaggerated on my face.

"One more thing," I said. "Reb Schvartz is going with me."

Dad's rush of fear washed over me, roiling the small amount of schnapps I had managed to swallow.

"That is a dangerous man, Cy. You need to keep your wits about you. You need to control your quick temper."

"I can take care of myself."

Dad shook his head. "I know you are a fighter. We had to pull you out of enough scrapes as a kid. But I'm not talking about your martial arts training. You can't let it come to something like that. You cannot antagonize Schvartz. Promise me, son. Don't start a fight you can't win."

I swallowed hard and nodded.

"Say nothing of this to your mother. Come. It's time for dinner."

It was Friday night and we lit the candles and recited the *shabbos* prayers. I no longer attended synagogue—the Test-Lits brand of religion had put me off that—but the traditions I had been raised with meant more to me now than they had at any time in my life. Mom had prepared my favorites: matzoh ball soup, brisket with potato kugel, and rugullah pastries for dessert. Dinner sat in my stomach like lead.

On Saturday morning, I promised my folks that I would visit before I shipped out. I merged my land drone onto the autoroad, let the autopilot connect with the road's traffic system, and sat back. I watched the pastoral scenery flow by. Golden grain fields and hay meadows stacked with bales were interspersed with verdant pastures dotted with cattle, goats, and sheep. Those animals and chickens came from earth during the diaspora in the giant, multi-generation seedships. They allowed Dovid's World to develop as a self-sustaining agricultural ecology. Even now, other than the roads, vehicles, and farm machinery, much of our world would have been familiar to Terrans of a thousand years ago.

Since the takeover by the Test-Lits, the latest technology was difficult to come by for the average citizen. The government and military restricted the use of winged aircraft, whirlydrones, and hovercraft to *approved* personnel. Antigravity propulsion technology was even more restricted, and space travel was out for all but the military. Most people made do with wheeled land drones. The Test-Lits monitored movement between local districts to keep tabs on revolutionaries, who were always thorns in the side of the government despite official pronouncements that they were of no concern.

Even as I thought this, my vehicle slowed for the first of a half dozen military checkpoints I would negotiate before I reached Jerusalem City. A camouflage-clad Zionist Guard member motioned me to roll down my windscreen. I wondered at the ubiquitous camouflage uniforms of the military. Did they hope someone might miss them standing in the middle of the road so they could unlimber their blasters to fry some rebel?

He stuck out his hand. "Papers."

I guess military mothers never taught their kids to say please. I handed over my documents. The guard looked at the folder, looked at my face, glanced back at the papers, and then returned them. Without another word, he waved me through.

The fields blended to an aureate blur and I closed my eyes. I wished I could be more like my dad, stoic and wise, never one to speak without careful forethought rather than the impulsive idiot I tended to be.

At school, I had never missed the opportunity to show off my smarts, which antagonized most other kids. My ability to read human emotions went beyond facial expressions and body language. I sensed what lay deep within, feelings no one was willing to show. This was more a curse than a blessing, since I perceived the hostile vibes I engendered. I learned that even supposed friends harbored negative feelings.

I isolated myself because I did not know how to deal with the perceived antipathy, and the resulting constant queasiness and headaches were intolerable. As an only child, I became a loner and a compulsive reader and watcher of Old Earth books and vids when I didn't have chores.

Almost everything ever written and filmed was preserved in digital format. Fortunately for me, that included even bad vids: some of those were a kick to watch, particularly the old science fiction flicks predicting the future I now inhabited. I laughed at the Fourth-of July sparkler spaceships of Flash Gordon, the ubiquitous and clunky robots, the inevitably big-headed aliens. I marveled at the predictions of the writings of Verne, Wells, Clarke, and Gibson. I shed tears at Simmons's portrait of a father watching his daughter aging backwards in *Hyperion.*

I remained a loner and, in some ways, looked forward to the isolation of space travel, though the thought of Reb Levi as my companion made my heart pound all the way to Jerusalem City.

***

Levi lectured me on my assignment in his office at his headquarters. I had never been in Government House. The Palmach storm troopers in every hallway sent shivers through me, but at least it was not the Inquisition prison. Levi's office was less intimidating than the interrogation room. It even included a generic landscape painting and a potted plant—no torture instruments, thankfully. He sat in a chair in front of a window, a black silhouette against the light.

"You will pursue your clinical duties and recruit students for the Academy on each world that we visit. I will tell you where to go. Our ship is well-equipped, so I expect you to impress the worlds we visit with veterinary medicine on Dovid's World. I will set the fees for these services, after all, we must pay for our travels.

"I will be your veterinary assistant, but remember *I* am in charge. You will obey my orders without question. You are responsible for what happens to your parents. Is that clear, Berger?"

I could only nod. The man had no clue as to what a veterinary assistant's job entailed. I looked forward to his education: how to collect urine and fecal samples and how to express infected anal sacs, among other grisly tasks.

The Galactic Circle Veterinary Service

My hospital ship—a converted space yacht from a time when private citizens could have space yachts—looked a bit like a giant, inverted "T," with the engines at the bottom of the cross-bar. It had been fitted with the latest antigravity drive for use within planetary atmospheres, an anti-matter drive for interplanetary travel, and an interstellar hyperspace jumpdrive. This voyage was obviously important to the Test-Lits. No way would we ever pay off the cost of this thing with veterinary services and new students. I puzzled over that quite a bit, especially since I assumed most human-settled worlds would already have veterinarians.

A wheeled land drone chassis with a rear compartment fitted as a combined examination room, surgery suite, and laboratory would give me mobility on planets. On the side of the spaceship and on the side of the land drone cabin was the symbol of veterinary medicine: the letter V super-imposed on the staff of Aesculapius. It overlaid a picture of a spiral galaxy and blood red letters surrounded this: *Galactic Circle Veterinary Service.*

The name seemed a bit presumptuous, but I liked it nonetheless. I thought of the ship as the *GCVS*. If not for the specter of Levi and the Inquisition, I would have been ecstatic. As it was, I felt like an ancient cartoon character I had seen: a man with a permanent thundercloud over his head who was the earth's greatest jinx.

***

As I nursed a drink in my favorite tavern, Furoletto Cohen asked to join me. I had not seen him since my arrest.

After some small talk, he said, "I worried about you after the night we met."

I told him about my opportunity. I did not mention the Inquisition, of course.

"That's remarkable. It says something about your abilities that they will speed up graduation and send you off on a mission of such importance. Congratulations." He looked at me with a furrowed brow. "But I'm confused. That night in the tavern, a member of the Rebbinical Council tore into you for your heresy. Why the change in heart?"

I took note that he recognized Reb Levi, but I brushed that aside and gave him part of the story, otherwise it would look as phony as a three-dollar bill, as the ancients used to say. "The Council decided I was better off someplace where I couldn't spread my seditious ideas. This was a way to get me out of their hair without making a martyr out of me. But it is a great chance for me to get experience."

Fur smiled. "I'm glad you didn't get targeted by the Inquisition."

"Um, yeah. Lucky, I guess."

Fur pursed his lips and tugged at his beard. "I almost envy you."

I snorted. "Yeah. Envy the fact that I am exiled—" I snapped my mouth shut. It had overridden my brain once again.

Fur leaned back in his seat. When I looked away and fiddled with my beer mug, he spoke. "Okay, you've got my attention."

"An experiment. That's what I meant. It's an experiment sending a new graduate on such a mission." My phony grin felt more like a grimace.

Fur stared at me.

I blinked first. Something about the big man's general demeanor and aura inspired my confidence, and I made a snap decision. I hoped I would not regret it as I did with my decisions all too often. In a low voice I said, "I'm being exiled. My parents and I have been threatened with the Inquisition if I don't do as they say."

Fur sat forward. "But why are they outfitting you for this space voyage?"

My hands trembled as I rolled my mug between them. "I've thought a lot about that. I'm guessing that it's a ploy to get a rebbe to other worlds as a spy. Reb Levi Schvartz is going with me as my assistant."

Fur's lips twisted in a grimace. "You might be right. Political representatives from Dovid's World have been *persona non grata* on other planets since the Test-Lits' attempt to subjugate Sammara." He referred to the only other inhabited planet in our solar system.

Too late, my caution kicked in and I started to panic. I grabbed his arm. "Please, don't say anything. I'm not supposed to tell anybody. I don't know what they'll do to me or my folks if Levi finds out."

Fur's paw covered my hand. "Don't worry. I won't get you in trouble." He let me have my hand back and shook his head. "Schvartz, huh? Not the most companionable of traveling partners."

I looked over my shoulder. Paranoia closed in on me. "You obviously recognized him. How well do you know Schvartz?"

"By reputation only."

"What have you heard?"

"That he's the top man in the Inquisition. He's a nasty piece of work. I knew a guy who was pulled in and interrogated. They thought he was a member of the resistance."

"Was he?"

"No, but he was crippled by the time they released him."

That did not ring true. Fur was not telling me something. I wondered if the guy in his story *was* connected to the resistance. Either way, the story gave me the creeps. Reb Levi was pure evil. I shuddered.

We spoke a bit more about the trip before I needed to leave for an appointment. As I rose, Fur asked if we might meet again. I sensed a strange excitement behind his words. I agreed.

The next couple of weeks, the Associate Dean for recruiting kept me busy. I had to learn all about the finances of the Academy, how students were selected, and how I was to act as the Academy's agent on the worlds that we would visit. I found that it was far more complicated than I had realized. The Associate Dean gave me speeches for different audiences. My spiel to students would be different from those I gave to school officials or local veterinary societies. I was not nearly as thrilled about that aspect of my job as I was about the real medical challenges I would face. After all, veterinary medicine is what I had studied for the past four years, not how to sign up new students. The Associate Dean finally cut me loose saying I was as prepared as I could be. That remained to be seen.

***

When I met Fur again, he seemed nervous. He finished his beer and lowered his voice, not an easy thing for him. "Cy, I-I have a request of you."

"Yeah?"

He looked around the room, then back at me. "Ten years ago I enrolled in the vet college, but I dropped out after two years. I decided that there were more important things than becoming a veterinarian. Family matters, you know? I settled for being an assistant."

I nodded, though I detected evasion in his thoughts.

"I've been working at a private clinic as a veterinary technician. I'm a damned good one, too. I want to go with you."

"It's not up to me—"

"I'll never get this opportunity again."

"I don't know."

"I can watch your back."

Astonished and not sure what to say, I sat silently for a few moments, but some of his excitement rubbed off on me. "Let me ask about it."

We finished our drinks over small talk and exchanged commlink data. I promised to get back to him.

I gave his offer lots of thought. I wondered what motivated the big guy. There was a deeper story than he was telling. If he knew that Levi was a sadistic son-of-a-bitch, why would he subject himself to a space voyage with the rebbe? On the other hand, it was easy to make the case for a real veterinary assistant besides Reb Levi. I would train and utilize the rebbe for routine tasks, but I doubted he would meet all the needs of my practice. I still needed someone like Fur to hold animals, to assist in surgery, to run the lab, and more, like watch my back.

I checked into Fur's background and confirmed his story about vet school and his job as a veterinary technician. His references were outstanding. He was the perfect choice; he had the background and there were few animals the big guy couldn't handle—or so I thought.

Levi remembered him from our tavern debate and was thrilled to have someone else along who saw eye-to-eye with him, at least with respect to religious matters. Fur passed the Rebbinical Council's screening, so I gained a real assistant and a badly needed ally. Maybe someone to keep Levi's venom from poisoning the whole trip.

***

Our spaceship had a brand-new Artificial Intelligence, although the ship itself was a reconstruction job. I guessed that was okay. They wouldn't put an expensive new AI and fancy drives in a questionable hull, I hoped.

As the first with access to the AI, I programmed and customized the interface. I added something that I did not tell anyone about: an override that would make the AI accept only my commands in case it came to a battle between me and Reb Levi, something I feared. I also named the AI *Ruthie* and gave her a seductive female voice to annoy the stiff-necked Levi.

"That is not acceptable," he fumed at me. "This is a computer. Computers do not have *names*."

Before I could respond, Ruthie chimed in. "But Cy gave me a name and I like it," she said in an excellent approximation of a whine.

Shit. That did not help. I switched off the AI's voice circuit. "A name will make it easier to give the ship commands," I argued. "Saying 'computer' all the time is awkward."

Levi scowled at me, but I did not back down, and the name stuck. I hoped I would not pay for that victory somewhere down the line, but I could not resist pulling his chain to achieve even a minuscule quantum of control.

The three of us, Levi, Fur, and I, took a crash course in operation of all the ship's systems. Although the AI handled everything, there was the outside chance that we humans would have to intervene. What if the AI failed? That fear lost me one night's sleep to a dream where the ship flew into the sun while Ruthie seduced me. "We will go out in a blaze of orgasmic glory," she said in her sexy contralto.

My first erotic nightmare, and I hoped the last.

Fur was more mechanical-minded than me. He said he had grown up fixing all the machinery on his farm, and been good enough that neighbors frequently enlisted him for help. He had also operated and repaired the medical equipment at his clinic. Levi came in a distant third in that regard. We sat around a small table in a room at the spaceport.

Levi pointed to a parts schematic of the air-processing unit. "What is this, here?"

His voice grated on my nerves. The trip hadn't even started yet and already his sour disposition and unpleasant aura bugged me. "That's the grabmitz valve."

I sensed Fur suppress a laugh at the name I'd pulled out of thin air.

"What does it do?" Levi asked.

"It's critical for the freebwhanil to scrub carbon dioxide out of the recycled air. If the freebwhanil fails, we suffocate to death."

"Suffocate?" Levi's voice rose as his eye twitched. He looked at Fur. "Can that happen?" He looked back at me, black eyes probing. "Is this one of your jokes, Berger?"

Fur remained mute as if to let the tension ratchet up a bit then jumped to my rescue. "It's no joke, Reb Levi. If the air scrubbers fail, carbon dioxide levels would rise and the air would become toxic."

He omitted reference to the grabmitz valve and freebwhanil because they did not exist. "The main thing we need to know is the oxygen-carbon dioxide ratio. That shows on the screen over here." He pointed to the drawing. "If that's good, we don't have to worry about the workings of the equipment. I'll handle repairs in case of a problem."

Levi nodded. "That is good. I will be busy with

spiritual matters. They are just as important as the mechanical ones."

Right. I would grab the extra oxygen tank while he prayed for deliverance.

***

Reb Levi had to make some major changes to accommodate his new role. It began with a clothing change, no more Darth Vader black-on-black like the old vids. He wore a white shirt, dark gray suit, and an over-the-top splash of color—a dark blue tie. His new look included a shave, but he looked uncomfortable shorn, and his scar stood out even more. However, his head was never without his fedora or a *yarmulke*, both black of course.

Levi's lessons as a veterinary assistant took place in the laboratory of the *GCVS*.

I motioned for Levi to move closer.

He flinched when I raised a scalpel to his face. "What are you doing?"

"Relax. I'm just going to take a skin scraping, for God's sake."

He scowled and adjusted his *yarmulke*. "Your continued use of our Lord's name in vain does you no good, Berger."

"Sorry. Just hold still."

I scraped the greasy, blackhead-dotted skin beside his nose. Nauseating, but worth the effort, I hoped. I had him place the scrapings on a slide and instructed him in further preparation of the sample. He examined it under the dual-headed microscope. I wondered that he could even focus through the eyepieces, his left eye twitched so violently.

"What is *that*?" He recoiled from the microscope.

"Those are mange mites. The *Demodex* mite is a

common inhabitant of the skin of people and animals. Ugly little things, aren't they?"

"They were in my skin?" His mouth turned down at the corners.

"They creep around in there and feed off your dead cells."

His ruddy face paled.

"Now let's take a look at the cultures you prepared from your skin a couple of days ago."

I brought out the Petri dishes from the incubator. Numerous bacterial colonies in sickly whites, yellows, browns, and blues dotted the gelatin surfaces of the plates.

As he stared at them, his face paled even more. "Yech," he mumbled.

His almost palpable queasiness delighted me even though I felt it as he did. I showed him how to make smears and stain them. At the microscope again, I said, "Those little round guys in chains are streptococci," as he peered into the lenses. "They can cause sore throats and meningitis."

His cheeks puffed out, fighting back his nausea.

"The round ones in bunches are staphylococci. They cause abscesses with thick nasty yellow pus."

I could *hear* faint gurgling in his stomach.

"Those rod-shaped ones are *E. coli*. You know, fecal bacteria?"

That did it. He stood, slammed his hand to his mouth, and rushed out of the lab.

Fur, who had observed us, said, "Our rebbe is not the only one with a sadistic streak, you know that? Be careful you don't take it too far."

"I don't know how else to fight back." I swallowed hard to remove the acid taste in my own mouth; my actions to gross out Levi was not without its side effects on me.

I sensed a rush of indecision from Fur, as if he were on the cusp of a major decision to reveal something, but it receded as quickly as it came.

Whatever that meant, he was right. Inconsequential triumphs like these did nothing but feed my need for revenge against Levi, and that could spell trouble for everyone.

***

My final visit to my parents was short, but difficult. Mom could not stop her tears no matter how I tried to assure her things would be fine. I wondered how much Dad had told her about my predicament.

My stomach squirmed and my head ached as I envisioned my failure to protect my folks. The thought of them subjected to torture made me fight to keep my own tears under control.

I prayed there would be no further reasons for Mom's tears.

***

To find out what happens next, go to www.twbpress.com/galacticcircle.html to find the links to purchase this novel in e-book or paperback from many fine booksellers.

Enjoy these short stories and novels from Stephen A Benjamin

The Galactic Circle Veterinary Service (TWB Press,
2014)
A sci-fi novel by Stephen A. Benjamin
http://www.twbpress.com/galacticcircle.html

A Change of Heart – A Galactic Circle Episode (TWB
Press, 2015)
A sci-fi short story by Stephen A. Benjamin
http://www.twbpress.com/achangeofheart.html

A Poetic Disorder – A Galactic Circle Episode (TWB
Press, 2015)
A sci-fi short story by Stephen A Benjamin
http://www.twbpress.com/apoeticdisorder.html

Howling at the Moons – A Galactic Circle Episode
(TWB Press, 2015)
A sci-fi short story by Stephen A Benjamin
http://www.twbpress.com/howlingatthemoons.html

Just Desserts (TWB Press, 2011)
A horror short story by Stephen A. Benjamin
http://www.twbpress.com/justdeserts.html

http://www.twbpress.com